The Patrioteer

THE PATRIOTEER

BY

HEINRICH MANN

AUTHORIZED TRANSLATION BY

 RNEST BOYD

NEW YORK

HARCOURT, BRACE AND COMPANY

1921

14)

PRINTED IN THE U S A. BY
THE QUINN & BODEN COMPANY
RAHWAY, N J

THE PATRIOTEER

THE PATRIOTEER

I

DIEDERICH HESSLING was a dreamy, delicate child, frightened of everything, and troubled with constant earache. In winter he hated to leave the warm room, and in summer the narrow garden, which smelt of rags from the paper factory, and whose laburnum and elder-trees were overshadowed by the wooden roofs of the old houses. Diederich was often terribly afraid when he raised his eyes from his story book, his beloved fairy tales. A toad half as big as himself had been plainly sitting on the seat beside him! Or over there against the wall a gnome, sunk to his waist in the ground, was staring at him! His father was even more terrible than the gnome and the toad, and moreover he was compelled to love him. Diederich did love him. Whenever he had pilfered, or told a lie, he would come cringing shyly like a dog to his father's desk, until Herr Hessling noticed that something was wrong and took his stick from the wall. Diederich's submissiveness and confidence were shaken by doubts so long as any misdeed remained undiscovered. Once when his father, who had a stiff leg, fell downstairs the boy clapped his hands madly—and then ran away at full speed.

The workmen used to laugh when he passed the workshops after having been punished, crying loudly, his face swollen with tears. Then Diederich would stamp his feet and put out his tongue at them. He would say to himself: "I have got a beating, but from my papa. You would be glad to be beaten by him, but you are not good enough for that."

He moved amongst the men like a capricious potentate.

3

Sometimes he would threaten to tell his father that they were bringing in beer, and at others he would coquettishly allow them to wheedle out of him the hour when Herr Hessling was expected to return. They were on their guard against the boss; he knew them, for he had been a workman himself. He had been a vat-man in the old mills where every sheet of paper was made by hand. During that time he had served in all the wars, and after the last one, when everybody made money, he was able to buy a paper machine. His plant consisted of one cylinder machine and one cutter. He himself counted the sheets. He kept his eye on the buttons which were taken from the rags. His little son often used to accept a few from the women, on condition that he did not tell on those who took some away with them. One day he had collected so many that he got the idea of exchanging them with the grocer for sweets. He succeeded—but in the evening Diederich knelt in his bed and, as he swallowed the last piece of barley sugar, he prayed to Almighty God to leave the crime undetected. He nevertheless allowed it to leak out. His father had always used the stick methodically, his weather-beaten face reflecting an old soldier's sense of honour and duty. This time his hand trembled and a tear rolled down, trickling over the wrinkles, onto one side of his grey upturned moustache. "My son is a thief," he said breathlessly, in a hushed voice, and he stared at the child as if he were a suspicious intruder. "You lie and you steal. All you have to do now is to commit a murder."

Frau Hessling tried to compel Diederich to fall on his knees before his father and beg his pardon, because his father had wept on his account. Diederich's instinct, however, warned him that this would only have made his father more angry. Hessling had no sympathy whatever with his wife's sentimental manner. She was spoiling the child for life. Besides he had caught her lying just like little Diederich. No wonder, for she read novels! By Saturday night her week's work was often not completed. She gossiped with the servant instead of exerting herself. . . . And even then Hessling did not know that his wife also pilfered, just like the child. At table she did not dare to eat enough and she crept surreptitiously to the cupboard. Had she dared to go into the workshop she would also have stolen buttons.

She prayed with the child "from the heart," and not according to the prescribed forms, and that always brought a flush to her face. She used to beat him also and gave him thorough thrashings, consumed with a desire for revenge. On such occasions she was frequently in the wrong, and then Diederich threatened to complain to his father. He would pretend to go into the office and, hiding somewhere behind a wall, would rejoice at her terror. He exploited his mother's tender moods, but felt no respect for her. Her resemblance to himself made that impossible, for he had no self-respect. The consequence was that he went through life with a conscience too uneasy to withstand the scrutiny of God.

Nevertheless mother and son spent twilight hours overflowing with sentiment. From festive occasions they jointly extracted the last drop of emotion by means of singing, pianoplaying and story-telling. When Diederich began to have doubts about the Christ Child he let his mother persuade him to go on believing a little while longer, and thereby he felt relieved, faithful and good. He also believed obstinately in a ghost up in the Castle, and his father, who would not hear of such a thing, seemed too proud, and almost deserving of punishment. His mother nourished him with fairy tales. She shared with him her fear of the new, animated streets, and of the tramway which crossed them and took him past the city wall towards the Castle, where they enjoyed delightful thrills. At the corner of Meisestrasse you had to pass a policeman, who could take you off to prison if he liked. Diederich's heart beat nervously. How gladly he would have made a détour! But then the policeman would have noticed his uneasy conscience and have seized him. It was much better to prove that one felt pure and innocent—so with trembling voice Diederich asked the policeman the time.

After so many fearful powers, to which he was subjected; his father, God, the ghost of the Castle and the police; after the chimney-sweep, who could slip him right up through the flue until he, too, was quite black, and the doctor, who could paint his throat and shake him when he cried—after all these powers, Diederich now fell under the sway of one even more terrible, which swallowed you up completely—the school. Diederich went there howling, and because he wanted to howl he could not give even the answers which he knew. Gradually he learnt how to exploit this tendency to cry whenever he had not learnt his lessons, for all his fears did not make him more industrious or less dreamy. And thus, until the teachers saw through the trick, he was able to avoid many of the evil consequences of his idleness. The first teacher who saw through it, at once earned his wholehearted respect. He suddenly stopped crying and gazed at him over the arm which he was holding bent in front of his face, full of timid devotion. He was always obedient and docile with the strict teachers. On the good-natured ones he played little tricks, which could with difficulty be proved against him and about which he did not boast. With much greater satisfaction he bragged of getting bad marks and great punishments. At table he would say: "To-day Herr Behnke flogged three of us again." And to the question: Whom? "I was one of them."

Diederich was so constituted that he was delighted to belong to an impersonal entity, to this immovable, inhumanly indifferent, mechanical organisation which was the college. He was proud of this power, this grim power, which he felt, if only through suffering. On the headmaster's birthday flowers were placed on the desk and the blackboard. Diederich actually decorated the cane.

In the course of the years two catastrophes, which befell the all-powerful, filled him with a holy and wonderful horror. An

assistant master was called down in front of the class by the
principal and dismissed. A senior master became insane. On
these occasions still higher powers, the principal and the lunatic asylum, made fearful havoc of those who had hitherto
wielded so much power. From beneath, insignificant but un-
harmed, one could raise one's eyes to these victims, and draw
from their fate a lesson which rendered one's own lot more
easy. In relation to his younger sisters Diederich replaced the
power which held him in its mechanism. He made them take
dictation, and deliberately make more mistakes than they naturally would, so that he could make furious corrections with
red ink, and administer punishment. His punishments were
cruel. The little ones cried—and then Diederich had to humble
himself in order that they should not betray him.

He had no need of human beings in order to imitate the
powers that be. Animals, and even inanimate objects, were
sufficient. He would stand at the rail of the paper-making
machine and watch the cylinder sorting out the rags. "So that
one is gone! Look out, now, you blackguards!" Diederich
would mutter, and his pale eyes glared. Suddenly he stepped
back, almost falling into the tub of chlorine. A workman's
footsteps had interrupted his vicious enjoyment.

Only when he himself received the punishment did he feel
really big and sure of his position. He hardly ever resisted
evil. At most he would beg a comrade: "Don't hit me on the
back, that's dangerous." It was not that he was lacking in
any sense of his rights and any love of his own advantage.
But Diederich held that the blows which he received brought
no practical profit to the striker and no 'real loss to himself.
These purely ideal values seemed to him far less serious than
the cream puff which the head waiter at the Netziger Hof
had long since promised him, but had never produced. Many
times Diederich wended his way, with earnest gait, up Meisestrasse to the market place, and called upon his swallow-tailed
friend to deliver the goods. One day, however, when the

waiter denied all knowledge of his promise, Diederich declared, as he stamped his foot in genuine indignation: "This is really too much of a good thing. If you don't give me it immediately, I'll report you to the boss!" Thereupon George laughed and brought him the cream puff.

That was a tangible success. Unfortunately Diederich could enjoy it only in haste and fear, for he was afraid that Wolfgang Buck, who was waiting outside, would come in on him and demand the share which had been promised to him. Meanwhile he found time to wipe his mouth clean, and at the door he broke out into violent abuse of George, whom he called a swindler who had no cream puffs at all. Diederich's sense of justice, which had just manifested itself so effectively to his own advantage, did not respond to the claims of his friend, who could not, at the same time, be altogether ignored. Wolfgang's father was much too important a personage for that. Old Herr Buck did not wear a stiff collar, but a white silk neckcloth, on which his great curly white beard rested. How slowly and majestically he tapped the pavement with his gold-topped walking-stick! He wore a silk hat, too, and the tails of his dress coat often peeped out under his overcoat, even in the middle of the day! For he went to public meetings, and looked after the affairs of the whole city. Looking at the bathing establishment, the prison and all the public institutions, Diederich used to think: "That belongs to Herr Buck." He must be tremendously wealthy and powerful. All the men, including Herr Hessling, took off their hats most respectfully to him. To deprive his son of something by force was a deed whose dangerous consequences could not be foretold. In order not to be utterly crushed by the mighty powers, whom he so profoundly respected, Diederich had to go quietly and craftily to work.

Only once did it happen, when he was in the Lower Third form, that Diederich forgot all prudence, acted blindly and became himself an oppressor, drunk with victory. As was the usual and approved custom, he had bullied the only Jew in his class, but then he proceeded to an unfamiliar manifestation. Out of the blocks which were used for drawing he built a cross on the desk and forced the Jew onto his knees before it. He held him tight, in spite of his resistance; he was strong! What made Diederich strong was the applause of the bystanders, the crowd whose arms helped him, the overwhelming majority within the building and in the world outside. He was acting on behalf of the whole Christian community of Netzig. How splendid it was to share responsibility, and to feel the sensation of collective consciousness.

When the first flush of intoxication had waned, it is true, a certain fear took its place, but all his courage returned to Diederich when he saw the face of the first master he met. It was so full of embarrassed good will. Others openly showed their approval. Diederich smiled up at them with an air of shy understanding. Things were easier for him after that. The class could not refuse to honour one who enjoyed the favour of the headmaster. Under him Diederich rose to the head of the class and secretly acted as monitor. At least, he laid claim, later on, to the latter of these honours also. He was a good friend to all, laughed when they planned their escapades, an unreserved and hearty laugh, as befitted an earnest youth who could yet understand frivolity—and then, during the lunch hour, when he brought his notebook to the professor, he reported everything. He also reported the nicknames of the teachers and the rebellious speeches which had been made against them. In repeating these things his voice trembled with something of the voluptuous terror which he had experienced as he listened to them with half-closed eyes. Whenever there was any disparaging comment on the ruling powers he had a guilty feeling of relief, as if something deep down in himself, like a kind of hatred, had hastily and furtively satisfied its hunger. By sneaking on his comrades he atoned for his own guilty impulses.

For the most part he had no personal feeling against the pupils whose advancement was checked by his activities. He acted as the conscientious instrument of dire necessity. Afterwards he could go to the culprit and quite honestly sympathise with him. Once he was instrumental in catching some one who had been suspected of copying. With the knowledge of the teacher, Diederich gave him a mathematical problem, the working out of which was deliberately wrong, while the final result was correct. That evening, after the cheater had been exposed, some of the students were sitting in the garden of a restaurant outside the gate singing, as they were allowed to do after gymnasium. Diederich had taken a seat beside his victim. Once, when they had emptied their glasses he slipped his right hand into that of his companion, gazed trustfully into his eyes, and began all alone to sing in a bass voice that quivered with emotion:

> " Ich hatt' einen Kameraden,
>   Einen bessern findst du nit. . . ."

For the rest, with increasing school experience he could make a good show in most subjects, without going beyond what was required of him in any one, or learning anything in the world which was not prescribed in the programme. German composition was his most difficult subject, and any one who excelled at it inspired him with an inexplicable mistrust.

Since he had been promoted to the highest class his matriculation was certain, and his father and teachers felt that he ought to continue his studies. Old Hessling, having marched through the Brandenburger Tor in 1866 and 1871, decided to send Diederich to Berlin.

As he did not care to venture far from the neighbourhood of Friederichstrasse he rented a room up in Tieckstrasse, so that he had only to walk straight down and could not miss the University. As he had nothing else to do, he went there twice a day, and in the intervals he often wept from homesickness.

He wrote a letter to his father and mother thanking them for his happy childhood. He seldom went out unless he had to. He scarcely dared to eat; he was afraid to spend his money before the end of the month, and he would constantly feel his pocket to see if it was still there.

Lonely as he felt, he still did not go to Blücherstrasse with his father's letter to Herr Göppel, the cellulose manufacturer, who came from Netzig and also did business with Hessling. He overcame his shyness on the fourth Sunday, and hardly had the stout red-faced man, whom he had so often seen in his father's office, waddled up to meet him than Diederich wondered why he had not come sooner. Herr Göppel immediately asked after everybody in Netzig, but especially old Buck. Although his beard was now grey he still respected old Buck as he had done when he was a boy like Diederich, only it was for different reasons. He took off his hat to such a man, one of those whom the German people should esteem more highly than certain persons whose favourite remedy was blood and iron, for which the nation had to pay so dearly. Old Buck was a Forty-Eighter, and had actually been condemned to death. "It is to such people as old Buck," said Herr Göppel, "that we owe the privilege of sitting here as free men." And, as he opened another bottle of beer: "nowadays we are expected to let ourselves be trampled on with jackboots. . . ."

Herr Göppel confessed himself a liberal opponent of Bismarck's. Diederich agreed with everything that Göppel said: he had no opinion to offer about the Chancellor, the young Emperor and freedom. Then he became uncomfortable, for a young girl had come into the room, and at the first glance her elegance and beauty frightened him.

"My daughter Agnes," said Herr Göppel.

A lanky youth, in his flowing frock-coat, Diederich stood there, blushing furiously. The girl gave him her hand. No doubt she wanted to be polite, but what could one say to her? Diederich said yes, when she asked him if he liked Berlin; and when she asked if he had been to the theatre yet, he said no. He was perspiring with nervousness, and was firmly convinced that his departure was the only thing which would really interest the young lady. But how could he get out of the place? Fortunately a third party stepped into the breach, a burly creature named Mahlmann, who spoke with a loud Mecklenburg accent, seemed to be a student of engineering and to be a lodger at Göppel's. He reminded Fräulein Agnes of a walk they had arranged to take. Diederich was invited to accompany them. In dismay he pleaded the excuse of an acquaintance who was waiting for him outside and went off at once. "Thank God," he thought, "she has some one," but the thought hurt him.

Herr Göppel opened the door for him in the dark hall and asked if his friend was also new to Berlin. Diederich lied, saying his friend was from Berlin. "For if neither of you know the city you will take the wrong bus. No doubt you have often lost yourself already in Berlin." When Diederich admitted it, Herr Göppel seemed satisfied. "Here it is not like in Netzig; you can walk about for half a day. Just fancy when you come from Tieckstrasse here to the Halle Gate you have walked as far as three times through the whole of Netzig. . . . Well now, next Sunday you must come to lunch."

Diederich promised to go. When the time came he would have preferred not to, he went only out of fear of his father. This time he had to undergo a tête-à-tête with the young lady. Diederich behaved as if absorbed in his own affairs and under no obligation to entertain her. She began again to speak about the theatre, but he interrupted her gruffly, saying he had no time for such things. Oh yes, her father had told her that Herr Hessling was studying chemistry.

"Yes. As a matter of fact that is the only science which can justify its existence," Diederich asserted, without exactly knowing what put that idea into his head.

Fräulein Göppel let her bag fall, but he stooped so reluctantly that she had picked it up before he could get to it. In spite of that, she thanked him softly and almost shyly. Diederich was annoyed. "These coquettish women are horrible," he reflected. She was looking for something in her bag.

"Now I have lost it—I mean my sticking-plaster. It is bleeding again."

She unwound her handkerchief from her finger. It looked so much like snow that Diederich thought that the blood on it would sink in.

"I have some plaster," he said with a bow.

He seized her finger, and before she could wipe off the blood, he licked it.

"What on earth are you doing?"

He himself was startled, and wrinkling his brow solemnly he said: "Oh, as a chemist I have to do worse things than that."

She smiled. "Oh yes, of course, you are a sort of doctor. . . . How well you do it," she remarked as she watched him sticking on the plaster.

"There," he said, pushing her hand away and moving back. The air seemed to have become close and he thought: "If it were only possible to avoid touching her skin. It is so disgustingly soft." Agnes stared over his head. After a time she tried again: "Haven't we got common relations in Netzig?" She compelled him to go over a few families with her and they discovered a cousin.

"Your mother is still living, isn't she? You should be glad of that. Mine is long since dead. I don't suppose I shall live long either. One has premonitions"—and she smiled sadly and apologetically.

Silently Diederich resolved that this sentimentality was ridiculous. Another long interval, and as they both hastened to speak, the gentleman from Mecklenburg arrived. He squeezed Diederich's hand so hard that the latter winced, and at the same time he looked into his face with a smile of triumph. He drew a chair unconcernedly close to Agnes's knee, and with an air of proprietorship began talking animatedly about all sorts of things which concerned only the two of them. Diederich was left to himself and he discovered that Agnes was not so terrible, when he could contemplate her undisturbed. She wasn't really pretty; her aquiline nose was too small, and freckles were plainly visible on its narrow bridge. Her light brown eyes were too close together, and they blinked when she looked at any one. Her lips were too thin, as indeed her whole face was. "If she had not that mass of reddish brown hair over her forehead and that white complexion. . . ." He noted, too, with satisfaction that the nail of the finger which he had licked was not quite clean.

Herr Göppel came in with his three sisters, one of whom was accompanied by her husband and children. Her father and her aunts threw their arms round Agnes and kissed her fervently, but with solemn composure. The girl was taller and slimmer than any of them, and as they hung about her narrow shoulders she looked down on them with an air of distraction. The only kiss which she returned, slowly and seriously, was her father's. As Diederich watched this he could see in the bright sunlight the pale blue veins in her temples overshadowed by auburn hair.

It fell to him to take one of the aunts into the dining-room. The man from Mecklenburg had taken Agnes's arm. The silk Sunday dresses rustled round the family table, while the gentlemen took precautions not to crush the tails of their frock-coats. While the gentlemen rubbed their hands in anticipation and cleared their throats, the soup was brought in.

Diederich sat at some distance from Agnes, and he could not see her unless he bent forward—which he carefully refrained from doing. As his neighbour left him in peace, he ate vast quantities of roast veal and cauliflower. The food was the subject of detailed conversation and he was called upon to testify to its excellence. Agnes was warned not to eat the salad, she was advised to take a little red wine, and she was requested to state whether she had worn her goloshes that morning.

Turning to Diederich Herr Göppel related how he and his sisters somehow or other had got separated in Friederichstrasse, and had not found one another until they were in the bus. "That's the sort of thing that would never happen in Netzig," he cried triumphantly to the whole table. Mahlmann and Agnes spoke of a concert to which they said they must go, and they were sure papa would let them. Herr Göppel mildly objected and the aunts supported him in chorus. Agnes should go to bed early and soon go for a change of air; she had over-exerted herself in the winter. She denied it. "You never let me go outside the door. You are terrible."

Diederich secretly took her part. He was swept by a wave of chivalry: He would have liked to make it possible for her to do everything she wished, to be happy and to owe her happiness to him. . . . Then Herr Göppel asked him if he would like to go to the concert. "I don't know," he said indifferently, looking at Agnes who leaned forward. "What sort of a concert is it? I go only to concerts where I can get beer."

"Quite right," said Herr Göppel's brother-in-law.

Agnes had shrunk back, and Diederich regretted his statement.

They were all looking forward to the custard but it did not come. Herr Göppel advised his daughter just to have a look. Before she could push away her plate Diederich had jumped up, hurling his chair against the wall, and rushed to the door. "Mary! the custard!" he bawled. Blushing, and without daring to look any one in the face, he returned to his seat, but he saw only too clearly how they smiled at one another. Mahlmann actually snorted contemptuously. With forced heartiness the brother-in-law said: "Always polite; as a gentleman should be." Herr Göppel smiled affectionately at Agnes, who did not raise her eyes from her plate. Diederich pressed his knees against the leaf of the table until it shook. He thought: "My God, my God, if only I hadn't done that!"

When they wished each other *"gesegnete Mahlzeit"* he shook

hands with everybody except Agnes, to whom he bowed awkwardly. In the drawing-room at coffee he carefully chose a seat where he was screened by Mahlmann's broad back. One of the aunts tried to take possession of him.

"What are you studying, may I ask, young man?" she said.

"Chemistry."

"Oh, I see, physics?"

"No, chemistry."

"Oh, I see."

Auspiciously as she had begun, she could not get any further. To himself Diederich described her as a silly goose. The whole company was impossible. In moody hostility he looked on until the last relative had departed. Agnes and her father had seen them out, and Herr Göppel returned to the room and found the young man, to his astonishment, still sitting there alone. He maintained a puzzled silence and once dived his hand into his pocket. When Diederich said good-bye of his own accord, without trying to borrow money, Göppel displayed the utmost amiability. "I'll say good-bye to my daughter for you," said he, and when they got to the door he added, after a certain hesitation: "Come again next Sunday, won't you?"

Diederich absolutely determined never to put his foot in the house again. Nevertheless, he neglected everything for days afterwards to search the town for a place where he could buy Agnes a ticket for the concert. He had to find out beforehand from the posters the name of the virtuoso whom Agnes had mentioned. Was that he? hadn't the name sounded something like that? Diederich decided, but he opened his eyes in horror when he discovered that it cost four marks fifty. All that good money to hear a man make music! Once he had paid and got out into the street, he became indignant at the swindle. Then he recollected that it was all for Agnes and his indignation subsided. He went on his way through the crowd feeling more

and more mellow and happy. It was the first time he had ever
spent money on another human being.

He put the ticket in an envelope, without any covering message, and, in order not to give himself away, he inscribed the
address in the best copper-plate style. While he was standing
at the letter-box Mahlmann came up and laughed derisively.
Diederich felt that he was discovered and looked earnestly at
the hand which he had just withdrawn from the box. But
Mahlmann merely announced his intention of having a look at
Diederich's quarters. He found that the place looked as if it
belonged to an elderly lady. Diederich had actually brought
the coffee pot from home! Diederich was hot with shame.
When Mahlmann contemptuously opened and shut his chemistry books Diederich was ashamed of the subject he was
studying. The man from Mecklenburg plumped down on the
sofa and asked: "What do you think of the little Göppel girl?
Nice kid, isn't she? Oh, look at him blushing again! Why
don't you go after her? I am willing to retire, if it is any
satisfaction to you, I have fifteen other strings to my bow."

Diederich made a gesture of indifference:

"I tell you she is worth while, if I am any judge of women.
That red hair!—and did you ever notice how she looks at you
when she thinks you can't see her?"

"Not at me," said Diederich even more indifferently. "I
don't care a damn about it anyhow."

"So much the worse for you!" Mahlmann laughed boisterously. Then he proposed that they should take a stroll, which
degenerated into a round of the bars. By the time the street
lamps were lit they were both drunk. Later on, in Leipziger-
strasse without any provocation, Mahlmann gave Diederich a
tremendous box on the ear. "Oh," he said, "you have an infernal ——." He was afraid to say "cheek." "All right, old
chap, amongst friends, no harm meant," cried the Mecklenburger, clapping him on the shoulder. And finally he touched

Diederich for his last ten marks. . . . Four days later he found him, weak from hunger, and magnanimously shared with him three marks from what he had meanwhile borrowed elsewhere. On Sunday at Göppel's—where Diederich would perhaps not have gone if his stomach had not been so empty—Mahlmann explained that Hessling had squandered all his money and would have to eat his fill that day. Herr Göppel and his brother-in-law laughed knowingly, but Deiderich would rather never have been born than meet the sad, inquiring eyes of Agnes. She despised him. In desperation he consoled himself with the thought: "She always did. What does it matter?" Then she asked if it was he who had sent the concert ticket. Every one turned to look at him.

"Nonsense! Why on earth should I have done that?" he returned, so gruffly that they all believed him. Agnes hesitated a little before turning away. Mahlmann offered the ladies sugar-almonds and placed what was left in front of Agnes. Diederich took no notice of her, and ate even more than on the previous occasion. Why not, since they all thought he had come there for no other reason? When some one proposed that they should go out to Grünewald for their coffee, Diederich invented another engagement. He even added: with "some one whom I cannot possibly keep waiting." Herr Göppel placed his closed hand on his shoulder, smiled at him, with his head a little on one side, and said in an undertone: "Of course you know the invitation includes you." But Diederich indignantly assured him that had nothing to do with it. "Well, in any case you will come again whenever you feel inclined." Göppel concluded, and Agnes nodded. She appeared to wish to say something, but Diederich would not wait. He wandered about for the rest of the day in a state of self-complacent grief, like one who has achieved a great sacrifice. In the evening he sat in an overcrowded beer-room, with his head in his hands, and wagged his head at his solitary glass from time to time, as if he now understood the ways of destiny.

What was he to do against the masterly manner in which Mahlmann accepted his loans? On Sunday the Mecklenburger had brought a bouquet for Agnes, though Diederich, who came with empty hands, might have said: "That is really from me." Instead of that he was silent, and was more incensed against Agnes than against Mahlmann. The latter commanded his admiration when he ran at night after some passer-by and knocked in his hat—although Diederich was by no means blind to the warning which this procedure contained for himself.

At the end of the month he received for his birthday an unexpected sum of money which his mother had saved up for him, and he arrived at Göppel's with a bouquet, not so large as to give himself away, or to challenge Mahlmann. As she took it the girl's face wore an embarrassed expression, and Diederich's smile was both shy and condescending. That Sunday seemed to him unusually gay and the proposal that they should go to the Zoological Gardens did not surprise him.

The company set out, after Mahlmann had counted them: Eleven persons. Like Göppel's sisters, all the women they met were dressed quite differently than on week-days, as if they belonged to-day to a higher class, or had come into a legacy. The men wore frock coats, only a few with dark trousers like Diederich, but many had straw hats. The side streets were broad, uniform and empty, not a soul was to be seen, nor any of the usual refuse. In one, however, a group of little girls in white dresses, and black stockings, bedecked with ribbons were singing shrilly and dancing in a ring. Immediately afterwards, in the main thoroughfare, they came on perspiring matrons storming a bus, and the faces of the shop assistants, who struggled ruthlessly with them for seats, looked so pale beside their strong red cheeks that one would have thought they were going to faint. Every one pushed forward, every one rushed to the one goal where pleasure would begin. On every face was plainly written: "Come on, we have worked enough!"

Diederich became the complete city man for the benefit of the ladies. He captured several seats for them in the tram. One gentleman was on the point of taking the seat when Diederich prevented him by stamping heavily on his foot. "Clumsy fool!" he cried and Diederich answered in appropriate terms. Then it turned out that Herr Göppel knew him, and scarcely had they been introduced when both exhibited the most courtly manners. Neither would sit down lest the other should have to stand.

When they sat down at table in the Zoological Gardens Diederich succeeded in getting beside Agnes—why was everything going so well to-day?—and when she proposed to go and look at the animals immediately after they had had their coffee, he enthusiastically seconded the proposal. He felt wonderfully enterprising. The ladies turned back at the narrow passage between the cages of the wild animals. Diederich offered to accompany Agnes. "Then you'd better take me with you," said Mahlmann. "If a bar really did break—"

"Then it would not be you who would put it back into its place," retorted Agnes, as she entered, while Mahlmann burst out laughing. Diederich went after her. He was afraid of the animals who bounded towards him on both sides, without a sound but the noise of their breathing which he felt upon him. And he was afraid of the young girl whose perfume drew him on. When they had gone some distance she turned round and said, "I hate people who boast."

"Really?" Diederich asked, joyfully moved.

"You are actually nice to-day," said Agnes; and he: "I always want to be nice."

"Really?"—and her voice trembled slightly. They looked at one another, each with an expression suggesting that they had not deserved all this. The girl said complainingly:

"I can't stand the horrible smell of these animals." Then they went back.

Mahlmann greeted them. "I was curious to see if you were going to give us the slip." Then he took Diederich aside. "Well, how did you find her? Did you get on all right? Didn't I tell you that no great arts are required?"

Diederich made no reply.

"I suppose you made a good beginning? Now let me tell you this: I shall be only two more terms in Berlin, then you can take her on after I am gone, but meanwhile, hands off— my little friend!" As he said this, his small head looked malicious on his immense body.

Diederich was dismissed. He had received a terrible fright and did not again venture in Agnes's neighbourhood. She did not pay much attention to Mahlmann, but shouted over her shoulder: "Father! it is beautiful to-day and I really feel well."

Herr Göppel took her arm between his two hands, as if he were going to squeeze it tight, but he scarcely touched it. His colourless eyes laughed and filled with tears. When the family had taken its departure, he called his daughter and the two young men, and declared that this was a day which must be celebrated; they would go along down Unter den Linden and afterwards get something to eat.

"Father is getting frivolous!" cried Agnes looking at Diederich. But he kept his eyes fixed on the ground. In the tram he was so clumsy that he got separated far from the others, and in the crowd in Friederichstrasse he walked behind alone with Herr Göppel. Suddenly Göppel stopped, fumbled nervously at his waistcoat and asked "Where is my watch?"

It had disappeared along with the chain. Mahlmann said: "How long have you been in Berlin, Herr Göppel?"

"Ah, yes,"—Göppel turned to Diederich,—"I have been living here for thirty years, but such a thing has never happened to me before." Then, with a certain pride: "such a thing couldn't happen in Netzig at all!"

Now, instead of going to a restaurant, they had to go to

the police station and lodge a complaint. Agnes began to cough, and Göppel gave a start. "It would make us too tired after this," he murmured. With forced good humour he said good-bye to Diederich, who ignored Agnes's hand, and lifted his hat awkwardly. Suddenly, with surprising agility, he sprang onto a passing bus, before Mahlmann could grasp what was happening. He had escaped. Now the holidays were beginning and he was free of everything. When he got to his house he threw his heaviest chemistry books to the ground with a crash, and he was preparing to send the coffee pot after them. But, hearing the noise of a door, he began at once to gather up everything again. Then he sat down quietly in a corner of the sofa, and wept with his head in his hands. If it had only not been so pleasant before! She had led him into a trap. That's the way girls were; they led you on solely for the purpose of making fun of you with another fellow. Diederich was deeply conscious that he could not challenge comparison with such a man. He contrasted himself with Mahlmann and would not have understood if any one had preferred him to the other. "How conceited I have been," he thought. "The girl who falls in love with me must be really stupid." He had a great fear lest the man from Mecklenburg should come and threaten him more seriously. "I don't want her at all. If I only could get away!" Next day he sat in deadly suspense with his door bolted. No sooner had his money arrived than he set off on his journey.

His mother, jealous and estranged, asked him what was wrong. He had grown up in such a short time. "Ah yes, the streets of Berlin!"

Diederich grasped at the chance, when she insisted that he should go to a small University and not return to Berlin. His father held that there were two sides to the question. Diederich had to give him a full account of the Göppels. Had he seen the factory? Had he been to his other business friends? Herr Hessling wished Diederich to employ his holidays in learning how paper was made in his father's workshops. "I am not so young as I used to be, and my old wound has not troubled me so much for a long time as lately."

Diederich disappeared as soon as he could, in order to wander in the Gäbbelchen wood, or along the stream in the direction of Gohse, and to feel himself one with Nature. This pleasure was now open to him. For the first time it occurred to him that the hills in the background looked sad and seemed full of longing. The sun was Diederich's warm love and his tears the rain that fell from heaven. He wept a great deal, and even tried to write poetry.

Once when he was in the chemist's shop his school friend, Gottlieb Hornung, was standing behind the counter. "Yes, I am doing a little compounding here during the summer months," he explained. He had even succeeded in poisoning himself by mistake, and had twisted himself backwards like an eel. It had been the talk of the town. But he would be going to Berlin in the autumn to set about the thing scientifically. Was there anything doing in Berlin? Delighted with his advantage, Diederich began to brag about his Berlin experiences. "We two will paint the town red," the chemist vowed.

Diederich was weak enough to agree. The idea of a small university was abandoned. At the end of the summer Diederich returned to Berlin. Hornung had still a few days to practise. Diederich avoided his old room in Tieckstrasse. From Mahlmann and the Göppels he fled out as far as Gesundbrunnen. There he waited for Hornung. But the latter, who had announced his departure, did not turn up. When he finally did come he was wearing a green yellow and red cap. He had been immediately captured by a fellow-student for a students' corps. Diederich would have to join them also; they were known as the Neo-Teutons, a most select body, said Hornung; there were no less than six pharmacists in it. Diederich concealed his fright under a mask of contempt, but to no effect.

Hornung had spoken about him and he could not let him down; he would have to pay at least one visit.

"Well, only one," he said firmly.

That one visit lasted until Diederich lay under the table and they carried him out. When he had slept it off they took him for the *Frühschoppen* for, although not a member of the corps, he had been admitted to the privilege of drinking with them. This suited him down to the ground. He found himself in the company of a large circle of men, not one of whom interfered with him, or expected anything of him, except that he should drink. Full of thankfulness and good will he raised his glass to every one who invited him. Whether he drank or not, whether he sat or stood, spoke or sang, rarely depended on his own will. Everything was ordered in a loud voice, and if you followed orders you could live at peace with yourself and all the world. When Diederich remembered for the first time not to close the lid of his beer mug, at a certain stage in the ritual, he smiled around at them all, as if his own perfection almost made him feel shy.

That, however, was nothing beside his confident singing. At school Diederich had been one of the best singers, and in his first song book he knew by heart the numbers of the pages where every song could be found. Now he had only to put his finger between the pages of the *Kommersbuch*, which lay in its nail-studded cover in the pool of beer, and he could find before any one else the song which they were to sing. He would often hang respectfully on the words of the president for a whole evening, in the hope that they would announce his favourite song. Then he would bravely shout: *"Sie wissen den Teufel, was Freiheit heisst."* Beside him he heard Fatty Delitzsch bellowing, and felt happily lost in the shadow of the low-ceilinged room, decorated in Old German style, with their students' caps on the wall. Around him was the ring of open mouths, all singing the same songs and drinking the same drinks, and the smell of beer and human bodies, from which the heat drew the beer again in the form of perspiration. He had sunk his personality entirely in the corps, whose will and brain were his. And he was a real man, who could respect himself and who had honour, because he belonged to it. Nobody could separate him from it, or get at him individually. Let Mahlmann dare to come there and try it. Twenty men, instead of one Diederich, would stand up to him! Diederich only wished he were there now, he felt so courageous. He should preferably come with Göppel, then they would see what Diederich had become. What a revenge that would be!

He got the greatest sympathy from the most harmless member of the whole crowd, Fatty Delitzsch. There was something deeply soothing about this smooth, white, humorous lump of fat, which inspired confidence. His corpulent body bulged far out over the edge of the chair and rose in a series of rolls, until it reached the edge of the table and rested there, as if it had done its uttermost, incapable of making any further movement other than raising and lowering the beer-glass. There Delitzsch was in his element more than any of the others. To see him sitting there was to forget that he had ever stood on his feet. He was constructed for the sole purpose of sitting at the beer table. In any other position his trousers hung loosely and despondently, but now they were filled out and assumed their proper shape. It was only then that his face lit up, bright with the joy of life, and he became witty.

It was a tragedy when a young freshman played a joke on him by taking his glass away. Delitzsch did not move, but his glance, which followed the glass wherever it went, suddenly reflected all the stormy drama of life. In his high-pitched Saxon voice he cried: "For goodness' sake, man, don't spill it! Why on earth do you want to take from me the staff of life! That is a low, malicious threat to my very existence, and I could have you jailed for it!"

If the joke lasted too long Delitzsch's fat cheeks sank in, and he humbled himself beseechingly. But as soon as he got his beer back, how all-embracing was his smile of forgiveness,' how he brightened up! Then he would say: "You are a decent devil after all. Your health! Good luck!" He emptied his mug and rattled the lid for more beer.

A few hours later Delitzsch would turn his chair round and go and bend his head over the basin under the water tap. The water would flow, Delitzsch would gurgle chokingly, and a couple of others would rush into the lavatory drawn by the sound. Still a little pale, but with renewed good humour, Delitzsch would draw his chair back to the table.

"Well, that's better," he would say; and: "what have you been talking about when I was busy elsewhere? Can you not talk of a damn thing except women? What do I care about women?" And louder: "They are not even worth the price of a stale glass of beer. I say! Bring another!"

Diederich felt he was quite right. He knew women himself and was finished with them. Beer stood for incomparably higher ideals.

Beer! Alcohol! You sat there and could always get more. Beer was homely and true and not like coquettish women. With beer there was nothing to do, to wish and to strive for, as there was with women. Everything came of itself. You swallowed, and already something was accomplished; you were raised to a higher sense of life, and you were a free man, inwardly free. Even if the whole place were surrounded by police, the beer that was swallowed would turn into inner freedom, and examinations were as good as passed. You were through and had got your degree. In civil life you held an important position and were rich, the head of a great postcard, or toilet-paper, factory. The products of your life's work were in the hands of thousands. From the beer table one spread out over the whole world, realised important connections, and became one with the spirit of the time. Yes, beer raised one so high above oneself that one had a glimpse of deity!

Diederich would have liked to go on like that for years.

But the Neo-Teutons would not allow him to. Almost from the very first day they had pointed out to him the moral and material advantages of full membership of the corps. But gradually they set about to catch him in a less indirect fashion. Diederich referred in vain to the fact that he had been admitted to the recognised position of a drinking guest, to which he was accustomed and which he found quite satisfactory. They replied that the aim of the association of students, namely, training in manliness and idealism, could not be fully achieved by mere drinking, important as that was. Diederich shivered, for he knew only too well what was coming. He would have to fight duels! It had always affected him unpleasantly when they had shown him the swordstrokes with their sticks, the strokes which they had taught one another; or when one of them wore a black skull cap on his head and smelt of iodoform. Panic-stricken he now thought: "Why did I stay as their guest and drink with them? Now I can't retreat."

That was true. But his first experience soothed his fears. His body was so carefully padded, his head and eyes so thoroughly protected, that it was impossible for much to happen to him. As he had no reason for not following the rules as willingly and as carefully as when drinking, he learned to fence quicker than the others. The first time he was pinked he felt weak, as the blood trickled down his cheek. Then when the cut was stitched he could have jumped for joy. He reproached himself for having attributed wicked intentions to his kind adversary. It was that very man, whom he had most feared, who took him under his protection and became his friendliest teacher.

Wiebel was a law student, and that fact alone insured Diederich's submissive respect. It was not without a sense of his own inferiority that he saw the English tweeds in which Wiebel dressed, and the coloured shirts, of which he always wore several in succession, until they all had to go to the laundry.

What abashed him most was Wiebel's manners. When the
latter drank Diederich's health with a graceful bow, Diederich
would almost collapse—the strain giving his face a tortured
expression—spill one half of his drink and choke himself with
the other. Wiebel spoke with the soft, insolent voice of a
feudal lord. "You may say what you will," he was fond of
remarking, "good form is not a vain illusion."

When he pronounced the letter "f" in form, he contracted
his mouth until it looked like a small, dark mousehole, and
emitted the sound slowly and broadly. Every time Diederich
was thrilled by so much distinction. Everything about Wiebel
seemed exquisite to him: his reddish moustache which grew
high up on his lip and his long, curved nails, which curled
downwards, not upward as Diederich's did; the strong masculine odour given out by Wiebel, his prominent ears, which
heightened the effect of his narrow skull, and the cat-like eyes
deeply set in his face. Diederich had always observed these
things with a wholehearted feeling of his own unworthiness.
But, since Wiebel had spoken to him, and become his protec-
tor, Diederich felt as if his right to exist had now been confirmed. If he had had a tail he would have wagged it gratefully. His heart expanded with happy admiration. If his
wishes had dared to soar to such heights, he would also have
liked to have such a red neck and to perspire constantly.
What a dream to be able to whistle like Wiebel.

It was now Diederich's privilege to serve him; he was his
fag. He was always in attendance when Wiebel got up, and
got his things for him. As Wiebel was not in the good graces
of the landlady, because he was irregular with his rent, Diederich made his coffee and cleaned his boots. In return, he was
taken everywhere. When Wiebel wanted privacy Diederich
went on guard outside, and he only wished he had his sword
with him in order to shoulder it.

Wiebel would have deserved such an attention. The honour
of the corps, in which Diederich's honour and his whole con-

sciousness were rooted, had its finest representative in Wiebel. ·
On behalf of the Neo-Teutons he would fight a duel with any
one. He had raised the dignity of the corps, for he was re-
puted to have once corrected a member of the swellest corps
in Germany. He had also a relative in the Emperor Francis
Joseph's second regiment of Grenadier Guards, and every time
Wiebel mentioned his cousin, von Klappke, the assembled Neo-
Teutons felt flattered, and bowed. Diederich tried to imagine
a Wiebel in the uniform of an officer of the Guards, but his
imagination reeled before such distinction. Then one day,
when he and Gottlieb Hornung were coming highly perfumed
from their daily visit to the barber's, Wiebel was standing at
the street corner with a quarter-master. There could be no
doubt that it was a quarter-master, and when Wiebel saw
them coming he turned his back. They also turned and walked
away stiffly and silently, without looking at one another or exchanging any remarks. Each supposed that the other had noticed the resemblance between Wiebel and the quarter-master.
Perhaps the others were long since aware of the true state of
affairs, but they were all sufficiently conscious of the honour of
the Neo-Teutons to hold their tongues and forget what they
had seen. The next time Wiebel mentioned "my cousin, von
Klappke," Diederich and Hornung bowed with the others, as
flattered as ever.

By this time, Diederich had learned self-control, a sense of
good form, *esprit de corps,* and zeal for his superiors. He ·
thought with reluctance and pity of the miserable existence
of the common herd to which he had once belonged. At regularly fixed hours he put in an appearance at Wiebel's lodgings,
in the fencing-hall, at the barber's and at *Frühschoppen*. The
afternoon walk was a preliminary to the evening's drinking,
and every step was taken in common, under supervision and
with the observance of prescribed forms and mutual deference,
which did not exclude a little playful roughness. A fellow-
student, with whom Diederich had hitherto had only official re-

lations, once bumped into him at the door of the lavatory, and although both of them were in a great hurry, neither would take precedence over the other. For a long time they stood bowing and scraping—until suddenly overcome by the same need at the same moment, they burst through the door, charging like two wild boars, and knocked their shoulders together. That was the beginning of a friendship. Having come together in such human circumstances, they drew nearer also at the official beer-table, drank one another's health and called each other "pig-dog" and "hippopotamus."

The life of the students' corps had also its tragic side. It demanded sacrifices and taught them to suffer pain and grief with a manly bearing. Delitzsch himself, the source of so much merriment, brought bereavement to the Neo-Teutons. One morning when Wiebel and Diederich came to fetch him, he was standing at his washstand and he said: "Well, are you as thirsty to-day as ever?" Suddenly, before they could reach him he fell down, bringing the crockery with him. Wiebel felt him all over, but Delitzsch did not move again.

"Heart failure," said Wiebel shortly. He walked firmly to the bell. Diederich picked up the broken pieces and dried the floor. Then they carried Delitzsch to his bed. They maintained a strictly disciplined attitude in the face of the landlady's vulgar tears. As they proceeded to attend to the usual formalities—they were marching in step—Wiebel said with stoical contempt for death: "that might have happened to any of us. Drinking is no joke. We should always remember that." Like the others, Diederich felt elevated by Delitzsch's faithful devotion to duty, by his death on the field of honour. They proudly followed the coffin, and every face seemed to say: "The Neo-Teutons for ever!" In the churchyard, with their swords lowered, they all wore the reflective expression of the warrior whose turn may come in the next battle, as his comrade's had come in the one before. And when the leader praised the deceased, who had won the highest prize in the

school of manliness and idealism, each of them was moved as
if the words applied to himself.

This incident marked the end of Diederich's apprenticeship.
Wiebel left in order to get called to the bar, and from now on
Diederich had to stand alone for the principles which he had
laid down, and inculcate them in the younger generation. He
did this very strictly and with a sense of great responsibility.
Woe to the freshman who incurred the penalty of drinking
so many pints in succession. He was obliged to do it for a
good deal longer than five minutes, and ended by groping his
way out along the wall. The worst offence was for one of them
to walk out of the door in front of Diederich. His punishment was eight days without beer. Diederich was not guided
by vanity or personal considerations, but solely by his lofty
idea of the honour of his corps. He himself was a mere individual, and therefore nothing; whatever rights, whatever dignity and importance he enjoyed, were conferred upon him by
the corps. He was indebted to it even for his physical advantages: his broad white face, his paunch which inspired the
freshmen with respect, and the privilege of appearing on festive
occasions in top boots and wearing a cap and sash, the joy of
a uniform! It is true he had still to give precedence to a lieutenant, for the corps to which the lieutenant belonged was obviously a higher one. But; at all events, he could fearlessly
associate with a tram conductor without running the risk of his
being impertinent. His manly courage was threateningly inscribed on his countenance in the slashes which grooved his
chin, streaked his cheeks and cut their way into his close-
cropped skull. What a satisfaction it was to exhibit these constantly to every one! Once unexpectedly a brilliant occasion
arose. He and two others, Gottlieb Hornung and the landlady's servant, were at a dance in Halensee. The two friends
had been sharing for some months a flat with which a rather
pretty servant was included. Neither gave her presents, and
during the summer they went out with her together. Whether

Hornung had gone as far with her as himself was a matter about which Diederich had his private opinion. Officially and as a member of the corps he knew nothing.

Rosa was rather nicely dressed and she found admirers at the ball. In order to dance another polka with her, Diederich had to remind her that it was he who had bought her gloves. He had made a polite bow as a preliminary to the dance when suddenly a third party thrust himself between them and danced off with Rosa. Considerably taken aback, Diederich looked after them with a sombre conviction that this was a case where he must assert himself. But, before he could move, a girl had rushed through the dancing couples, slapped Rosa, and dragged her roughly from her partner. It was the work of a moment for Diederich, when he had seen this, to dash up to Rosa's ravisher.

"Sir," he said looking him straight in the eye, "your conduct is unworthy of a gentleman."

"Well, what about it?"

Astonished by this unusual turn to a dignified conversation Diederich stammered: "Dog."

"Hog," replied the other promptly with a laugh.

Completely demoralised by this absence of good form, Diederich prepared to bow and retire. But the other gave him a punch in the stomach and immediately they rolled on the floor. Amidst screams and encouraging shouts they fought until they were separated. Gottlieb Hornung, who was helping to find Diederich's eyeglasses, cried, "there he goes"—and rushed after him, with Diederich following. They were just in time to see him and a companion getting into a cab, and they took the next one. Hornung declared that the corps could not allow such an insult to pass unpunished. "The swine pinches and does not even trouble to look after his lady," Diederich explained.

"As far as Rosa is concerned, I consider the matter closed."

"So do I."

The chase was exciting. "Shall we overtake them? Our old nag is lame. Suppose this commoner is not of high enough rank to fight a duel with?" In that case they decided that the affair would be officially considered never to have happened.

The first carriage stopped before a nice looking house in the West End. Diederich and Hornung got to the door just as it was shut. They posted themselves with determination in front of it. It grew cold and they marched up and down in front of the house, twenty paces to the right and twenty paces to the left, always keeping the door in view and repeating the same profound and serious remark. This was a case for pistols! This time the Neo-Teutons would buy their honour dearly! Provided he was not a commoner!

At last the concierge appeared, and they consulted him. They tried to describe the two gentlemen, but found that neither of them had any special marks. Hornung maintained, even more passionately than Diederich, that they must wait, and for two more hours they marched up and down. Then two officers came out of the house. Diederich and Hornung stared, uncertain whether there might not be some mistake. The officers started, and one of them seemed to turn slightly pale. That settled the matter for Diederich. He walked up to the one who had turned pale.

"I beg your pardon, sir—"

His voice faltered. The embarrassed lieutenant replied, "You must be mistaken."

Diederich managed to say: "Not at all. I must have satisfaction. You have—"

"I don't know you at all," stammered the lieutenant. But his comrade whispered something in his ear: "That won't do," and taking his friend's card, together with his own, he handed them to Diederich. The latter gave his, and then he read:

"Albrecht Count Tauern-Bärenheim." He did not delay to read the other card, but began dutifully to make little bows. Meanwhile the second officer turned to Gottlieb Hornung.

"Of course, my friend meant no harm by the little joke. Needless to say, he is perfectly ready to give you satisfaction, but I wish to state that no insult was intended."

The other, at whom he glanced, shrugged his shoulders. Diederich stuttered: "Thank you very much."

"That settles the matter, I suppose," said the friend; and the two gentlemen went off.

Diederich remained standing there, with moist brow and choking voice. Suddenly he gave a deep sigh and smiled slowly.

This incident was the sole subject of conversation afterwards at their drinking parties. Diederich praised the true knightly conduct of the count to his comrades.

"A real nobleman always reveals himself."

He contracted his mouth until it was the size of a mouse-hole and brought out in a slow crescendo: "Good f—form is not a vain illusion."

He repeatedly appealed to Gottlieb Hornung as the witness of his great moment. "He wasn't a bit stuck up, was he? Even a rather daring joke is nothing to a gentleman like that. He preserved his dignity all through. Simply *marvellous*, I tell you! His Excellence's explanation was so thoroughly satisfactory that it was impossible for me to—you know, I am no roughneck."

Every one understood and assured Diederich that the tradition of the Neo-Teutons had been adequately maintained in this affair. The cards of the two noblemen were handed round by the juniors and were stuck between the crossed swords over the Emperor's portrait. There was not a Neo-Teuton that night who went home sober.

That was the end of the term, but Diederich and Hornung

had no money to travel home. For some time past they had no money for most things. In view of his duties as a corps member, Diederich's cheque had been raised to two hundred and fifty marks, but still he was up to his eyes in debt. All sources from which a loan could be expected were exhausted, and only the most harried prospect stretched out forbiddingly before them. Finally they were obliged to consider the question of recovering what they themselves had lent in the course of time to their comrades, little as this accorded with knightly practice. Many old chums must meanwhile have come into money. But Hornung could find none. Diederich remembered Mahlmann.

"He is a good mark," he declared. "He was not a member of any corps, a common outsider. I'll beard him in his den." As soon as Mahlmann saw him, he at once burst into that tremendous laugh which Diederich had almost forgotten, and which immediately had an irresistible effect upon him. Mahlmann had no tact. He should have felt that all the Neo-Teutons were morally present in his office with Diederich, and on their account he should have shown more respect for Diederich. The latter had the sensation of having been roughly torn from that powerful unit, and of standing here as one isolated individual before another. This was an unforeseen and uncomfortable position. He felt all the less compunction in mentioning his business. He did not want any money back, such conduct would be unworthy of a comrade. He simply asked if Mahlmann would be so kind as to back a bill for him. Mahlmann leaned back in his desk-chair and said plain and straight: "No."

Diederich was astonished: "Why not?"

"It is against my principles to back a bill," Mahlmann explained.

Diederich blushed with annoyance. "But I have gone security for you, and then the bill came to me and I had to fork out a hundred marks. You took care not to show up."

"So you see! And if I were to go security for you now, you wouldn't pay up either."

Diederich was more surprised than ever.

"No, my young friend," Mahlmann concluded, "if I ever want to commit suicide I can do so without your help."

Diederich pulled himself together and said in a challenging fashion: "I see you have no conception of a gentleman's honour."

"No," Mahlmann repeated, laughing heartily.

With the utmost emphasis Diederich declared: "You appear to be a general kind of swindler. I understand that there is a good deal of swindling in the patent business."

Mahlmann stopped laughing. The expression of his eyes in his little head had become threatening, and he stood up. "Now, get out of here," he said quietly. "Between ourselves, I suppose, it doesn't matter, but my employés are in the next room, and they must not hear such talk." He seized Diederich by the shoulders, turned him around, and shoved him along. Every time he tried to break loose Diederich received a powerful cuff. "I demand satisfaction," he shrieked, "I challenge you to a duel!"

"I am at your service. Have you not noticed it? Then I'll get somebody else for you." He opened the door. "Frederick!" Then Diederich was handed over to one of the packers, who led him down the stairs. Mahlmann shouted after him: "No harm done, my young friend. Whenever you have anything else on your mind, be sure to call again."

Diederich put his clothes in order and left the building in proper style. So much the worse for Mahlmann if he made such an exhibition of himself. Diederich had nothing to reproach himself with, and would have been brilliantly vindicated by a court of honour. The fact remained that it was most objectionable that one person could allow himself such liberties. Every corps had been insulted in the person of Diederich. At the same time it could not be denied that Mahlmann had considerably increased Diederich's self-esteem. "A low dog," Diederich reflected. "But people are like that. . . ."

At home he found a registered letter.

"Now we can be off," said Hornung.

"How do you mean, we? I need my money for myself."

"You must be joking. I can't stay here alone."

"Then go and find some one else to keep you company!" Diederich burst into such a laugh that Hornung thought he was crazy. Thereupon he took his departure.

On the way he noticed for the first time that his mother had addressed the letter. That was unusual. . . . Since her last card, she said, his father had been much worse. Why had Diederich not come?

"We must be prepared for the worst. If you want to see your dearly-beloved father again, do not delay any longer, my son."

These expressions made Diederich feel uncomfortable. He assured himself that his mother was not trustworthy. "I never believe women anyhow, and mother is not quite right in her mind."

Nevertheless, Herr Hessling was breathing his last when Diederich arrived.

Overcome by the sight, Diederich immediately burst into a most undignified howl as he crossed the threshold. He stumbled to the bedside, and his face at that moment was as wet as if he had been washing it. He flapped his arms a number of times, like a bird beating his wings, and let them fall helplessly to his side. Suddenly he noticed his father's right hand on the coverlet, and knelt down and kissed it. Frau Hessling, silent and shrinking, even at the last breath of her master, did the same to his left hand. Diederich remembered how this black, misshapen finger-nail had hit his cheek, when his father boxed his ears, and he wept aloud. And the thrashings when he had stolen the buttons from the rags! This hand had been terrible, but Diederich's heart ached now that he was about to lose it. He felt that the same thought was in his mother's mind and she guessed what was passing in his. They fell into one another's arms across the bed.

When the visits of condolence came, Diederich was himself again. He stood before the whole of Netzig as the representative of the Neo-Teutons, firm and unbending in his knowledge of gentlemanly behaviour. He almost forgot he was in mourning so great was the attention he aroused. He went right out to the hall-door to receive old Herr Buck. The bulky person of Netzig's great man was majestic in his fine frock-coat. With great dignity he carried his upturned silk-hat in front of him in one hand, while the other, from which he had taken his black glove to shake hands with Diederich, felt extraordinarily soft. His blue eyes gazed warmly at Diederich and he said:

"Your father was a good citizen. Strive to become one, too, young man. Always respect the rights of your fellow-citizens. Your own human dignity demands that of you. I trust that we shall work here together in our town for the common welfare. You will continue your studies, no doubt?"

Diederich could scarcely answer yes, he was so disturbed by a sense of reverence. Old Buck asked in a lighter tone: "Did my youngest son look you up in Berlin? No? Oh, he must do that. He is also studying there now. I expect he'll soon have to do his year's military service. Have you got that behind you?"

"No"—and Diederich turned very red. He stammered his excuses. It had been quite impossible for him hitherto to interrupt his studies. But old Buck shrugged his shoulders as if the subject were hardly worth discussing.

By his father's will Diederich was appointed, with the old book-keeper Sötbier, as the guardian of his two sisters. Sötbier informed him that there was a capital of seventy thousand marks which was to serve as a dowry for the two girls. Even the interest could not be touched. In late years the average net profit of the factory had been nine thousand marks. "No more?" asked Diederich. Sötbier looked at him, horrified at first and then reproachful. If the young gentleman only knew how his late lamented father and Sötbier had worked up the business! Of course there was still room for improvement. . . .

"Oh, all right," said Diederich. He saw that many changes would have to be made here. Was he expected to live on one-quarter of nine thousand marks? This supposition on the part of the deceased made him indignant. When his mother stated that the dear departed had expressed the hope on his death-bed that he would live on in his son Diederich, that Diederich would never marry, and always care for the family, then Diederich burst out. "Father was not a sickly sentimentalist like you," he shouted, "and he wasn't a liar either." Frau Hessling thought she could hear the voice of her husband again and bowed to the inevitable. Diederich seized the opportunity to raise his monthly cheque by fifty marks.

"First of all," he said roughly, "I must do my year's military service. That's an expensive business. Afterwards you can come to me with your petty money questions."

He insisted on reporting himself in Berlin. The death of his father had filled him with wild notions of freedom. But at night he had dreams in which the old man came out of his office with his grey face as when he lay in his coffin—and Diederich awoke in a sweat of terror.

He departed with his mother's blessing. He had no further use for Gottlieb Hornung and their common property Rosa, so he moved. He exhibited his changed circumstances in due form to the Neo-Teutons. The happy days of student life were over. The farewell party! They drank toasts of mourning which were intended for the old gentleman, but which also applied to Diederich and the first flowering of his freedom. Out of sheer devotion he finished up under the table, as on the night when he had first drunk with them as a guest. He had now joined the ranks of the old boys.

A couple of days later, still suffering from a bad head, he was standing before the military doctor with a crowd of other young men, all stark naked like himself. The medical officer looked disgustedly at all this manly flesh exposed to view, but when he saw Diederich's paunch his expression was one of contempt. At once they all grinned, and Diederich could not help looking down at his stomach, which was blushing. . . . The surgeon-major had become quite serious again. One of them, who did not hear as sharply as was prescribed in the regulations, had a bad time, as they knew the tricks of the shirkers. Another, who had the misfortune to be called Levysohn, was told: "If you ever come to bother me here again, you might at least take a bath first!" To Diederich he said: "We'll soon massage the fat off you. After four weeks' training I guarantee you'll look like a civilised man."

With that he was accepted. Those who had been rejected hastened into their clothes as if the barracks was on fire. The men who were considered fit for service looked at one another suspiciously out of the corners of their eyes and went off sheepishly, as if they expected to feel a heavy hand come down on their shoulders. One of them, an actor, who looked as if everything was a matter of indifference, went back again to the doctor and said in a loud voice, carefully enunciating each word: "I beg to add that I am also homosexual."

The medical officer started back and went very red. In an indifferent tone he said: "We certainly don't want such swine here."

To his future comrades Diederich expressed his indignation at this shameless conduct. Then he spoke again to the sergeant who had previously measured his height against the wall, and assured him that he was delighted. Nevertheless he wrote home to Netzig to the general practitioner, Dr.

Heuteufel, who used to paint his throat as a boy, asking if he could not certify that he was suffering from scrofula and rickets. Diederich could not be expected to destroy himself with drudgery. But the reply was that he should not complain, that the training would do him no end of good. So Diederich gave up his room again and drove off to the barracks with his portmanteau. Since he had to put in fourteen days there, he might as well save that much rent.

They at once began with horizontal-bar exercises, jumping, and other breathless exertions. They were herded in companies into corridors, which were called "departments." Lieutenant von Kullerow displayed a supercilious indifference, screwing up his eyes whenever he looked at the volunteers. Suddenly he shouted, "Instructor!" and gave his orders to the sergeant and turned on his heels contemptuously. When they exercised in the barrack square, forming fours, opening out, and changing places, the sole object was to keep these "dogs" on the jump. Diederich fully realised that everything here, their treatment, the language used, the whole military system, had only one end in view, to degrade the sense of self-respect to the lowest level. And that impressed him. Miserable as he felt, indeed precisely on that account, it inspired him with deep respect and a sort of suicidal enthusiasm. The principle and the ideal were obviously the same as with the Neo-Teutons, only the system was carried out more cruelly. There were no more comfortable intervals when one could remember one's manhood. Slowly and inevitably one sank to the dimensions of an insect, of a part in the machine, of so much raw material, which was moulded by an unlimited will. It would have been ruin and folly to raise oneself up, even in one's secret heart. The most that one could do, against one's own convictions, was to shirk occasionally. When they were running Diederich fell and hurt his foot. It was not quite bad enough to make him limp, but he did limp, and when the company went out route marching, he was allowed

to remain behind. In order to do this he had first gone to
the captain in person. "Please, captain—" What a catastrophe! In his innocence he had boldly addressed a power
from which one was expected to receive orders silently and
metaphorically on one's knees! A power whom one could
approach only through the intermediary of a third person.
The captain thundered so that the noncommissioned ranks
started, with expressions of horror at having witnessed a crime.
The result was that Diederich limped still more and had to
be relieved of duty for another day.

Sergeant Vanselow, who was responsible for the misde-
meanour of his recruits, only said to Diederich: "And you
profess to be an educated man!" He was accustomed to seeing all misfortunes coming from the volunteers. Vanselow
slept in their dormitory behind a screen. When lights were
out they would tell dirty stories until the outraged sergeant
yelled at them: "And you fellows set up to be men of education!" In spite of his long experience he always expected
more intelligence and better conduct from the one-year volunteers than from the other recruits, and every time he was
disappointed. Diederich he regarded as by no means the
worst. Vanselow's opinion was not influenced solely by the
number of drinks they bought him. He set even more store
by the military spirit of ready submission, and that Diederich
had. When they received instruction he could be held up
as a model for the others. Diederich showed himself entirely
filled with the military ideals of bravery and honour. When
it came to differences of rank and stripes, he seemed to have
an innate sense of these things. Vanselow would say: "Now
I am the general commanding," and immediately Diederich
would act as if he believed it. When he said: "Now I am a
member of the Royal Family," then Diederich's attitude was
such as to make the sergeant smile with the illusion of grandeur.

In private conversation in the canteen Diederich confided

in his superiors that military life filled him with enthusiasm.
"To be swallowed up in a great unit," he would say. He
would ask for nothing better in the world than to stay in the
army. He was sincere, but that did not prevent him, when
they were exercising in the parade ground that afternoon,
from having no other wish than to lie down in his grave and
die. The uniform which was cut to fit closely, for reasons
of smartness, became a real instrument of torture after eating. It was no consolation that the captain appeared un-
speakably warlike and daring as he gave his commands from
his horse, when one could feel the undigested soup slopping
about in one's stomach as one ran around breathlessly. The
enthusiasm which Diederich was fully prepared to feel was
tempered by his personal hardships. His foot was aching
again, and Diederich waited for the pain in the anxious hope,
mixed with self-contempt, that it would get worse, so bad
that he could not go route marching again. Perhaps he might
not even have to exercise any more in the barrack square,
and they would have to give him his discharge.

Things came to the point where he called one Sunday on
the father of one of his college friends, who was an advisory
member of the Medical Council. Red with shame Diederich
confessed that he had come to ask for his support. He loved
the army, the whole system, and would gladly follow that
career. He would be part of a great mechanism, an element
in its strength, so to speak, and would always know what
he had to do, which was a delightful feeling. But now his
foot was paining him. "I can't let it go so far until it is
useless. After all, I have to support my mother and sisters."
The doctor examined him. "The Neo-Teutons for ever,"
said he. "It so happens your surgeon-major is a friend of
mine." That fact was known to Diederich through his friend.
He took his leave full of anxious hope.

The effect of this hope was that he could hardly stand the
next morning. He reported sick. "Who are you? and why

do you bother me?"—And the medical officer looked him over. "You look as fit as a fiddle and your waist line has diminished." But Diederich stood to attention and remained sick. The officer in charge had to come and make an examination. When the foot was uncovered the latter declared that if he did not light a cigar he would be ill. Still, he could find nothing wrong with the foot. The doctor pushed him impatiently from the chair. "Fit for duty, that's all, dismissed"— and Diederich was released. In the middle of drill he gave a sudden cry and collapsed. He was taken into the sick ward for slight cases where there was nothing to eat and a powerful smell of humanity. In this place it was difficult for the volunteers to procure their own food, and he got none of the other men's rations. Driven by hunger he reported himself cured. Cut off from all human protection, and from all the social privileges of civil life, he wore a gloomy look. But one morning, when he had lost all hope, he was called away from drill to the room of the surgeon-major-general. This important official wished to examine him. He spoke in an embarrassing, human kind of way, and then broke again into military gruffness which was not any more calculated to put one at one's ease. He too seemed to find nothing definite, but the result of his examination sounded somewhat different. Diederich was only to carry on "temporarily" until further notice. "With a foot like that . . ."

A few days later a hospital orderly came to Diederich and took an impression of this fateful foot on black paper. Diederich was ordered to wait in the consulting-room. The surgeon-major happened to be passing and took the opportunity to express his complete contempt. "The foot is not even flat! all it wants is to be washed!" Just then the door was pushed open and the surgeon-major-general made his entry with his cap on his head. His step was firmer and surer than usual, he looked neither to the right nor to the left, stood silently in front of his subordinate, and glared gloomily and severely at his cap. The latter was embarrassed. He obviously found himself in a position which did not permit the usual comradeship of colleagues. But he realised the situation, took off his cap and stood at attention. His superior then showed him the paper with the tracing of Diederich's foot, spoke to him in a low tone but with an emphasis which commanded him to see something that was not there. The surgeon-major blinked alternately at his commanding officer, at Diederich and at the paper. Then he clicked his heels; he had seen what he was ordered to see.

When the major-general had gone, the major approached Diederich. With a slight smile of understanding he said politely:

"Of course, the case was clear from the beginning. Because of the men we had to . . . you understand, discipline. . . ."

Diederich stood at attention as a sign that he understood.

"But," continued the major, "I need hardly say I knew how your case stood."

Diederich thought: "If you didn't know it before you know it now." Aloud he said: "I trust you will pardon me for asking, sir, but shall I not be allowed to continue my service?"

"I cannot guarantee that," said the doctor, turning away.

From that time on Diederich was relieved of heavy duty. He went for no more route marches. His conduct in barracks was all the more friendly and willing. At roll-call in the evening the captain came from the mess, with a cigar in his mouth and slightly tipsy, to confine to cells those who had wiped their boots instead of polishing them. He never found fault with Diederich. On the other hand, he vented his righteous wrath all the more severely on a volunteer who, now in his third month, had to sleep in the men's dormitory as a punishment because he had not slept there, but at home, during his first fortnight's service. He had had at the time fourteen degrees of fever and would probably have died if he had done his duty. Well, let him die! The captain's face assumed an expression of proud satisfaction every time he looked at this volunteer. Standing in the background, small and unnoticed, Diederich thought: "You see, my boy, the Neo-Teutons and an Advisory Member of the Medical Council are more useful than fourteen degrees of fever. . . ." As far as he was concerned the official formalities were one day happily fulfilled, and Sergeant Vanselow informed him that he had received his release. Diederich's eyes at once filled with tears and he shook his hand warmly.

"Just my luck for a thing like that to happen to me, and I had"—he sobbed—"such a happy time."

Then he found himself outside in the street.

He remained at home four whole weeks and studied hard. When he went out to meals he looked round anxiously lest an acquaintance should see him. Finally he felt he would have to show himself to the Neo-Teutons. He assumed a challenging attitude.

"Until you have been in the army you have no idea what it's like. There, I can tell you, you see the world from a very different standpoint. I would have stayed altogether, my qualifications were so excellent that my superior officers advised me to do so. But then"—here he stared moodily in front of him—"came the accident with the horse. That is the result of being too good a soldier. The captain used to get some one to drive in his dog-cart to exercise the horse, and that is how the accident happened. Of course I did not nurse my foot properly and resumed duty too soon. The thing got very much worse, and the doctor advised me to prepare my relatives for the worst."—The words came sharply and with manly restraint.—"You should have seen the captain; he came to see me himself every day, after the long marches, just as he was, with his uniform covered with dust. During those days of suffering we became real comrades. Here, I still have one of his cigars. When he had to confess that the doctor had decided to send me away, I assure you it was one of those moments in a man's life which he can never forget. Both the captain and I had tears in our eyes." The whole company was deeply moved. Diederich looked bravely around at them.

"Well, now I suppose I must try and find my way back into civilian life. Your health."

He continued to cram and on Saturdays he drank with the Neo-Teutons. Wiebel also turned up. He had become an assistant judge, on the way to becoming a state's attorney, and could only talk of "subversive tendencies," "enemies of the fatherland" and "Christian socialist ideas." He explained to the freshmen that the time had come to take politics seriously. He knew it was considered vulgar, but their opponents made it necessary. Real feudal aristocrats, like his friend, von Barnim, were in the movement. Herr von Barnim would shortly honour the Neo-Teutons with his company.

When he came he won all hearts, for he treated them as equals. He had dark, closely cropped hair, the manner of a conscientious bureaucrat, and spoke in matter-of-fact tones, but at the end of his address his eyes had a look of ecstasy, and he said good-bye quickly, pressing their hands fervently. After his visit the Neo-Teutons all agreed that Jewish liberalism was the first fruits of social democracy and German Christians should rally to the Royal Chaplain, Stöcker. Like the others, Diederich did not connect the expression "first fruits" with any definite idea, and he understood "social democracy" to mean a general division of wealth. And that was enough for him. But Herr von Barnim had invited those who desired further information to come to him, and Diederich would never have pardoned himself if he had missed so flattering an opportunity.

In his cold, old-fashioned, bachelor apartment Herr von Barnim held a private and confidential conclave. His political objective was a permanent system of popular representation as in the happy Middle Ages: knights, clergy, craftsmen and artisans. As the Emperor had rightly insisted, the crafts would have to be restored to the dignity which they enjoyed before the Thirty Years' War. The guilds were to cultivate religion and morals. Diederich expressed the warmest approval. The idea fully corresponded with his tendency, as a registered member of a profession and a gentleman of rank, to take his stand in life collectively rather than personally. He already pictured himself as the delegate of the paper industry. Herr von Barnim frankly excluded their Jewish fellow-citizens from his social order. Were they not the root of all disorder and revolution, of confusion and disrespectfulness, the principle of evil itself? His pious face was convulsed with hatred and Diederich felt with him.

"When all is said and done," he remarked, "we wield the power and can throw them out. The German army—"

"That's just it," cried Herr von Barnim, who was walking up and down the room. "Did we wage the glorious war in order to sell my family estate to a gentleman named Frankfurter?"

While Diederich maintained a disturbed silence, there was a ring and Herr von Barnim said: "This is my barber; I must tackle him also." He noticed Diederich's look of disappointment and added:

"Of course with such a man I talk differently. But each one of us must do his bit against the Social Democrats, and bring the common people into the camp of our Christian Emperor. You must do yours!" Thereupon Diederich took his leave. He heard the barber say:

"Another old customer, sir, has gone over to Liebling just because Liebling now has marble fittings."

When Diederich reported to Wiebel the latter said:

"That is all very well, and I have a particular regard for the idealistic viewpoint of my friend, von Barnim, but in the long run it will not get us anywhere. Stöcker, you know, also made his damned experiments with democracy at the Ice Palace. Whether it was Christian or un-Christian democracy, I don't know. Things have got too far for that. To-day only one course is still open: To hit out hard so long as we have the power."

Greatly relieved Diederich agreed with him. To go round converting Christians had at once struck him as rather laborious.

"I will attend to the Social Democrats, the Emperor has said." Wiebel's eyes gleamed with a cat-like ferocity. "Now what more do you want? The soldiers have been given their orders, and it may happen that they will have to fire on their beloved relatives. What of it? I tell you, my dear fellow, we are on the eve of great events."

Diederich showed signs of excited curiosity.

"My cousin, von Klappke—" Wiebel paused and Diederich clicked his heels—"has told me things which are not yet ripe for publication. Suffice it to say that His Majesty's statement yesterday, that the grumblers should kindly shake the dust of Germany from the soles of their feet, was a damnably serious warning."

"Is that a fact? Do you really think so?" said Diederich. "Then it is the devil's own luck that I have to leave His Majesty's service just at this moment. I am not ashamed to say that I would have done my whole duty against the domestic enemy. One thing I do know, the Emperor can rely upon the army."

During those icy cold days of February, 1892, he went about the streets a great deal, in the expectation of great events. Along Unter den Linden something was afoot, but what it was could not yet be seen. Mounted police held the ends of the streets and waited. Pedestrians pointed to this display of force. "The unemployed!" People stood still to watch them approaching. They came from a northerly direction, marching slowly in small sections. When they reached Unter den Linden they hesitated, as if lost, took counsel by an exchange of glances, and turned off towards the Castle. There they stood in silence, their hands in their pockets, while the wheels of the cars splashed them with mud, and they hunched up their shoulders beneath the rain which fell on their faded overcoats. Many of them turned to look at passing officers, at the ladies in their carriages, at the long fur coats of the gentlemen hurrying from Burgstrasse. Their faces were expressionless, neither threatening nor even curious: not as if they wanted to see, but as if they wanted to be seen. Others never moved an eye from the windows of the Castle. The rain trickled down from their upturned faces. The horse of a shouting policeman drove them on further across the street to the next corner—but they stood still again, and the world seemed to sink down between those broad hollow faces, lit by the livid gleam of evening, and the stern walls beyond them which were already enveloped in darkness.

"I do not understand," said Diederich, "why the police do not take more energetic measures. That is certainly a rebellious crew."

"Don't you worry," Wiebel replied, "they have received exact instructions. Believe me, the authorities have their own well-developed plans. It is not always desirable to suppress at the outset such excrescences on the body politic. When they have been allowed to ripen, then a radical operation can be performed."

The ripening process to which Wiebel referred increased daily, and on the 26th it was completed. The demonstrations of the unemployed seemed more conscious of their objective. When they were driven back into one of the northern streets they overflowed into the next, and, before they could be cut off, they surged forward again in increased numbers. The processions all met at Unter den Linden, and as often as they were separated they ran together again. They reached the Castle, were driven back, and reached it again, silent and irresistible, like a river overflowing its banks. The traffic was blocked, the stream of pedestrians was banked up until it flowed over slowly into the flood which submerged the square; into this turbid, discoloured sea of poverty, rolling up in clammy waves, emitting subdued noises and throwing up, like the masts of sunken ships, poles bearing banners: "Bread! Work!" Here and there a more distinct rumbling broke out of the depths: "Bread! Work!" Swelling above the crowd it rolled off like a thunder-cloud: "Bread! Work!" The mounted police attack, the sea foams up and subsides, while women's voices shrilly cry like signals above the uproar: "Bread! Work!"

They are swept along, carrying with them the curious spectators standing on the Friederich monument. Their mouths are wide open; dust rises from the minor officials whose way to the office has been blocked, as if their clothes had been beaten. A distorted face, unknown to Diederich, shouts at him: "Here's something different! Now we are going for the Jews!"—and the face disappears before he remembers that it is Herr von Barnim. He tries to follow him, but in a big rush is thrown far across the road in front of a café, where he hears the crash of the broken windows and a workman shouting: "They fired me out of here lately with my thirty pfennig, because I had not got a silk hat on."—With him Diederich is forced in through the window, between the overturned tables and on to the floor, where they trip over broken glass, crushing against one another and howling. "No more in here! We must have air!" But still they clamber in. "The police are charging!" In the middle of the street, a free passage is miraculously made, as if for a triumphant procession. Then someone cries: "There goes Emperor William!"

Diederich found himself once more on the street. No one knew how it happened that they could suddenly move along in a solid mass the whole width of the street, and on both sides, right up to the flanks of the horse on which the Emperor sat—the Emperor himself. The people looked at him and followed him. Shouting masses were dissolved and swept along. Every one looked at him. A dark pushing mob without form, without plan, without limit, and bright above it a young man in a helmet: the Emperor. They looked. They had brought him down from his Castle. They had shouted: "Bread! Work!" until he had come. Nothing had been changed, except that he was there, and yet they were marching as if to a review of the troops at the Tempelhof.

On the outskirts, where the crowds were thinner, respectable people were saying to each other: "Well, thank God, he knows what he wants!"

"What does he want then?"

"To show that mob who is master! He tried treating them kindly. He even went too far in remitting sentences two years ago; they have become impertinent."

"It certainly must be admitted that he is not afraid. My word, this is an historical moment!

Diederich listened and was thrilled. The old gentleman who had spoken turned to him. He had white side-whiskers and wore an iron cross.

"Young man," said he, "what our magnificent young Emperor is now doing will be learned one day by the children in their schoolbooks. Wait till you see!"

Many people threw out their chests with an air of reverence. The gentlemen who rode behind the Emperor kept their eyes fixed in front of them, but they guided their horses through the crowd as if all these folk were supers ordered to appear in some royal spectacle. At times they glanced sideways at the public to see how the latter were impressed. The Emperor himself saw only his own personality and his own performance. Profound seriousness was stamped upon his features and his eyes flashed over the thousands whom he had fascinated. He measured himself against them, he, the master by the grace of God, and his rebellious slaves. Alone and unprotected he had dared to come amongst them, strong only in the sense of his mission. They might lay violent hands upon him if that were the will of the Almighty. He offered himself as sacrifice to his sacred trust. He would show them whether God was on his side. Then they would carry away the impression of his action and the eternal memory of their own powerlessness.

A young man wearing a wide-brimmed hat passed near Diederich and said: "Old stuff. Napoleon in Moscow fraternising alone with the people."

"But it is fine," asserted Diederich, and his voice faltered with emotion. The other shrugged his shoulders.

"Melodrama, and no good, at that."

Diederich looked at him and tried to flash his eyes like the Emperor.

"I suppose you are one of that rabble yourself."

He could not have explained what the rabble was. He simply felt that here, for the first time in his life, he had to defend law and order against hostile criticism. In spite of his agitation, he had another look at the man's shoulders; th·y were not imposing. The bystanders, too, were expressing disapproval. Then Diederich asserted himself. With his huge stomach he pressed the enemy against the wall and battered in his hat. Others joined in pummelling him, his hat fell to the ground, and soon the man himself lay there. As he moved on, Diederich remarked to his fellow-combatants: "That fellow has certainly not done his military service. He hasn't even got scars on his face; he has never fought a duel."

The old gentleman with the side-whiskers and the iron cross turned up again and shook Diederich's hand.

"Bravo, young man, bravo!"

"Isn't it enough to make you mad," said Diederich, still

furious, "when the fellow tries to spoil our historical moment?"

"You have been in the army?" queried the old gentleman.

"I would have liked nothing better than to stay there," Diederich replied.

"Ah, yes, it isn't every day that we have a Sedan." The old gentleman touched his iron cross. "That's what we did!"

Diederich stretched himself and pointed to the Emperor and the subdued crowd.

"That is as good as Sedan!"

"Hm, hm," said the old gentleman.

"Allow me, sir," cried some one, waving a notebook. "We must get that. A touch of atmosphere, y'understand? I suppose it was a damned radical you bashed?"

"Oh, a mere trifle"—Diederich was still boiling. "As far as I am concerned this would be the time to go straight for the domestic enemy. We have our Emperor with us."

"Fine," said the reporter as he wrote: "In the wildly agitated throng people of all classes were heard expressing their devoted loyalty and unshakable confidence in His Majesty."

"Hurrah!" shouted Diederich, for every one was shouting, and, caught in a great surge of shouting people, he was carried right along to the Brandenburger Tor. A few steps in front of him rode the Emperor. Diederich could see his face, its stony seriousness and flashing eyes, but he was shouting so much that his sight was blurred. An intoxication, higher and nobler than that which beer procured, raised his feet off the ground and carried him into the air. He waved his hat high above all heads, in a sphere of enthusiastic madness, in a heaven where our finest feelings move. There on the horse rode Power, through the gateway of triumphal entries, with dazzling features but graven as in stone. The Power which transcends us and whose hoofs we kiss, the Power which is beyond the reach of hunger, spite and mockery!

Against it we are impotent, for we all love it! We have it in our blood, for in our blood is submission. We are an atom of that Power, a diminutive molecule of something it has given out. Each one of us is as nothing, but massed in ranks as Neo-Teutons, soldiers, bureaucrats, priests and scientists, as economic organisations and unions of power, we taper up like a pyramid to the point at the top where Power itself stands, graven and dazzling. In it we live and have our being, merciless towards those who are remote beneath us, and triumphing even when we ourselves are crushed, for thus does power justify our love for it!

. . . One of the policemen lined up to keep a clear passage through the gateway gave Diederich a blow in the chest that took his breath away, but his eyes were full of the tumult of victory, as if he himself were riding away over all these wretches who had been cowed into swallowing their hunger. Let us follow him! Follow the Emperor! They all felt as Diederich did. A chain of policemen was too weak to restrain so much feeling. The people broke through. Beyond the gate was another chain, so they had to make a détour, find a gap, and reach the Tiergarten by a roundabout way. Only a few succeeded, and Diederich was alone when he stumbled onto the riding alley in the direction of the Emperor, who was also alone. A man in a very dangerous state of fanaticism, dirty and torn, with wild eyes—from his horse the Emperor gave him a piercing glance which went through him. Diederich snatched his hat off, his mouth was wide open but not a sound came from it. As he came to a sudden stop he slipped and sat down violently in a puddle, with his legs in the air, splashed with muddy water. Then the Emperor laughed. The fellow was a monarchist, a loyal subject! The Emperor turned to his escort, slapped his thigh and laughed. From the depths of his puddle Diederich stared after him, open-mouthed.

II

HE brushed his clothes carefully and turned away. A lady was sitting on a seat, and Diederich did not feel anxious to pass in front of her. To make matters worse, she kept looking towards him. "Silly fool," he thought angrily, but then he noticed an expression of great astonishment on her face and he recognised that it was Agnes Göppel.

"I have just met the Emperor," he began at once.

"The Emperor?" she asked abstractedly. With large, unaccustomed gestures he began to pour out the emotions which were choking him. Our magnificent young Emperor, all alone in the midst of a mob of revolutionaries! They had smashed up a café, and Diederich himself had been in it! He had fought bloody fights Unter den Linden for his Emperor! They ought to have turned machine guns on them!

"I suppose the people are hungry," said Agnes gravely. "They, too, are human beings."

"Do you call them human?" Diederich rolled his eyes indignantly. "They are the domestic enemy, that's what they are!" But he grew a little calmer when he saw Agnes start again with fear.

"No doubt it amuses you to find all the streets barred on account of that mob."

No, that was most inconvenient for Agnes. She had had some errands in the city, but when she wanted to go back to Blücherstrasse there were no more buses running, and she could not get through anywhere. She had been pushed back to the Tiergarten. It was cold and wet; her father would be anxious; what was she to do? Diederich assured her that he would make it all right. They continued their way to-

gether. All of a sudden he felt tongue-tied and kept looking
about as if he had lost his way. They were alone amongst
the leafless trees and the wet, withered foliage. Where was
all the manly rapture which had previously filled him? Diederich felt embarrassed, as he had been during that last walk
with Agnes, when Mahlmann had warned him, and he had
jumped on a bus, torn himself away and disappeared. Agnes
was just saying: "It is a very, very long time since you came
to see us. Didn't papa write to you?" Somewhat confused,
Diederich explained that his own father had died. Now Agnes
hastened to express her sympathy, then she went on to ask
why he had suddenly disappeared three years ago.

"Isn't that so? It is nearly three years now."

Diederich recovered his self-possession and explained that
his student life had taken up all his time, that it was a jolly
strenuous business. "And then I had to do my military
service."

"Oh!"—Agnes stared at him. "What a great man you have
become! And now I suppose you have got your doctor's
degree?"

"That will come very soon now."

He gazed discontentedly in front of him. The scars on
his face, his broad shoulders, all the signs of his well-earned
manliness—were these nothing to her? Did she not even notice them?

"But what about you?" he said suddenly. A faint blush
suffused her thin, pale face and even the bridge of her small,
aquiline nose, with its freckles.

"Yes, sometimes I don't feel very well, but I'll be all right
again."

Diederich expressed his regrets.

"Of course I meant to say that you have become prettier"
—and he looked at her red hair which escaped from under
her hat, and seemed thicker than formerly because her face
had become so thin. He was reminded of his former humilia-

tions and of how different things were now. Defiantly he asked: "How is Herr Mahlmann?"

Agnes assumed an air of contempt. "Do you still remember him? If I were to see him again, I should not be particularly pleased."

"Really? But he has a patent office and could very easily marry."

"Well, what of it?"

"But you used to be greatly interested in him."

"What makes you think that?"

"He was always giving you presents."

"I would have preferred not to take them, but then—" she looked down at the ground, at the wet fallen leaves—"then I could not have accepted your presents." She was frightened and said nothing more. Diederich felt that something serious had happened and was silent also.

"They were not worth talking about," he said finally, "a few flowers." And, with returning indignation: "Mahlmann even gave you a bracelet."

"I never wear it," said Agnes. His heart began to beat violently as he managed to say: "And if I had given it to you?"

Silence. He held his breath. Softly he heard her whisper: "In that case, yes."

Then they walked on more quickly and without speaking a word. They came to the Brandenburger Tor, saw that Unter den Linden was full of police and hurried past it, turning into Dorotheenstrasse. Here there were few people about. Diederich slowed their pace and began to laugh.

"It is really very funny. Every present Mahlmann gave you was paid for with my money. I was still a greenhorn and he took everything from me."

She stood still. "Oh!"—and she gazed at him, her blue brown eyes tremulous. "That's dreadful. Can you forgive me?"

He smiled in a superior way, and said that was ancient history, youthful follies.

"No, no," she said, quite disturbed.

Now, he said, the principal thing was: how was she to get home? They could not go any further this way either, and there were no more buses to be seen. "I am very sorry, but you will have to put up with my society a little longer. In any case, I live just near here. You could come up to my apartment, at least you would be dry there. But, of course, a young lady can't do such a thing."

She still had that beseeching look of hers. "You are too kind," said she, breathlessly. "You are so noble." And as they entered the house, she added: "I know I can trust you, can't I?"

"I know what I owe to the honour of my corps," Diederich declared.

They had to pass the kitchen, but there was no one in it. "Won't you take off your things until you go out again?" said Diederich graciously. He stood there without looking at Agnes, and while she was taking off her hat he stood first on one foot and then on the other.

"I must go and find the landlady and get her to make some tea." He had turned towards the door, but started back, for Agnes had seized his hand and kissed it. "Agnes," he murmured, terribly frightened, and he put his arm around her shoulder to console her. Then she nestled against his. He pressed his lips to her hair, and pressed them fairly hard, because he felt that was the right thing to it. Under that pressure her whole being quivered and shook, as if she had been struck. Through her thin blouse her body felt warm and moist. Diederich felt hot. He kissed Agnes's neck, but suddenly her face was turned up to his, with her lips parted, her eyes half closed and an expression which he had never seen before. It turned his head. "Agnes! Agnes! I love you," he cried, as if compelled by some deep emotion. She

did not answer. Short, hot panting breaths came from her
open mouth, and he felt that she was falling; as he carried
her, she seemed to melt away.

She sat on the sofa and cried. "Don't be angry with me,
Agnes," Diederich begged. Her eyes were wet as she looked
at him. "I am crying with joy," said she. "I have waited
so long for you."

"Why?" she asked, when he began to button her blouse,—
"why do you cover me so soon? Do you no longer find me
beautiful?"

He protested: "I am fully conscious of the responsibility
I have undertaken."

"Responsibility?" Agnes queried. "Whose is it? I have
loved you for three years, but you did not know it. It must
have been our fate."

With his hands in his pockets Diederich was thinking that
such is the fate of light-minded women. At the same time,
he felt the need of hearing her repeat her protestations. "So
I am really the only man you ever loved?"

"I saw that you did not believe me. It was terrible when
I knew that you had stopped coming, and that everything was
over. It was really awful. I wanted to write to you, to
go and see you. I lost courage each time, because you might
not want me any more. I was so run down that papa had
to take me away."

"Where to?" asked Diederich, but Agnes did not answer.
She drew him to her again. "Be good to me, I have no one
but you!"

"Then you haven't got much," thought Diederich, embarrassed. Agnes appeared greatly diminished in his eyes, and
lowered in his estimation, since he had proof that she loved
him. He also said to himself that one could not believe everything a girl said who behaved like that.

"And Mahlmann?" he queried mockingly. "There must

have been something between you and him— Oh, well, we'll say no more about it," he concluded, as she drew herself up, dumbfounded with horror. He tried to make things right again, saying he was still completely mastered by his joy.

She dressed herself very slowly. "Your father will not know at all what has happened to you," said Diederich. She merely shrugged her shoulders. When she was ready, and he had opened the door, she stood for a moment and looked back into the room with a long glance, full of fear.

"Perhaps," she said, as if talking to herself, "I shall never see this room again. I feel as if I were going to die to-night."

"Why do you say that?" asked Diederich aggrievedly. Instead of replying she clung to him again, her lips pressed to his, their two bodies so closely held together that they seemed but one. Diederich waited patiently. She broke away from him, opened her eyes and said: "You must not think that I expect anything from you. I love you and that is enough."

He offered to call a cab for her, but she preferred to walk. On the way he inquired after her family and other acquaintances. But by the time they had reached the Belle Alliance Platz he began to feel uneasy, and in rather muffled tones he said: "Of course you must not think that I want to evade my responsibility to you. But, you understand, for the moment I am not earning anything, and I must get fixed up and get into harness at the factory. . . ."

Agnes answered quietly and gratefully, as if a favour had been conferred upon her: "How nice it would be if I could become your wife later on."

When they turned into Blücherstrasse he stopped. Hesitatingly he suggested it would probably be better if he turned back.

"Because some one might see us? That wouldn't matter at all, for I must explain at home that I met you and that we waited together in a café till the streets were clear."

"She is certainly a clever liar," thought Diederich. She added: "You are invited to dinner on Sunday, you must be sure to come."

This was too much for him, he started. "I must—? I am invited to—?" She smiled softly and shyly. "It cannot be avoided. If any one ever saw us— Do you not want me to come to you again?"

Oh, yes, he did. Nevertheless, she had to persuade him until he promised to put in an appearance. In front of her house, he said good-bye with a formal bow, and turned quickly away. "Women of that type," he thought, "are terribly subtle. I won't have too much to do with her." Meanwhile he noticed with reluctance that it was time to meet his friends for a drink. For some reason he was longing to be home. When he had shut the door of his room behind him he stood and stared into the darkness. Suddenly he raised his arms, turned his face upwards and breathed a long sigh: "Agnes!"

He felt entirely changed, as light as if he trod on air. "I am terribly happy," was his thought, and "never in my life again shall I experience anything so wonderful!" He was convinced that until then, until that moment, he had looked at things from a wrong angle, and had wrongly estimated them. Now his friends were drinking and giving themselves an air of importance. What did it matter about the Jews and the unemployed? Why should he hate them? Diederich even felt prepared to love them! Was it really he who had spent the day in a struggling mob of people whom he had regarded as enemies? They were human beings; Agnes was right. Was it really he who, for the sake of a few words, had beaten somebody, had bragged, lied and foolishly over-exerted himself, and who had finally thrown himself, torn and stunned, in the mud before a gentleman on horseback, the Emperor, who had laughed at him? He recognised that, until Agnes came, his life had been helpless, poor and meaningless. Efforts which seemed those of another than himself, feelings which shamed him, and nobody whom he could love—until Agnes came! "Agnes! my sweet Agnes, you do not know how much I love you!" But she would have to know. He felt that he would never again be able to tell her so well as in this hour, and he wrote a letter. He wrote that he, too, had waited for her these three years, and that he had had no hope because she was too fine, too good, too beautiful for him; that he had said what he did about Mahlmann out of cowardice and spite, that she was a saint, and, now that she had condescended to him, he lay at her feet. "Lift me up, Agnes, I can be strong, I know I can, and I will dedicate my whole life to you!" He began to cry, pressing his face into the sofa cushion where her perfume still lingered, and sobbing like a child he fell asleep.

In the morning, it is true, he was astonished and irritated at not finding himself in bed. His great adventure came back to his mind and sent a delicious thrill through his blood to his heart. At the same time the suspicion seized him that he had been guilty of unpleasant exaggerations. He re-read his letter. It was all right and a man could really lose his head when he suddenly had an affair with such a fine girl. If she had only been there now he would have treated her tenderly. Still it was better not to send that letter. It was imprudent in every way. In the end Papa Göppel would intercept it. . . . Diederich shut the letter up in his desk. "I forgot all about eating yesterday!" He ordered a substantial breakfast. "I did not smoke either in order to preserve her perfume. But that's absurd; such things aren't done." He lit a cigar and went off to the laboratory. He resolved to release what was weighing on his heart in music rather than in words, for such lofty words were unmanly and uncomfortable. He hired a piano and tried his hand at Schubert and Beethoven with much more success than at his music lessons.

On Sunday when he rang at Göppel's it was Agnes herself
who opened the door. "The girl seemed in no hurry to leave
the kitchen range," said she; but her glance told the real reason. Not knowing what to say, Diederich allowed his eyes
to wander to the silver bracelet which she rattled as if to
draw his attention.

"Do you not recognise it?" Agnes whispered. He blushed.
"The present from Mahlmann?"

"The present from you. This is the first time I have worn
it." Suddenly he felt the warm pressure of her hand, then
the door of the drawing-room opened. Herr Göppel turned
to meet him: "Here is the man who deserted us!" But
scarcely had he seen Diederich than his manner altered and
he regretted his familiarity. "Really, Herr Hessling, I should
hardly have known you again!" Diederich looked at Agnes
as much as to say: "You see, he notices that I am no longer
a callow youth."

"Everything is unchanged with you," Diederich observed,
and he greeted the sisters and brother-in-law of Herr Göppel.
In reality he found them all appreciably older, especially Herr
Göppel, who was not so lively, and whose cheeks were un-
healthily fat. The children were bigger and some one seemed
to be missing from the room. "Yes, indeed," concluded Herr
Göppel, "time passes, but old friends always meet again."

"If you only knew in what circumstances," Diederich
thought contemptuously as they went in to dinner. When
the roast veal was brought on, it finally dawned upon him who
used to sit opposite to him. It was the aunt who had so
haughtily asked him what he was studying, and who did not
know that chemistry and physics were two entirely different
things. Agnes, who sat on his right, explained to him that
this aunt had been dead for two years. Diederich murmured
words of sympathy, but his private reflection was: "One more
chatterbox the less." It seemed to him as if every one present
had been punished and buffeted by fate, he alone had been

raised in accordance with his merits. He swept Agnes from head to foot with a glance of possession.

As on the former occasion, they had to wait this time for the sweets. Agnes kept looking uneasily at the door and Diederich saw a shadow in her lovely blue eyes, as if something serious had happened. He suddenly felt the deepest sympathy for her and an immense tenderness. He rose and shouted through the door: "Marie! the custard!"

When he returned Herr Göppel drank to him. "You did the same thing before. Here you are like one of the family. Isn't that so, Agnes?" Agnes thanked Diederich with a glance which stirred his heart to the depths. He had to control himself to prevent tears from coming into his eyes. How kindly her relatives smiled at him. The brother-in-law clinked glasses with him. What good-hearted people! and Agnes, darling Agnes, loved him! He was unworthy of so much kindness! His conscience pricked him and he vaguely resolved to speak to Herr Göppel afterwards.

Unfortunately, after dinner Herr Göppel began again to talk about the riots. When we had at last shaken off the pressure of the Bismarckian jackboot there was no necessity to irritate the workers with flamboyant speeches. The young man (that was how Herr Göppel referred to the Emperor!) will talk until he has brought a revolution upon our heads. . . . Diederich found himself compelled to repudiate most sharply such fault-finding, on behalf of the young men who stood steadfast and true by their magnificent young Emperor. His Majesty himself had said: "I welcome heartily those who want to help me. I will smash those who oppose me." As he said this Diederich tried to flash his eyes. Herr Göppel declared that he would await events.

"In these difficult times," Diederich continued, "every one must stand forth in his true colours." He struck an attitude in front of the admiring Agnes.

"What do you mean by difficult times?" Herr Göppel asked.

"The times are difficult only when we make life difficult for one another. I have always got on perfectly well. with my workmen."

Diederich expressed his determination to introduce entirely different methods at home in his factory. There will be no room for social democrats, and on Sunday the people would have to go to church!—"So that is also included," said Herr Göppel. He could not expect such a thing from his people, when he himself went only on Good Friday. "Am I to fool them? Christianity is all right, but nobody believes any more all the stuff the parsons talk." Then Diederich's countenance assumed the most superior expression.

"My dear Herr Göppel, all I can say is this: what the powers that be, and especially my esteemed friend, Assessor von Barnim, consider it right to believe, I also believe—unconditionally. That's all I have to say."

The brother-in-law, who was a civil servant, suddenly took Diederich's side. Herr Göppel was already considerably excited when Agnes interrupted with coffee. "Well, how do you like my cigars?" Herr Göppel tapped Diederich's knee. "Don't you see, we are at one where human things are concerned." Diederich thought: "Especially as I am, so to speak, one of the family."

He gradually relaxed his uncompromising attitude, it was all so very cosy and comfortable. Herr Göppel wanted to know when Diederich would be "finished" and a doctor. He could not understand that a chemistry thesis took two years and more. Diederich launched into phrases which nobody understood about the difficulties of reaching a solution. He had the notion that Herr Göppel, for definite reasons of his own, was most anxious that he should receive his degree. Agnes seemed to notice this, too, for she intervened and turned the conversation on to other topics. When Diederich had said good-bye she accompanied him to the door and whispered: "To-morrow, at three o'clock at your rooms."

From sheer joy he seized her and kissed her, between the two doors, while immediately beside them the servant was clattering the dishes. She asked sadly: "Do you never think of what would happen to me if some one were to come now?" He was taken aback, and as a proof that she had forgiven him, he asked for another kiss. She gave it to him.

At three o'clock Diederich used to return to the laboratory from the café. Instead he was back in his room at two, and she did come before three o'clock. "Neither of us could wait! we love one another so much!" It was nicer, much nicer than the first time. No more tears nor fears, and the room was flooded with sunshine. Diederich loosened Agnes's hair in the sun and buried his face in it.

She stayed until it was almost too late to make the purchases which had served as an excuse at home. She had to run. Diederich, who ran with her, was greatly concerned lest any harm should come to her. But she laughed, looked rosy, and called him her bear. And so ended every day on which she came. They were always happy. Herr Göppel noticed that Agnes was looking better than ever and this made him feel younger. For that reason the Sundays were also jollier. They stayed on till evening, then punch was made. Diederich played Schubert or he and the brother-in-law sang students' songs while Agnes accompanied them. Sometimes these two glanced at each other and it seemed to them both that it was their happiness which was being celebrated.

It came about that in the laboratory the porter would come and inform him that a lady was waiting outside. He got up at once, blushing proudly under the knowing looks of his colleagues. Then they wandered off, went to the cafés and to the picture gallery. As Agnes was fond of pictures Diederich discovered that there were such things as exhibitions. Agnes loved to stand in front of a picture that pleased her, a picture of a tender, festive landscape from more beautiful countries, and with half-closed eyes to share her dreams with Diederich.

"If you look properly you'll see that it is not a frame, it is a gate with golden stairs and we are going down them and across the road; we are bending back the hawthorn bushes and stepping into the boat. Don't you feel how it rocks? That's because we're trailing our hands in the water, it is so warm. Up there, on the hill, the white point, you know, is our house, that is our destination. Look, do you see?"

"Oh, yes," said Diederich with enthusiasm. He screwed up his eyes and saw everything that Agnes wished. He got so enthusiastic that he seized her hand to dry it. Then they sat in a corner and talked of the journeys they would make, of untroubled happiness in distant sunny lands, and of love without end. Diederich believed everything he said. At bottom he knew very well that he was destined to work and to lead a practical existence without much leisure for superfluities. But what he said here was true in a higher sense than everything that he knew. The real Diederich, the man he should have been, spoke the truth. But when they stood up to go Agnes was pale and seemed tired. Her lovely blue eyes had a brightness which made Diederich feel uncomfortable, and in a trembling whisper she asked: "Supposing our boat overturned?"

"Then I would rescue you!" replied Diederich with resolution.

"But it is far from the shore and the water is frightfully deep." And when he seemed powerless to make any suggestion: "We'd have to drown. Tell me, would you like to die with me?"

Diederich looked at her and shut his eyes. "Yes," he said with a sigh.

Afterwards he regretted having talked like that. He had noticed the reason why Agnes suddenly had to get into a cab and drive home. She was flushed and pale by turns and tried to hide how much she was coughing. Then Diederich regretted the whole afternoon. Such things were unhealthy, led nowhere except to unpleasantness. His professor had begun to hear about the lady's visits. It wouldn't do for her to take him from his work whenever the whim seized her. He explained the whole matter to her patiently. "I suppose you are right," she said. "Normal people must have regular hours. But what if I must come to you now at half-past five when I feel inclined to love you most at four?"

He sensed a joke in this, perhaps even contempt, and was rude. He had no use for a sweetheart who wished to hinder him in his career. He had not counted on that. Then Agnes begged his pardon. She would be quite humble and would wait for him in his room. If he still had anything to do, he need have no consideration for her. Diederich was shamed by this, he softened and abandoned himself with Agnes in complaints against the world which was not made entirely for love. "Is there no alternative?" Agnes asked. "You have a little money and so have I. Why worry about making a position for yourself? We could be so happy together." Diederich agreed, but afterwards he cherished a grievance against her. He used to keep her waiting deliberately. He even declared that going to political meetings was a duty which took precedence over his meetings with Agnes. One evening in May, as he returned home late, he met a young man at the door in a volunteer's uniform, who looked at him in a hesitating manner. "Herr Diederich Hessling?"—"Oh, yes," Diederich stammered. "You are Herr Wolfgang Buck, aren't you?"

The youngest son of the great man of Netzig had at last decided to obey his father's orders and call on Diederich. The latter took him upstairs, as he could not think at once of an excuse to get rid of him, and there sat Agnes! On the landing he raised his voice so that she could hear him and hide. In fear and trembling he opened the door. There was nobody in the room, even her hat was not on the bed, but Diederich knew very well that she had been there a moment previously. He knew it by the chair which was not in its exact place. And he felt it in the air which seemed still to vibrate gently from the swish of her skirts. She must have gone into the little windowless room where his washstand was. He pushed a chair in front of it and with peevish embarrassment grumbled about his landlady who hadn't cleaned out his room. Wolfgang Buck hinted that perhaps his visit was untimely. "Oh, no!" Diederich assured him, and he asked his visitor to be seated and got some cognac. Buck apologised for calling at such an unusual hour, but his military service left him no choice. "Oh, I quite understand that," said Diederich, and, in order to anticipate awkward questions, he began at once to explain that he had a year's service behind him, that he was delighted with the army, for it was the life. How lucky were those who could stay in it! He, unfortunately, was called by family duties. Buck smiled, a gentle, sceptical smile which irritated Diederich. "Well, of course, there were the officers, they, at least, were people with good manners."

"Do you frequent them?" Diederich asked with ironical intention. Buck explained simply that he was invited from time to time to the officers' mess. He shrugged his shoulders: "I go because I think it is useful to look at everything. On the other hand, I mix a good deal with socialists." He smiled again. "Sometimes I think I'd like to be a general, and sometimes a Labour leader. I am curious to know myself on which side of the fence I shall come down," he concluded, emptying his second glass of cognac. "What a disgusting person," thought Diederich. "And Agnes is in the dark room!" Then he said: "With your means it is open to you to get elected to the Reichstag or anything else you like. I am destined for practical work. Anyhow, I regard the Social Democrats as my enemies, for they are the enemies of the Emperor."

"Are you quite sure about that?" queried Buck. "I rather

suspect the Emperor of having a secret affection for the Social Democrats. He himself would like to have become the chief Labour leader. But they wouldn't have him."

Diederich was frantic with indignation, saying it was an insult to His Majesty. But Buck was not in the least put out. "Don't you remember how he threatened Bismarck that he would withdraw military protection from the rich. In the beginning, at least, he had the same grudge against the rich as the workers, though, of course, for very different reasons, namely, because he cannot stand any one else having power."

Buck anticipated the protest which he read in Diederich's face. "Please don't imagine," he said with animation, "that I speak with any hostility. It is tenderness, rather, a sort of hostile tenderness, if you wish."

"I am afraid I don't understand," said Diederich.

"Well, you know, the sort of thing one feels for a person in whom one recognises one's own defects or, if you like, virtues. At all events, we young men are all like our Emperor nowadays, we want to realise our own personality, but we know very well that the future is to the masses. There will be no more Bismarcks and no more Lassalles. Probably it is the most gifted among us who would deny this to-day. He would certainly deny it. When power comes into the hands of such a multitude, it would be really suicidal not to exaggerate one's personal value. But in the depths of his soul he must certainly have his doubts about the part which he has arrogated to himself."

"The part?" Diederich asked, but Buck did not hear him.

"It is a rôle which can lead him very far, for it must appear a damned paradox in the world as it is to-day. The world expects nothing more from any individual than from its neighbours. The general level is important, not the exceptional, and least of all, great men."

"I beg your pardon!" cried Diederich, striking his chest. "And what about the German Empire? Should we have had that without great men? The Hohenzollerns are always great men." Buck screwed up his mouth in a melancholy and sceptical smile. "Then they had better look out for themselves and so had we. In his own sphere the Emperor is facing the same question as I. Shall I become a general and fashion my whole life in view of a war which, so far as we can see, will never happen? Or shall I become a more or less gifted Labour leader, while the people are at the stage where they can do without men of genius? Both would be romantic, and romance notoriously ends in bankruptcy." Buck drank two more glasses of cognac in succession.

"What, then, am I to do?"

"A drunkard," thought Diederich. He debated with himself whether it was not his duty to pick a quarrel with Buck. But Buck was in uniform, and perhaps the noise would have frightened Agnes out of her hiding-place. Then, goodness knows what might happen! In any case he determined to make an exact note of Buck's remarks. Holding such opinions, did the man really believe that he could get on? Diederich remembered that in school Buck's German compositions had aroused in him a deep, if inexplicable, mistrust; they were too clever. "That's it," he thought, "he has remained the same, an intellectual, and so is the whole family." Old Buck's wife was a Jewess and had been an actress. After the event Diederich felt humiliated by the benevolent condescension of old Buck at his father's funeral. The son also humiliated him constantly and in all things: by his superior phrases, by his manners, by his intercourse with the officers. Was he a von Barnim? He was only from Netzig like Diederich himself. "I hate the whole lot of them!" From beneath his half-closed eyelids Diederich observed his fleshy face with its gently curved nose and moist, shining eyes, full of dreams. Buck rose: "Well, we'll meet again at home. I shall pass my examination next term, or the term after, and then what is there to do but be a lawyer in Netzig? And you?" he asked.

Diederich solemnly explained that he did not intend to waste his time and would finish his doctor's thesis by summer. Then he saw Buck to the door. "You are only a silly fool after all," he said to himself, "you didn't notice that I had a girl with me." He returned, pleased at his superiority to Buck, and to Agnes who had waited in the darkness and had not uttered a sound.

When he opened the door, however, she was leaning over a chair, her breast was heaving and with her handkerchief she was stifling her gasps. She looked at him with reddened eyes, and he saw that she had almost choked in there, and had cried —while he was sitting out here drinking and talking a lot of nonsense. His first impulse was one of immense remorse. She loved him! There she sat, loving him so much, that she bore everything! He was on the point of raising his arms and throwing himself before her, weeping and begging her pardon. He restrained himself just in time from fear of the scene and the sentimental mood which would follow, and would cost him more of his working time and would give her the upper hand. He would not give her that satisfaction. For, of course, she was exaggerating on purpose. So he kissed her hastily on the forehead and said: "Here already? I did not see you arriving at all." She gave a start, as if she were going to reply, but she remained silent. Whereupon he explained that some one had just gone out. "One of those young Jews trying to make himself important! Simply disgusting." Diederich rushed about the room. In order not to look at Agnes, he went quicker and quicker and talked with increasing violence. "Those people are our deadliest enemies! With their so-called refined education they paw everything which is sacred to us Germans! A damn Jew like that may consider himself fortunate when we put up with him. Let him swot his law books and keep his mouth shut. I don't care a rap for his high-brow smartness!" He screamed still louder, with the intention of hurting Agnes. As she did not answer, he tried a new line of attack. "It all comes because every one now finds me at home. On your account I am constantly obliged to hang around the place!"

Agnes replied timidly: "We have not seen one another for six days. On Sunday again, you didn't come. I am afraid you don't love me any more." He came to a standstill in front of her: Very condescendingly: "My dear child, I imagine it is hardly necessary for me to assure you that I love you. But it is quite another question whether I, therefore, wish to watch your aunts at their crochet every Sunday, and to talk politics with your father, who doesn't understand the slightest thing about it." Agnes bowed her head. "It used to be so nice. You got on so well with papa." Diederich turned his back on her and looked out of the window. That was just it: he was afraid of being on too good terms with Herr Göppel. He knew from his bookkeeper, old Sötbier, that Göppel's business was going down. His cellulose was no good, and Sötbier no longer gave him any orders. Clearly a son-in-law like Diederich would have suited him most beautifully. Diederich had the sensation of being involved with these people. With Agnes, too. He suspected her of working in conjunction with the old man. Indignantly he turned to her again. "Another thing, my dear child, let us be honest: what we two do is our affair, isn't it? So don't drag your father into it. The relations which exist between us must not be mixed up with family friendship. My moral sense demands that the two shall be kept entirely separate." A moment passed, then Agnes rose as if she at last understood. Her cheeks were crimson. She walked towards the door and Diederich caught up on her. "But I didn't mean it that way, Agnes. It was only because I had too much respect for you —and I shall really be able to come on Sunday." She let him talk, unmoved. "Now, do be pleasant again," he begged. "You haven't even taken off your hat." She did so. He asked her to sit down on the sofa and she obeyed. She

kissed him, too, as he desired. But though her lips smiled
and kissed, her eyes were staring and unresponsive. Suddenly she seized him in her arms; he was frightened, for he
did not know if it was hate that moved her. But then he
felt that she loved him more passionately than ever.

"To-day was really beautiful, wasn't it, my dear, sweet little
Agnes?" Diederich asked, happy and contented. "Good-bye,"
said she, hastily seizing her bag and umbrella while he was
still dressing himself.

"You're in a great hurry.—I suppose there is nothing more
I can do for you?" She was already at the door, when suddenly she fell with her shoulders against the door post and
did not move. "What's wrong?" When Diederich approached
he saw that she was sobbing. He touched her. "Yes, what is
the matter with you?" Then she began to cry loudly and
convulsively. She did not stop. "Agnes, dear," said Diederich
from time to time. "What has happened all of a sudden?
We were so happy." He did not know what to do. "What
have I done to you?" Between spasms of crying which half
choked her, she managed to say: "I can't help it. Forgive
me." He carried her to the sofa. When the crisis was over
Agnes was ashamed. "Forgive me, it is not my fault."—"It
is mine!"—"No, no. It is my nerves. I am sorry!"

Full of patience and sympathy he saw her to a cab. Looking back on it, however, the affair seemed to him half play-
acting, and one of the tricks which would catch him in the
end. He could not get rid of the feeling that plans were being laid against his freedom and his future. He defended himself with rude behaviour, insistence upon his manly independ-
ence, and by his coldness whenever her mood was sentimental.
On Sundays at Göppel's he was on his guard as if in an enemy's country; he was correct and unapproachable. When
would his research work be finished, they would ask. He
might find a solution the next day or in two years, he himself didn't know. He stressed the fact that in the future he

would be financially dependent upon his mother. For a long time yet he would have no time for anything but business. When Herr Göppel reminded him of the ideal values in life, Diederich repelled him sharply. "Only yesterday I sold my Schiller. My head is screwed on the right way and I can't be fooled." Whenever, after such speeches, he felt the silent reproach of Agnes's glance upon him, he would feel for a moment as if some one else had spoken and he was living in a fog, speaking falsely and acting against his own will. But that feeling passed off.

Whenever he ordered her, Agnes came, and she left whenever it was time for him to go off to work or to drink. She no longer enticed him to day-dreams in front of pictures after he had once stopped in front of a sausage shop, and had declared that this spectacle was for him the highest form of artistic enjoyment. At last it occurred even to him that they saw one another very seldom. He reproached her because she no longer insisted on coming more often. "You used to be quite different." "I must wait," said she. "Wait for what?" "Until you are again like you used to be. Oh, I am quite certain that you will be."

He remained silent for fear of having explanations. Nevertheless, things came about as she had predicted. His work was finally finished and accepted. He had still to pass only an unimportant oral examination, and he was in the exalted frame of mind of one who has passed a turning point. When Agnes came with her congratulations and some roses he burst into tears and vowed that he would love her always and for ever. She announced that Herr Göppel was just starting on a business trip for several days. "And the weather is so perfectly lovely just now. . . ." Diederich at once accepted the hint. "We have never had such an opportunity. We must make use of it." They decided to go out into the country. Agnes knew of a place called Mittenwalde; it must be lonely there and as romantic as the name. "We shall be together all day long!"—"And the whole night, too," added Diederich.

Even the station from which they started was out of the way and the train was small and old-fashioned. They had the carriage to themselves. The day slowly darkened, the guard lit a dim lamp for them, and held close in one another's arms they gazed silently with wide-open eyes at the flat, monotonous fields. Oh, to go out there on foot, far away, and lose oneself in the kindly darkness! They almost got out at a little village with a handful of houses. The jovial guard held them back, asking if they wanted to sleep under a hayrick all night. Then they reached their destination. The inn had a great yard, a spacious dining-room lit with oil lamps hanging from the rafters, and a genial innkeeper, who called Agnes *"gnädige Frau,"* with a sly, Slavic smile, full of secret sympathy and understanding. After eating they would have liked to go upstairs at once, but they did not dare to do so and obediently turned the pages of the magazines which their host laid before them. As soon as he had turned his back, they exchanged a glance and in the twinkling of an eye they were on the stairs. The lamp had not yet been lit in the room and the door was still open, but they already lay in one another's arms.

Very early in the morning the sun streamed into the room. Down in the yard the fowl were pecking and fluttering on the table in front of the summer house. "Let us have breakfast there!" They went downstairs. How delightfully warm it was. A delicious smell of hay came from the barn. Coffee and bread tasted fresher to them than usual. Their hearts were so free and life stood open before them. They wanted to walk for hours and the innkeeper had to tell them the names of the streets and villages. They joyfully praised his house and his beds. He assumed they were on their honeymoon. "Quite right," they said, laughing heartily.

The cobblestones of the main street stretched themselves upwards and were gaily coloured by the summer sun. The houses were uneven, crooked, and so small that the roads between them gave the impression of a field dotted with stones. The bell in the general dealer's shop tinkled for a long time after the strangers had left. A few people, dressed in semi-fashionable style, glided amongst the shadows and turned to look after Agnes and Diederich, who felt proud, for they were the most elegantly dressed in the place. Agnes discovered the milliner's shop with the hats of the fine ladies. "It is incredible! Those were the fashion in Berlin three years ago!" Then they went through a shaky looking gateway out into the country. The mowers were at work in the fields. The sky was blue and oppressive, and the swallows swam in the heavens as if in stagnant water. The peasants' cottages in the distance were bathed in a warm haze, and a wood stood out darkly with blue pathways. Agnes and Diederich took one another's hands and without premeditation they began to sing a song for wandering children, which they remembered from their school-days. Diederich assumed a deep voice to excite Agnes's admiration. When they could not remember any more their faces met and they kissed as they walked.

"Now I can see properly how pretty you are," said Diederich, looking tenderly into her rosy face, her bright eyes glittering like stars beneath their fair lashes. "Summer weather always agrees with me," replied Agnes with a deep breath which filled out her lungs. She looked slim as she walked along, with slender hips, her blue scarf floating behind her. It was too warm for Diederich, who first took off his coat, then his waistcoat, and finally admitted that he would have to walk in the shade. They found shelter along the edge of a field in which the corn was still standing, and under an acacia which was in bloom, Agnes sat down and laid Diederich's head in her lap. They played for a while with each other and joked: suddenly she noticed that he had fallen asleep.

He woke up, looked about him, and when he saw Agnes's

face he beamed with delight. "Dearest," said she, "what a good-natured, silly old face you have."—"Come now, I can't have slept more than five minutes. What, really, have I been asleep for an hour? Were you bored?" But she was more astonished than he that the time had passed so quickly. He withdrew his head from beneath the hand which she had laid upon his hair when he fell asleep.

They went back amongst the fields. In one place a dark mass was lying. When they peered through the stalks, they saw it was an old man in a fur cap, rusty coat and corduroy trousers also of reddish hue. He was crouching on his haunches and had twisted his beard round his knees. They bent down lower to get a better look at him. Then they noticed that he had been gazing at them for some time with dark, glowing eyes like live coals. In spite of themselves they hastened on, and in the glances which they exchanged they read the fear of frightened children. They looked about them: they were in a vast strange land, away in the distance behind them the little town looked unfamiliar as it slept in the sun, and by the sky it seemed as if they had been travelling day and night.

What an adventure! Lunch was in the summer house of the inn, with the sun, the fowl, and the open kitchen window through which the plates were passed out to Agnes! Where was the bourgeois orderliness of Blücherstrasse, where Diederich's hereditary *Kneiptisch?* "I will never leave here," declared Diederich, "and I won't let you leave." "Why should we?" she answered. "I will write to father and have the letter sent to him by my married friend in Küstrin. Then he will think I am there."

Later they went out for a walk again in the other direction, where the water ran and the sails of three windmills stood out on the horizon. A boat lay on the canal, and they hired it and drifted along. A swan came towards them, and their boat and the swan glided past one another noiselessly,

coming to a stop of its own accord beneath the overhanging
bushes. Suddenly Agnes asked about Diederich's mother and
sisters. He said that they had always been good to him and
that he loved them. He was going to have his sisters' photo-
graphs sent. They had grown up into pretty girls, or perhaps
not pretty, but so nice and gentle. One of them, Emma, read
poetry like Agnes. Diederich was going to look after them
both and get them married. But he would keep his mother
with him, for he owed to her all that was best in his life until
Agnes came. He told her about the twilight hours, the fairy
tales beneath the Christmas trees of his childhood, and even
about the prayers which he said "from his heart." Agnes listened, sunk in thought. At last she sighed: "I would like to
meet your mother. I never knew my own." Full of pity he
kissed her respectfully and with an obscure sense of uneasy
conscience. He felt that he had now to say but one word
which would console her for ever. But he could not speak,
and put it off. Agnes gave him a profound look. "I know,"
she said slowly, "but you are good at heart, only sometimes
you must act differently." Her words made him start. Then
she concluded by way of apology: "I am not afraid of you
to-day."

"Are you afraid at other times?" he questioned remorse-
fully.

"I am always afraid when other people are jolly and in the
highest spirits. Formerly with my friends I often used to
feel as if I could not keep pace with them, and that they
would notice it and despise me. But they did not notice anything. When I was a child I had a doll with big, blue glass
eyes, and when my mother died I had to sit in the next room
with my doll. It kept staring at me with its hard, wide-open
eyes that seemed to say to me: 'Your mother is dead. Now
every one will look at you as I do.' I would like to have laid
it on its back so that the eyes would close. But I didn't

dare to do so. Could I have laid the people too on their backs? They all have such eyes and sometimes—" She hid her face on his breast, "Even you have."

He felt a lump in his throat. His hand sought her neck and his voice trembled. "Agnes! my sweetest, you cannot know how much I love you. . . . I was afraid of you, indeed I was! For three whole years I longed for you, but you were too beautiful for me, too fine, too good. . . ." His heart melted and he told her everything that he had written to her after her first visit, in the letter which still lay in his desk. She had raised herself and was listening to him enchanted, with her lips parted. Softly she rejoiced: "I knew it, you are like that, you are like me!"

"We belong to one another," said Diederich, pressing her to him, but he was frightened by his own words. "Now," he thought, "she will expect me to speak!" He wanted to do so, but felt powerless. The pressure of his arms around her back grew weaker. . . . She made a movement and he knew that she no longer expected him to speak. They drew away from one another with averted faces. Suddenly Diederich buried his face in his hands and sobbed. She did not ask why, but soothingly stroked his hair. That lasted quite a while.

Speaking over his head into space, Agnes said: "Did I ever say that I thought it would last? It must end badly because it has been so beautiful." He broke out in desperation. "But it is not over!"

"Do you believe in luck?" she asked.

"Never again, if I lose you!"

She murmured: "You will go away out into the world and forget me."

"I would rather die!"—and he drew her closer. She whispered against his cheek:

"Look how wide the water is here, like a lake. Our boat has got loose of itself and has led us far out. Do you still remember that picture? and that lake on which we once sailed in a dream? Whither, I wonder?" And more softly: "Whither are we drifting?"

He did not answer any more. Wrapped in one another's arms, and lips pressed against lips, they sank backwards deeper and deeper over the water. Was he dragging her? Was she pushing him? Never had they been so united. Now, Diederich felt, it was right. He had not been noble enough, not trustful enough, not brave enough, to live with Agnes. Now he had risen to her, now all was well.

Suddenly came a bump and they started up. Diederich's movement was so violent that Agnes had fallen from his arms to the bottom of the boat. He drew his hand across his forehead. "What on earth was that?" Shivering with fright he looked away from her, as if he had been insulted. "One should not be so careless in a boat." He allowed her to get up by herself, seized the oars at once and rowed back. Agnes kept her face turned towards the shore. Once she ventured a glance at him, but he looked at her with such harsh, mistrustful eyes that she shuddered.

In the darkening twilight they walked faster and faster back along the high road. Towards the end they were almost running. It was not until it was so dark as to hide their faces that they spoke. Perhaps Herr Göppel was coming home early the next morning. Agnes had to get back. . . . As they arrived at the inn, the whistle of the train could be heard in the distance. "We can't even eat together again," cried Diederich, with forced regret. In a terrible fluster their things were got, the bill was paid and they were off. They had scarcely taken their seats when the train started. It was fortunate that it took them some time to get their breath and to talk over the hasty questions of the last quarter of an hour. They had nothing more to say, and there they sat alone under the dim light as if stunned by a great mishap. Was it that sombre country out there which had once enticed them and promised happiness?

That must have been yesterday? It was now irrevocably past. Would the lights of the city never come to release them?

By the time they had arrived they had agreed that it was not worth while getting into the same cab. Diederich took the tram. With the merest glance and touch of the hands they separated.

"Phew!" exclaimed Diederich, when he was alone. "That has settled it." He said to himself: "It might just as well have gone wrong." Then, indignantly: "Such an hysterical person!" She herself would probably have clung to the boat. He would have taken a bath alone. She only hit on the trick because she wanted to be married at all costs! "Women are so impetuous and they are without restraints. We men cannot keep up with them. This time, by God, she led me an even worse dance than formerly with Mahlmann. Well, let it be a lesson to me for life. Never again!" With assured gait he betook himself to the Neo-Teutons. Henceforth he spent every evening there, and in the day time he ground for his oral examination, not at home, as a precaution, but in the laboratory. When he did come home he found it laborious to mount the stairs, and he had to admit that his heart was beating abnormally. Tremblingly he opened the door of his room—nothing. In the beginning, after it had become a little easier, he ended regularly by asking the landlady if any one had called. Nobody had called.

A fortnight later a letter came. He opened it without thinking, then he felt inclined to throw' it into the drawer of his writing table without reading it. He did so, but then took it out again and held it in front of his face at arm's length. His hasty and suspicious glance caught a line here and there. "I am so unhappy. . . ." "We've heard all that before," Diederich thought in reply. "I am afraid to come to you. . . ." "So much the better for you!" "It is dreadful to think we have become strangers to one another. . . ." "Well, you've grasped that much anyhow." "Forgive me for what has happened, if anything has happened. . . ." "Quite enough!" "I cannot go on living. . . ." "Are you beginning that all over again?" Finally he hurled the sheet of paper into the drawer with that other letter which he had filled with exaggerations during a night of madness, but which he had fortunately not posted.

A week later, as he was coming home late, he heard steps behind him which sounded peculiar. He turned round with a start and the figure stood still with raised hands stretched out empty before it. While he opened the street door and stepped in he could still see it standing in the shadow. He was afraid to turn on the light in the room. While she stood out there in the dark, looking up, he was ashamed to light up the room which had belonged to her. It was raining. How many hours had she been waiting? She was probably still there, waiting with her last hope. This was more than he could stand. He was tempted to open the window, but he refrained. Then he suddenly found himself on the stairs with the key of the street door in his hand. He had just enough will power to turn back. He shut his door and undressed. "Pull yourself together, old chap!" This time it would not be so easy to extricate oneself from the affair. No doubt the girl was to be pitied, but after all it was her doing. "Above all things, I must remember my duty to myself." The next morning, having slept badly, he even held it as a grievance against her that she had once more tried to make him deviate from his proper course. Now, of all times, when his examination was imminent! It was very like her to behave in this unconscionable fashion. That scene in the night, when she had seemed like a beggar in the rain, had transformed her into a suspicious and uncanny apparition. He regarded her as definitely fallen. "Never again, not on your life!" he assured himself, and he decided to change his lodgings for the short time which he still had to stay, "even at a pecuniary sacrifice." Fortunately, one of his colleagues was just looking for a room. Diederich lost nothing and moved at once far out onto the North Side. Shortly afterwards he passed his examination. The Neo-Teutons celebrated the occasion with a *Frühschoppen* which lasted until the evening. When he reached home, he was told that a gentleman was waiting in his room. "It must be Wiebel," thought Diederich, "coming to congratulate me." Then with swelling hope, "Perhaps it is Assessor von Barnim?" He opened the door and jumped back, for there stood Herr Göppel.

The latter was at a loss for words at first. "Well, well, why in evening dress?" he said, then with hesitation: "were you by any chance at our house?"

"No," replied Diederich, starting again in fear. "I have only been passing my doctor examination."

"My congratulations," said Göppel. Then Diederich managed to say: "How did you find out my address?" And the other replied, "certainly not from your former landlady, but there are other sources of information." Then they looked at one another. Göppel's voice had not been raised, but Diederich felt terrible threats in it. He had always refused to think about this catastrophe, and now it had happened. He would have to brace himself up.

"As a matter of fact," began Göppel, "I have come because Agnes is not at all well."

"Oh, really," said Diederich with an effort of frantic hypocrisy. "What's wrong with her?" Mr. Göppel wagged his head sorrowfully. "Her heart is bad, but, of course, it is only her nerves . . . of course," he repeated, after he had waited in vain, for Diederich to say something. "Now worry has driven her to melancholia and I would like to cheer her up. She is not allowed to go out. But won't you come and see us, to-morrow will be Sunday?"

"Saved!" thought Diederich. "He knows nothing." He was so pleased that he became quite diplomatic and scratched his head. "I had fully determined to do so, but now I am urgently required at home, our old manager is ill. I cannot even pay farewell calls on my professors, for I am leaving first thing in the morning."

Göppel laid his hand upon his knee. "You should think it over, Herr Hessling. Often one has duties to one's friends." He spoke slowly and his glance was so searching that Diederich's eyes could not meet it. "I only wish I could come," he stammered. Göppel replied: "You can. In fact, you can do everything that the present situation requires."

"What do you mean?" Diederich shivered inwardly. "You know very well, what I mean," said the father, and, pushing back his chair a little: "I hope you do not think that Agnes has sent me here. On the contrary, I had to promise her I would do nothing and leave her in peace. But then I began to think that it would be really too silly for us two to go on playing hide and seek with one another, seeing that we are friends, and that I knew your late lamented father, and that we have business connections and so forth."

Diederich thought: "These business connections are a thing of the past, my dear man." He steeled himself.

"I am not playing hide and seek with you, Herr Göppel."

"Oh, well, then everything is all right. I can easily understand, no young man, especially nowadays, wants to take the plunge into matrimony without going through a period of hesitation. But then the matter is not always so simple as in this case, is it? Our lines of business fit into one another, and if you wanted to extend your father's business Agnes's dowry would be very useful." In the next breath, he added while his glance faltered: "At this moment, it is true I can only put my hands on twelve thousand marks in cash, but you can have as much cellulose as you want."

"So, you see," thought Diederich, "and even the twelve thousand would have to be borrowed—that is, if you could raise a loan." . . . "You misunderstand me, Herr Göppel," he explained. "I am not thinking of marriage, that would require too much money." Herr Göppel laughed, but his eyes were full of anxiety as he said: "I can do more than that. . . ."

"It doesn't matter," said Diederich in a tone of dignified refusal.

Göppel became more and more bewildered.

"Well, then, what do you really want?"

"I? Nothing. I thought you wanted something, since you have called on me."

Göppel pulled himself together. "That won't do, my dear Hessling, after what has happened, especially as it has gone on for so long."

Diederich looked at the father up and down, and the corner of his mouth curled. "So, you knew about it, did you?"

"I was not certain," murmured Göppel. With great condescension Diederich retorted: "That would have been rather remarkable."

"I had every confidence in my daughter."

"That's where you were mistaken," said Diederich, determined to use every weapon in self-defence. Göppel's forehead flushed. "I also had confidence in you."

"In other words, you thought I was naïve." Diederich stuck his hands in his trousers' pocket and leant back.

"No!" Göppel jumped up. "But I did not take you for the dirty cad that you are!"

Diederich stood up with an air of formal restraint. "Do you challenge me to a duel?" he asked. Göppel shouted, "No doubt that is what you'd like! To seduce the daughter and shoot the father. Then your honour would be satisfied."

"You understand nothing about honour." Diederich, in his turn became excited, "I did not seduce your daughter. I did what she wanted, and then I could not get rid of her. In this she takes after you." With great indignation: "How do I know that you were not in league with her from the beginning? This is a trap!"

Göppel's face looked as if he were going to shout still louder.

He gave a sudden start, and in his ordinary tone, but with a voice that shook, he said: "We are becoming too heated, the subject is too important for that. I promised Agnes that I would remain quiet."

Diederich laughed derisively. "You see what a swindler you are, you said before that Agnes did not know you were here."

The father smiled apologetically. "In the end people can always agree in a good cause, isn't that so, my dear Hessling?"

But Diederich felt that it was dangerous to become amiable again.

"What the hell do you, mean by your 'dear Hessling'!" he yelled. "To you I am Doctor Hessling!"

"Of course," retorted Göppel stiff with rage. "I suppose this is the first time that you have been able to get yourself called Doctor. You may be proud of so auspicious an occasion." "Do you wish to make any insinuations against my honour as a gentleman?" Göppel made a gesture of dissent.

"I make no insinuations. I am simply wondering what we have done to you, my daughter and I. Must you really have so much money with your wife?"

Diederich felt that he was blushing, and he proceeded with all the more assurance.

"Since you insist upon my telling you: my moral sense forbids me to marry a girl who does not bring her maidenly purity as her marriage portion."

Göppel was obviously on the point of breaking out again, but his strength failed him, he could only just stifle a sob.

"If you had seen her misery this afternoon. She confessed to me because she could not stand it any longer. I believe she does not even love me any more, only you. I suppose it is natural, you are the first."

"How do I know that? Before me a gentleman named Mahlmann frequented your house." Göppel shrank as if he had received a blow on the chest.

"Yes, how can you tell? A person who tells lies cannot be believed."

He continued: "Nobody can expect me to make such a woman the mother of my children. My sense of duty to society is too strong." With this, he turned round and, stooping over the trunk that stood open, he began to fill it with his things.

Behind him he could hear the father who was now really sobbing—and Diederich could not help feeling moved himself by the manly noble sentiments which he had expressed, by the unhappiness of Agnes and her father which his duty forbade him to alleviate, by the painful memory of his love and this tragic fate. . . . His heart almost stopped beating as he listened to Herr Göppel opening and closing the door, creeping along the passage, and as he heard the noise of the street door closing behind him. Now it was all over—then Diederich fell on his knees and wept passionately into his half-packed trunk. That evening he played Schubert.

That was a sufficient concession to sentiment. He must be strong. Diederich speculated as to whether Wiebel had ever become so sentimental. Even a common fellow like Mahlmann, without manners, had given Diederich a lesson in ruthless energy. It seemed to him almost unlikely that any of the others had still perhaps some soft spots left in them. He alone was so afflicted by the influence of his mother. A girl like Agnes, who was just as foolish as his mother, would have rendered him unfit for these difficult times. These difficult times, the phrase always reminded Diederich of Unter den Linden with its mob of unemployed, women and children, of want and fear and disorder—and all that quelled, tamed into cheering, by the power, the all-embracing superhuman power, massive and flashing, which seemed to place its hoofs upon those heads.

"It can't be helped," he said to himself in an ecstasy of

submission. "One must act like that." So much the worse for those who could not, they fell under the hoofs. Had the Göppels, father and daughter, any claims upon him? Agnes was of age and he had not given her a child. What then? "I should be a fool if I did anything to my own disadvantage which I cannot be compelled to do. I can get nothing for nothing." Diederich was proud and glad of his excellent training. The students' corps, his military service and the atmosphere of imperialism, had educated him and made him fit. He resolved to give effect to his well-earned principles at home in Netzig, and to become a pioneer of the spirit of the times. In order to show an outward and visible sign of this resolution on his person he betook himself the following morning to the court hairdresser, Haby, in Mittelstrasse, and had a change made which he had more and more frequently noticed of late in officers and gentlemen of rank. Hitherto it had seemed to him too distinguished to be imitated. By means of a special apparatus he had the ends of his moustache turned up at right angles. When this was done he could hardly recognise himself in the glass. When no longer concealed by hair, his mouth had something tigerish and threatening about it, especially when his lips were drawn, and the points of his moustache aimed straight at his eyes, which inspired fear in Diederich himself, as though they flashed from the countenance of the All-Powerful.

III

In order to avoid further trouble from the Göppel family he departed at once. The heat made the railway carriage intolerable. Diederich, who was alone, gradually removed his coat, waistcoat and shoes. A few stations before Netzig, people got in, two foreign-looking ladies, who seemed to be offended by the sight of Diederich's flannel shirt. In a language which he could not understand they began to complain to him, but he shrugged his shoulders and put his stockinged feet up on the seat. The ladies held their noses and shouted for help. The ticket-collector came and the guard himself, but Diederich showed them his second-class ticket and maintained his rights. He even gave these functionaries to understand that they had better be careful, as they could never tell with whom they had to do. When he had gained his victory and the ladies had withdrawn, another came in their place. Diederich gave her a challenging stare, but she calmly took a sausage out of her bag and began to eat it out of her hand, smiling at him at the same time. This disarmed him, and beaming broadly he returned her overtures and spoke to her. It turned out that she was from Netzig. He told her his name and she rejoiced at the fact that they were old acquaintances. "Was that so?" Diederich looked at her searchingly: her fat, rosy face, with fleshy lips and small impudently retroussé nose, her bleached hair, neat, smooth and carefully done, her plump youthful neck, and her mittened hands, whose fingers holding the sausage were themselves like pink little sausages. "No," he decided, "I do not recognise you, but you are a jolly nice girl, as delicious as a sucking pig." He put his arm around her waist and immediately received a box on the ear. "Good for you," he said, rubbing his cheek. "Have you many more like that?"

91

—"Enough for every impertinent puppy." She laughed in her throat and her small eyes twinkled naughtily. "You can have a piece of sausage, but nothing else." Involuntarily he compared her ability to defend herself with the helplessness of Agnes, and he said to himself: "It would be no harm to marry a girl like that." In the end she herself told her Christian name, and as he still could not guess who she was, she asked after his sisters. Suddenly he cried: "Guste Daimchen!" They both shook with laughter. "You always used to give me buttons from the rags in your paper factory. I shall always be grateful to you for that, Dr. Hessling! Do you know what I used to do with those buttons? I collected them, and whenever my mother gave me money for buttons I used to buy sweets for myself."

"You are a practical person, too!" Diederich was delighted. "Then you used to climb over the garden wall to us, you little rogue! Most of the time you did not wear knickers, and when your dress slipped up there was a view from behind."

She shrieked; no decent man would remember such things. "Now, it must be much more interesting," added Diederich. She at once became more serious.

"Now, I am engaged to be married."

It was to Wolfgang Buck that she was engaged. Diederich was silent and his face expressed his disappointment. Then he declared reluctantly that he knew Buck. She said cautiously: "I suppose you mean that he is rather eccentric? But the Bucks are a very distinguished family. Of course, in other families there is more money," she concluded. Feeling that this shot was directed at him, Diederich looked at her. She twinkled. He wanted to ask her something, but he had lost courage.

Just before they reached Netzig Fräulein Daimchen asked: "and what about your heart, Dr. Hessling, is it still free?"

"So far I have avoided an engagement." He nodded his head seriously. "Oh, you must tell me all about it," she cried, but their train was now entering the station. "I hope we'll meet soon again," said Diederich. "I can only say that a young man often comes damned near burning his fingers. A yes or a no can spoil his whole life."

His two sisters were waiting in the station. When they caught sight of Guste Daimchen, they first made a wry face but then rushed up and helped to carry her luggage. As soon as they were alone with Diederich they explained their zeal. Guste had come in for some money and was a millionairess. So that was it! He was filled with timid respect.

The sisters related the story in detail. An elderly relative in Magdeburg had left all the money to Guste as a reward for the way she had looked after him. "And she earned it," remarked Emma, "towards the end, he was simply disgusting, they say." Magda added: "and, of course, you can draw your own conclusions, for Guste was a whole year in the house with him alone."

Diederich at once became indignant. "A young girl should not say such things," he cried righteously, but Magda assured him that Inge Tietz, Meta Harnisch and every one said it. "Then I command you most emphatically to contradict such talk." There was a moment's silence, then Emma said: "Guste, you know, is already engaged."—"I know that," muttered Diederich.

They met a number of acquaintances. Diederich heard them addressing him as "Doctor," beamed proudly, and walked on between Emma and Magda, who cast admiring glances from each side at his new style of wearing his moustache. When they reached the house, Frau Hessling received her son with open arms and shrieks like those of a drowning person calling for help. Diederich also wept, much to his own surprise. All at once he realised that the solemn hour of fate had come, in which he entered the room for the first time as the real head of the family, completely fitted out with the title of Doctor, and determined to guide the factory and the family according to his own well considered views. He took the hands of his mother and sisters all together, and said in earnest tones: "I shall never forget that I am responsible before God for you."

Frau Hessling, however, was uneasy. "Are you ready, my boy?" she asked. "Our people are waiting for you." Diederich finished his beer and went downstairs at the head of his family. The yard had been swept clean and the entrance to the factory was framed with wreaths of flowers which surrounded the inscription "Welcome!" In front stood the old bookkeeper Sötbier who said: "Well, good day, Dr. Hessling. I ain't had a chance to come up, there were still some things to do."

"On a day like this you might have left it," replied Diederich walking past him. Inside, in the rag room he found the work people. They all stood clustered together; the twelve workmen who looked after the paper machine, the cylinder machine and the cutter, the three bookkeepers together with the women whose job it was to sort the rags. The men coughed, there was an awkward pause until several of the women pushed forward a little girl who held a bouquet of flowers in front of her and in a piping voice wished the Doctor welcome and good luck. With a gracious air Diederich accepted the flowers. Now it was his turn to clear his throat. First he turned towards his own family, then he looked sharply into the faces of his workers, one after another, even the black-bearded machinist, although this man's look made him feel uncomfortable. Then he began:

"Men and women! As you are my dependents, I will simply say to you that in the future you must put your shoulders to the wheel. I am determined to put some life into this business. Lately, as there was no master here, many of you probably thought you could take things easily. You never were more mistaken. I say this particularly for the older people who belong to my lamented father's time."

He raised his voice and spoke still more sharply and commandingly, looking all the while at old Sötbier:

"Now I have taken the rudder into my own hands. My course is set straight and I am guiding you to glorious times. Those who wish to help me, are heartily welcome, but whoever opposes me in this work I will smash."

He tried to make his eyes flash and the ends of his moustache rose still higher.

"There is only one master here, and I am he. I am responsible only to God and my own conscience. You can always count on my fatherly benevolence, but revolutionary desires will be shattered against my unbending will. Should I discover any connection between one of you"—he caught the eye of the black-bearded machinist, who looked suspicious—"and the Social Democratic clubs, our relationship will be severed. I regard every Social Democrat as an enemy of my business and his country. . . . So now return to your work and consider well what I have told you.

He turned round sharply and marched off, breathing heavily. His strong words produced in him a kind of dizziness which made him incapable of recognising any face. Disturbed and respectful, his family followed him, while the workers stared at one another in dumb amazement, before they attacked the bottles of beer which stood ready for the feast.

Upstairs Diederich was explaining his plans to his mother and sisters. The factory would have to be enlarged by taking in the house of their neighbour at the back. They would have to go into competition with their rivals. A place in the sun! Old Klüsing over there in the Gausenfeld paper factory probably imagined that he would go on forever getting all the business. . . . Finally Magda raised the question as to where he expected to get the money, but Frau Hessling interrupted her. "Your brother knows all about that better than we do." Cautiously she added: "Many a girl would be happy if she could win his heart."—Fearing his anger she pressed her hand to her mouth. But Diederich merely blushed. Then she had enough courage to kiss him. "It would be such a terrible blow to me," she sobbed, "if my son, my dear son, went away from home. It is doubly hard for a widow. Frau Daimchen feels it too, now that her Guste is going to marry Wolfgang Buck."

"Perhaps not," said Emma, the elder girl. "They say that Wolfgang has an affair with an actress." Frau Hessling completely forgot to chide her daughter. "But where so much money is at stake! A million, people say."

Diederich said contemptuously that he knew Buck, that he was not normal. "It must run in the family. The old man also married an actress."

"The results are easily seen," said Emma. "You hear all sorts of things about the daughter, Frau Lauer."

"Children!" begged Frau Hessling nervously. But Diederich quieted her.

"That's all right, mother, it is high time to bell the cat. I take the view that the Bucks have long since become unworthy of their position in this town. They are a decadent family."

"The wife of Maurice, the eldest son," said Magda, "is nothing but a peasant. They were lately in town, and he, too, looked quite countrified." Emma was full of indignation.

"And what about the brother of old Herr Buck? Always so elegant, and his five unmarried daughters? They have soup brought from the public kitchen, I know that for a fact."

"Yes, Herr Buck founded the public kitchen," explained Diederich. "Also the Discharged Prisoners' Aid, and goodness knows what besides. I'd like to know when he has time to look after his own business."

"I should not be surprised," said Frau Hessling, "if he hadn't very much more business left. Though, of course, I have the greatest respect for Herr Buck. He is so well thought of."

Diederich laughed bitterly. "Why, then? We have all been

brought up to honour old Buck. The great man of Netzig!
Sentenced to death in Forty Eight!"

"But that was an historic service, your father always used
to say."

"Service," shouted Diederich. "When I know that any one
is against the government that is quite enough for me. Why
should high treason be a service?"

Before the astonished women he launched into politics.
These old Democrats who still led the regiment, they were a
positive disgrace to Netzig! Unpatriotic slackers, at odds with
the government! They were a mockery of the spirit of the
time. Because old Judge Kühlemann was their representative
in the Reichstag, and was a friend of the notorious Eugene
Richter, business here was at a standstill and nobody got any
money. Of course, there would be no railway connections or
soldiers for such a radical hole. No traffic and no influx of
population! The legal appointments were always in the hands
of the same couple of families, that was well-known, and they
passed round the jobs among themselves and there was nothing for any one else. The Gausenfeld paper factory furnished
all the supplies for the town, for Klüsing, the owner, also belonged to old Buck's gang.

Magda had something else to add. "Recently the amateurs'
show at the Civic Club had been put off because Herr Buck's
daughter, Frau Lauer, was ill. That is simply absolutism."
"Nepotism, you mean," said Diederich sharply. He rolled his
eyes. "And into the bargain, Herr Lauer is a socialist. But
Herr Buck had better look out! We shall keep a sharp eye
on him."

Frau Hessling raised her hands entreatingly. "My dear son,
when you go now to pay your calls in the town, promise me
you will also go to Herr Buck's. After all he is so influential."
But Diederich promised nothing. "Other people want their
turn," he cried.

Nevertheless he did not sleep well that night. By seven
o'clock he was down in the factory and at once raised a row
because the beer bottles of the day before were still lying
about. "No boozing here, this is not a barroom. Surely that
is in the regulations, Herr Sötbier?"—"Regulations?" said the
old bookkeeper. "We have none." Diederich was speechless.
He shut himself up with Sötbier in the office. "No regulations? Then, of course, nothing more can surprise me. What
are those ridiculous orders on which you are working?" and
he scattered the letters about on the desk. "It seems to be
high time that I took charge. The business is going to the
dogs in your hands."

"To the dogs, Master Diederich?"

"Doctor Hessling to you!"

He insisted that they should underbid all the other factories.

"We cannot do that for long," said Sötbier. "In fact we
are not in position at all to execute such large orders as
Gausenfeld."

"And you set up to be a business man? We'll simply install
more machinery."

"That costs money," replied Sötbier.

"Then we'll get some! I'll bring some style into this business. Wait till you see. If you don't want to back me up,
I'll do it alone."

Sötbier shook his head. "Your father and I always agreed,
Master Diederich. Together we worked up this business."

"Times are changed, and don't you forget it. I am my own
manager."

"Impetuous youth," sighed Sötbier as Diederich slammed
the door. He walked through the room in which the mechanical drum, beating loudly, was washing the rags in chlorine
and went into the smaller room where the large boiling machine was. In the doorway he unexpectedly met the black-
bearded machinist. Diederich started and almost made way
for him, but he brushed past him with his shoulder before

the man could step aside. Snorting with impatience, he watched the machine at work, the cylinders turning and the knife cutting, which separated the material into threads. Weren't the people who attended the machine grinning at him slyly, because he had been frightened by that dark fellow? "He is an impudent dog! He must be fired!" A bestial hate arose in Diederich, the hatred of his fair flesh for the thin dark man of another race, which he would have liked to regard as inferior and which looked sinister. Diederich made a sudden movement.

"The cylinder is not in the right position, the knives are working badly!" As the hands merely stared at him, he yelled: "where is the machinist?" When the man with the black beard came along, Diederich said: "look how this has been bungled. The cylinder is much too close to the knives and they are cutting everything to pieces. I will hold you responsible for the damage."

The man bent over the machine. "No harm done," he said quietly, and again Diederich wondered if a smile was not hidden by that black beard. The machinist gave him a surly mocking look, which Diederich could not stand. He stopped blustering and simply made a gesture with his arms. "I hold you responsible."

"What's wrong now?" asked Sötbier, who had heard the noise. Then he explained that the rags were not being cut too fine, that they were always done in this way. The men nodded their heads in approval and the machinist stood there indifferently. Diederich did not feel equal to a discussion about his competence in such matters, so he shouted: "In the future, you will kindly see that it is done differently!" and he turned away.

He reached the rag room, and he recovered his composure as he watched with an expert eye the women who were sorting the rags on the sieve plates of the long tables. One little dark-eyed woman was bold enough to smile at him from beneath her coloured kerchief, but her glance met such a stony stare that she shrank back and bent upon her work. Brightly-coloured rags streamed out of the sacks, the whispering of the women was stilled under the master's eye, and in the warm stuffy atmosphere nothing else could be heard but the gentle rattling of the blades as they came down upon the tables and cut off the buttons. But Diederich, who was examining the hot water pipes, heard something suspicious. He looked over a heap of sacks—and started back, with blushing cheeks and quivering moustache. "Stop that now," he shouted, "come out here!" A young workman crept out. "The female, too!" shouted Diederich. "Look lively!" Finally, when the girl appeared, he struck an attitude. Nice goings on, indeed! Not only was the place a bar room but it was something else! He swore so loudly that all the workers gathered about him. "Well, Herr Sötbier, I suppose this also has always been done in this way. I congratulate you on such success. These people are accustomed to waste my time amusing themselves behind the sacks. How did this man get in here?" The young man said she was engaged to be married to him. "Married? Here, we know nothing about marriage, only about work. You are both stealing my time, for which I pay you. You are swine and thieves. I shall give you both the sack and lodge a complaint against you for indecent conduct." He gave a challenging glance all around.

"In this place I insist upon German virtue and decency. Do you understand?" Then he caught the eye of the machinist. "And I will see that they are observed, whether you like it or not."

"I haven't made any objections," said the man quietly, but Diederich could not contain himself any longer. At last, he had got something against him.

"Your conduct has been all along most suspicious. If you had been doing your duty, I should not have caught these two people."

"It is not my business to look after people," the man interrupted.

"You are very insubordinate and you have encouraged those beneath you in insubordination. You are preparing for the revolution. What's your name, anyhow?"

"Napoleon Fischer," said the man. Diederich stammered. "Nap— Well, I'm damned! Are you a Social Democrat?"

"I am."

"I thought so. You're fired."

He turned round to the others. "Remember what you have seen—" And he bounced out of the room. In the yard Sötbier ran after him. "Master Diederich!" He was greatly excited, and he would not speak until the door of the private office had been closed behind him. "This won't do," said the bookkeeper, "he is a union man."—"For that very reason he is fired," replied Diederich. Sötbier explained that it would not do, because all the others would strike. Diederich could not understand this. Were they all in the Union? No. Well, then. But Sötbier explained that they were afraid of the Reds, even the older people could not be relied upon.

"I'll kick them all out!" cried Diederich, "bag and baggage, with all their belongings!"

"Then it would be a question if we could get others to take their places," said Sötbier with a pale smile, looking from under his green eye shade at his young master who was knocking the furniture about in his rage. "Am I master in my own factory or not? I will show them—"

Sötbier waited until his rage had evaporated, then he said: "You need not say anything to Fischer, he won't leave us, for he knows that it would lead to too much trouble."

Diederich flared up again: "Really! So it is not necessary for me to beg him to have the kindness to stay. Napoleon the Great! I need not invite him to dinner on Sunday, I suppose? It would be too great an honour for me!"

His face was red and swollen, the room seemed to stifle him, and he threw the door open. It so happened that the machinist was just passing. Diederich gazed after him and his hatred made his impressions sharper than usual. He noticed the man's thin, crooked legs, his bony shoulders, and his arms which hung forward. As the machinist spoke to the men, he could see his strong jaws working underneath his thin, black beard. How Diederich hated that mouth and those knotted hands! The black devil had long since passed and still Diederich was conscious of his odour.

"Just look, Sötbier, how his arms reach down to the ground. He will soon run on all fours and eat nuts. Just you watch, we'll trip up that ape! Napoleon! The name in itself is a provocation. He had better look out for himself, for there's one thing certain, either he or I will go under."

With head erect, he left the factory. Putting on a morning-coat he made preparations to pay a call on the most important people of the town. From Meisestrasse, in order to reach the house of Dr. Scheffelweis, the Mayor, in Schweinichenstrasse, he had simply to go along Kaiser Wilhelmstrasse. He wished to do so, but at the decisive moment, as if by a secret agreement with himself, he turned aside into the Fleischhauergrube. The two steps in front of old Herr Buck's house were removed from the traffic of the passers-by, and always had been. The bell-handle on the yellow glass door caused a prolonged rattling noise in the empty interior. Then a door opened in the background and the old servant crept along the floor. But long before she could reach the outer door, the master of the house himself stepped out of his office and opened it. He seized Diederich, who bowed deeply, by the hand and dragged him in.

"My dear Hessling, I have been expecting you. I heard that you'd arrived. Welcome back to Netzig, my dear Doctor." Tears sprang into Diederich's eyes and he stammered.

"You are too kind, Herr Buck. I need hardly say, Herr Buck, that you are the first person on whom I wanted to call, and to assure that I am always—I am always—at your service," he concluded, smiling like a diligent schoolboy. Old Herr Buck still held him fast with his hand which was warm yet light and soft in its pressure.

"My service"—he shoved forward a chair for Diederich —"you mean, of course, the service of your fellow citizens, who will be grateful to you. I think I can promise you that they will shortly elect you to the Town Council, for that would be a mark of respect to a family which deserves it, and then" —old Buck made a gesture of dignified generosity—"I rely upon you to give us an early opportunity of seeing you raised to the bench."

Diederich bowed, smiling happily, as if he already had been raised to the honour. "I do not say," continued Herr Buck, "that public opinion in our town is sound in every respect"— his white beard sank onto his necktie—"but there is still room" —his beard rose again—"and God grant it may long be so, there is still room for genuine Liberals."

"I need hardly tell you I am thoroughly liberal," Diederich assured him.

Old Buck ran his hand over the papers on his desk. "Your lamented father often used to sit opposite to me here, and particularly at the time when he was building the paper mill. To my great joy I could be of use to him in that matter. It was a question of the stream which now flows through your yard."

Diederich said in a grave voice: "How often, Herr Buck, my father has told me that he owed to you the stream without which we could not exist."

"You must not say that he owed it only to me, but rather to the happy circumstances of our civic life." Looking earnestly at Diederich, the old gentleman raised his white forefinger: "But certain people and a certain party would like to make many changes as soon as they could." With deep feeling: "The enemy is at the gate; we must stand together."

A moment passed in silence, then in lighter tones and with

a slight smile, he said: "are you not, my dear Dr. Hessling, in the same position as your father then was? Don't you want to extend your business? Have you any plans?"

"Certainly, I have." With great eagerness Diederich set forth what he would like to see happen. The other listened carefully, nodded, and took a pinch of snuff. . . . Finally, he said: "This much I can see; the alterations will not only cause you great expense, but under certain conditions, may give rise to difficulties under the city building laws, with which I, by the way, am concerned as a magistrate. Take a look, my dear Hessling, at what I have here on my desk."

Diederich recognised an exact plan of his property with that which lay behind it. His astonished face produced a smile of satisfaction in old Buck. "I have no doubt that I can see that no oppressive conditions are raised." And in reply to Diederich's profuse thanks: "We do a service to the whole community when we help on each one of our friends, for all except tyrants are friends of the people's party."

After these words he leant back deeper in his chair and folded his hands. His expression had relaxed and he nodded his head in a grandfatherly fashion. "As a child you had such lovely fair curls," said he. Diederich understood that the official part of the conversation was over. He took the liberty of saying, "I still remember how I used to come to this house as a small boy, when I used to play soldiers with your son Wolfgang."

"Ah, yes, and now he is playing soldiers again."

"Oh, he is very popular with the officers. He told me so himself."

"I wish, my dear Hessling, that he had more of your practical disposition . . . but he will settle down once I have got him married."

"I believe your son has a streak of genius in him. For that reason he is never contented with anything, and does not know whether he would like to become a general or a great man in some other field."

"Meanwhile, unfortunately, he gets into silly scrapes." The old gentleman gazed out of the window. Diederich did not dare to show his curiosity.

"Silly scrapes? I can hardly believe it. He always impressed me by his intelligence, even at college; his compositions. And his recent statement to me about the Emperor, that he would really like to be the first labour leader. . . ."

"God save the workers from that."

"What do you mean?" Diederich was absolutely astounded.

"Because it would do them no good. It has not done the rest of us any good either."

"Yet, it is thanks to the Hohenzollerns that we have a united German Empire."

"We are not united," said old Buck, rising from his chair with unaccustomed haste. "In order to prove our unity we ought to be able to follow our own impulse, but can we? You call yourselves united because the curse of servility is spreading everywhere. That is what Herwegh, a survivor like myself, cried to those who were drunk with victory in the spring of 1870. What would he say now!" Diederich's reply to this voice from another world was to stammer: "Ah, yes, you belong to Forty-Eight."

"My dear young friend, you mean that I have lost and that I am a fool. Yes, we were beaten, because we were foolish enough to believe in the people. We believed that they would achieve for themselves what they now receive from their masters at the cost of liberty. We thought of this nation as powerful, wealthy, full of understanding for its own affairs and consecrated to the future. We did not see that, without political education, of which it has less than any other, it was fated to fall the victim of the powers of the past, after the first flush of freedom. Even in our time there were far too many people who pursued their own personal interests, unconcerned about the common weal, and who were contented when they could fulfil the ignoble needs of a selfish life of pleasure by basking

in the sun of some one's approval. Since that time their name
is legion, for they have been relieved of all care for the public
welfare. Your masters have already made you into a world-
power, and, while you're earning money whatever way you can,
and spending whatever way you like, they will build the fleet
for you—or rather for themselves—which we ourselves at that
time would have built. Our poet then knew what you are
now only learning: the future of Germany will spring from
the furrows which Columbus ploughed."

"So Bismarck has really accomplished something," said
Diederich in mild triumph.

"That is just the point, that he has been allowed to do it!
At the same time he has done it all in such a matter-of-fact
manner, but nominally in the name of his master. We citizens
of Forty-Eight were more honest, it seems to me, for then I
myself paid the price of my own daring."

"Oh, yes, I know, you were condemned to death," said
Diederich, once more impressed.

"I was condemned because I defended the supremacy of the
National Parliament against individual authority, and I led
the people to revolt in their hour of need. Thus the unity
of Germany was in our hearts. It was a matter of conscience,
the personal obligation of every individual, by which he was
prepared to stand. No! we had no thought of sacrificing German unity. When, defeated and betrayed, I was waiting in
this house with my last remaining friends for the King's soldiers, I was still a man, nevertheless, who himself had created
an ideal, one of many, but a man. Where are they now?"

The old gentleman stopped and his face assumed an expression as if he were listening. Diederich felt uncomfortably
warm, and that he ought not to remain silent any longer. He
said: "God be praised, the German people is no longer the
nation of poets and thinkers; it has modern and practical ends
in view." The other was drawn from his thoughts and pointed
to the ceiling.

"At that time the whole town thronged this house. Now it is as lonely as the grave. Wolfgang was the last to go. I would abandon everything, but we must respect our past, young man, even when we have been beaten."

"No doubt," said Diederich. "You're still the most influential man in the town. People always say Herr Buck owns the town."

"But I do not want that, I want it to belong to itself." He sighed deeply. "That is a long story, you will gradually learn it when you get an insight into our administration. Every day we are more hardly pressed by the government and their Junker taskmasters. To-day they want to compel us to supply light to the landlords who pay us no taxes. To-morrow we shall have to build roads for them. Finally they will take away our right to self-government. We are living in a beleaguered town as you will see."

Diederich gave an embarrassed smile. "It cannot be as bad as all that, for the Emperor has such modern ideas."

"Hm, yes," replied old Buck, shaking his head. He stood up—and then decided to say nothing. He offered Diederich his hand. "My dear Doctor, your friendship will be as precious to me as your father's was. After this conversation I have the hope that we shall be able to work together in all things."

Moved by the glance of those friendly blue eyes Diederich laid his hand upon his heart. "I am a thorough-going Liberal!"

"Above all, I warn you against Governor von Wulckow. He is the enemy who has been sent here into the city against us. The municipal authorities maintain only such relations with him as are absolutely unavoidable. I personally have the honour to be cut by him in the street."

"Oh!" cried Diederich genuinely disturbed.

The old gentleman had already opened the door for him, but he seemed to be hesitating about something. "Wait a moment!" He hastened back into the library, bent down and then rose up out of the dusty depths with a small quarto volume. He hastily pressed it into Diederich's hands, with shy pride in his glowing face. "There, take this. A copy of my 'Storm Bells.' We were also poets—at that time." He gently pushed Diederich out into the street.

The Fleischhauergrube was pretty steep, but that was not the only reason why Diederich was out of breath. At first he was somewhat dazed, but gradually he had the feeling of having allowed himself to be bluffed. "An old chatter-box like that is nothing more than a scarecrow, and yet he impresses me." He vaguely recalled his childhood when old Herr Buck, who had been condemned to death, inspired him with as much respect and the same fear as the policeman at the corner or the spectre in the Castle. "Am I always going to be so weak? Another man would not have allowed himself to be treated in this fashion." The fact that he had been silent, or had feebly contradicted, so many compromising speeches, might have unpleasant consequences. He prepared the most effective reply for the next occasion. "The whole thing was a trap, he wanted to catch me and render me harmless . . . but I'll show him!" Diederich clenched his fist in his pocket as he marched erect along Kaiser Wilhelmstrasse. "For the present I must put up with him, but let him beware when I am the stronger!"

The Mayor's house had been newly painted and the plate glass windows shone as of yore. A pretty servant received him. She took him up the stairs, passing by a friendly boy in biscuit holding a lamp, through an anteroom in which a small rug lay in front of almost every piece of furniture, and left him in the dining-room. It was furnished in light colours, with attractive pictures and in the midst of it all the Mayor and another gentleman sat at lunch. Dr. Scheffelweis extended a white hand to Diederich and looked at him over the edge of his pince-nez. Nevertheless, you never knew if he was looking at you, his glance was so vague, and his eyes were as colourless as his face and his scanty side-whiskers, which were cut in mutton-chop fashion. Several times the Mayor attempted to talk before he finally found something which it was safe to say. "What fine scars," said he; and turning to the other gentleman, "Don't you think so?"

The other gentleman looked so Jewish that Diederich maintained a reserve at first. But the Mayor introduced him: "Herr Assessor Jadassohn of the Public Prosecutor's Office." This made a respectful greeting indispensable.

"Come and sit down," said the Mayor, "we are just beginning." He poured out some porter for Diederich and helped him to *Lachsschinken*. "My wife and her mother have gone out, the children are at school, I am a bachelor. Your health!"

The Jewish gentleman from the Public Prosecutor's Office had eyes only for the servant. While she was busy at the table near him his hand disappeared. Then she left the room and he was anxious to talk of public affairs, but the Mayor would not be interrupted. "The two ladies will not be back to lunch. My mother-in-law is at the dentist's, and I know what that means, it is not an easy business with her. Meanwhile the whole house is at our disposal." He fetched a liqueur from the sideboard, sang its praises, made his guests confirm its merits, and continued to boast of his idyllic mornings, in a monotonous voice interrupted by chewing. In spite of his contentment, his expression gradually became more and more anxious, as he felt that the conversation could not continue in this fashion. After all three had been silent for a minute he made up his mind.

"I suppose I may assume, Dr. Hessling—my house is not in the immediate vicinity of yours and I should think it quite natural if you had called on other gentlemen before coming to me."

Diederich was already blushing for the lie he had not yet told. "It would come out," he thought, just in time, and so he replied: "As a matter of fact I took the liberty—that is to say, my first thought of course, was to call on you, Mr. Mayor, but in memory of my father, who had such a high opinion of old Herr Buck. . . ."

"Quite so, quite so." The Mayor nodded emphatically. "Herr Buck is the oldest of our deserving citizens and therefore exercises a doubtless legitimate influence."

"Only for the time being," said the Jewish gentleman from the Public Prosecutor's Office in an unexpectedly harsh tone, as he looked defiantly at Diederich. The Mayor had bent his head over his cheese, and Diederich, finding himself helpless, blinked. As the gentleman's look demanded a response, he mumbled something about "innate respect" and even began to cite memories of his childhood as an excuse for having gone first to Herr Buck. While he was speaking he gazed in terror at the huge, red, prominent ears of the gentleman from the Public Prosecutor's. The latter allowed Diederich to stammer on to the end, as if he were a prisoner in the dock giving himself away. Finally he retorted cuttingly: "There are certain cases where respect is a habit which one must lose."

Diederich stopped short and then ventured to laugh meaningly. The Mayor with a pale smile and a conciliatory gesture said: "Dr. Jadassohn likes to be witty—a thing which I personally esteem him for particularly. In my position, of course, I am compelled to consider things impersonally and without prejudice. Therefore I must admit, on the one hand. . . ."

"Let us get at once to, 'on the other hand'," demanded Jadassohn. "As a representative of the State authorities, and as a convinced supporter of the existing order, I regard Herr Buck and his comrade, Deputy Kühlemann, as revolutionaries, both on their past record and their present opinions. That is enough for me. I do not conceal my thoughts; I hold that to be un-German. Let them set up public kitchens by all means, but the best nourishment for the Crown is sound opinions. A lunatic asylum might also be very useful."

"But it must be a loyal one!" Diederich added. The Mayor made signs as if to pacify them. "Gentlemen!" he entreated, "gentlemen, if we must discuss the matter, then it is certainly right, with all due respect to the gentleman named, that we confess, on the other hand—"

"On the other hand!" repeated Jadassohn sternly.

"—the deepest regret for our unfortunately most unfavourable relations with the representatives of the State administration. It is right that I should ask you to remember that the unwonted harshness of Governor Von Wulckow towards the city authorities—"

"Towards disaffected organisations," interjected Jadassohn. Diederich ventured: "I am a thoroughly liberal man but I must say. . . ."

"A town," explained the Assessor, "which opposes the wishes of the government certainly cannot be surprised when the government turns a cold shoulder to it!"

"We could travel from Berlin to Netzig," Diederich declared, "in half the time if we were in better odour with the powers that be."

The Mayor allowed them to finish their duet. He was pale and his eyes were closed behind his pince-nez. Suddenly he looked at them with a wan smile.

"Gentlemen, do not worry. I know that opinions more in harmony with the spirit of the times prevail elsewhere. Pray, do not believe that it was my fault that no telegram of greeting was sent to His Majesty on the occasion of his last visit to the provinces during the manœuvres last year. . . ."

"The refusal of the authorities was thoroughly un-German," Jadassohn declared emphatically.

"The national flag must be held aloft," Diederich insisted. The Mayor threw up his hands.

"I know it, gentlemen. But I am only the chairman of the board and must carry out its decisions, unfortunately. Change the conditions. Dr. Jadassohn remembers our row with the government about the Social Democratic teacher, Rettich. I could not control the man. Herr von Wulckow knows"—the Mayor winked his eye—"that I would have done it if I could."

They looked at one another in silence for a while. Jadassohn blew his nose as if he had heard enough. But Diederich could not be silent any longer. "Liberalism is the beginning of Social Democracy. Such people as Buck, Kühlemann, Eugen Richter, make our workers impudent. My factory imposes upon me the heaviest sacrifices in work and responsibilities, and on top of that I have conflicts with my workers. Why? Because we are not united against the Red peril, and there are certain employers with socialistic leanings, as, for example, the son-in-law of Herr Buck. Herr Lauer's workmen have a share in whatever profits the factory earns. That is immoral. It undermines law and order, and I hold that order is more necessary than ever in these difficult times. Therefore we need a strong government like that which is led by our glorious young Emperor. I declare that I stand fast by His Majesty in all circumstances. . . ." Here the two others bowed profoundly and Diederich replied, his eyes flashing. Unlike the democratic balderdash in which the departing generation still believed, the Emperor was the representative of youth, the most individual personality, charmingly impulsive and a highly original thinker. "One man must be master, and master in every field!" Diederich made a full confession of the strongest and most strenuous opinions, and declared that an end must be made, once and for all, in Netzig of the old liberal routine. "Now comes the new age!"

Jadassohn and the Mayor listened quietly until he had finished, Jadassohn's ears growing longer all the time. Then he crowed: "There are loyal Germans in Netzig also." And Diederich shouted: "We will go after those who are not loyal. We shall see whether certain families are to enjoy the position they now have. Apart from old Buck, who are his supporters?

His sons are peasants or ne'er do wells, his son-in-law is a socialist, and they say his daughter. . . ."

They looked at one another, and the Mayor sniggered and went pale with excitement. He was bursting with delight, as he cried: "And you didn't know that Herr Buck's brother is bankrupt!"

They loudly expressed their satisfaction. That man with his five elegant daughters! The President of the Harmony Club! But, as Diederich knew, they got their meals from the public kitchen. At this stage the Mayor poured out some more cognac and passed round the cigars. All at once he became certain that they were on the eve of a big change. "The Reichstag elections will take place in eighteen months. Between now and then you gentlemen will have to work."

Diederich proposed that the three of them should there and then constitute themselves an inner election committee.

Jadassohn explained that it was absolutely essential to get into touch with Governor von Wulckow. "In the strictest confidence," added the Mayor, winking. Diederich regretted that the "Netzig Journal," the chief newspaper in the town, was tarred with the liberal brush. "A damned Semitic rag!" said Jadassohn. On the other hand, the loyal government county paper had practically no influence in the town. But old Klüsing in Gausenfeld supplied paper to both. As he had money in the "Netzig Journal," it did not seem improbable to Diederich that its attitude might be influenced through him. They would have to frighten him into thinking that otherwise he would lose the county paper. "After all, there is another paper factory in Netzig," said the Mayor, grinning. Then the maid came in and announced she would have to set the table for dinner, as the mistress would soon be back—and also Frau Hauptmann, she added. When he heard this title the Mayor at once jumped up. As he accompanied his guest to the door, his head drooped, and in spite of all the cognac, he looked quite pale. On the stairs he caught Diederich by the sleeve. Jadassohn had remained behind, and the screams of the maid could be heard. There was already a ring at the door.

"My dear Doctor," whispered the Mayor, "I hope you have not misunderstood me. In everything we discussed I have, of course, only the interests of the town at heart. It goes without saying that I have no intention of undertaking anything in which I am not sure of the support of the organisations of which I have the honour to be the chief."

He blinked earnestly, but before Diederich had collected his thoughts, the ladies were entering the house, and the Mayor released his arm to hasten to meet them. His wife, who was dried up and wrinkled with care, had scarcely time to greet the gentlemen. She had to separate the children who were fighting. Her mother was a head taller and still youthful looking, and she looked sternly at the flushed faces of the luncheon guests. Then, with Juno-like majesty, she descended upon the Mayor who grew visibly smaller. . . . Assessor Jadassohn had already disappeared. Diederich made formal bows which were not returned and hastened away. He felt uncomfortable and looked uneasily about him in the street. He was not listening to what Jadassohn said and suddenly he turned back. He had to ring loudly several times, for there was a great deal of noise inside. The family was still standing at the foot of the stairs, where the children were pushing one another and screaming. A discussion was in progress. The Mayoress wanted her husband to take some action against a headmaster who had mishandled her son. His mother-in-law, on the contrary, was insisting that the master should be promoted because his wife had the greatest influence on the committee of the Bethlehem Asylum for fallen girls. The Mayor entreated them in turn with his hands. At last, he got a word in.

"On the one hand. . . ."

At this point Diederich had seized him by the arm. With

many apologies to the ladies, he took him aside and tremblingly whispered: "My dear Mr. Mayor, I am most anxious to avoid misunderstanding. I must repeat that I am a thoroughly liberal man."

Dr. Scheffelweis hastily assured him that he was no less certain of this than of his own sound Liberalism. Then he was called and Diederich somewhat relieved left the house. Jadassohn awaited him with a grin.

"I suppose you got frightened. Wait a bit! Nobody can ever compromise himself with the head of our city. Like God Almighty he is always on the side of the strongest battalions. To-day I just wanted to find out how far he had gone with von Wulckow. Things are not doing badly, we can move a step forward."

"Please do not forget," said Diederich reservedly, "that I am at home amongst the citizens of Netzig and I am naturally also a liberal."

Jadassohn gave him a sidelong glance. "A Neo-Teuton?" he asked. Diederich turned to him in astonishment, as he added: "How is my old friend Wiebel?"

"Do you know him? He was my fag."

"Do I know him? I arranged a duel with him."

Diederich seized the hand which Jadassohn held out to him and they shook warmly. That settled the matter and arm in arm they went down to the Ratskeller to dine.

The place was empty and dimly lighted. The gas was turned on for them at the end of the room, and while they were waiting for the soup they discovered mutual college friends. Fatty Delitzsch! As an eye-witness Diederich gave a circumstantial account of his tragic end. They drank the first glass of Rauenthal to his memory. It turned out that Jadassohn had also been through the February riots, and, like Diederich, he had learned to respect power. "His Majesty," said the Assessor, "showed such courage as would take your breath away. Several times I thought, by God—" He stopped and they gazed shuddering into each other's eyes. In order to banish the dreadful spectacle they raised their glasses. "The best of luck," said Jadassohn. "The same to you," replied Diederich. "To the very good health of your family." And Diederich answered, "I shall certainly convey the compliment to them at home."

Although his food was getting cold, Jadassohn launched into an elaborate eulogy of the Emperor's character. The Philistines, the fault-finders, and the Jews might pick holes in him as they liked, taking him all in all our glorious young Emperor is the most individual personality, charmingly impulsive and a highly original thinker. Diederich fancied that he had already established this fact and nodded contentedly. He said to himself that a person's outward appearance was sometimes deceptive, and that the length of one's ears did not determine one's loyal sentiments. They drained their glasses to the success of the struggle for throne and altar against revolution in every shape and form.

Then they got back to conditions in Netzig. They were both agreed that the new national spirit to which they must convert the town need have no other programme than the name of His Majesty. Political parties were so much rubbish, as His Majesty himself had said. "I know only two parties, those who are with me and those who are against me." Those were his words and they expressed the facts. Unfortunately in Netzig the party which was against him was still on top, but that would have to be changed, and it would be—of this Diederich was certain—by means of the Veterans' Association. Jadassohn, who was not a member, undertook nevertheless to introduce Diederich to the leading people. First and foremost there was Pastor Zillich, a member of Jadassohn's corps and a true-born German! They would call on him as soon as they had finished. They drank his health. Diederich also drank to his captain, the captain who, from being his stern superior, had become his best friend. "My term of military service is the year which I would least like to lose out of my life." All of a sudden, with flushed cheeks, he shouted: "And it is such noble memories which these Democrats would like to spoil for us!"

Old Buck! Diederich could not contain his rage as he stammered: "Such a creature would prevent us from serving in the army, saying that we are slaves! Because he once took part in a revolution. . . ."

"That is all over now," said Jadassohn.

"Are we all to get condemned to death on that account? If they had only chopped his head off! . . . And the Hohenzollerns, they say, are no use to us!"

"Certainly not to him," said Jadassohn taking a long drink.

"But I declare," continued Diederich rolling his eyes, "that I listened to all his vicious humbug only in order to find out what type of mind he has. I call you as witness, Herr Assessor! If that old schemer ever asserts that I am his friend, and that I approve of his infamous treason to the Emperor, then I will call upon you to witness that I protested this very day."

He broke into perspiration as he thought of the affair with the Building Commission and of the protection which he was to enjoy. . . . Suddenly he threw onto the table a small book, almost square in shape, and broke into a mocking laugh.

"He goes in for poetry also!"

Jadassohn turned over the pages. "Songs of the Athletes." "In Captivity." "All Hail to the Republic!" "By the lake lay a youth, sad to see" . . . "Quite so that's what they were. Sentimentalizing about jail birds while rocking the foundations of society. Revolutionary sentimentality, subversive ideas and flabby bearing. Thank God, we are differently constituted."

"Let us hope so, indeed," said Diederich. "Our student life taught us manliness and idealism, that is enough; poetry is superfluous."

"Away with your altar candles!" declaimed Jadassohn. "That sort of thing is for my friend Zillich. Now that he has finished his siesta, we can clear off."

They found the Pastor drinking coffee. He wanted immediately to send his wife and daughter out of the room, but Jadassohn gallantly detained the mistress of the house. He also tried to kiss the young lady's hand, but she turned her back on him. Diederich, who was rather tight, begged the ladies most urgently to stay and they did so. He explained to them that after Berlin Netzig seemed remarkably quiet. "The ladies are rather behind the times. I give you my word of honour, *gnädiges Fräulein*, you are the first person I have seen here who could easily stroll Unter den Linden without any one noticing that you were from Netzig." Then he learned that she had really been once in Berlin, and had even been to Ronacher's. Diederich profited by the occasion to recall a song he had heard there, but which he could only whisper into her ear.

"Unsre lieben süssen Dam'n,
Zeigen alles, was sie ham'n."

As she gave him a bold glance he kissed her lightly on the neck. She looked at him beseechingly, whereupon he assured her with the utmost frankness that she was a nice little girl. With downcast eyes she fled to her mother who had been watching the entire proceedings. The Pastor was in earnest conversation with Jadassohn. He was complaining that church attendance in Netzig had fallen off terribly.

"On the third Sunday after Easter, just think of it! On the third Sunday after Easter, I had to preach to the sexton and three old ladies from the home for decayed gentlewomen. Everybody else had influenza."

Jadassohn replied: "In view of the lukewarm, not to mention hostile, attitude which the party in power adopts towards matters of church and religion, it is a wonder the three old ladies were there. Why do they not go to the Free Thought lectures of Doctor Heuteufel?"

The Pastor shot up out of his chair. He snorted so much that his beard looked like foam, and his frock-coat flapped wildly. "Herr Assessor!" he cried vehemently, "this man is my brother-in-law, and vengeance is mine saith the Lord. But also this person is my brother-in-law and the husband of my own sister, I can only pray to God, pray with clasped hands, that He shall strike him with the lightning of his vengeance. Otherwise, He will one day be obliged to rain fire and brimstone upon the whole of Netzig. Heuteufel, do you understand, gives coffee, coffee for nothing, to the people so that they will come to him and let him capture their souls. And then he tells them that marriage is not a sacrament, but a contract—as if I were ordering a suit of clothes." The Pastor laughed bitterly.

"Disgusting," said Diederich in a deep voice, and while Jadassohn was assuring the Pastor of the positive nature of his Christianity, Diederich began again to make obvious efforts to approach Käthchen by changing his chair. Fräulein Käthchen," he said, "I can assure you most seriously that to me marriage is really a sacrament." Käthchen replied:

"You ought to be ashamed of yourself, Dr. Hessling."

He turned hot all over. "Don't look at me so crossly!"

Käthchen sighed. "You are so frightfully designing. I am sure you are no better than Herr Assessor Jadassohn. Your sisters have told me all the things you used to do in Berlin, they are my best friends."

Then they would meet soon again?—Yes, at the Harmony Club. "But you needn't think that I believe anything you say. You arrived together with Guste Daimchen at the station."

Diederich asked what that proved, and said that he protested against any conclusions which might be drawn from that purely accidental fact. Besides, Fräulein Daimchen was already engaged.

"Oh, her!" sneered Käthchen. "That doesn't make any difference to her, she is such a shocking flirt."

The Pastor's wife also confirmed this. That very day she had seen Guste in patent-leather shoes and lilac-coloured stockings. That promised nothing good. Käthchen's lip curled.

"And then that inheritance of hers—"

This insinuation reduced Diederich to perturbed silence. The Pastor had just admitted to Jadassohn the necessity of discussing once again more fully with them the position of the Christian Church in Netzig. He asked his wife for his hat and coat. It was already dark on the staircase, and as the two others went in front Diederich had a chance to kiss Käthchen's neck again. She said languishingly: "Nobody in Netzig has a moustache that tickles like yours"—which flattered him at first, but immediately awoke in him painful suspicions. So he let her go and disappeared. Jadassohn was waiting for him downstairs and whispered: "Never say die! The old boy did not notice anything and the mother pretends not to." He winked impressively.

When they had passed St. Mary's Church the three men wanted to get to the market place, but the Pastor stood still and indicated something behind him with a movement of his head. "You gentlemen doubtless know the name of the alley to the left of the church round the corner. That dirty hole of an alley, or rather a certain house in it."

"Little Berlin," said Jadassohn, for the Pastor would not move on.

"Little Berlin," he repeated, laughing painfully, and again he shouted with a gesture of holy wrath, so that many people turned round: "Little Berlin . . . in the shadow of my church! Such a house! and the Town Council will not listen to me. They make fun of me. But they make fun of some one else,"—here the Pastor moved on again—"and He will not allow Himself to be made fun of."

Jadassohn was of that opinion. But, while his companions were arguing heatedly, Diederich saw Guste Daimchen approaching from the Rathaus. He raised his hat to her with formal politeness and she smiled disdainfully. It occurred to him that Käthchen Zillich was just as fair and that she also had that small, impertinently retroussé nose. As a matter of fact, one or the other would do. Guste, it is true, was more broadly built. "And she knows well how to take care of herself. She will slap your face before you know where you are." He turned round to look after Guste. From behind she looked extraordinarily round and she waddled. In that moment Diederich decided: either her or nobody!

The other two had eventually also noticed her. "Was that not the little daughter of Frau Daimchen?" the Pastor asked, adding: "Our Bethlehem Home for fallen girls is still waiting for the gifts of the generous. I wonder if Fräulein Daimchen is generous? People say she has inherited a million."

Jadassohn hastened to declare that this was greatly exaggerated. Diederich contradicted him, saying that he knew the circumstances. The deceased uncle had made much more out of chicory than you would think. He was so positive that the Assessor was forced to promise to have an inquiry made as to the truth by the authorities in Magdeburg. Diederich said no more, for he had achieved his purpose.

"Anyhow," said Jadassohn, "the money will only go to the Bucks, that is to say, to the revolution." But Diederich insisted that he was better informed. "Fräulein Daimchen and I arrived here together," he said, by way of a feeler.— "Oh, I see. May we congratulate you?" returned Jadassohn. Diederich made a deprecating movement of his shoulders. Jadassohn apologised; he had simply imagined that young Buck—

"Wolfgang?" queried Diederich. "I saw a lot of him in Berlin. He is living there with an actress."

The Pastor coughed disapprovingly. As they just reached the square on which the theatre stood he looked sternly across the building and said: "Little Berlin, it is true, is beside my church, but it is in a dark corner at least. This den of iniquity flaunts itself on the public square, and our sons and daughters rub sleeves with common prostitutes,"—he pointed to the stage door where some members of the company were standing.

With a grieved expression Diederich agreed that this was very sad, while Jadassohn waxed indignant against the "Netzig Journal," which had rejoiced because four illegitimate children had occurred in the plays of the last season, and had regarded this as sign of progress.

Meanwhile they had turned into Kaiser Wilhelmstrasse and were obliged to salute various gentlemen who were just going into the Masonic Hall. When they had passed and had put on again the hats which they had so respectfully removed, Jadassohn said: "We shall have to keep an eye on the people who take part in that Masonic humbug. His Majesty most decidedly disapproves of it."

"So far as my brother-in-law Heuteufel is concerned," declared the Pastor, "even the most dangerous sect would not surprise me."

"Well, and what about Herr Lauer?" Diederich inquired. "A man who does not hesitate to share his profits with his workmen, is capable of anything."

"The worst of all," declared Jadassohn, "is Landgerichtsrat Fritzsche, who dares to show himself in that company, one of His Majesty's judges, arm in arm with Cohn, the money-lender. Vat does dat mean, Cohn?" Jadassohn mimicked, turning up the palms of his hands.

Diederich continued: "Since he and Frau Lauer . . ." He

stopped short and began to explain that he could easily understand how these people always won their cases in the courts. "They stick together and close their ranks." Pastor Zillich muttered something about orgies which were said to be celebrated in that building, and at which unspeakable things had happened. Jadassohn smiled significantly:

"Well, it is fortunate that their windows are overlooked by Herr von Wulckow." And Diederich nodded approvingly at the government building on the opposite side of the street. Next door stood the military depot, in front of which a sentinel was marching up and down. "It does your heart good to see the glint of the rifle of one of those fine fellows," cried Diederich. "With them we can hold that gang in check."

As a matter of fact, the rifle did not shine, because it was dark. Groups of returning workmen were already making their way home through the evening crowd. Jadassohn proposed that they should go and take a drink at Klappsch's, round the corner. It was comfortable there, for at that hour there were no customers. Klappsch was also a loyal citizen, and while his daughter was bringing the beer he expressed his warmest thanks to the Pastor for the good work which he was doing for his youngsters in the Bible class. It was true that the eldest had again stolen some sugar, but he had not been able, in consequence, to sleep at night, and had confessed his sins to God so loudly that Klappsch had heard him and had given him a good hiding. From that the talk drifted to the government officials whom Klappsch supplied with lunch. He was able to report how they spent church-time on Sundays. Jadassohn took notes while, at the same time, his hand disappeared behind Fräulein Klappsch. Diederich discussed with Pastor Zillich the founding of a Christian workman's club. "Any of my men who won't join will have to go," he promised. This prospect cheered up the Pastor. After the girl had brought beer and cognac several times he found himself in the same state of hopeful determination to which his two companions had attained in the course of the day.

"My brother-in-law Heuteufel," he cried, banging the table, "may preach as much as he likes about our being descended from monkeys. I shall get back my congregation in spite of him."

"Not only yours," Diederich assured him.

"Yes, there are too many churches in Netzig," the Pastor admitted. "Too few, man of God, too few," said Jadassohn sharply. He called Diederich to witness how things had developed in Berlin. There also the churches were standing empty until His Majesty intervened. He had issued a command to the city authorities: "See to it that churches are built in Berlin." Then they were built, religion became fashionable again, they got customers. The Pastor, the publican, Jadassohn and Diederich all grew enthusiastic over the profound piety of the monarch. Then a loud report was heard.

"Some one has fired a shot!" Jadassohn jumped up first and they all turned pale as they looked at one another. Like a flash of lightning Diederich saw in his mind's eye the bony face of Napoleon Fischer, the machinist with the black beard through which his grey skin was visible. "The revolution! it has started!" he stammered. Outside was the patter of running feet, and suddenly they all seized their hats and ran out.

The people who had collected were standing in a frightened semicircle, from the corner of the military depot to the steps of the Masonic Hall. On the other side, where the circle was open, some one was lying face downwards in the middle of the street. The soldier, who had previously been marching up and down so gaily, was now standing motionless in the sentry box. His helmet was a little on one side and he was visibly pale. With his mouth wide open he was staring at the fallen figure, while he held his rifle by the barrel and let it drag along the ground. There was a muffled murmur from the crowd, consisting chiefly of workmen and women of the people. Suddenly a man's voice said very loudly: "Ah, ah!" Then there was a deep silence. Diederich and Jadassohn exchanged a glance of fear and understanding as to the critical nature of the occasion.

Down the street ran a policeman, and in front of him a girl, her dress flying in the wind, who cried while still some distance away: "There he is! the soldier fired!"

She came up, threw herself on her knees and shook the man. "Up! Do stand up!"

She waited. His feet seemed to move convulsively, but he lay there, his arms and legs stretched out over the pavement. Then she began to cry: "Karl!" There was a scream which made everybody start. The women joined in the crying, and several men pushed forward with clenched fists. The crowd had become denser. From between the cars, which had come to a halt, reinforcements overflowed. In the midst of the threatening mob the girl worked herself free, her loosened hair streaming, her face distorted with tears. It could be seen that she was screaming, but not a sound could be heard, for it was drowned in the general noise. The solitary policeman pushed the crowd back with outstretched arms, for they would have trodden on the prostrate figure. He shouted at them in vain, tramping on their toes, and, losing his head, he began to gaze around wildly for help.

It came. A window was opened in the government building, an immense beard appeared, and a voice was heard, a formidable bass voice, which reached the ears of every one above the outcry, like the rumbling of distant cannons, even when the words could not be understood.

"Wulckow," said Jadassohn. "At last."

"I forbid this!" thundered the voice. "Who dares to make this noise here in front of my house?" And as it became a little quieter: "Where is the sentry?"

Now, for the first time, most of the people noticed that the soldier had withdrawn into the sentry box, as deeply as possible so that only the barrel of his rifle projected.

"Come out, my man!" the bass voice commanded from above. "You have done your duty. He provoked you. His Majesty will reward you for your bravery. Do you understand?"

Every one had understood and was dumb with amazement, including even the girl. All the more formidably he boomed.

"Disperse, or I'll have you shot!"

A moment passed and some had already begun to run. The workmen broke up into groups, lingered . . . and then went a little further on, with downcast heads. The governor shouted down again:

"Paschke, go and get a doctor."

Then he slammed the window. At the entrance of the building, however, there was a movement of people. Gentlemen suddenly emerged to give orders, a mass of policemen was running about on all sides, pushing the people who still remained, and shouting on their own account. Diederich and his companions, who had stepped back around their corner, noticed some gentlemen standing on the steps of the Masonic Hall. Now Dr. Heuteufel was making his way between them. "I am a doctor," he said in a loud voice, as he went quickly across the street and bent over the wounded man. He turned him over, opened his waistcoat and pressed his ear to his chest. At that moment there was complete silence, even the police stopped shouting. But the girl stood there, leaning forward with her shoulders hunched as if she feared the threat of a blow, and with her fist clenched to her heart as if that was the heart which had stopped beating.

Dr. Heuteufel stood up. "The man is dead," he said. Simultaneously he noticed that the girl was tottering, and he made a move to seize her. But she stood erect again, looking down at the face of the dead man, and said simply:

"Karl." More softly: "Karl." The doctor looked round and asked: "What's to become of this girl?"

Then Jadassohn stepped forward. "I am Assessor Jadassohn of the Public Prosecutor's Office. This girl must be removed. As her lover provoked the sentry, there is ground for suspicion that she was concerned in the offence. Inquiries will be instituted."

He made a sign to two policemen who seized the girl. Dr. Heuteufel raised his voice: "Herr Assessor, as a doctor I certify that the condition of this girl will not permit her arrest." Somebody said: "Why don't you arrest the corpse also!" But Jadassohn croaked: "Herr Lauer, I forbid all criticism of such measures as I may officially take."

Meanwhile Diederich had shown signs of great excitement. "Oh! . . . Ah! . . . Why, that is—" He was quite pale, and began again: "Gentlemen. . . . Gentlemen, I am in a position to . . . I know these people, the man and the girl. My name is Dr. Hessling. Up till to-day they were both employed in my factory. I had to discharge them on account of indecent behaviour in public."

"Ah, indeed!" said Jadassohn. Pastor Zillich made a movement. "This is truly the hand of God," he remarked. Herr Lauer's face went deep red under his grey beard, his burly figure was shaking with anger.

"We won't be so sure about the hand of God. What seems likely, Dr. Hessling, is that the man took his dismissal to heart and was guilty of disorderly conduct. He had a wife and perhaps children, too."

"They were not married at all," said Diederich, indignant in his turn. "He told me so himself."

"What difference does that make?" Lauer asked. The Pastor raised his hands in horror. "Have we reached the stage," he cried, "when it makes no difference whether God's moral law is followed or not?"

Lauer declared that it was unseemly to argue about moral

laws in the street when somebody had been shot with the connivance of the authorities. He turned to the girl and offered her employment in his workshop. Meanwhile an ambulance had come up and the dead man was raised from the ground. When they were placing him in the car the girl started out of her stupor, threw herself upon the stretcher, tore it from the grasp of the bearers before they could prevent her, and it fell on the pavement. Clasping the dead man convulsively, and with wild screams she rolled on the ground. With great difficulty she was separated from the corpse and placed in a cab. The assistant surgeon, who had accompanied the ambulance, drove off with her.

Jadassohn advanced threateningly towards Lauer, who was moving off with Heuteufel and the other members of the Masonic Lodge. "One moment, please. You stated just now that with the connivance of the authorities—I call these gentlemen to witness that that was your expression—with the connivance of the authorities somebody had been shot here. I call upon you to answer whether this was intended as a criticism of the authorities."

"Do you really, now," replied Lauer, looking at him. "I suppose you would like to have me jailed, too?"

"At the same time," continued Jadassohn, in loud cutting tones, "I draw your attention to the fact that the conduct of a sentry, firing upon a person who molests him, was defined in authoritative quarters as praiseworthy and justifiable, a few months ago in the Lück affair. It was rewarded by marks of official distinction and approval. Beware how you criticise the actions of the supreme authorities."

"I have not done so," said Lauer. "I have merely expressed my disapproval of the gentleman there with the dangerous moustache."

"What?" asked Diederich, who was still staring at the pavement where the man had fallen, which was stained with blood. Finally he understood that it was he who had been challenged.

"His Majesty wears a moustache like that. It is a German fashion. Moreover, I decline all discussion with an employer who encourages revolution."

Lauer opened his mouth in a rage, although old Buck's brother, Heuteufel, Cohn and Judge Fritzsche tried to drag him off. Jadassohn and Pastor Zillich ranged themselves beside Diederich, ready for the fray. Then a detachment of infantry arrived at a quick march and closed off the street, which was quite empty. The lieutenant in charge called upon the gentlemen to move on. They lost no time in obeying, but they observed how the lieutenant went up to the sentry on duty and shook his hand.

"Bravo!" said Jadassohn, and Dr. Heuteufel added: "Tomorrow, I suppose, it will be the turn of the captain, the major and the colonel to pronounce his eulogy and reward the fellow with money."

"Quite right!" said Jadassohn.

"But—" Heuteufel stood still—"gentlemen, let us understand one another. What is the sense in all that? Just because this lout of a peasant could not understand a joke. A joking reply, a good-humoured laugh, and he would disarm the workman who wanted to challenge him, his comrade, a poor devil like himself, instead of that, he is ordered to shoot. And afterwards come the grandiloquent phrases." Judge Fritzsche agreed, and counselled moderation. Then said Diederich, still pale and with a voice that trembled:

"The people must learn to feel power! The life of one man is not too much to pay for the sensation of imperial power!"

"Provided it is not your life," retorted Heuteufel.

"Even if it were mine!" he returned, placing his hand upon his heart.

Heuteufel shrugged his shoulders. While they continued on their way Diederich, who was a little behind with Pastor Zillich, tried to explain his feelings to the latter. Breathing heavily with emotion, he said: "For me, the incident partakes of the sublime, of the majestic, so to speak. That a person who is impertinent can be simply shot down in the public street, without trial,—think of it! It brings something heroic into the dulness of civil life. It shows people what power means."

"When exercised by the grace of God," added the Pastor.

"Of course. That's just it. That's why the thing gives me a real sense of religious exaltation. From time to time one notices evidence of the existence of higher things, of powers to which we are all subjected. For example, in the Berlin riots last February, when His Majesty ventured into the seething tumult with such phenomenal coolness—I can tell you—" As the others had stopped in front of the Ratskeller, Diederich raised his voice. "If the Emperor on that occasion had ordered the soldiers to close off Unter den Linden, and to fire on the whole crowd of us, straight into the middle of us, I say . . ."

"You would have shouted hooray," concluded Dr. Heuteufel.

"Would you not?" asked Diederich, attempting a flashing glance. "I do hope that we are all inspired by national feeling!"

Herr Lauer was on the point of again replying incautiously, but was restrained. Instead, Cohn said: "I, too, am patriotic. But do we pay our army for such pleasantries?" Diederich looked him up and down.

"Your army, do you say? Herr Cohn, the department store owner, has an army. Did you hear that, gentlemen?" He laughed loftily. "Hitherto I have only heard of the army of His Majesty the Emperor!"

Dr. Heuteufel murmured something about the rights of the

people, but in the hectoring tone of a drill sergeant Diederich declared that he had no use for a mere figurehead of an Emperor. A people without stern discipline would fall into decay. . . . By this time they had reached the cellar where Lauer and his friends were already seated. "Well, are you going to sit with us?" Heuteufel asked Diederich. "In the last analysis, I suppose, we are all liberals." Then Diederich solemnly declared: "Liberals, of course. But where great national issues are concerned I am not in favour of half measures. In such matters there are for me only two parties, which His Majesty himself has defined: Those who are with him and those who are against him. Therefore, it is pretty evident to me that my place is not at your table."

He made a formal bow and went over to an unoccupied table. Jadassohn and Pastor Zillich followed him. People seated in the neighbourhood turned round, and a general silence ensued. In the exuberance of what he had been through Diederich conceived the idea of ordering champagne. At the other table there was whispering, then some one moved his chair. It was Fritzsche. He said good-bye, came over to Diederich's table to shake hands with his party and went out.

"He was well advised to do that," remarked Jadassohn. "He recognised in time that his position was untenable." Diederich answered: "I should have preferred an honest break. No one who has a clear conscience in matters of patriotism has any reason to fear those people." But Pastor Zillich seemed embarrassed. "The righteous man must suffer much," said he. "You have no idea what an intriguer Heuteufel is. God knows what atrocious story he will tell about us to-morrow." At this Diederich gave a start. Dr. Heuteufel was one of the initiated in that still obscure incident of his life, when he tried to escape military service! In a mocking letter he had refused to give a certificate of ill-health. He held him in the hollow of his hand and could destroy him! In his sudden terror Diederich began to fear revelations from his school-days, when Dr. Heuteufel had painted his throat and accused him of being a coward. He broke into a sweat, but called all the more loudly for lobster and champagne.

The Masonic brethren at the other table had worked themselves up again over the violent death of the young workman. What were the military and the Junkers thinking about when they ordered it? They acted as if they were in a conquered country! When they had become more heated they rose to the point of demanding that the conduct of the State should be in the hands of the civilians, who, as a matter of fact, did all the work. Lauer wanted to know in what respect the ruling caste was any better than other people. "They are not even superior in race," he declared, "they are all infested with Jews, even including the princely family." But he added: "I mean no offence to my friend, Cohn."

It was time to intervene, Diederich felt. He hastily swallowed another glass, then stood up, marched heavily into the middle of the room beneath the Gothic chandelier, and said sharply:

"Herr Lauer, allow me to ask whether German princes are included in the princely houses which, according to your personal opinion, are infested with Jews?"

Quietly, and in an almost friendly fashion, Lauer replied: "Why, certainly."

"Indeed," said Diederich, drawing a deep breath before delivering his final stroke. The entire restaurant was all attention as he asked:

"Amongst these Jewish princely families in Germany do you include one which I do not need to specify?" Diederich said this with an air of triumph. He was perfectly certain that his opponent would now lose his head, stammer and crawl under the table. But he found himself met with unexpected cynicism.

"Oh, why not?" said Lauer.

Now it was Diederich's turn to lose his bearings from sheer horror. He looked around as if asking whether his ears had deceived him. The expressions of those present assured him that he had not. He muttered that time would show what would be the consequences of this statement of Herr Lauer, and withdrew in tolerable order into the friendly camp. Simultaneously Jadassohn appeared again upon the scene, after having disappeared no one knew where.

"I was not an eye-witness of what had just happened here," he said at once. "I want to make this point absolutely clear, as it may be of the greatest importance in the later developments of the case." He then obtained an exact account of what had happened. Diederich related the story with great heat. He claimed as his service that he had cut off the enemy's retreat. "Now we have him in our power!"

"Certainly," confirmed Jadassohn, who had been taking notes.

An elderly gentleman with a stiff leg and a grim face approached from the entrance. He saluted both tables and prepared to join the advocates of revolution. But Jadassohn was in time to prevent him. "Major Kunze, just a word!" He talked to him in an undertone, his eyes indicating people to the right and to the left. The major seemed to be in doubt. "Do you give me your word of honour that such a statement was actually made?" While Jadassohn was giving him his word, Herr Buck's brother came up, tall and elegant, and smiling easily, he offered a satisfactory explanation of everything to the major. But the latter regretted that he could not see how there could be any explanation for such a statement, and his face wore an expression of the most terrible gloom. Nevertheless, he continued to look over with regret at his old *Stammtisch*. Then, at the decisive moment, Diederich lifted the champagne bottle out of the pail. The major saw it and decided to obey the call of duty. Jadassohn introduced: "Dr. Hessling, the manufacturer."

The two gentlemen clasped hands fervently. They gazed into each other's eyes with mute promises of strength and loyalty. "Sir," said the major, "you have behaved like a real German patriot." Bowing and scraping, they settled their chairs in their places, presented their glasses to one another, and finally drank. Diederich immediately ordered another bottle. The major emptied his glass as regularly as it was filled, and between drinks he assured them that he too could take his stand when it was a question of German loyalty. "Even though my King has now relieved me of active service—"

"The major," Jadassohn explained, "was last stationed at the military depot."

"—I have still got the heart of an old soldier"—striking his breast—"and I shall always oppose unpatriotic tendencies, with fire and sword!" As he shouted these words his fist came down heavily upon the table. At that moment Herr Cohn hastened out behind his back, pulling his hat down upon his head. In order that his departure should look less like a retreat Herr Buck's brother first went to the lavatory. "Ha, ha!" said Jadassohn. Then in a louder tone: "Major, the enemy is in flight." Pastor Zillich was still uneasy.

"Heuteufel is still there. I do not trust him."

As Diederich ordered the third bottle he looked round contemptuously at Lauer and Dr. Heuteufel, who were sitting alone and staring shamefacedly at their beer glasses.

"We have the power," said he, "and those gentlemen over there are well aware of it. They have already resigned themselves to the fact that the sentry fired. They now look as if they were afraid that it would be their turn next. And their turn will come!" Diederich explained that he would lodge a complaint with the Public Prosecutor against Herr Lauer because of his previous statement. "And I shall see," Jadassohn assured him, "that the complaint is followed up. I shall

personally appear at the trial. You gentlemen know that I am
not concerned as a witness, as I was not present when the thing
happened."

"We will clean out the Augean stables," said Diederich, and
he began about the Veterans' Association, to which every true
patriot and loyal supporter of the Emperor would have to rally.
The major assumed a professional air. Yes, indeed, he was
on the committee of the Association. They served their King
as best they could; he was ready to propose Diederich as a
member, so that the loyal element might be strengthened;
hitherto, there was no use denying it, the damned Democrats
predominated even there. In the major's opinion, the authorities were far too considerate towards the peculiar conditions
in Netzig. He himself, if he had been appointed commanding
officer of the District, would have kept a sharp check on the
officers of the Reserve at the elections, he guaranteed that.
"But, unfortunately, my King did not give me the opportunity,
so—" In order to console him Diederich filled his glass again.
While the major was drinking Jadassohn leaned over to Diederich and whispered: "Don't believe a word of it! He is a spineless creature and crawls before old Buck. We must make an
impression on him."

Diederich proceeded to do so at once. "I may tell you that
I have already made formal arrangements with Governor
von Wulckow." And as the major opened his eyes in astonishment: "Next year, major, come the Reichstag elections.
Then we loyal citizens will have a heavy task. The fight is
already on."

"Forward," said the major grimly. *"Prost!"*

"The same to you!" replied Diederich. "Gentlemen, however powerful the subversive elements in the country may be,
we are stronger, for we have one agitator whom our opponents
have not, and that is His Majesty."

"Bravo!"

"His Majesty has issued the command to every part of his country, and therefore to Netzig, that the citizens shall at last awake from their slumbers. That is what we want, too!"

Jadassohn, the major and Pastor Zillich manifested their wakefulness by thumping the table, shouting their applause, and toasting one another. The major shouted: "To us officers His Majesty said: 'These are the gentlemen upon whom I can rely!'"

"And to us," cried Pastor Zillich, "he said, if the Church has need of princes—"

They abandoned all restraint, for the restaurant was quite empty, Lauer and Heuteufel had slipped away unnoticed, and the gas had been turned out at the end of the room.

"He also said—" Diederich puffed out his cheeks until they were fiery red and his moustache seemed to stick into his eyes, but still he thundered impressively. "We stand under the emblem of commerce, and so we do. Under his exalted leadership we are determined to get trade."

"And to make a career!" Jadassohn crowed. "His Majesty has said that everybody is welcome who wishes to help him. Does anybody suggest that this does not include me?" he asked in a challenging tone, his bloodshot eyes gleaming. The major bellowed once more:

"My King can rely on me for a dead certainty. He dismissed me too soon, as an honest German citizen I am not afraid to say that to his face. He will have bitter need of me when trouble begins. I have no intention of only firing off crackers at club balls for the rest of my life. I was at Sedan!"

"God bless me soul, so was I!" cried a shrill piping voice out of the invisible depths, and out the shadows appeared a little old man with long grey hair. He tottered up, his spectacles glitering, his cheeks glowing, and he shouted: "Major Kunze! Well, well! my old pal, you are as well as when we

were together in France. That's what I always say: 'Live
well and the longer the better!'" The major introduced him.
"Professor Kühnchen, of the High School." The little man
entered into lively explanations as to how he had come to be
forgotten there in the dark. Earlier he had been with some
people. "I suppose I must have dozed off a bit, and then
the damned fellows left me in the lurch." His sleep had not
dulled the fire of what he had drunk, and with boastful cries
he reminded the major of their mutual achievements in the
iron year. "The frank-tiroors!" he yelled, and moisture ran,
out of his wrinkled, toothless mouth. "Those were the boy-os!
As sure as you gentlemen are looking at me, I have still got
a stiff finger where a frank-tiroor bit me, just because I wanted
to slit his throat a bit with my sword. A dirty trick the fellow played on me!" He showed the finger round the table
and elicited cries of admiration. Diederich's feeling of enthusiasm was frankly mixed with fear. Involuntarily he saw
himself in the position of the *franc-tireur:* the fiery little man
was kneeling on his chest and pointing the blade at his throat.
He had to go outside for a moment.

When he returned the major and the professor, each trying
to shout louder than the other, were telling the story of a
wild battle. Neither of them could be heard properly. Kühnchen, however, yelled more piercingly than the other bellowed,
until he had reduced him to silence and could take up the
story undisturbed. "No, my old friend, you have a mind for
detail. If you fell downstairs you wouldn't miss a step. But
it was Kühnchen who set fire to the house when the frank-
tiroors were inside, there's no doubt about that. I employed
a ruse of war and pretended to be dead, so that the silly idiots
did not notice anything. Once it was burning of course, they
had no more desire to defend their country, and thought only
of getting out, of soofe-qui-pooh. Then you should have
seen us Germans! We shot them off the wall as they tried
to clamber down! They bucked like rabbits!"

Kühnchen had to interrupt his inventions, he was choking with laughter, while the whole table boomed in unison.

Kühnchen recovered. "The treacherous swine had also caught us napping! And the women! Upon my word, gentlemen, there is nothing can touch the French women for viciousness. They poured boiling water on our heads. Now, I ask you, was that lady-like? When the house was on fire they threw the children out of the window, and expected us to catch them. Nice, wasn't it? But foolish! On our bayonets we caught the little devils. And then the women!" Kühnchen bent his gouty fingers as if they held the butt end of a gun and looked up as if there was still some one to be empaled. His glasses shone and he continued to lie. "At last a real fat one came along. She could not get through the window frontways, so she tried if she could go backwards. But you didn't know your Kühnchen, my child. I wasn't slow in getting up on the shoulders of two comrades, and with my bayonet I tickled her fat French—"

The last word was drowned in the applause. The professor added: "Every Sedan anniversary I tell the story in noble words to my class. The youngsters must learn what heroic forebears they had."

They were all agreed that this could only strengthen the loyal sentiments of the younger generation, and they toasted Kühnchen. In their enthusiasm none had noticed that a newcomer had approached the table. Suddenly Jadassohn saw the modest grey figure of a man in a long military cape, and made a friendly sign to him. "Why, come along, Herr Rothgroschen!" In the exuberance of his spirit Diederich asked overbearingly: "Who are you?"

The stranger answered cringingly: "Rothgroschen, editor of the 'Netzig Journal.'"

"Ah, a hungry intellectual," said Diederich, his eyes flashing. "Broken-down college men, poor scholars, a menace to us!"

They all laughed and the editor smiled humbly.

"His Majesty has described your type," said Diederich. "Well, come and sit down."

He poured out champagne for him, and Rothgroschen drank it gratefully. He looked round in a cool but shy manner at the company, whose self-consciousness had been greatly heightened by the empty bottles which lay on the ground. They soon forgot him. He waited patiently till somebody asked him how he had blown in there in the middle of the night. "I had to make the paper ready," he explained with an air of importance. "To-morrow morning you will want to read in the paper all about the workman who was shot."

"We know that better than you," cried Diederich. "You have to write it up like a starving penny-a-liner."

The editor smiled apologetically and listened dutifully while they all related at the same time what had happened. When the noise subsided he continued: "As that gentleman there—"

"Dr. Hessling," said Diederich sharply.

"Rothgroschen," murmured the editor. "As you mentioned the name of the Emperor just now, it will interest these gentlemen to know that he has made another proclamation."

"I will not stand any joking!" shouted Diederich. The editor bowed and placed his hand on his heart. "There is a letter from the Emperor."

"I suppose," Diederich asked, "that could only have reached your desk through some infamous betrayal of confidence." Rothgroschen extended a deprecating hand. "The Emperor himself has designed it for publication. You'll read it to-morrow in the newspapers. I have a proof here."

"Go ahead, Doctor," the major ordered. Diederich cried: "What is that? Doctor? Are you a Doctor?" But no one was interested in anything but the letter. They snatched the proof from the editor's hand. "Hurrah!" cried Jadassohn, who could still read without much difficulty. "His Majesty has definitely identified himself with the Christian Church."

Pastor Zillich rejoiced so heartily that he got a hiccup. "That's one in the eye for Heuteufel! At last that impudent scientist, hic, will get what's coming to him. These fellows dare to discuss the question of divine revelation, which I myself, hic, can hardly understand, and I have studied theology!" Professor Kühnchen threw the proof sheets up into the air. "Gentlemen, if I do not make my class read that letter, and set it as a subject for composition, then my name is not Kühnchen!"

Diederich was very serious. "Hammurabi was truly an instrument of God! I should like to know who would deny it." He glared round angrily. Rothgroschen bent his shoulders. "And Emperor William the Great," Diederich continued, "I insist on him. If he was not an instrument of the Lord, then the Lord does not know what an instrument is!"

"That is absolutely my opinion," the major confirmed. Fortunately nobody contradicted him, for Diederich was determined to go to extremes. Clinging to the table he staggered up from his chair. "What about our magnificent young Emperor?" he asked threateningly. From every side the answer came: "Personality, impulsive . . . versatile . . . an original thinker." Diederich was not satisfied.

"I move that he is also an instrument!"

The motion was passed unanimously.

"And I further move that His Majesty be informed by telegram of this resolution!"

"I second the motion!" bellowed the major. Diederich declared: "Passed unanimously and with enthusiasm!" He flopped back into his seat. Kühnchen and Jadassohn assisted one another in drawing up the telegram. They read out what they had concocted.

"A meeting held in the Ratskeller at Netzig—"

"Gathered in session," corrected Diederich. They continued:

"A meeting of loyal citizens—"

"Loyal, hic, and Christian," added Pastor Zillich.

"Are you gentlemen really serious?" asked Rothgroschen in a voice of gentle entreaty. "I thought it was a joke."

Then Diederich lost his temper.

"We do not trifle with sacred things! Do you want me to prove it to you in acts as well as words, you broken-down scholar?"

As Rothgroschen's gestures indicated complete submission, Diederich quieted down again and said: "Your health!" The major shouted as if he would burst: "We are the gentlemen on whom His Majesty can rely!" Jadassohn begged him to be quiet and began to read.

"This meeting of loyal and Christian citizens, gathered in session at the Ratskeller in Netzig, humbly extends to Your Majesty its unanimous and enthusiastic approval of Your Majesty's Royal testimony to revealed religion. We register our deepest loathing of revolution in every form, and in the courageous act of a sentry in Netzig to-day we greet the gratifying evidence that Your Majesty, no less than Hammurabi and Emperor William the Great, is the instrument of Almighty God." Jadassohn gave a flattered smile when they all applauded.

"Let us sign!" cried the major. "Or has any gentleman anything to say?" Rothgroschen cleared his throat. "With the utmost deference, just one point."

"I cannot allow that," said Diederich. The alcohol had given the editor courage, and he rolled on his seat, sniggering senselessly.

"I have nothing to say against the sentry, gentlemen. In fact, I have always held that soldiers are there to shoot."

"Well, what then?"

"Yes, but how do you know that the Emperor thinks so?"

"Of course, he does! Look at the Lück case."

"Precedents—he, he—are all very well, but we know that the Emperor is an original thinker and—he, he—and very impulsive. He does not like to be forestalled. If I were to write in the paper that you, Dr. Hessling, should be appointed minister, then—he, he—you would certainly never be appointed."

"The perverted reasoning of a Jew," cried Jadassohn. The editor became indignant. "Every time there is a High Church festival I write a column and a half of appropriate sentiment. The sentry, however, may be accused of murder. Then we shall have put our foot in it."

A silence ensued. Abstractedly the major laid the pencil on the table. Diederich seized it. "Are we loyal citizens?" and he signed his name furiously. Then the enthusiasm was renewed. Rothgroschen wanted to sign his name second.

"To the telegraph-office!"

Diederich gave orders to have the bill sent to him the next day and they left the restaurant. All of a sudden Rothgroschen was full of the wildest hopes. "If I can get the Emperor's reply it will be a real journalistic scoop."

The major bellowed: "Now we shall see whether I am to continue arranging charity bazaars!"

Pastor Zillich could already see his church swarming with people and Heuteufel being stoned by the mob. Kühnchen was dreaming of the streets of Netzig bathed in blood. "Does any one dare to question my loyalty to the Emperor?" crowed Jadassohn. And Diederich: "Old Buck had better look out! and Klüsing and Gausenfeld, too! We are awakening from our sleep!"

The gentlemen held themselves very straight, and from time to time one of them shot forward unexpectedly. They made a great noise with their sticks on the closed shutters of the shops, and they sang the "Watch on the Rhine" without making the slightest effort to keep in time with one another. At the corner of the Courthouse stood a policeman, but fortunately he did not move. "Do you want anything, little man?" should Rothgroschen, who was oblivious of all consequences. "We are telegraphing to the Emperor!" In front of the Post Office an accident befell Pastor Zillich, who had the weakest stomach. While the others endeavoured to ease his plight, Diederich rang the bell and handed in the telegram. When the postal official had read it, he looked hesitatingly at Diederich, but the latter glared so fiercely that he shrank back and did his duty. Meanwhile Diederich, without any reason, continued to glare and strike an attitude as if he were the Emperor when an aide-de-camp reported the heroic deed of the sentry, and the prime minister handed him the telegram of greeting. Diederich felt the helmet on his head, he tapped the sword at his side and said: "I am very powerful!" The telegraphist thought he was making some complaint and counted his change again. Diederich took the money, went up to a desk and scribbled some lines on a piece of paper. He put it in his pocket and returned to his companions.

They had called a cab for the Pastor, and he was just driving off, making tearful signs from the window as if it were a final farewell. Jadassohn turned round the corner into a side street near the theatre, although the major shouted after him that his home lay in a different direction. Soon the major disappeared also, and alone with Rothgroschen he reached Lutherstrasse. The editor refused to go any further when they reached the Valhalla Theatre. In the middle of the night he wanted to see "The Electric Marvel," a lady who was supposed to emit sparks. Diederich had to reason earnestly with him that this was not the hour for such frivolities. For the rest, Rothgroschen forgot all about the Electric Marvel as soon as he beheld the offices of the "Netzig Journal." "Stop!" he shouted. "Stop the presses! The telegram of the loyal citizens must be inserted. . . . You'll want to see it in the newspapers to-morrow morning," he remarked to a passing watchman. Then Diederich grasped him firmly by the arm.

"Not only that telegram," he whispered sharply. "I have another one." He drew a piece of paper out of his pocket. "The night telegraphist is an old acquaintance of mine, and he gave it to me. You must promise me the utmost discretion as to its origin, otherwise the man will lose his post."

As Rothgroschen at once promised everything, Diederich continued without looking at the paper:

"It is addressed to the military depot and must be communicated by the colonel himself to the sentry who shot the workman. It reads as follows: 'For your valour on the field of honour against the domestic enemy we are pleased to extend our approval and hereby promote you to the rank of lance-corporal. . . .' Here, look for yourself"—and Diederich handed the paper to the editor. But Rothgroschen did not look at it, he only stared at Diederich in blank amazement, at his adamant bearing, at his moustache pointing upwards and his flashing eyes.

"It almost seems to me—" stammered Rothgroschen. "You look so very like—His . . ."

IV

DIEDERICH would like to have slept until the afternoon, as in the good old days of the Neo-Teutons, but the Ratskeller presented its bill, which was considerable enough to compel him to get up and go to the office. He felt very badly, and everything conspired to irritate him, even the family. His sisters demanded their monthly dress allowance, and, when he said he hadn't it, they contrasted him with old Sötbier, who had never failed them. Diederich dealt energetically with this attempt at revolt. In the hoarse tones of one who is suffering from a bad head he gave the girls to understand that they would have to accustom themselves to a different state of affairs. Sötbier, of course, had been very free with the money and had let down the whole business. "If I had to pay you your shares to-day you'd be damnably surprised at how little it would amount to." While he spoke he became impressed by the injustice of his ever being obliged to give the two girls a share in the business. That would have to be prevented, was his reflection. They, on the other hand, became more insistent. "So, we cannot pay the dressmaker, but you drink one hundred and fifty marks' worth of champagne." Thereupon Diederich's wrath was terrible to behold. They were opening his letters! They were spying on him! He wasn't master in his own house, but just a clerk, a slave, who had to toil hard for the ladies so that they might loaf about all day doing nothing! He shouted and stamped until the glasses tinkled. Frau Hessling begged plaintively for peace; only their fear prompted the two sisters to answer back, but there was no stopping Diederich now that he had started.

"How dare you dictate to me, you pack of silly women?

How do you know whether that hundred and fifty marks is not an excellent investment of capital? Yes, a capital investment! Do you think that I would go boozing on champagne with those idiots, if I did not want to get something out of them? Here in Netzig you know nothing of how these things are done, this is the modern way. It is"—he hesitated for the right phrase—"in the grand manner!"

He went out, slamming the door. Frau Hessling followed him cautiously, and when he had thrown himself down on the parlour sofa, she took his hand. "My dear son, I am with you," she said, looking at him as if she wanted to "pray from the heart." Diederich asked for a salted herring and then began to complain angrily of the difficulty of introducing the new spirit into Netzig. At least in his own home they should not thwart his efforts! "I have big things in store for you, but you must kindly leave all that to my superior judgment. There can be only one master, and of course he must be filled with a spirit of enterprise and have large views. Sötbier does not fit the part. I'll give the old man a little while more to potter about, then he gets the sack."

Softly Frau Hessling said she was sure that, for his mother's sake, her dear son would always do exactly what was best. Then Diederich went off to the office and wrote a letter to Büschli & Co., machinery manufacturers, of Eschweiler, in which he ordered a "New Patent Two-Cylinder Machine, fitted on the Maier system." He left the letter lying open on his desk and went out. When he returned Sötbier was standing at the desk, and it was evident that he was crying under his green eye-shade. His tears were falling on the letter. "You must have that copied," said Diederich coldly. Then Sötbier began:

"Master Diederich, our old cutting machine is not a Patent Two-Cylinder, but it belongs to the earliest days of the old master. He began with that machine, and with that machine the business grew up. . . ."

"Well, in my turn I wish to develop the business with my own machine," replied Diederich sharply. Sötbier entreated. "The old one has always been good enough for us."

"Not for me."

Sötbier swore that it could do as much as the very latest machines, which were only foisted on the market by lying advertisements. As Diederich remained unmoved, the old man opened the door and shouted: "Fischer! Come here a moment!" Diederich began to feel uneasy. "What do you want with that fellow? I forbid him to interfere!" But Sötbier appealed to the testimony of the machinist, who had worked in the largest factories. "Look here, Fischer, tell Dr. Hessling what our cutting machine can do." Diederich would not listen. He walked rapidly up and down, convinced that the man would jump at the opportunity to annoy him. Instead of that, Napoleon Fischer began with a generous acknowledgment of Diederich's expert knowledge, and then added every possible unfavourable comment on the old machine. If they would believe Napoleon Fischer, he was on the point of chucking up his job, he was so dissatisfied with the old machine. Diederich said snappishly that he really congratulated himself on the prospect of now being able to retain the invaluable services of Herr Fischer. Ignoring this irony, however, the machinist explained to him all the advantages of the new Patent Two-Cylinder as set out in the prospectus, especially the ease with which it worked. "Provided I can save you trouble," sneered Diederich, "I have no other desire. Thanks, Fischer, you can go."

When the machinist had left, Sötbier and Diederich were each busied with his own calculations. Suddenly Sötbier asked: "Where is the money coming from to pay for it?" Diederich's face was scarlet, for he, too, had been thinking only of that the whole time. "Oh, it doesn't matter about paying," he shouted. "In the first place, I shall set a long period for delivery. Then, do you think I would buy such an expensive machine if I had no use for it? No, sir. In that case it is most likely that I have definite plans for the extension of the business in the near future—but I will not discuss that to-day."

He left the office with an air of buoyancy, in spite of private misgivings. That fellow, Napoleon Fischer, had looked back, as he went out, with a glance which suggested that he had let the boss down nicely. "When surrounded by enemies," thought Diederich, "then we show our real strength," and he held himself more erect than ever. He would show them the sort of man he was, and he decided to carry out a suggestion which had occurred to him when he awoke in the morning. He called on Dr. Heuteufel, but it was the hour when the latter received patients, so he had to wait. When the Doctor did see him it was in the consulting-room where everything, the smell and the furniture, reminded Diederich of former unpleasant visits. Dr. Heuteufel took up the newspaper from the table and said, with a short laugh: "Well, I suppose you've come to triumph. Two successes at one blow! Your champagne-inspired greetings are mentioned—and the Emperor's telegram to the sentry leaves nothing further to be desired, from your point of view."

"What telegram?" asked Diederich. Dr. Heuteufel showed him, and Diederich read: "For your valour on the field of honour against the domestic enemy we are pleased to extend our approval and hereby promote you to the rank of lance-corporal!" Standing there in print it gave him the impression of complete authenticity. He was actually moved, and said with manly reserve: "Those sentiments will find an echo in the heart of every true patriot." While Heuteufel shrugged his shoulders Diederich recovered his breath. "I did not come here on that account, but in order to clear up our mutual relations." "I thought they were already settled," replied Heuteufel. "No, not at all." Diederich assured him that he desired to make an honourable peace. He was prepared to work along reasonably liberal lines, provided his strong feeling of devotion to King and country were respected. Dr. Heuteufel declared that this was merely playing with words. Whereupon Diederich lost his head. This man held him in the hollow of his hand, and with the help of a certain document could show him up as a coward! The mocking smile on his yellow Chinaman's face, this attitude of superiority, these were a perpetual threat. He remained silent and allowed the sword to dangle a little longer over Diederich's head. This could not last! "I command you," said Diederich, hoarse with excitement, "to give me back my letter." Heuteufel feigned astonishment. "What letter?"—"The one I wrote you about my military service, when I was called up."

The Doctor thought back.

"Oh, I remember, when you wanted to evade service!"

"I knew you would distort my thoughtless statements into something insulting to me. Once again I demand the return of the letter." Diederich stepped forward threateningly, but Heuteufel stood his ground.

"Don't bother me. I haven't got your letter any more."

"I demand your word of honour."

"I do not give that to order."

"Then I warn you of the consequences of your dishonourable conduct. Should you ever try to cause me trouble with that letter, it will be a case of violating professional secrets. I will denounce you to the Medical Council, bring proceedings against you, and use all my influence to make your further career impossible!" In the tensity of his excitement his voice dropped to a whisper. "I tell you I am prepared for the worst! Between us, from now on there can be only war to the knife!"

Dr. Heuteufel looked at him curiously, and shook his head, shaking his long Chinese moustache. "You are hoarse," he said.

Diederich started, and stammered: "What does that matter to you?"

"Oh, nothing," said Heuteufel. "It just interests me from early times because I always prophesied that of you."

"What is it? Kindly explain yourself." But Heuteufel declined. Diederich glared at him. "I must insist most emphatically upon your doing your duty as a physician!"

Heuteufel replied that he was not Diederich's doctor. Whereupon the latter's commanding air collapsed, and he begged plaintively. "Sometimes I have pains in my throat. Do you think it will get worse? Is there anything to be afraid of?"

"I advise you to consult a specialist."

"But you are the only one here! For God's sake, Doctor, do not have this on your conscience, I have a family to support."

"Then you should smoke less and drink less. You had too much last night."

"Oh, is that all?" Diederich drew himself up. "You begrudge me the champagne, and then the greetings to the Emperor."

"If you suspect me of doubtful motives, you need not ask my opinion."

Diederich began to cringe again. "You might, at least, tell me whether I am liable to get cancer."

Heuteufel remained stern. "Well, you were always subject to scrofula and rickets as a child. You should have had your military training, then you would not now have so much flesh."

The end of it was that the Doctor consented to examine him and decided to paint his larynx. Diederich choked, rolled his eyes in terror and clutched the Doctor's arm. Heuteufel withdrew the brush. "If you go on like that, I can do nothing. You were always the same," he tittered.

As soon as Diederich had recovered his composure he made

off as quickly as possible from this chamber of horrors. In front of the house, while his eyes were still full of tears, he ran into Judge Jadassohn. "Hello!" said Jadassohn. "Did the liquor disagree with you? I see you are off to consult Heuteufel?"

Diederich assured him that he never felt better. "But I was concerned about the fellow, and I went to him because I thought it my duty to demand a satisfactory explanation of what this man, Lauer, said yesterday. I need hardly say that the idea of meeting Lauer directly does not appeal to a man of my loyal principles."

Jadassohn proposed that they should adjourn to Klappsch's beer saloon.

"As I was saying," continued Diederich when they were seated inside, "I went to him with the intention of clearing up the whole matter by attributing it to the fact that the gentleman in question was drunk. Or, at the worst, to a temporary aberration of his mind. What do you think happened? Heuteufel got impertinent, put on a superior air, and made cynical comments on our greeting to the Emperor. In fact, you will hardly believe me, but he even criticised His Majesty's telegram!"

"Well, what next?" asked Jadassohn, whose hand was busy with Fräulein Klappsch.

"There is no 'next' for me. I have done with the gentleman for the rest of my life!" cried Diederich, in spite of his painful consciousness of the fact that he would have to return on Wednesday to have his throat painted. Jadassohn broke in sharply:

"I haven't finished with him." Diederich stared at him. "There are authorities, known as the Public Prosecutor's Department, who take a considerable interest in persons like Messrs. Lauer and Heuteufel." At this point he released Fräulein Klappsch and told her to make herself scarce.

"What do you mean, exactly?" asked Diederich uneasily. "I am thinking of taking proceedings for *lèse-majesté*."

"You?"

"Certainly I am. State Attorney Feiser is away on sick leave and I am in charge. As I pointed out yesterday, immediately after the incident, and in the presence of witnesses, I was not present when the offence was committed. I am not, therefore, disqualified from representing the prosecuting authorities at the trial."

"But if nobody lodges a complaint?"

Jadassohn smiled grimly. "The Lord be praised, that is not necessary. . . . In any case, let me remind you that yesterday you yourself offered to appear as a witness."

"I know nothing about it," said Diederich quickly. Jadassohn clapped him on the shoulder. "I trust you will be able to remember everything when you are put on your oath." Then Diederich became indignant, and his voice became so loud that Klappsch glanced into the room discreetly.

"Herr Assessor, I am greatly astonished that my private remarks— Obviously it is your intention to secure rapid promotion by means of a political trial, but I fail to see why I should be concerned with your career."

"And does yours concern me?" asked Jadassohn.

"I see. Then we are opponents?"

"I hope that may be avoidable," and Jadassohn proceeded to prove that he had no reason to be afraid of the trial. All the witnesses of what happened at the Ratskeller would have to give the same evidence as himself, including Lauer's friends. Diederich would not have to thrust himself too much to the fore in any way. . . . Diederich replied that he had unfortunately done so already, for it was he, after all, who had had the row with Lauer. But Jadassohn quieted his fears. "Nobody will bother about that. The question is whether the incriminating words were spoken by Herr Lauer. You will simply make your statement, like the other witnesses, but use a little discretion, if you like."

"With the utmost discretion!" Diederich assured him. Then, prompted by Jadassohn's Mephistophelian air: "How do I come to be the means of landing a decent man like Lauer in jail? After all, he is a decent man. In my eyes there is no shame in professing certain political opinions!"

"Especially when they are professed by the son-in-law of old Buck, whom you need for the moment," concluded Jadassohn—and Diederich bowed his head. This Jew climber was exploiting him shamelessly and he was helpless. And then, people talked of friendship! Again he reminded himself that everybody else was much more brutal and unscrupulous in life than he was. The great task was to be hard. He drew himself up stiffly in his chair and glared, but he preferred to leave it at that. With these officials of the Public Prosecutor's you never could tell. . . . For the rest, Jadassohn turned the conversation into other channels.

"I suppose you know that in the government offices and in the courts there are curious rumours afloat about His Majesty's telegram to the commanding officer of the regiment? The colonel is said to have denied that he ever received a telegram."

Although he was quaking inwardly, Diederich kept his voice in control. "But it was published in the press!" Jadassohn grinned ambiguously. "You can't believe everything you read in the papers." He ordered Klappsch, who again shoved his head in the doorway, to bring the "Netzig Journal." "Look here, this number is devoted exclusively to His Majesty. The leading article deals with the declaration of the All Highest concerning revealed religion. Then comes the telegram to the colonel, then the local news of the sentry's act of heroism, mixed up with three anecdotes about the Royal Family."

"They are very touching stories," remarked Klappsch, rolling his eyes.

"No doubt, they are!" Jadassohn affirmed. And Diederich: "Even that radical propagandist rag is forced to admit the importance of His Majesty."

"It is, of course, possible that, in their praiseworthy zeal, they prematurely published the telegram of the All Highest—before it was despatched. "That is out of the question," said Diederich decisively. "His Majesty's style is unmistakable." Even Klappsch could recognise it. "Well that may be, . . ." admitted Jadassohn. "You never can tell, so we have issued no official denial. Although the colonel has heard nothing, the 'Netzig Journal' may have had it direct from Berlin. Wulckow sent for Rothgroschen, the editor, but the fellow refuses to make any statement. The governor came to us in person to see about invoking against Rothgroschen the law compelling witnesses to speak. Finally we decided to take no action, but to wait for a denial from Berlin—for you never can tell."

When Klappsch was called into the kitchen, Jadassohn continued: "Funny, isn't it? The thing seems fishy to everybody, but no one will take any action, because in this case—in this very peculiar case"—he emphasised these words maliciously, and his whole bearing, even his ears, seemed malicious —"the improbable is most likely to happen."

Diederich was paralysed with fear. He had never dreamed of such a dark betrayal. Jadassohn noticed his dismay and, mistaking the cause of it, he began to prevaricate. "Between ourselves, you know, the man has his weaknesses." In threatening and hostile tones Diederich retorted. "Last night you were of a very different opinion." Jadassohn pleaded as his excuse the uncritical frame of mind induced by the champagne, and asked if Dr. Hessling had really taken so seriously the enthusiasm of the other gentlemen. Nobody was more critical, as a matter of fact, than Major Kunze. . . . Diederich drew back his chair, and his blood ran cold, as if he had suddenly found himself in a den of thieves. With the utmost conviction he said: "I trust I can rely as implicitly upon the patriotic sentiments of the other gentlemen as upon my own, as to which I most emphatically repudiate any doubts."

Jadassohn had recovered his offensive tone. "If that implies any insinuation regarding myself, I deny it with all the scorn it deserves." His voice rose to a scream, which brought Klappsch to the door: "Remember who I am, Dr. Hessling, one of His Majesty's judges. I am at your disposal whenever you want me."

Diederich could only murmur that he had not intended anything of that kind. But he called for the bill, and they parted on almost unfriendly terms.

On his way home Diederich was perturbed. Should he not have been more frank with Jadassohn, in case Rothgroschen should tell? Still, he was indispensable to Jadassohn in the Lauer case. At all events, it was a good thing that Diederich now knew exactly the sort of person this gentleman was. "Real patriotic feeling is incompatible with ears like his. I always suspected them."

As soon as he reached the house he seized the Berlin "Lokal-Anzeiger." There he found the anecdotes about the Emperor which would appear to-morrow in the "Netzig Journal." Perhaps they would not appear until the day after to-morrow, for there was not room for everything. He continued his search with trembling hands. Here it was! He was obliged to sit down. "Is there anything wrong with you, my boy?" asked Frau Hessling. Diederich was staring at the printed words which were like a fairy tale come true. There it stood, amongst other indubitable facts, in the one paper which was read by the Emperor himself! Deep within the depths of his soul he murmured, so that he himself could hardly hear it: "My telegram." He could hardly contain himself with sheer joy. Was it possible? Had he really anticipated what the Emperor would say? Was his ear so acute? Did his brain work in unison with . . . ? He was overpowered by a sense of mystic relationship. . . . But there might still be a denial, he might be hurled back into his own obscurity! Diederich passed a night of anxiety, and the next morning he rushed for the "Lokal-Anzeiger." The anecdotes. The unveiling of a monument. The speech. "From Netzig." There was the report of the recognition bestowed upon Lance-Corporal Emil Pacholke for his bravery in the face of the domestic enemy. All the officers, led by the colonel, had shaken his hand. He had received presents of money. "It is well known that yesterday the Emperor telegraphed, promoting the brave soldier to the rank of lance-corporal." There! not a denial but a confirmation! He had adopted Diederich's own words and had taken action in the sense Diederich had indicated! . . . Diederich spread out the newspaper, and gazed into its mirrored reflection of himself draped in royal ermine.

Unfortunately no word could reveal this victory and Diederich's dizzy promotion, but his own bearing sufficed, his inflexible mien and speech, his commanding glance. His family and his workmen were cowed into respectful silence. Even Sötbier had to admit that a creative breath had put new vigour into the business. The more clearly Diederich's dominating figure emerged the more ape-like seemed the manner in which Napoleon Fischer crept about, with his arms hanging in front of him, his eyes averted and his teeth gleaming above his scraggy black beard. He was the spirit of suppressed revolt. . . . Now was the time to make a move in the direction of Guste Daimchen. Diederich paid her a visit.

At first Frau Daimchen received him alone, seated on the old plush-covered sofa, but attired in a brown silk dress, much beribboned. She folded her hands, which were red and swollen like those of a washerwoman, across her stomach in such a way that her new rings could not escape the visitor's gaze. Out of sheer embarrassment he began to admire them, whereupon Frau Daimchen was only too glad to explain that now she and Guste need want for nothing, thank God. The only thing that worried them was whether to furnish in Old German or "Louis Kangze" style. Diederich warmly recommended Old German; he had seen it in the best houses in Berlin. But Frau Daimchen was suspicious. "Who knows whether you have called on such nice people as us. You can't tell me, I know what it means when people make a show as if they had money, when they haven't." At a loss what to reply, Diederich remained silent, while Frau Daimchen complacently drummed with her fingers on her stomach. Fortunately Guste came in, with a great rustling of petticoats. Diederich sprang gracefully from his chair, and said, with a bow, as he kissed her hand: *"Gnädigstes Fräulein!"* Guste laughed. "Mind you don't break anything!" But she consoled him at once. "It is easy to recognise a real gentleman. Lieutenant von Brietzen always does that, too."

"Yes, indeed," said Frau Daimchen, "all the officers visit us. Only yesterday I was saying to Guste: 'Guste, says I, we could have a crest embroidered on every chair, for members of the nobility have sat on every one of them.'"

Guste made a grimace. "As far as birth is concerned, and everything else, for that matter, Netzig is awfully so-so. I think we'll move to Berlin." To this Frau Daimchen agreed. "We shouldn't indulge these people," she said. "Only to-day old Frau Harnisch nearly burst her sides laughing when she saw my silk dress."

"That's mother all over," said Guste. "As long as she can brag it is all right. But I am thinking of my fiancé. Do you know that Wolfgang has passed his final examination? But what can he do here in Netzig? With our money he can get somewhere in Berlin." Diederich said: "He always wanted to become a minister of state, or something." With a faint sneer he added: "That's so easy, they say!"

Guste immediately bridled up. "Old Herr Buck's son is a

cut above the average," she said sharply. With the superior air of a man of the world Diederich explained that nowadays qualifications were demanded which could not be supplied through old Buck's influence: personality, a spirit of large scale enterprise, and, above all, an unimpeachable sense of patriotism. The girl no longer interrupted him, but even gazed respectfully at his aggressive moustache. But his consciousness of the impression he was making betrayed him. "I have not noticed any of those qualities in Herr Wolfgang Buck," he said. "That fellow philosophises and finds fault with everything, and for the rest, he leads a pretty gay life. . . . After all," he concluded, "his mother was an actress." He stared in front of him, although he felt that Guste's threatening glance sought to catch his eye.

"What do you mean?" she asked. He feigned astonishment.

"I? Oh, nothing. I was only referring to the way in which rich young men live in Berlin. After all, the Bucks are a distinguished family."

"I should hope so, indeed," said Guste sharply. Frau Daimchen, who had been yawning, remembered an appointment with a dressmaker; Guste looked expectantly at Diederich, and there was nothing for him to do but to stand up and bow himself out. In view of the tension, he made no effort to kiss the ladies' hands. In the ante-room Guste caught up on him. "Now, will you kindly tell me what you meant about the actress?"

He opened his mouth, stuttered and shut it again, blushing deeply. He had almost given away what his sisters had told him about Wolfgang Buck. In sympathetic tones he said: "We are old friends, Fräulein Guste. . . . All I meant to say was that Buck is not a fit match for you. He has an hereditary taint, so to speak, from his mother. The old man, too, was condemned to death. What are the Bucks, in any case? Take it from me, one should never marry into a family that is on the down grade. That is a sin against oneself," he added. But Guste was standing with her hands on her hips.

"Oh, the down grade? And you, I suppose, are on the up grade? Because you go boozing in the Ratskeller and get into rows with people? The whole town is talking about you, and you try to slander a most respectable family. On the down grade, indeed! There will be no question of the down grade with whoever gets my money. You are just jealous. Do you think I can't see that?"—and she glared at him with tears of rage in her eyes. He felt exceedingly uncomfortable and would have liked to fall on his knees and kiss her little chubby fingers, and then the tears from her eyes—but would that do? Meanwhile she screwed up her fat, pink face into an expression of contempt, turned her back and slammed the door. With beating heart Diederich stood for a while on the spot, then he made off, feeling very small.

He reflected that there had been no chance for him in that quarter anyhow; the matter did not concern him. For all her money, Guste was just a silly goose—and this thought quieted him. When he heard one evening what Jadassohn had learnt in the courts at Magdeburg, Diederich had his moment of triumph. Only fifty thousand marks! And with that, putting on the airs of a countess! A girl who bluffed on that scale was obviously more suitable for second-raters, like the Bucks, than for a solid, right-thinking citizen like Diederich! Käthchen Zillich would be preferable. She was like Guste in appearance, her charms were almost as irresistible, and moreover her good temper and easy manners were a recommendation. He began to come more frequently to afternoon coffee and diligently made love to her. She warned him against Jadassohn, which Diederich recognised as only too well justified. She also spoke with extreme dislike of Frau Lauer, whose conduct with Landgerichtsrat Fritzsche. . . . In the Lauer case Käthchen Zillich was the only person who wholly took Diederich's part.

This affair was assuming a threatening appearance for
Diederich. Jadassohn had succeeded in getting the Public
Prosecutor's Department to summon before a court of inquiry
the witnesses of what happened that night. In spite of Diederich's reluctant deposition, the others held him responsible
for bringing them into this dilemma. Cohn and Fritzsche
avoided him, Herr Buck's brother forgot his natural politeness so far as to cut him dead, and Heuteufel painted his
throat ferociously while refusing to talk to him in private. On
the day when it became known that the court had served
Herr Lauer with a summons, Diederich's table in the Ratskeller
was deserted. Professor Kühnchen was just putting on his
overcoat and Diederich had just time to seize him by the collar.
But Kühnchen was in a hurry, he had to speak against the
new Army Bill to the Liberal Voters' Association. He slipped
away, and Diederich remembered bitterly that night of victory, when the blood of the domestic enemy had flowed outside in the street and champagne inside in the restaurant,
while Kühnchen was the most militant of the patriots present.
Now he was opposing the increase of our glorious army! . . .
Alone and forsaken, Diederich gazed into his mug of afternoon beer. Suddenly Major Kunze appeared.

"Hello, Major," said Diederich with forced joviality, "you
have been keeping very quiet lately."

"Well, that's more than can be said about you," the major
growled, as he stood in his hat and coat, looking about him as
if in a desert. "Not a soul about!" "Perhaps you will join
me in a glass of wine—" ventured Diederich, but he met a
speedy rebuff. "Thanks, I haven't yet got over your champagne." The major ordered beer and sat down in silence, his
expression as dark as thunder. Just to break the terrible silence, Diederich suddenly burst out: "I say, Major, what
about the Veterans' Association? I thought I should hear
something of my election."

The major looked hard at him, as if he would like to kill

him. "Oh, really. You thought that, did you? I suppose
you also thought it would be an honour for me to be mixed
up in your scandal?"

"My scandal?" stuttered Diederich. "Yes, sir, yours!"
thundered the major. "Herr Lauer may have said a hasty
word; that can happen, even to old soldiers who have lost a
limb in the service of their King. But you led Herr Lauer,
with malice aforethought, into making a rash statement. I
am ready to swear that in the witness-box. I know Lauer.
He was with us in France and is a member of our Veterans'
Association. You, sir, who are you? How do I know
whether you were ever in the army? Produce your
papers!"

Diederich's hand went at once to his pocket-book. He
would have stood to attention, if the major had ordered him.
The major held the discharge papers at arm's length in front
of him. Then he threw them down with a grim laugh. "Ah!
ha! Assigned to the Landsturm. I thought so. Flat feet,
I suppose." Diederich was pale, and trembled at every word
of the major's. He said, holding out a beseeching hand:
"Major, I give you my word of honour that I have done my
service. In consequence of an accident, which was entirely
to my credit, I was demobilised after three months. . . ."

"We know those accidents. . . . How much did you pay?"

"Otherwise I would have stayed on permanently," added
Diederich, in a whining tone. "I was absolutely devoted to
the army. You can ask my superior officers."

"Evening." The major had put on his overcoat. "All I
have to say to you, sir, is this: What the devil business is it
of a slacker when other people commit *lèse-majesté?* His
Majesty has no use for slackers. . . . Grützmacher," he said
to the proprietor, "you should be more particular about your
customers. Because of one too many Herr Lauer has been
almost arrested, and I, with my stiff leg, must appear in court
as a witness for the prosecution, and get myself into bad odour

with everybody. The dance at the Harmony Club has been called off, I have nothing to do, and when I come here"—he again looked round as if the place were a desert—"there is nobody to be seen. Except, of course, the informer!" he shouted from the steps.

"My word of honour, Major . . ." said Diederich, running after him, "it was not I who lodged the complaint; it is all a misunderstanding." But the major had already reached the street. "At least, I rely upon your discretion!" cried Diederich after him. He wiped his forehead. "Herr Grützmacher," he said tearfully, "you at least will admit . . ." As he ordered wine, the proprietor admitted everything.

Diederich drank and shook his head mournfully. He could not understand this miscalculation. His intentions had been pure, only the wiles of his enemies had obscured them. . . . Then Judge Fritzsche turned up, and looked round hesitatingly. When he saw that Diederich was really quite alone, he came up to him. "Dr. Hessling!" he said as he shook hands, "you look as if you had just buried your best friend." Diederich murmured that there was always a lot of trouble in a big business. But he opened his heart fully when he saw the other's sympathetic expression.

"I don't mind telling you, Judge, this business with Herr Lauer is damnably unpleasant for me."

"Still more so for him," said Fritzsche severely. "If it were not that he is above suspicion of flight, we should have had to arrest him to-day." He saw Diederich blanch and added: "And that would have been painful even to us judges. After all, we are all human and it takes all sorts to make a world. But of course—" He steadied his *pince-nez* and assumed a wooden expression. "The law must be obeyed. If on that evening—I myself had already left—Lauer actually did use those unprecedented expressions concerning His Majesty, as stated by the prosecution, and as to which you are chief witness—"

"I?" Diederich started up in desperation. "I heard nothing, not a word!"

"That does not accord with your testimony before the court of inquiry."

Diederich became confused. "At first one doesn't know what to say. But now, when I think over the questionable incident, it seems to me we were all pretty merry, particularly myself."

"Particularly yourself," repeated Fritzsche.

"Yes, and I probably put leading questions to Herr Lauer. What his answers were I am no longer prepared to swear. Anyhow, the whole thing was a joke."

"Oh, I see: a joke." Fritzsche breathed more freely. "Well, what is to prevent you from simply telling the judge that?" He raised a warning finger. "Not that I have any desire to influence your testimony."

Diederich raised his voice. "I shall never forgive Jadassohn for this trick!" He described the manœuvres of this gentleman, who had purposely gone out during the scene, so that he could not be cited as a witness; who had then begun immediately to assemble evidence for the prosecution, taking advantage of the more or less irresponsible condition of those present, and binding them in advance with their testimony. "Herr Lauer and I know each other to be men of honour. What right has this Jew to egg us into a quarrel?"

Fritzsche carefully explained that Jadassohn personally was not concerned in this; that it was the Public Prosecutor who had taken action. Of course, it must be admitted that Jadassohn was perhaps inclined to be overzealous. Lowering his voice he continued: "You see, that is why we do not like working with these Jewish gentlemen. A man like that never asks himself what impression it will make upon the public, when an educated man, an employer of labour, is condemned for *lèse-majesté*. His radical methods take no account of material considerations."

"The radical methods of the Jew," added Diederich. "He never hesitates to shove himself forward—although I do not deny that he believes he is discharging a patriotic and a professional duty."

"How do you mean?" cried Diederich. "A vulgar upstart who is trafficking in our most sacred possessions!" "That's putting it in rather strong terms"—Fritzsche gave a smile of satisfaction, and drew his chair nearer. "Suppose I were the judge in charge of the inquiry. There are cases in which one is justified, to a certain degree, in handing in one's resignation." "You are a close friend of the Lauer family," said Diederich, nodding significantly. Fritzsche assumed the air of a man of the world. "But, you understand, in so doing I would definitely confirm certain rumours."

"That won't do," said Diederich. "It would be contrary to the code of honour."

"Then I have no choice but to do my duty, quietly and impartially." "To be impartial is to be German," said Diederich.

"Especially as I may assume that the witnesses will not render my task unnecessarily difficult." Diederich laid his hand on his heart. "Judge Fritzsche, one may be carried away where great issues are at stake. I have an impulsive nature, but I am aware that I owe an accounting to God for everything." He dropped his eyes. Then, in manly tones: "I too am susceptible to remorse." This appeared to be enough for Fritzsche, for he paid the bill. The two gentlemen shook hands solemnly and in perfect understanding.

The very next day Diederich was called before the judge in charge of the inquiry, and found himself in the presence of Fritzsche. "Thank God," he said to himself, and he made his statement in a spirit of honest impartiality. Fritzsche's only care seemed also to be the truth. Public opinion, it is true, lost none of its partiality for the accused. Apart from the Social Democrat newspaper, it reached the point of sarcastic references to Diederich's private life, which were certainly inspired by Napoleon Fischer. But even the usually docile "Netzig Journal" chose this moment to publish a speech of Herr Lauer's to his workmen, in which the manufacturer stated that he was sharing honestly the profits of his business with all who had co-operated in it, a quarter to the office staff and a quarter to the men. In eight years they had had the sum of 130,000 marks to share amongst themselves, in addition to their salaries and wages. This produced a most favourable and widespread impression. Diederich encountered unfriendly faces. Rothgroschen, the editor, to whom he stopped to speak, actually smiled offensively and said something about social progress which could not be arrested by patriotic claptrap. The consequences to his business were particularly irritating. Orders, upon which Diederich could usually count, did not come in. Cohn, the proprietor of the big stores, frankly informed him that he had given preference to the Gausenfeld Paper Factory for his Christmas catalogues, because he could not get mixed up in politics, out of consideration for his customers. Diederich now began to turn up quite early at the office in order to intercept such communications, but Sötbier was always there first, and the reproachful silence of the old manager only increased his rage. "I'll let the whole show go to the devil!" he yelled. "Then you and the rest of them will see where you are, with my doctor's degree I can get a post as managing director to-morrow, with 40,000 marks!"— "I am sacrificing myself for you," he shouted at the men when they drank beer against the rules. "I am paying out money to keep you employed."

Towards Christmas, however, he was compelled to pay off a third of the men. Sötbier showed him by calculation that they could not otherwise meet the obligations which fell due at the beginning of the year, "since we must deduct 2,000 marks as an instalment on the new cylinder machine," and he insisted on this, although Diederich seized the ink-pot. In the faces of those who remained he saw a lack of confidence and respect. Whenever several were standing together, he fancied he heard the word "informer." Napoleon Fischer's knotted, dark, hairy hands did not hang down so close to the ground, and he looked as if his cheeks had actually some colour in them.

On the last Sunday in Advent—the courts had just decided on holding the public trial—Pastor Zillich preached in St. Mary's on the text: "Love your enemies." Diederich shrank at the first words. Soon he felt that the whole congregation was becoming uneasy. "Vengeance is mine, saith the Lord." Pastor Zillich addressed the words pointedly in the direction of the Hesslings' pew. Emma and Magda bowed their heads out of sight; Frau Hessling sobbed. Diederich defiantly answered the glances which sought him. "Whosoever speaketh of vengeance, so he shall be judged!" Then everybody turned round and Diederich collapsed.

His sisters made a scene when they got home. They were being badly received in society. Young Professor Helferich no longer sat near Emma, he had eyes only for Meta Harnisch, and she knew why. "Because you are too old for him," said Diederich. "No, because you make us unpopular!"—"The five daughters of Herr Buck's brother won't know us any more!" cried Magda. "I'll give them five boxes on the ear," said Diederich.—"You will kindly not interfere. We have enough with your lawsuit." Then he lost patience. "You? What business of yours are my political fights?"

"We shall become old maids because of your political fights!"

"There is no need for you to talk of becoming so. You loll uselessly about the house here, while I slave for you, and into the bargain you presume to find fault and to turn me from my most sacred duties. You can shake the dust of the place off your feet! You can become nursemaids for all I care!" He slammed the door in spite of Frau Hessling's beseeching gesture.

Thus a dismal Christmas approached. The sisters refused to speak to their brother. Whenever Frau Hessling left the locked room in which she was decorating the Christmas tree, her eyes were red and swollen with tears. And on Christmas Eve, when she brought the children in, she sang all alone and with quavering voice, "Stille Nacht." "This is a present from little Diederich to his dear sisters," she said, and her glance begged him not to give her the lie. Emma and Magda thanked him with embarrassment, and he was equally embarrassed as he looked at the gifts which were supposed to have come from him. He regretted that, in spite of Sötbier's emphatic advice, he had refused the accustomed Christmas-tree celebration for the workmen in order to punish the unruly crew. Otherwise he might now be with them. Here in the family the thing was artificial, a revamping of old, dead sentiments. Only one person could have made it real, Guste, and she was not there. . . . The Veterans' Association was closed to him, and he would have found nobody in the Ratskeller, at least none of his friends. Diederich felt neglected, misunderstood and persecuted. How remote were the innocent days of the Neo-Teutons, when in long ranks, inspired by good-will, they sang and drank beer. Now, in the rough world, sturdy college friends no longer exchanged slashes in honourable duels, but a crowd of treacherous rivals flew at one another's throats. "I do not belong to this cruel age," thought Diederich as he ate the marzipan on his plate, and dreamed in the candle light of the Christmas tree. "I am really a good-hearted fellow. Why do they drag me into horrible things like this trial, and injure me even in my business, so that, my God, I shall not be able to pay for the cylinder machine which I ordered."

A cold shiver ran through him, tears came into his eyes, and so that they might not be seen by his mother, who was watching his worried face, he crept into the dark room adjoining. Resting his arms on the piano, he buried his face in his hands and wept. Outside Emma and Magda were quarrelling about a pair of gloves, and their mother did not dare to decide on whom they had been bestowed. Diederich sobbed. Everything had gone wrong, in politics, business and love. "What is left to me?" He opened the piano. He shivered, he felt so uncannily alone that he was afraid to make a noise. The sounds came of their own accord, his hands were unconscious of them. Folk songs, Beethoven and drinking songs rang out in the twilight, which was thereby cosily warmed so that a comfortable drowsiness filled the brain. At one moment it seemed to him that a hand was stroking the top of his head. Was it only a dream? No, for suddenly a glass full of beer stood on the piano. His good mother! Schubert, what loyal integrity, the soul of the mother country. . . . All was silent, and he did not notice it, until the clock struck: an hour had passed. "That was my Christmas," said Diederich, and he went out to join the others. He felt consoled and strengthened. As the girls were still jawing about the gloves, he declared that they had no sense of the fitness of things, and placed the gloves in his pocket, to have them changed for a pair for himself.

The whole Christmas season was overclouded by worry about the new machine. Six thousand marks for a New Patent Cylinder Machine, Maier System! He had no money in hand and, as things were, none was available. It was an incomprehensible fatality, a shabby perversity of men and circumstances which embittered Deiderich. When Sötbier was not there he banged the lid of his desk and threw the letter files about the room. As the new master, who had firmly grasped the reins of the business, he felt he must immediately launch into new enterprises; success awaited him and events would have to shape themselves to his personality! . . . He was angry and humble by turns, and took precautions in case of a catastrophe. He softened towards Sötbier; perhaps the old chap might yet be of some use. He also humbled

himself before Pastor Zillich and begged him to tell the people
that the sermon, which had excited so much comment, was not
aimed at him. The Pastor was obviously remorseful and
promised to do so, under the reproachful glance of his wife,
who confirmed his promise. Then the parents left Käthchen
alone with Diederich, and he felt so grateful to them in his
depression that he almost proposed to her. Käthchen's consent, which hovered on her dear, plump lips, would have been
a success for him, and would have brought him allies against
a hostile world. But that machine which he had to find the
money for! It would have swallowed up a quarter of her
dowry. . . . Diederich said, with a sigh, that he would have
to be getting back to the office, and Käthchen pressed her
lips together without having had an opportunity of saying
"yes."

A decision had to be made, for the arrival of the machine
was imminent. · Diederich said to Sötbier: "I advise those
people to deliver it punctually to the minute, otherwise I shall
have no hesitation in returning it." But Sötbier reminded
him of the custom which gave the manufacturers a few days'
grace. He insisted, in spite of Diederich's wrath. In any
case, the machine arrived punctually. It had not yet been
unpacked when Diederich began to fuss and fume. "It is too
large. They guaranteed that it would be smaller than the old
pattern. Why should I buy it when it does not even save
space?" As soon as it had been installed he went over the
machine with a foot-rule. "It is too big. They can't swindle
me. Look at it, Sötbier; isn't it too large?" But with imper-
turbable accuracy Sötbier explained the errors in Diederich's
measurements. Diederich retired, raging, to devise another
method of attack. He sent for Napoleon Fischer. "Where
is the man to adjust the new machine? Did they not send
any one with it?" Then he grew indignant. "I ordered him
to come," he lied. "These people have a nice way of doing
business. I should not be surprised if I have to pay twelve

marks a day for this fellow, and he is conspicuous by his absence. Who will set up the damned machine for me?"

The machinist said he knew all about it. Diederich suddenly developed the utmost cordiality towards him. "I need hardly say I would rather pay you overtime than squander good money on a stranger. After all, you are an old employé." Napoleon Fischer raised his eyebrows, but said nothing. Diederich laid his hand on his shoulder. "Look here, my man," he said confidentially, "I don't mind telling you I am disappointed in this machine. It looked different in the pictures of the prospectus. The blades of the cutter were supposed to be much wider. Where is the greater efficiency which those people promised? What do you think? Do you think the drive is strong? I am afraid the stuff will stick half way." Napoleon Fischer looked at Diederich inquiringly, but he began to see what he was driving at. They would have to try it out, he said hesitatingly. Diederich avoided his glance, as he said encouragingly: "Well, all right. You will put the thing together, I will pay you an additional twenty-five per cent. for overtime, and for Heaven's sake, run some stuff through it at once. Then we'll see how it cuts."

"It will be a queer cut," said the mechanic, obviously seeking to conciliate Diederich, who seized his arm, before he realised what he was doing. Napoleon Fischer was his friend and saviour! "Come on, my good man"—his voice trembled with emotion. He took Napoleon Fischer into the house, and Frau Hessling had to pour him out a glass of wine. Without looking at him Diederich pressed fifty marks into his hand. "I rely on you, Fischer," he said. "The makers would take me in, if I hadn't you. I have already put two thousand marks into the rapacious pockets of those people."

"They will have to pay them back," said the machinist pleasantly. "You think that, too?" Diederich asked earnestly.

A day or two later, after having spent the lunch hour on the machine, Napoleon Fischer informed his employer that the new acquisition was no good. The stuff did not move and had to be shoved on with the stirring-pole, just as in the oldest style of machine. "So it is a common swindle," Diederich cried. It was also more than twenty horsepower. "That is not in the contract. Do we have to accept it, Fischer?"

"We must not allow that," he decided, stroking his black-bearded chin with his knotted hand. For the first time Diederich looked him squarely in the face.

"Then, you can prove to me that the machine does not fulfil the terms of purchase?"

A pale smile seemed to hover around Napoleon Fischer's spare beard. "You bet," he replied. Diederich noticed the smile and said with all the more emphasis: "I'll show those people who I am!" He wrote at once in the strongest terms to Büschli & Co. in Eschweiler. The reply came by return. They could not understand his contentions, the New Patent Cylinder Machine, Maier pattern, had been installed and given a trial by several paper manufacturers, whose testimonials were enclosed. It was, therefore, out of the question for them to take it back, much less return the 2,000 marks paid on account, and the balance of the agreed purchase price must be settled forthwith. Whereupon Diederich wrote an even sharper letter than the first and threatened proceedings. Then Büschli & Co. endeavoured to pacify him, and recommended another trial. "They are afraid," said Napoleon Fischer, to whom Diederich showed the communication, and his teeth flashed. "They cannot stand a lawsuit, for their machine is not sufficiently well known." "That's right," said Diederich, "we have them at our mercy!" His heart hardened by the certainty of victory, he refused peremptorily every compromise and their offer to reduce the price. When nothing happened for several days, however, he began to feel uncomfortable. Perhaps they were waiting for him to take legal action! Perhaps they were doing so themselves! Many times a day his uncertain glance sought Napoleon Fischer, who furtively returned the look. They no longer spoke to one another. One morning at eleven o'clock, when Diederich was sitting at early lunch, the servant brought in a visiting card: Frederich Kienast, Manager, Büschli & Co., Eschweiler. While Diederich was still turning it round between his fingers, the visitor entered. "Excuse me," he said, "there must be some mistake. I have been shown in here, but I have come on a matter of business."

Diederich had recovered his presence of mind. "Very likely, but it doesn't matter. Won't you come right in? I am Dr. Hessling. This is my mother and my sisters, Emma and Magda."

The gentleman approached and bowed to the ladies. "My name is Frederich Kienast," he murmured. He was short, with a fair beard, and wore a brown morning suit of woolly material. The three ladies smiled amiably. "May I set a place for you?" Frau Hessling asked. "Of course," said Diederich, "you will have lunch with us, Herr Kienast, won't you?"

"I cannot refuse," declared the representative of Büschli & Co., rubbing his hands. Magda helped him to some kippered herring, which he praised while the first mouthful was still on his fork.

Laughing innocently, Diederich asked: "Don't you like to have a little something to drink when you are doing business?" Herr Kienast also laughed. "I never drink much when on business." Diederich grinned. "Well, in that case we shall not quarrel." "It all depends, doesn't it?" And Kienast's slily challenging words were accompanied by a glance at Magda, who blushed.

Diederich filled the guest's glass with beer. "I suppose you have other business in Netzig?" "You never can tell," said Kienast evasively.

Tentatively Diederich remarked: "You won't do anything with Klüsing in Gausenfeld, he's had a slump." As the other did not reply, Diederich thought: "They have sent him here specially about the machine; they are afraid of a lawsuit." Then he noticed that Magda and Büschli's representative were raising their glasses at the same time, and toasting each other with their eyes. Emma and Frau Hessling looked on in rigid silence. Diederich bent his head over his plate in a rage— but all at once he began to sing the praises of domestic life. "You are in luck, my dear Herr Kienast, for this lunch hour is by far the pleasantest time in the day. Coming up here, right in the middle of one's work, has a humanising effect, so to speak, and one needs it."

Kienast agreed that it was needed. To Frau Hessling's inquiry whether he was married he replied in the negative, looking, as he did so, at the top of Magda's head, for it had modestly drooped. Diederich stood up at attention, bringing his heels together. "Herr Kienast," he said sharply, "I am at your disposal."

"You will take a cigar, Herr Kienast," said Magda invitingly. Kienast allowed her to light it for him and hoped that he would have the pleasure of seeing the ladies again—this with a significant smile at Magda. Outside in the yard his tone changed completely. "Hm, these are small, cramped premises," he remarked in frigid tones of depreciation. "You should see our works."

"In a hole like Eschweiler," replied Diederich, equally contemptuous, "that is no wonder. Just you try to pull down this block of houses!" Then he shouted in the tones of a martinet for the machinist to set the new cylinder machine in motion. As Napoleon Fischer did not come at once, Diederich stormed down upon him. "Are you deaf, sir?" But as soon as he came in front of him he stopped shouting. In an imploring whisper, his eyes staring with anxiety, he said: "Fischer, I have been thinking things over. I am satisfied with your work, and from the first of the month your salary is raised to one hundred and eighty marks." Napoleon

Fischer gave a short, understanding nod and moved away. Diederich began at once to shout. Some one had been smoking! They told him it was only his own cigar which he smelt. To the representative of Büschli & Co. he said: "Anyway, I am insured, but we must have discipline. Aren't these works fine?"

"Old stuff," retorted Herr Kienast, with a hostile glance at the machines. "All right, my friend," sneered Diederich, "but they're as good as your cutting machine, in any case." Ignoring Kienast's protest, he began to belittle the capacity of the domestic manufacturers. He was waiting until his trip to England before installing his new fittings. He was forging ahead at a great rate. Business had developed enormously since he took charge. "And there is still room for development." He drew on his imagination. "I have now contract with twenty local newspapers. The Berlin houses will drive me mad. . . ." Kienast interrupted him brusquely:

"Then you must just have despatched all your orders, for I don't see any finished goods about." Diederich became indignant. "Sir! Allow me to tell you that only yesterday I sent a circular to all my smaller customers, informing them that I could promise no more deliveries until our new building was completed."

The machinist came to fetch the gentlemen. The new Patent Cylinder machine was half full, but the material still passed through it very slowly, and had to be helped by a man with the stirring-pole. Diederich held his watch in his hand. "Now, let us see. You state that in your machine the stuff takes twenty to thirty seconds to go right round. I have already counted fifty. Machinist, pay out more material. . . . What is wrong, it is taking ages."

Kienast was bending over the bowl. He straightened up and smiled facetiously. "Of course, if the valves are stopped up. . . ." He gave Diederich a searching look which the other's eyes failed to meet. "I cannot say offhand what else

may have been done to the machine." Diederich started up,
suddenly very red. "Do you wish to insinuate that I and
the machinist have—?"

"I have said nothing," replied Kienast primly.

"I must emphatically repudiate that insinuation," Diederich
thundered, but it seemed to leave Kienast unimpressed. His
eyes were calm and a sly grin hovered about his beard, which
was brushed in a parting on his chin. If he had shaved and
trained the ends of his moustache to grow upright he would
have looked like Diederich! He was a Force! Diederich's
attitude became all the more truculent. "My machinist is a
Social Democrat. The idea of his doing me a favour is absurd. Moreover, as an officer of the reserve I warn you of
the consequences of your statements!"

Kienast walked out into the yard. "Never mind about that,
Dr. Hessling," he said calmly. "I am a sober man when it
comes to business, as I told you at lunch. All I have to repeat
to you is that we delivered the machine in excellent condition,
and we do not propose to take it back." They would see about
that, said Diederich. Doubtless Büschli & Co. would not consider a lawsuit particularly helpful in introducing their new
merchandise. "I will give you a special testimonial in the
trade papers!" Whereupon Kienast retorted that he took no
account of attempted blackmail. And Diederich declared that
the only thing to be done with a vulgarian was to throw him
out, since he was not fit to fight a duel. In the midst of this
Magda appeared in the doorway of the dwelling house.

She was wearing her Christmas fur coat and gave them a
rosy smile. "Are you gentlemen not finished yet?" she asked
roguishly. "It is such a lovely day, I felt I must go out for
a bit before dinner. By the way," she added volubly,
"mother wants to know if Herr Kienast will be with us for
supper?" As Kienast regretted that he must say no, she
smiled more persuasively. "And would you refuse me, too?"
Kienast gave a harsh laugh. "I would not refuse. But I

don't know whether your brother . . ." Diederich snorted, and Magda looked at him beseechingly. "Herr Kienast," he managed to say, "I shall be delighted. Perhaps we may yet come to an understanding." Kiénast said he hoped so, and offered gallantly to escort the young lady for a while. "If my brother has no objection," she said with demure irony. Diederich allowed this also. Then he gazed after her in amazement as she went off with the representative of Büschli & Co. How that girl got her way, when she liked!

When he came in to dinner he heard the sisters talking in sharp tones in the sitting-room. Emma was accusing Magda of behaving disgracefully. "You shouldn't do such things." "No," cried Magda, "I suppose I must ask your permission. This is my turn, anyway! Is there anything else worrying you?" And Magda burst into a mocking laugh. She stopped immediately, when Diederich entered. Diederich glanced around disapprovingly, but Frau Hessling need not have wrung her hands behind her daughters' backs. It was beneath his dignity to intervene in this feminine quarrel.

At table they spoke of their visitor. Frau Hessling testified to the impression of reliability which he had made. Emma declared that such a person might at least be reliable. But he had no idea of how to talk to a lady. Magda indignantly asserted the contrary. As they all were waiting for Diederich's decision, he pronounced judgment. The gentleman was certainly not exactly good form. He was admittedly no substitute for a university education. "But I have learnt to know him as a first-rate man of business." Emma could no longer contain herself.

"If Magda intends to marry that man, I declare I will have nothing more to do with you. He ate stewed fruit with a knife!"

"She's a liar!" Magda broke into tears. Diederich took compassion on her, and said rudely to Emma:

"You, marry your reigning duke and then leave us in peace."

Then Emma put down her knife and fork and went out. In the evening, before the office closed, Kienast appeared. He was wearing a frock-coat and his manner was more social than commercial. By tacit agreement they both refrained from speaking until old Sötbier had packed up his things. When he had retired, with a mistrustful glance, Diederich said: "I have placed the old man on the retired list. I attend to all the more important things alone."

"Well, have you thought over our little affair?" asked Kienast.

"Have you?" returned Diederich. Kienast's eyes twinkled confidentially.

"My powers do not really extend so far, but I will take the risk. For Heaven's sake, return the machine. I have no doubt some defect will be discovered in it."

Diederich understood. "You will find one," he promised. Kienast said in a matter of fact tone:

"In return for this concession you undertake to order all your machines from us whenever required. One moment!" he commanded, as Diederich started to protest. "And in addition you will defray our costs and my travelling expenses to the extent of five hundred marks, which we shall deduct from your first instalment."

"Oh, I say, this is sheer robbery!" Diederich's outraged sense of justice raised his voice. Kienast, too, began again to speak loudly. "Dr. Hessling! . . ." With an effort Diederich controlled himself. He laid his hand on the manager's shoulder. "Let us go up to the house, the ladies are waiting." Somewhat mollified Kienast said: "So far we have understood one another perfectly." "This little difference will also be made up," Diederich assured him.

There was a festive odour upstairs. Frau Hessling shone in

her black satin dress. Through Magda's lace blouse more was visible than she usually displayed for the benefit of the family circle. Emma alone retained the drab demeanour and dress of ordinary weekdays. Magda showed the guest his place and seated herself on his right. They were hardly seated, and were still clearing their throats, when she began to speak, her eyes shining with feverish animation: "Now you gentlemen have finished with your stupid business." Diederich explained that they had come to a very satisfactory agreement. Büschli & Co. were thoroughly fair people.

"With such an immense business as ours," declared the manager. "Twelve hundred workmen and clerks, a whole town, with a hotel of our own for customers." He invited Diederich. "You must come along, you will live in the best style and free of charge." As Magda, beside him, was hanging on his lips, he began to brag about his position, his power and privileges, the villa of which he shared one-half. "If I marry I get the other half."

Diederich laughed impressively. "Then the simplest thing would be for you to get married. Well, good health!" Magda dropped her eyes and Herr Kienast turned to other topics. Did Diederich know why he had met his wishes so easily? "The fact is, Dr. Hessling, as soon as I saw you I knew that there would be big things to be done with you later on—even though the circumstances here at present are rather narrow," he added condescendingly. Diederich would have liked to assure him of his grandiose ideas and of the possibilities of developing his business, but Kienast would not allow his train of thought to be interrupted. His specialty was sizing up men, he said. It was specially important to see in his home a man with whom one has to do business. "If everything there is so well ordered as here—"

At this point the fragrant goose was brought on, towards which Frau Hessling had several times glanced out surreptitiously. At once she assumed an air as if the goose were a very common occurrence. Herr Kienast, however, stopped a moment in silent admiration. Frau Hessling wondered if he was really gazing at the goose or, under cover of its delicious steam, at Magda's open-work blouse. Then he recalled himself and raised his glass. "And now to the Hessling family, to the respected mother and head of the household and her charming daughters." Magda's bosom swelled to make the charm more noticeable, and Emma looked all the more suppressed. It was Magda's glass which Mr. Kienast touched first.

Diederich answered the toast. "We are a German family. The guest we take into our home we also take to our hearts." He had tears in his eyes, while Magda blushed once more. "And even if our house is modest, our hearts are true." He wished the visitor long life, and the latter, in his turn, declared that he had always been in favour of modesty, "specially in families where there are young girls."

Frau Hessling intervened. "Isn't that so? How otherwise would a young man have the courage to—? My daughters make all their own clothes." Herr Kienast took this as his cue to bend over Magda's blouse on the pretext of making a detailed examination.

At dessert she peeled an orange for him and in his honour took a taste of Tokay. When they went into the sitting-room Diederich stopped in the doorway with his arms around his two sisters. "Yes, indeed, Herr Kienast," he said in a deep voice, "this is family happiness, Herr Kienast, look at it!" Magda nestled against his shoulder, all submission, but Emma tried to break away from him and received a blow from the rear. "We are always like this," continued Diederich. "All day long I work for my family, and the evening sees us united here beneath the shade of the lamp. The outside world and the cliques of our so-called Society we avoid as much as possible. We have enough in ourselves."

At this point Emma succeeded in breaking loose, and she

was heard slamming a door outside. The picture of Diederich and Magda was all the more tender, as they sat down beside the softly lighted table. Herr Kienast thoughtfully contemplated the arrival of the punch in a large bowl, which Frau Hessling, smiling softly, carried in. While Magda was filling the guest's glass Diederich explained how, thanks to this devotion to quiet domesticity, he was in a position to do well by his sisters when they married. "The expansion of business is to the advantage of the girls, for they are part owners of the factory, quite apart from their mere dowries. And if one of my future brothers-in-law cares to put his capital into the concern, then . . ."

Magda, however, noticed that Herr Kienast was beginning to wear a worried look, and changed the subject. She asked after his own people and whether he was all alone. At this his glance became tender and he moved nearer. Diederich sat on, drinking, and twiddling his thumbs. He tried several times to take part again in the conversation of the pair, who seemed to feel as if there were nobody present but themselves. "Oh, I see you got through your year of military service all right," he said ingratiatingly, as he puzzled over the signs which Frau Hessling was making to him behind their backs. It was not until she had crept out of the room that he understood, took his glass, and went into the dark adjoining room to the piano. He ran his fingers over the keys a while, glided suddenly into the students' songs and sang impressively to his own accompaniment:

Sie wissen den Teufel, was Freiheit heisst.

When he came to the end he listened; everything was still in the next room as if they had fallen asleep, and although he would like to have filled up again from the bowl of punch, he began again, from a sense of duty:

Im tiefen Keller sitz' ich hier.

In the middle of the verse a chair fell and a loud noise followed, whose cause was not difficult to guess. In an instant Diederich had sprung into the sitting-room. "Hello," he said, with immense joviality, "you seem to have serious intentions." The couple separated, and Herr Kienast answered: "I do not say that I haven't." Whereupon Diederich was deeply moved, and, his eyes gazing earnestly into those of Kienast, he shook the latter's hand, while with his disengaged hand he drew Magda towards them. "This *is* a surprise! Herr Kienast, make my dear little sister happy. You will always find in me the best of all brothers, as I have been up to this, I may say."

Wiping his eyes he shouted: "Mother! Something has happened." Frau Hessling was standing right outside the door, but so excessive was her emotion that her limbs refused to obey her. Leaning on Diederich's arm, she tottered in, fell upon Herr Kienast's neck, and dissolved into tears. Meanwhile Diederich was knocking at Emma's bedroom door, which was locked. "Come out, Emma; something has happened!" Finally she pulled open the door, her face flaming with rage. "What are you waking me up for? I can easily guess what has happened. Leave me out of your indecencies!" She would have slammed the door again, if Diederich had not inserted his foot. He sternly pointed out to her that, for her churlish behaviour, she deserved never to get a husband. He would not even allow her to dress, but dragged her along, in her dressing-jacket, with her hair down. At the door she escaped from his grasp. "You are making us ridiculous," she hissed. She reached the engaged couple before he did and, holding her head high, she gave them a mocking glance of critical inspection. "So you were afraid to wait until the morning?" she inquired. "Of course, time has no meaning for the happy." Kienast looked at her. She was taller than Magda, and her face, now flushed, looked fuller beneath her loosened hair, which was long and thick. Kienast held her hand longer than was necessary, and when she withdrew it he turned from her to Magda in obvious doubt. Emma gave a laugh of triumph at her sister, turned about, and, holding herself very erect, she disappeared. Meanwhile Magda had anxiously seized Kienast's arm, but Diederich came with a glass full of punch in his hand and insisted upon Kienast's cementing the new relationship by their drinking out of each other's glasses with intertwined arms.

The next morning he called for him at his hotel to come and have an early glass of beer. "Please restrain your longing for the little girl until midday. Now we must have a few words as one man to another." In Klappsch's *Bierstube* he explained the situation in detail: Twenty-five thousand marks in cash on the day of the wedding—the documents could be inspected at any time—and one-fourth of the business in common with Emma. "So it's only one-eighth," Kienast observed. To which Diederich retorted: "Am I to slave for you people for nothing?" And an uneasy silence ensued.

Diederich restored the proper mood. "Your health, Friederich!" "Here's to you, Diederich!" replied Kienast. Then something seemed to occur to Diederich. "Of course you have an easy means of increasing your share in the business by putting your money into it. How about your savings? With a huge salary like yours!" Kienast declared that he did not object to the idea on principle, but his contract with Büschli & Co. was still valid. He also expected a considerable increase of salary in the course of the year, and it would be a crime against himself to give notice now. "But if I do produce the money I must have an active hand in the business myself. Although I have every confidence in you, my dear Diederich . . ."

Diederich admitted his point, and Kienast in his turn made a suggestion. "If you were simply to fix the dowry at fifty thousand, then Magda would renounce her share in the business." To this Diederich returned an unconditional refusal.

"That would be contrary to the last wishes of my late lamented father, and they are sacred to me. And I work on such a large scale that in a few years Magda's share may be ten times as much as you now demand. I will never consent to injure my poor sister." At this the brother-in-law grinned a little. Diederich's devotion to the family did him credit, but large ideas alone were not enough. With noticeable heat Diederich retorted that, thank Heaven, he was answerable to nobody but God for the conduct of his business. "Twenty-five thousand cash and one-eighth of the net profits—that is all." Kienast drummed on the table. "I am not sure that I can accept your sister on those terms," he declared. "I will reserve my final decision for the moment." Diederich shrugged his shoulders and they finished their beer. Kienast returned with him to lunch. Diederich had begun to fear that he would refuse. Fortunately, Magda was even more seductively attired than the day before—"as if she knew that the whole game was at stake," thought Diederich as he admired her. By the time the sweets came on she had so inflamed Kienast's ardour that he was demanding the wedding in four weeks. "Is this your final decision?" asked Diederich teasingly. Kienast's reply was to take the ring out of his pocket.

After lunch Frau Hessling went on tiptoe out of the room where the engaged couple were sitting, and Diederich also decided to retire. But they fetched him to join them in a walk. "Where would you like to go, and where are mother and Emma?" Emma had refused to come and therefore Frau Hessling stayed at home. "Otherwise, it would look queer, you know," said Magda, and Diederich agreed with her. He even brushed away a little dust which had clung to her fur coat when she came into the factory. He treated Magda with respect, because she had achieved success.

They went off in the direction of the Rathaus. It was no harm, you know, to let people see you. The first person, it

is true, whom they met right in Meisestrasse was only Napoleon
Fischer. He bared his teeth at the fiancé and gave Diederich
a nod with a look which said that he knew a thing or two.
Diederich blushed deeply, and he would have stopped the
man, and had a row with him in the public street. But did
he dare to? "It was a bad mistake to have indulged in confidences with that shifty proletarian. Everything would have
gone all right without him. Now he creeps about the place
to remind me that he has me in his power. He will try to
blackmail me yet." But, thank God, everything which had
passed between himself and the machinist had been en tête-à-
tête. Whatever Napoleon Fischer might say about him was
a libel. Diederich would simply have him locked up. All
the same, he hated him because he shared his secret, and made
him perspire with fear when the thermometer showed twenty
degrees of cold. He looked back. Why did a tile not fall on
Napoleon's Fischer's head?

In Gerichtstrasse Magda realised that the whole thing was
worth while, for Meta Harnisch and Inge Tietz were looking
out from behind the shutters at Landgerichtsrat Harnisch's,
and Magda knew for certain that their faces had betrayed
great disturbance when they got a glimpse of Kienast. In
Kaiser Wilhelmstrasse, unfortunately, there were very few
people about that day; the only thing was the fact that Major
Kunze and Dr. Heuteufel, who were going into the Harmony
Club, stared from a distance with great curiosity. But at
the corner of Schweinichenstrasse something occurred, which
Diederich had not anticipated; right in front of them walked
Frau Daimchen and Guste. At once Magda hastened her
steps and talked with greater animation. Sure enough, Guste
looked around and Magda had a chance to say: "My dear
Frau Daimchen, allow me to introduce my fiancé, Herr
Kienast." The prospective bridegroom was looked over and
seemed to come up to expectations, for Guste, who remained
a few steps behind with Diederich, asked with a certain re-

spect: "Where did you discover him?" Diederich joked. "You know, every woman cannot find hers as near at hand as you did, but he is all the more sound." "Are you beginning that again?" cried Guste, but without resentment. She even gave Diederich a tender glance and said with a gentle sigh: "Mine is still off, goodness knows where. It makes one feel like a widow." She looked thoughtfully at Magda, who was hanging on Kienast's arm. Diederich gave food for reflection: "Out of sight, out of mind. There are as good fish in the sea as ever came out of it." As he said this he pushed Guste close to the wall and gazed pleadingly into her face. And for a whole minute there was really a responsive smile on her dear, chubby face.

By this time, unfortunately, they had reached 77 Schweinichenstrasse, and had to say good-bye. As there was nothing to be seen beyond the Saxon Gate, they turned homewards again with Herr Kienast. Magda, who had taken her fianée's arm, said to Diederich encouragingly: "Well, what do you think?" At which he turned red and began to breathe hard. "What is there to think about?" he managed to say, and Magda laughed.

In the empty street it was rapidly growing dusk when they saw some one coming towards them. "Isn't that . . . ?" said Diederich uncertainly. The figure approached, stout, evidently still young, with a large, soft hat, fashionably dressed, and walking with the feet turned inwards. " 'Pon my word, Wolfgang Buck!" He reflected disappointedly: "And Guste tried to make out that he is at the other end of the world. I must cure her of lying."

"Is that you?"—Young Buck shook Diederich's hand—"Delighted to see you."—"So am I," replied Diederich, in spite of his disappointment with Guste, and he introduced his future brother-in-law to his school-friend. Buck congratulated the happy pair and then walked behind them with Diederich. "I am sure you were on your way to your fiancée's," Diederich remarked, "she is at home, for we have just accompanied her there."—"Is that so?" said Buck, shrugging his shoulders. "Well, there is always plenty of time to see her," he added indifferently. "For the present I am delighted to meet you again. Our talk in Berlin, the only one, I think was so . . . stimulating."

Diederich now confessed to a similar recollection, though at the time it had merely annoyed him. This meeting had quite cheered him up. "Indeed, I still owe you a return visit, but you know how in Berlin so many things turn up to prevent one. Here, at all events, one has leisure. Dull, though, isn't it? And to think that we must waste our lives here"— and Diederich pointed up to the row of bleak houses. Wolfgang Buck sniffed the air with his gently retroussé nose, he seemed to taste it on his full lips and he assumed a thoughtful expression. "A lifetime in Netzig," he began slowly, "well, it all depends. People like us are not in a position to live only for excitement. In every case, there is some here." He smiled suspiciously. "That sentry created some excitement which reached the most exalted circles."

"Oh, I see"—Diederich protruded his paunch—"you want to tease me again. I insist that I am absolutely on the side of His Majesty in that affair."

Buck swept this aside with a gesture. "Don't try that on me. I know all about him."

"I know him even better," Diederich declared. "Any one who has stood alone with him, face to face, as I did in the Tiergarten last February, after the big riot, and has seen those eyes flashing, that truly imperial glance—can have no doubts as to our future."

"No doubts as to the future . . . because a man's eyes flashed!" Buck's mouth and jaws fell pessimistically. Diederich snorted impatiently. "Of course, I know, you do not believe in any personality of this era. Otherwise you would have become a Lassalle or a Bismarck."

"In the end I may indulge in some such luxury. Why not? Just as well as he. . . . Even if I am less favoured by external circumstances." His voice became more animated and assured. "What matters personally to each of us is not that we should really change the world very much, but that we should create in ourselves a sense of life, as if we were doing so. That only requires talent, and he has plenty."

Diederich was looking about him uneasily. "Here we are alone, more or less, for the company in front of us has more important matters to discuss, yet I do not think—"

"How you keep on believing that I have something against him. I really do not dislike him any more than I dislike myself. In his place I would have taken Lance-Corporal Lück and our Netzig sentry just as seriously. Would that represent a Force if it were not threatened? Power can be realised only when there is a revolt. What would become of him if he had to admit to himself that the Social Democrats do not aim at him, but, at most, at a more practical distribution of profit?"

"Oh, oh!" cried Diederich.

"Don't you see? That would seem to you an outrage, and to him also. To move along, beside the main current of events, to be caught up in their development instead of guiding it—would that be tolerable? . . . To have unlimited power in one's inner consciousness, and to be incapable, at the same time, of even arousing hatred except through words and gestures! What, after all, do the fault-finders seize upon? Has anything more tangible happened? Even the Lück affair was only another gesture. When his hand is lowered, everything is as before; only the actor and his audience have had a thrill. And that, my dear Hessling, is the only thing that matters to all of us to-day. The man himself, about whom we are speaking, would be most astonished, believe me, if the war, which he is so constantly announcing, or the revolution, which he has imagined a hundred times, were really to break out!"

"You won't have to wait so long for that," cried Diederich. "And then you will see how all loyal patriots will rally faithfully and steadfastly to their Emperor!"

"No doubt." Buck was shrugging his shoulders more frequently. "That is the traditional sequence, as he himself has prescribed it. You people allow him to prescribe phrases for you, and never was opinion so well drilled as now. But deeds? My excellent contemporary, our age is not prepared for deeds. In order to exercise one's capacity for adventure it is necessary, first of all, to live, and deeds are dangerous to life."

Diederich drew himself up. "Are you trying to associate the accusation of cowardice with—?"

"I have expressed no moral judgment. I have mentioned a fact of the inner history of these times which concerns us all. For the rest, we are not responsible. All action is settled for the mummer on the stage, for it is he who has carried out his part. What more can reality demand of him? I suppose you do not know whom history will designate as the representative type of this era?"

"The Emperor," said Diederich.

"No," Buck replied. "The actor."

At this Diederich burst into such a roar of laughter that the engaged couple in front started away from each other and turned around. But they had reached the Theaterplatz, an icy wind was blowing across it, and they went on.

"Why, of course," Diederich ejaculated, "I might have guessed how you came by such notions. You are connected with the theatre." He slapped Buck on the shoulder. "Have you finally gone on the stage yourself?"

Buck's eyes were troubled. He shook off the hand that slapped him with a movement which Diederich found unfriendly. "I? Not at all," said Buck, and after they had reached Gerichtstrasse in uneasy silence: "So you don't know why I am in Netzig?"

"Presumably because of your fiancée."

"That is not the real reason. It is chiefly because I have undertaken the defence of my brother-in-law, Lauer."

"You are . . . ? In the Lauer case . . . ?" It took Diederich's breath away and he came to a standstill.

"Well, why not?" said Buck, shrugging his shoulders. "Does that surprise you? I have recently been admitted to practice at the Netzig County Court. Did my father not tell you about it?"

"I rarely see your father. . . . I don't go out much. Business cares. . . . My sister's engagement. . . ." Diederich began to stammer incoherently. "Then you must often. Perhaps you are settled here altogether?"

"Only temporarily—I fancy."

Diederich pulled himself together. "I must say, I have often failed to understand you properly, but never so little as now when we have been walking half way through Netzig together." Buck blinked at him. "Because in the trial tomorrow I am counsel for the accused and you are the chief witness for the prosecution? That is just chance. The situation might just as well have been reversed."

"I beg your pardon!" cried Diederich, indignantly. "Every man in his right place. If you have no respect for your profession—"

"Respect? What do you mean? I am delighted to act for the defence. I do not deny it. I shall let myself go and give the people something for their money. I shall have unpleasant things to say to you, Dr. Hessling. I trust you will take everything in good part. It is part of my profession."

Diederich grew frightened. "Pardon me, do you know my sworn statement? It is by no means unfavourable to Lauer."

"Leave all that to me." There was a threatening touch of irony in Buck's attitude.

By this time they had reached Meisestrasse. "The trial!" thought Diederich breathlessly. He had completely forgotten it in the excitement of the last few days. Now he felt as if he were going to have both legs amputated within the next twenty-four hours. So Guste, the treacherous creature, had purposely said nothing to him about her fiancé. He was to get the shock at the last moment! . . . Diederich took leave of Buck before they got to the house. Provided Kienast did not notice anything! Buck proposed that they should adjourn somewhere. "Apparently your future wife does not draw you irresistibly," said Diederich. "At this moment I'd much sooner have a cognac." Diederich laughed mockingly. "You always seem to be anxious for that." So that Kienast should not learn anything, he turned back again with Buck. "You see," he began abruptly, "my fiancée is another of the questions which I put to Fate." And as Diederich asked, "How do you mean?" he continued: "If I really become a lawyer in Netzig, then Guste Daimchen will be in her right place in my home. But is that certain? In view of other . . . circumstances which may come into my life, I have some one else in Berlin . . ."

"I heard something about an actress." Diederich blushed for Buck, who so cynically admitted this. "That is to say," he stammered, "I may have been mistaken."

"So you know," Buck concluded. "Now the situation is this. For the present I am tied up there and cannot look after Guste as I should. Would you not like to take charge of the poor girl a bit?" he asked with cool innocence.

"I am to—"

"Keep the pot stirred, so to speak, in which I have left things simmering . . . while I am busy elsewhere. We hit it off very well together. . . ."

"Thanks," said Diederich coldly. "Not quite so well as all that. Give somebody else the job. I take a more serious view of life." He turned and left him.

Besides Buck's immorality, his undignified familiarity was outrageous, after they had just proved themselves opponents once more both in theory and practice: An insufferable person, from whom nothing could be learned! "What has he up his sleeve for me to-morrow?"

At home he relieved his feelings. "A fellow as spineless as a jellyfish, and intellectually benighted! God preserve our home from an all-consuming lack of principle, the sure sign of decadence in any family!" He made sure that Kienast had to leave that night. "Magda will have nothing alarming to write to you," he said, à *propos* of nothing, and laughed. "So far as I am concerned, there may be fire and slaughter in the town, I stick to my office and my family."

Kienast had hardly left when he confronted Frau Hessling. "Well, where is the summons for me to appear in court to-morrow?" She had to admit that she had intercepted the ominous letter. "I would not let it spoil your share in the family happiness, my dear son." But Diederich would hear of no excuses. "Dear son, be damned! I suppose it is for love of me that the food gets worse and worse, except when we have strangers, and the housekeeping money goes on your fiddle-faddle. Do you think you can fool me that Magda made that lace blouse herself? Tell that to the marines!" Magda raised a protest against the insult to her fiancé, but it was no good. "Shut up, you! Your fur coat is half stolen. You women are in league with the servant. When I send her for wine, she brings cheap stuff, and you pocket the difference. . . ."

The three women were horrified, and Diederich shouted all the louder. Emma declared he was mad just because he was going to make a fool of himself the next day before the whole town. All Diederich could do in reply was to hurl a plate onto the ground. Magda stood up, went out, shouting over her shoulder: "Thank the Lord, I don't need you any more!" At once Diederich ran after her. "Please, mind what you are saying. If you have got a husband at last, you have only me to thank and the sacrifices I am making. Your intended haggled over your dowry in a way that was positively shameful. Anyway, you are nothing but a makeweight!"

At this juncture he received a resounding smack in the face and before he could recover his breath Magda was in her room and had locked the door. In rueful silence Diederich rubbed his cheek. Then his indignation boiled up again, but a kind of satisfaction ensued. The crisis was over.

During the night he had quite made up his mind to appear in court rather late, and to show by his whole demeanour how little the whole thing affected him. But he could not contain himself. When he entered the particular court which had been specified an entirely different case was still being heard. Jadassohn, who presented an uncommonly sinister appearance in his black gown, was just engaged in demanding two years in the reformatory for a poor young lad who was scarcely more than a child. The judge granted only one, it is true, but the youthful criminal broke out into such screams that Diederich, himself in a state of great anxiety, felt ill out of sheer compassion. He went outside and entered a lavatory, although a notice on the door read: "For members of the Bar only." Immediately after him Jadassohn appeared. When he saw Diederich he wanted to retire, but the latter at once asked what sort of a place a reformatory was, and what a pimp like that would do there. "As if we could be bothered with those details!" was Jadassohn's only reply, as he disappeared. Diederich's qualms increased still more, as if a ghastly abyss yawned between Jadassohn, representing the authorities, and himself, and he had ventured too near the edge. It had happened with the most pious intentions in an excess of zeal for authority. However, now he would have to take himself in hand, lest he be seized and ground to powder. He would have to kneel and cringe in the hope of escaping. Lucky the man who lived in the obscurity of private life! Diederich vowed to pursue in the future only his own inconsiderable but well-understood advantage.

People were now standing outside the corridor: some of the common herd and some of the *élite*. The five Buck girls, dressed up as if the trial of their brother-in-law, Lauer, was the greatest honour for the family, were chattering in a group with Käthchen Zillich, her mother and the wife of Mayor Scheffelweis. The Mayor, however, could not get rid of his mother-in-law, and from the glances which she darted at Herr Buck's brother and his friends, Cohn and Heuteufel, it was evident that she had set him against the Bucks' cause. Major Kunze, in uniform, was standing by with a gloomy air, and declined to talk. Just then Pastor Zillich and Professor Kühnchen appeared, but when they saw the big group they remained in the shelter of a pillar. The grey figure of Rothgroschen, the editor, moved unnoticed from one group to another. Diederich looked in vain for some one to whom he could attach himself. Now he regretted that he had forbidden his own people to come. He stood in the shadow, behind a turn in the corridor, and cautiously looked out! Suddenly he drew back. Guste Daimchen and her mother! She was immediately surrounded by Buck's daughters, as a valuable reinforcement to their party. At the same moment a door opened in the background, and Wolfgang Buck emerged, in cap and gown, and wearing patent-leather shoes which he turned noticeably inwards. He smiled festively, as if at a reception, shook hands with every one and kissed his fiancée. Everything would go beautifully, he assured them. The Public Prosecutor was well disposed and so was he. Then he went up to the witnesses whom he had called and whispered to them. At that instant everybody stopped talking, for at the head of the stairs the accused, Herr Lauer, appeared and with him his wife. The Mayoress fell upon her neck. How brave she was! "Not at all," she answered in a deep musical voice, "we have nothing to reproach ourselves with, have we, Karl?"

Lauer said: "Certainly not, Judith." Just then Judge
Fritzsche passed, and there was silence. When he and old
Buck's daughters exchanged bows, people winked at each other,
and the Mayor's mother-in-law muttered something half aloud,
which could be more easily read in her eyes.

Diederich had been discovered in his sheltered post by
Wolfgang Buck, who dragged him forward and led him up
to his sister. "My dear Judith, I wonder if you know our
honourable enemy, Dr. Hessling? To-day he will destroy us."
But Frau Lauer neither laughed nor returned Diederich's
bow. She simply stared at him with ruthless curiosity. It
was hard to meet those sombre eyes, and still harder because
she was so beautiful. Diederich felt the blood rushing to his
face, his glance wandered and he stammered. "Your brother
likes his joke. As a matter of fact, there must be some mistake. . . ." · The eyebrows met in that pale face, the corners
of the mouth drooped expressively, and Judith Lauer turned
her back on Diederich.

A court-crier came along and Wolfgang Buck went into the
courtroom beside his brother-in-law, Lauer. As the door did
not open easily, the whole crowd pushed through in haste,
and the better class people got the best of the nobodies. The
petticoats of the five sisters Buck rustled mightily in the
struggle. Diederich was the last to get in, and had to sit down
on the bench provided for witnesses beside Major Kunze, who
at once moved away a bit. The president of the court, Herr
Sprezius, who looked like a worm-eaten vulture, from his lofty
eminence declared the session open, called upon the witnesses
to stand up and warned them of the sacredness of their oath—
whereat Diederich at once assumed the expression he used to
wear in Sunday-school. Judge Harnisch was putting papers in
order and looked in the audience for his daughter. More
attention was paid to old Judge Kühlemann, who had left his
sick room to take his place on the bench to the left of the
president. People thought he did not look well. The Mayor's

mother-in-law professed to know that he intended to resign his seat in the Reichstag—and where would all his money go if he died? To the other witnesses Pastor Zillich expressed the hope that he would leave his millions for the erection of a church, but Professor Kühnchen doubted this in a penetrating whisper. "He'll not separate himself from the money even when he's dead. He has always believed in getting what was his, and if possible what belonged to others, as well. . . ." Then the judge ordered the witnesses to leave the courtroom.

As there was no room for them to wait in, they found themselves again in the corridor. Messrs. Heuteufel, Cohn and Buck, junior, annexed a window-sill. Beneath the ferocious gaze of the Major, Diederich reflected painfully: "Now the defendant is being heard. If I only knew what he is saying! I would like him to be free just as much as his friends." He tried in vain to convince Pastor Zillich of his softened mood, that he had always said the whole affair was trumped up. Zillich turned away in his embarrassment, and Kühnchen went off, whistling through his teeth: "Just you wait, my boy-o, we'll cook your goose." The silent oppression of general dislike weighed upon Diederich. At length, the usher appeared. "Dr. Hessling!"

Diederich pulled himself together so as to pass through the audience in a manner worthy of a gentleman. He stared fixedly in front of him, but he felt just then that Frau Lauer was looking at him. He breathed hard and swerved a little to one side. To the left, beside the junior counsel who was admiring his nails, stood Jadassohn, standing erect and menacing. The light from the window behind him shone through his prominent ears, which glowed bloodily, and his expression postulated such selfless submission on Diederich's part that the latter began to look around for a way of escape. On the right of the accused and below him he saw Wolfgang Buck sitting carelessly, his fists resting on his plump thighs, from which his gown had fallen. He looked as smart and as cheerful as if

he represented the spirit of Light. Justice Sprezius administered the oath to Diederich, saying only two words at a time,
with great condescension. Diederich swore dutifully; then he
had to describe the sequence of events that evening in the
Ratskeller. He began: "We were a lively party. There at the
table sat also Messrs. . . ."

As he had already come to a full stop, there was laughter
in court. Sprezius jumped up, snapped his vulture's beak and
threatened to have the room cleared. "Is that all you remember?" he asked testily. Diederich begged him to take into consideration that, in consequence of business and other cares,
the facts had meanwhile become a little obscured in his memory. "Then, to refresh your memory, I will read out your
sworn statement before the examining magistrate "—and the
judge had the affidavit handed up to him. From this document Diederich learned to his disagreeable surprise that he
had made the definite charge, in the presence of the examining
judge, Justice Fritzsche, of the County Court, that the accused
was guilty of uttering a serious libel upon His Majesty the
Emperor. What had he to say to this? "That may be," he
stammered, "but there were a number of gentlemen there.
Whether it was exactly the accused who said it. . . ."
Sprezius leaned forward over his desk. " Think back. Remember you are on your oath. Other witnesses will testify
that you went up quite alone to the accused and had with him
the conversation in question." "Was it I?" asked Diederich,
blushing crimson, and the whole court rocked with laughter.
Even Jadassohn's face was distorted by a grin of contempt.
Sprezius had opened his mouth to let himself go, but Wolfgang Buck stood up. His soft features, by a visible effort, assumed an energetic look, and he asked Diederich: "I suppose
you were distinctly under the influence of liquor that evening?" Immediately the presiding judge and the Public Prosecutor fell upon him. "I appeal that the question be disal-
lowed?" cried Jadassohn shrilly. "Counsel for the defence will

submit the question to me," croaked Sprezius. "Whether I put it to the witness or not is for me to decide." But Diederich observed with astonishment that both had found a determined adversary. Wolfgang remained on his feet. In the ringing tones of an orator he demurred to the stand taken by the presiding judge, which was prejudicial to the rights of the defence. He moved that the court make a ruling as to whether the right of cross-examining witnesses directly was not conferred upon him by the rules of criminal procedure. Sprezius snapped his beak in vain. He had no alternative but to withdraw into the consulting room with the four judges. Buck looked around in triumph. His cousins moved their hands as if applauding. But in the meantime his father had also come in, and people noticed how old Buck made a sign of disapproval to his son. The accused, for his part, shook his counsel's hand, his apoplectic face expressing angry excitement. Diederich, who was exposed to the gaze of all, struck an attitude and surveyed the scene. But, alas, Guste Daimchen avoided his glance! Old Buck was the only one who gave a friendly nod. He was pleased with Diederich's evidence. He even forced his way out of the crowded auditorium in order to proffer his soft, white hand to Diederich. "Many thanks, dear friend," he said. "You have treated the matter as it deserved." In his loneliness Diederich felt the tears coming to his eyes in the presence of such kindness from the great man. Only after Herr Buck had gone back to his seat again did it dawn on Diederich that here he was promoting the other's interests. And the son, Wolfgang, too was by no means the weakling Diederich had imagined. Probably he had indulged in those political debates just in order to use them against him here. Loyalty, true German loyalty, did not exist any more. Nobody could be trusted. "How long am I to stand here and be gaped at from all sides?"

Fortunately the judges were returning. Old Kühlemann exchanged a glance of regret with old Buck, and Sprezius, with remarkable self-control, read out the decision. Whether counsel for the defence had the right of cross-examining witnesses remained undecided, for the question itself: was the witness intoxicated on that occasion? was ruled out as irrelevant. Then the judge asked whether the prosecution had any question to put to the witness. "Not just now," said Jadassohn indifferently, "but I demand that the witness shall not be dismissed for the present," and Diederich was allowed to sit down. "I further demand that Dr. Fritzsche, the examining judge, be called upon immediately to give evidence as to the nature of the witness, Hessling's earlier allegations against the defendant." Diederich cowered. The public all turned towards Judith Lauer. Even the junior members of the bar present looked in her direction. . . . Jadassohn's request was granted.

Then Pastor Zillich was called, took the oath, and proceeded to give his account of the fateful evening. He declared that it had been a time of crowded impressions, and his conscience as a Christian had been sorely troubled, for just that afternoon blood had been spilled in the streets of Netzig, even though it was for patriotic reasons. "That has nothing to do with the case," said Sprezius decisively—and at that very moment Governor von Wulckow entered the courtroom, dressed in hunting clothes, with great, muddy boots. Every one turned around, the presiding judge bowed from the bench, and Pastor Zillich trembled. The judge and the Public Prosecutor harassed him alternately. Jadassohn even said in tones of dreadful insinuation: "Reverend Sir I need hardly remind you, as a minister of God's word, of the sanctity of the oath you have taken." Then Zillich collapsed and admitted that he had certainly heard the expression alleged to have been employed by the defendant. The latter jumped up and struck his fist on the seat. "I never mentioned the name of the Emperor at all! I took care not to!" His counsel made a sign to him to be quiet and said: "We shall produce evidence to prove that only the provocative intention of the witness, Dr. Hessling, caused the accused to make the statements which have here been misrepresented."

For the present he would ask the president to put the question to the witness as to whether he had not preached a sermon which was specifically directed against the persecution instigated by the witness Hessling. Pastor Zillich stammered that he had only counselled peace in general and done his duty as a servant of the church. Then Buck asked another question. "Has the witness Zillich not a particular interest in maintaining good relations with the chief witness for the prosecution, Dr. Hessling, for the reason that his daughter—" Jadassohn at once intervened: he protested against that question. Sprezius ruled it out and in the audience there was a disapproving murmur of women's voices. The Governor leant over the seat to old Buck and said in an audible voice:

"That's a nice way your son is putting his foot in it!"

Meanwhile Kühnchen was called into the witness-box. The little old man rushed into the room, his glasses gleaming, and he was hardly across the threshold when he began to shout out his name, address and profession. He rattled off the form of the oath before it was read to him, but after that he could not be induced to say anything, except that the tide of national enthusiasm was running high on that evening. First, the sentry's glorious deed! Then His Majesty's magnificent letter with its confession of positive Christianity! "What of the row with the defendant? Well, gentlemen, I know nothin' about it. I just happened to doze off at that moment."—"But, afterwards the matter was discussed," the judge insisted. "Not by me," cried Kühnchen. "All the same, I spoke about our glorious deeds in 1870. The frank tiroors! says I. There was a crowd, for you! My stiff finger is where a frank tiroor bit me, just because I wanted to give him a little jab in the throat with my sword. A low trick for the fellow to play!" Kühnchen tried to submit his finger to the bench inspection. "That will do!" croaked Sprezius and he threatened again to have the court cleared.

Major Kunze stepped up stiffly, as if he were walking on

stilts, and he repeated the oath in a tone as if it were the deadliest insult directed against Sprezius. Then he declared briefly that he had nothing to do with the whole spree; that he had arrived at the Ratskeller afterwards. "All I can say is that Dr. Hessling's conduct savours to me of the informer."

But for some time the atmosphere of the room had savoured of something else. Nobody knew where the smell came from, and the members of the public suspected one another. With their handkerchiefs to their mouths they moved discreetly a little bit away from each other. The presiding judge sniffed the air, and old Kühlemann, whose chin had long since sunk on his breast, stirred uneasily in his sleep.

When Sprezius argued that the gentlemen who had reported the circumstances to him at the time were all loyal patriots, the major simply replied that he did not care, that Dr. Hessling was a person quite unknown to him. Then, however, Jadassohn intervened. His ears twitched and in a voice which cut like a knife he said: "Witness, I ask you if the defendant is not much better known to you. Will you deny that you borrowed a hundred marks from him a week ago?" The whole courtroom became still with horror, and every one stared at the major in uniform, who stood there fumbling for an answer. Jadassohn's boldness was making an impression. He lost no time in pressing his advantage and succeeded in dragging out of Kunze that the indignation of the loyal citizens at Lauer's statements was genuine, and that he himself shared it. Without a doubt, the defendant had meant His Majesty— Here Wolfgang Buck could not resist an opportunity. "Since the president holds it unnecessary to censure the Public Prosecutor when he insults his own witnesses, my client and I can hardly complain, I suppose." Sprezius snapped at him at once. "Counsel for the defence will permit me to censure or not, as I think fit." Unruffled, Buck retorted: "That is just the point I wish to establish. So far as the charge itself is concerned, we assert, and we have witnesses to prove, that there was no reference to the Emperor."—"I took care not to!" interjected the defendant. Buck continued. "Should the imputation, however, be proven, then I will move that the publisher of the Almanach de Gotha be called as an expert witness to testify as to what German princes are of Jewish blood." Whereupon he sat down again, pleased at the sensational murmur which swept the court. "Monstrous!" said a formidable bass voice. Sprezius was on the point of breaking forth, but looked just in time to see who it was. Wulckow! It even aroused Kühlemann. The judges consulted together and the presiding judge announced that the motion of the counsel for the defence could not be admitted, as the truth of the libel was not the question before the court. The mere expression of disrespect was sufficient to establish the fact of guilt. Buck was beaten, and his plump cheeks puckered like those of a sad child. People tittered and the Mayor's mother-in-law laughed outright. In his seat among the witnesses Diederich was grateful to her. Listening anxiously he felt that public opinion was veering round quietly to the side of those who were more clever and powerful. He exchanged glances with Jadassohn.

It was the turn of the editor, Rothgroschen. He suddenly appeared, a grey, inconspicuous figure, and began to function like a machine, like a commissioner for oaths. Every one who knew him was surprised. He had never seemed so sure of himself. He knew everything, made the gravest allegations against the accused, and spoke fluently, as if he were reciting a leading article. The only difference was that the judge gave him his cue at the end of every paragraph, with a word of encouragement, as if to a model pupil. Buck, who had recovered, raised the point against him that the "Netzig Journal" had championed Lauer. "Ours is a liberal and impartial paper," declared the editor. "We reflect public opinion. Since here and now opinion is unfavourable to the defendant—" He must have informed himself as to this outside in the corridor! Buck began in ironical tones: "I beg to draw attention to the

curious conception of his oath which this witness betrays."
But Rothgroschen could not be browbeaten. "I am a jour-
nalist," he explained. "I appeal to the presiding judge to
protect me from the insults of counsel on the opposite side."
Sprezius did not hesitate and he allowed the editor to retire
with flying colours.

It struck twelve, and Jadassohn drew the president's attention to the fact that Dr. Fritzsche, the examining judge, was
at the disposal of the court. He was called, and scarcely had
he appeared at the door when all eyes glanced back and forth
from him to Judith Lauer. She had become even paler and the
sombre glance, which accompanied him to his place on the
bench, became intensified. It had an insistent, silent appeal,
but Fritzsche avoided it. He also looked unwell, but he walked
with an air of determination. Diederich decided that of his
two habitual expressions he had chosen the most matter-of-
fact for this occasion.

What impressions of the witness Hessling had he received
during the preliminary inquiry? The witness had made his
statement absolutely freely and independently, in the form of
a narrative still coloured by his recent experiences. The reliability of the witness, which Fritzsche had an opportunity of
testing by means of his further inquiries, was beyond all question. That the witness to-day should no longer have distinct
recollections could be explained by the excitement of the moment. . . . And the accused? At this question a pin might
have been heard falling in court. Fritzsche swallowed a lump
in his throat. The defendant also had made a rather favourable impression upon him, in spite of the many damaging circumstances. "In a conflict of evidence would you hold that
the defendant was capable of the crime with which he is
charged?" asked Sprezius.

Fritzsche replied: "The defendant is an educated gentleman.
He would have taken care not to use specifically insulting
words." "That is what the defendant says himself," remarked

the judge severely. Fritzsche began to talk more rapidly. By reason of his civil activities the accused was accustomed to associate authority with liberal leanings. He obviously regarded himself as more enlightened and more entitled to criticise than most other people. It was, therefore, conceivable that, in a state of exasperation—and he felt exasperated by the shooting of the workman by the sentry—he may have given such expression to his political opinions as would suggest an offensive intention, although outwardly free from reproach.

The presiding judge and the Public Prosecutor gave a visible sigh of relief. Justices Harnisch and Kühlemann glanced at the public, amongst which there was a lively sensation. The junior counsel sitting to the left again examined his nails, his colleague on the right hand, however, a thoughtful looking young man, observed the accused, who was just in front of him. The hands of the defendant clutched the rail of the seat, and his prominent brown eyes were turned towards his wife. She was looking steadily at Fritzsche, with parted lips, as if in a dream, and her expression was one of suffering, weakness and shame. The Mayor's mother-in-law said distinctly: "And she has two children at home!" Suddenly Lauer seemed to notice the whispering all round him, all these glances which turned away when they met his own. He crumpled up, and his face became so pale that the young barrister moved anxiously in his chair.

Diederich who was feeling better and better, was probably the only person who still followed the dialogue between the presiding and examining judges. Poor Fritzsche! At first the affair could not have been more painful to any one than to Diederich, for good reasons. Had he not exercised an influence over Diederich as witness which was almost a violation of professional etiquette? And yet in affidavit form, Diederich's testimony was very damaging, and Fritzsche's own evidence even more so. He had not been any less ruthless than Jadassohn. His close and peculiar relations with the Lauer house-hold had not made him falter in the task before him, the de-fence of authority—what a lesson for Diederich! Even Wolf-gang Buck admitted it after his own fashion. He looked up at Fritzsche with an expression of nausea on his face.

As the examining judge made his way towards the exit by shoving vigorously, the whispering grew louder. The Mayor's mother-in-law pointed her lorgnon at Frau Lauer and said: "A nice crowd!" Nobody contradicted her, for people had be-gun to abandon the Lauers to their fate. Guste Daimchen bit her lip and Käthchen Zillich gave Diederich a quick look from under her eyelashes. Dr. Scheffelweis bent over to the head of the Buck family, pressed his hand and said sweetly: "I hope, my dear friend and supporter, that all may yet be well."

The judge gave an order to the usher. "Bring in the wit-ness Cohn!" The witnesses for the defence were to have their turn. The judge sniffed: "There is a most unpleasant smell here," he remarked. "Krecke, open that window behind there!" He gazed searchingly at the poorer public, which was sitting closely packed. On the other hand, there was plenty of room in the lower seats, and most of all in the vicinity of Gov-ernor von Wulckow, whose hunting jacket reeked of stale per-spiration. . . . The icy draught through the open window caused complaints amongst the out of town journalists, who were sitting stowed away in the rear. But Sprezius merely snapped his beak at them, and they huddled up in their over-coat collars.

Jadassohn looked at the witness with an air of conscious victory. Sprezius allowed him to speak for a while, then Jadassohn cleared his throat and he held up a deed in his hand. "You have been the tenant since 1889 of the shop bearing your name?" Then, without warning: "Do you admit that just at that time one of the people who supplied you with goods, a certain Lehmann, committed suicide by shooting him-self in your neighbourhood?" With fiendish satisfaction he looked at Cohn, for the effect of his words was extraordinary. Cohn began to fidget and to gasp for air. "The old libel!" he screamed. "He didn't do it on my account! He was unhappily married! People broke me once before with that story and now they are beginning again! Counsel for the defence also protested. Sprezius snapped at Cohn. The Public Prosecutor was not an ordinary individual, and the witness would be fined fifty marks for contempt of court because of the expression "libel." That settled Cohn. Herr Buck's brother was called. He was asked point blank by Jadassohn: "Your business is notoriously failing; what is your means of livelihood?" At this there was such a murmur of protest that Sprezius quickly intervened. "Does counsel for the prosecution really think this question pertinent?" But Jadassohn was worthy of the occasion. "The prosecution is interested in establishing the fact that the witness is financially dependent upon his relations, and particularly upon his brother-in-law, the accused. The reliability of his evidence can be measured by that." Tall and elegant, Herr Buck stood there with bowed head. "That is all," said Jadassohn and Sprezius dismissed this witness. Under the glances of the crowd his five daughters huddled together on their seat like a herd of lambs in a storm. The poorer section of the audience laughed in a hostile way. Sprezius amiably called for silence and ordered Heuteufel to come into the witness-box.

When Heuteufel raised his hand to swear Jadassohn thrust forward his own with a dramatic effort.

"First I must ask the witness one question. Does he admit that he approved of the expressions which constitute the crime of *lèse-majesté*, and even improved upon them?" Heuteufel replied: "I admit nothing." Whereupon, Jadassohn confronted him with his statement at the preliminary hearing, and said in a loud voice: "I appeal for a ruling that this witness be not allowed to take the oath, because he is suspected of complicity in the crime." Still more sharply: "The opinions of the witness cannot be ignored by this court. He is one of those people whom His Majesty the Emperor has rightly called men without a country. Further, at regular meetings, which he calls Sunday festivals for free men, he is actively engaged in spreading the crassest atheism, which is sufficient to define his attitude towards a Christian monarch." Jadassohn's ears glowed with an ardour which was in itself a confession of faith. Wolfgang Buck stood up, smiled sceptically and said they all knew that the religious convictions of counsel for the prosecution were monastic in their severity, and that nobody could expect him to give any credence to a non-Christian. His Lordship, however, would think differently and refuse the appeal of the prosecution. Then Jadassohn rose in his wrath. For contempt of his person he demanded that counsel for the defence be fined one hundred marks. The judges withdrew for consultation. Immediately an animated exchange of opinion broke out in the courtroom. Dr. Heuteufel put his hands in his pockets and looked Jadassohn up and down with deliberate contempt. Deprived of the protection of the bench, the latter was panic-stricken and cowered against the wall. It was Diederich who came to his rescue, for he had an important communication to make to him. . . . Soon the judges returned. First the oath was administered to Heuteufel. For contempt of the Public Prosecutor counsel for the defence was fined eighty marks.

When the hearing was resumed counsel for the defence intervened to ask the witness what was his opinion, as an intimate friend of the defendant, of his domestic life. Heuteufel made a move, there was a rustle of excitement among the public, who understood. Would Sprezius allow the question? He had already opened his mouth to refuse, but understood just in time that a sensation should be encouraged. Thereupon Heuteufel sang the praises of the model conditions which prevailed in Lauer's household. Jadassohn absorbed the witness's words, trembling with impatience. Finally he had an opportunity of asking his question in tones of unspeakable triumph. "Will the witness state with what kind of women he has had the personal intercourse from which he derives his knowledge of family life. Does he not frequent a certain establishment known in the vernacular as 'Little Berlin'?" As he was speaking he made sure that the ladies in the audience and the judges also, were giving looks of disgust. The chief witness for the defence was ruined! Heuteufel tried to answer. "You probably know that better than any one else. We must have met there many a time." But that only resulted in a fine of fifty marks being imposed by Sprezius. Finally the judge decided: "The witness must remain in court. He is required for further elucidation of the facts of the case." Heuteufel declared: "As far as I am concerned, this business here is sufficiently elucidated, and I would prefer to leave." At once his fine of fifty marks was raised to one hundred.

Wolfgang Buck looked about uneasily. His lips seemed to taste the mood of the court. He drew them back as if that mood were expressed in the remarkable smell which had again arisen since the window was closed. Buck saw that the sympathy which had accompanied him there was dulled and destroyed, that his weapons were wasted. And the yawning faces drawn with hunger, the impatience of the judges who were eyeing the clock, all boded him no good. He jumped up to save what could still be rescued! He assumed an energetic tone as he moved that witnesses be called for the afternoon session. "Since the Public Prosecutor systematically doubts the credibility of our witnesses, we are prepared to prove the good name of the accused by means of the most prominent citizens of Netzig. No less person than his Honour Mayor Scheffelweis will testify to the services which the accused has rendered the city. Governor von Wulckow could not refuse to bear witness to his sense of civic and national duty. "Well, I never!" said the formidable basso from the empty space behind. Buck steadied his voice.

"As for the social virtues of the defendant, all his employés will vouch for them."

Buck was gasping as he sat down. Jadassohn remarked icily: "My learned friend for the defence is asking for a plebiscite." The judges consulted in whispers, and Sprezius announced that the court could only allow counsel's motion in so far as it related to the summoning of Mayor Scheffelweis. As the latter was present he was called at once. He worked his way out of his seat. His wife and mother-in-law held him firmly on both sides and gave him hurried recommendations which must have been contradictory, for the Mayor reached the witness-box visibly perturbed. What attitude did the defendant display in the civic life of the community? Dr. Scheffelweis was able to report favourably. For example, the defendant had voted at the board meetings of the City Council for the restoration of the famous old presbytery where was preserved the hair which Dr. Martin Luther, as well known, had pulled from the Devil's tail. It was true, he had supported the building of "secular Sunday-schools," and had undoubtedly created offence in so doing. Then, he was universally esteemed in business circles; the social reforms which he had introduced into his own factory were generally admired— although it must be confessed there had also been objections to them, on the ground that they increased the demands of the workers to an unlimited degree and thus hastened perhaps the day of revolution. "Would you consider the defendant capable of the crime with which he is charged?" asked counsel for the defence. "In one sense," Scheffelweis replied, "certainly not. "But in another sense?" queried counsel for the prosecution. The witness replied: "In another sense, yes, certainly."

After this answer the Mayor was allowed to retire. His two ladies received him, each equally dissatisfied. The presiding judge was preparing to adjourn the session when Jadassohn cleared his throat. He moved that the witness, Dr. Hessling, be heard again, as he wished to amplify his testimony. Sprezius blinked his eyelids peevishly and the public, who were just scrambling out of their seats, complained aloud. But Diederich had already stepped forward confidently, and had begun to speak in a clear voice. After mature consideration he had come to the conclusion, he said, that he could strengthen the substance of his evidence at the preliminary hearing. He repeated it, but in stronger and more detailed form. He began with the shooting of the workman and retailed the critical comments of Lauer and Heuteufel. The audience, oblivious of their desire to leave, followed the clash of opinions along the blood-stained Kaiser Wilhelmstrasse as far as the Ratskeller, watched the hostile ranks lining up for the decisive battle, and saw Diederich spring forward under the gothic chandelier with drawn sword, so to speak, and challenge the accused to mortal combat.

"Then, gentlemen, I will not deny it, I challenged him! Would he say the word with which I could convict him? He did, gentlemen, and I convicted him. In so doing I only fulfilled my duty, and I would do so again to-day, even though I should suffer greater social and financial losses than I have had to bear of late. Disinterested idealism, gentlemen, is the privilege of a German, and he will follow it unswervingly, even though his courage falter at times in the face of the multitude of his enemies. When I previously hesitated in my statement, it was not, as the examining judge so charitably assumed, because my memory was confused. I am not afraid to confess that it was because of a perhaps pardonable dread of the weight of the combat which I would have to undertake. But I am undertaking it, for none less than His Majesty our noble Emperor demands it of me. . . ." Diederich went on fluently, with a swing to his phrases which took the breath away. Jadassohn discovered that the witness was beginning to anticipate the effect of his own peroration, and looked anxiously at the presiding judge. Sprezius, however, had no intention of

interrupting Diederich. His vulture-like features were unmoved, he did not bat an eyelid, as he watched Diederich's
grim face in which the eyes flashed threateningly. Even old
Kühlemann listened with gaping mouth. Wolfgang Buck leant
forward in his chair and gazed up at Diederich, with the excited interest of an expert, his glance betraying a fearful joy.
That was a mob oration! A sure hit! A winner! "Let our
citizens," cried Diederich, "awake from the sleep in which
they have so long been lulled, and not abandon to the State
and its instruments the task of fighting the revolutionary elements, but do their own part! That is His Majesty's command, gentlemen, can I hesitate? Revolution is raising its
head; a gang of people unworthy of the name of Germans dares
to drag in the dust the sacred person of the King. . . ."

Somebody laughed among the poorer members of the
audience. Sprezius snapped his beak and threatened to fine
the person who laughed. Jadassohn sighed. Now it was
frankly no longer possible to interrupt the witness.

In Netzig, unfortunately, the imperial call to battle had
awakened only a feeble response! Here people were closing
their eyes and ears to the danger and clinging to the commonplace views of democracy and humanity which made the way
easy for the unpatriotic enemies of the divine order of the
world. Here they did not yet understand virile national sentiment and far-seeing imperialism. "The task of modern thinkers is to win even Netzig to the new spirit, as defined by our
glorious young Emperor, who has appointed every true patriot
whether noble or commoner, to be the instrument of his exalted
purpose." And Diederich concluded: "Therefore, gentlemen, I
was justified in challenging the defendant with the greatest
decision, when he began to criticise. I have acted without personal malice, for the sake of the cause. To be impartial is to
be German! I for my part"—he glared across at Lauer—
"admit my actions, for they spring from an exemplary life,

which rests upon honour in the home and knows neither untruth nor immorality!"

There was a great sensation in court. Diederich was swept off his feet by the noble sentiments which he expressed, and, intoxicated by his success he continued to glare at the accused. Suddenly he shrank back, for the defendant was helping himself up by the rail of his seat, trembling and shaking. His eyes were wild and blood-shot and his jaws moved convulsively, as if he had had a stroke. "Oh!" cried the women's voices, shivering with expectation. Meanwhile the presiding judge announced that the Public Prosecutor would begin his address at four o'clock, and disappeared together with his colleagues. Half-dazed Diederich found himself suddenly surrounded by Kühnchen, Zillich and Rothgroschen, who were congratulating him. Strangers shook him by the hand and assured him that a verdict of guilty was absolutely certain, that Lauer might as well prepare to leave. Major Kunze reminded the victorious Diederich that there had never been a difference of opinion between them. In the corridor old Buck passed by quite close to Diederich, who was just then surrounded by a crowd of women. He was putting on his black gloves and he looked the young man full in the face as he did so, without replying to Diederich's involuntary salute, with a sad, searching glance, so sad that Diederich, in the midst of his triumph, looked after him sadly.

All of a sudden he became aware that the five Buck girls did not scruple to pay him compliments. They fluttered with rustling skirts and inquired why he had not also brought his sisters to this thrilling trial. He looked these five over-dressed dolls up and down in turn, and explained sternly and shortly that there were things which were to be taken more seriously than a theatrical performance. They walked off in blank amazement. The corridor began to empty; the last to appear was Guste Daimchen. She made a movement in Diederich's di-

rection, but Wolfgang Buck caught up on her, smiling as if
nothing had happened, and with him were Herr and Frau
Lauer. Guste quickly threw a glance at Diederich which
stirred his tender emotions. He stepped back behind a pillar
and with beating heart allowed the vanquished to pass.

As he turned to go Governor von Wulckow came out of one
of the offices. Hat in hand, Diederich took up his position and
at the right moment clicked his heels together and stood at attention. And Wulckow actually stopped! "Well, well!" he
rumbled from the depths of his beard, clapping Diederich on
the shoulder. "You have set the pace. Most excellent sentiments. You'll hear from me again." He went off in his muddy
boots, his paunch quivering in his riding-breeches, which were
soaked with perspiration and left behind him, as penetrating
as ever, that overpowering odour of masculinity which per-
meated everything that happened in the court.

Downstairs at the entrance door the Mayor still lingered,
with his wife and mother-in-law who harassed him from both
sides, and whose demands he tried to reconcile, a hopeless expression on his pale face.

At home they had already heard everything. The three
women had waited in the vestibule for the end of the hearing,
and had got Meta Harnisch to tell them what happened.
Weeping silently Frau Hessling embraced her son. The sisters looked on feeling rather small, for only yesterday they
had had nothing but contempt for Diederich's part in the affair, which had now turned out so brilliantly. But in the
happy oblivion of victory Diederich ordered wine for dinner,
and assured them that this day would assure their social position in Netzig for all time. "The five Buck girls will be
careful not to cut you in the street. They may consider themselves lucky if you answer their salutes." Lauer's condemna-
tion, he explained, was now only a matter of form. It had
already been decided and, at the same time, Diederich's irresistible advance! "Naturally"—he nodded into his glass—

"even while faithfully discharging my duty I might have made a wrong move, and then, my dears, I don't mind telling you, it would have been all up with me and with Magda's marriage, too!" As Magda turned pale he touched her arm. "Now we have come through very nicely," he said, raising his glass in manly joy. "How things have turned out under God's guidance!" He ordered the two girls to make themselves pretty and come along with him. Frau Hessling begged them to be careful, she was very much afraid of the excitement. On this occasion Diederich could afford to wait and his sisters could take as long to dress as they liked. By the time they arrived every one was in court, but they were not the same people. All the Buck family was missing, and also Guste Daimchen, Heuteufel, Cohn, the whole masonic lodge and the Independent Voters' Association. They admitted their defeat! The whole town knew it and crowded there to witness their annihilation. The poorer people were thrust forward into the front seats. Those of the erstwhile clique who were still visible, Kühnchen and Kunze, took care that every one should read their unimpeachable sentiments in their faces. There were a few suspicious looking figures scattered about: young men with a tired, soulful air, together with several loud young women, with unnaturally radiant complexions, and they all exchanged greetings with Wolfgang Buck. The State Theatre! Buck had actually dared to invite them to hear his oration.

Every time any one entered Lauer turned his head anxiously. He was expecting his wife! "If he imagines that she will come again!" thought Diederich. But there she came, even paler than in the morning, greeted her husband with an imploring look, and sat down quietly at the end of a seat, her eyes staring fixedly in front of her at the Bench, proud and silent, as if awaiting Destiny. . . . The judges had entered the courtroom, the presiding justice opened the session and called upon counsel for the prosecution to speak.

Jadassohn launched forth at once with extreme vehemence;

after a few sentences his effects were exhausted and he lost his grip on the audience. The theatrical people smiled at one another contemptuously. Jadassohn noticed this and began to swing his arms until his gown whirled about him; his voice rose to a shriek and his ears glowed. The painted ladies fell on the rails of their seat in a paroxysm of uncontrollable giggling. "Is Sprezius blind?" asked the Mayor's mother-in-law. But the Bench was fast asleep. Diederich inwardly rejoiced. This was his revenge on Jadassohn, who could devise nothing except what he had already employed in setting the pace! It was all over, as Wulckow knew; and Sprezius knew it, therefore he slept with his eyes open. Jadassohn knew it best of all, and the noisier he became the more ineffective he was. When he finally called for a penalty of two years' imprisonment, all the people he had bored disagreed with him, even the judges, as it seemed. Old Kühleman gave a snore and awoke with a start. Sprezius blinked his eyes several times to arouse himself, and then called upon counsel for the defence.

Wolfgang Buck stood up slowly. His curious friends in the audience gave a murmur of applause and Buck calmly waited until they had finished, in spite of the threatening beak of Sprezius. Then he declared lightly, as if it would be all over in two minutes, that the evidence had shown the defendant in a thoroughly favourable light. Counsel for the prosecution was wrong in his view that the testimony of witnesses had any value, who had been intimated by ruthless attacks upon their own private lives. Or rather, it had the value of proving incontrovertibly the innocence of the defendant, since so many well-known friends of truth could only be blackmailed into— Of course he was not allowed to continue. When the judge had calmed down Buck imperturbably resumed. Even if they accepted as proven, that the defendant had really uttered the expression with which he was charged, then the idea of guilt was untenable. The witness Hessling had publicly admitted that deliberately and with malice aforethought he had provoked the defendant. He would ask rather if the witness Hessling, because of his provocative intention, were not really guilty of incitement to commit an offence, which he had carried out with the involuntary co-operation of another party, by consciously taking advantage of the latter's excited condition. Counsel recommended the witness Hessling to the further investigations of the Public Prosecutor. Every one turned towards Diederich, who began to feel uncomfortably warm. But the deprecatory air of the judge restored his courage.

Buck's voice became tender and impassioned. No. He did not wish any ill to the witness Hessling, whom he regarded as the victim of one more exalted. "Why do the charges of *lèse-majesté* multiply in these times? You may say: as a result of such occurrences as the shooting of the workman. I answer: No. But as a result of the speeches which accompany those occurrences." Sprezius moved his head, sharpened his beak, but drew back. Buck refused to be disturbed, and a strong, virile note crept into his voice.

"Threats and exaggerated claims on the one side bring forth their appropriate response on the other. The principle: he who is not with me is against me, draws too sharp a line between sycophants and calumniators."

Then Sprezius snapped. "Counsel for the defence cannot be permitted to criticise the words of His Majesty in this place. If he continues to do so the court will impose a fine."

"I accept the ruling," said Buck and his tone became softer and more emphatic. "I will not speak of the prince, but of the loyal subject, whom he has moulded; not of William II but of Diederich Hessling. You have seen what he is like! An average man, with a commonplace mind, the creature of circumstance and opportunity, without courage so long as things were going badly for him here, and tremendously self-important as soon as they had turned in his favour."

Diederich fumed in his seat. Why did Sprezius not protect

him? It was his duty. He allowed a loyal patriot to be made little of at a public hearing—and by whom? By counsel for the defence, the professional champion of subversive tendencies! There was something rotten in the State!—He began to boil with rage as he looked at Buck. There was the enemy, his antithesis. There was only one thing to do: smash him! There was some insulting quality of humanity in Buck's fat profile! One could feel in him a kind of patronising affection for the phrases which he was weaving to describe Diederich.

"At all times," said Buck, "there have been many thousands such as he, who mistook their business and developed political opinions. What is added, and makes of him a new type, is simply the gesture, the swaggering manner, the aggressiveness of an alleged personality, the craving for effect at any price, even at the expense of others. Those who differ in opinion are to be branded enemies of their country, though they constitute two-thirds of the nation. Class interests, no doubt, but romanticised out of all recognition. Romantic prostration at the feet of a master who just confers enough of his power upon his subjects to enable them to crush lesser men. And as neither master nor slave exists, either in law or in fact, public life takes on an air of wretched mummery, opinion appears in costume parts, speeches fall as from the lips of crusaders, while all the time these people are led by merchants or paper manufacturers. The *papier mâché* sword is drawn for an idea like that of majesty, which nobody can any longer experience outside fairy tales. Majesty! . . ." Buck repeated the word, rolling it on his tongue, and some of its listeners enjoyed the taste of it. The theatre people, who were clearly more interested in the sound than the sense of the words, listened eagerly and murmured approvingly. For the others Buck's language was too choice, and they were disappointed because he made no use of dialect. Sprezius, however, sat bolt upright in his chair and was eager for prey. "For the last time I must warn counsel not to bring the person of the King into this discussion." There was a sensation amongst the audience. When Buck began again to speak, some one tried to applaud. Sprezius snapped his beak just in time. It was one of the loud young women.

"The presiding judge has been the first to mention the person of the King. But, now that it has been mentioned, I may be permitted, with all due respect, to observe that his person so perfectly expresses and represents the tendencies of the country at this moment as to be almost awe-inspiring. You will not interrupt me when I say that the Emperor is a great artist. Can I say more? We know nothing loftier. . . . And for that very reason it should be forbidden for every contemporary mediocrity to ape him. Amidst the splendour of the throne an undoubtedly unique personality may have full play; he may make speeches without arousing in us any expectation of more than mere words; he may flash and dazzle; he may provoke the hatred of imaginary rebels and the applause of the parterre, which never loses sight of its own bourgeois realities. . . ."

Diederich trembled, and all eyes and mouths were opened in tense excitement, as if Buck were walking on a tight rope between two towers. Would he fall? Sprezius held his beak in readiness to pounce, but not a trace of irony could be seen in the expression of the speaker, into which a suggestion of embittered enthusiasm had crept. Suddenly the corners of his mouth drooped and all the colour was extinguished about him.

"But a paper manufacturer in Netzig?" he queried. He had not tumbled, and was once more on solid ground! Everybody turned to look at Diederich and smiled. Emma and Magda also smiled. Buck secured his effect and Diederich admitted to himself sadly that their conversation yesterday in the street had been a general rehearsal for this. He cowered under the open scorn of the speaker.

"Nowadays paper-makers have ambitions; they aspire to a

rôle for which they were never manufactured. Let us hoot
them off the stage! They have no talent. The æsthetic level
of our public life, which has been gloriously raised since the
advent of William II, has nothing to gain from the co-operation of such persons as the witness Hessling. . . . And the
moral level, gentlemen, rises and falls with the æsthetic. Lying
ideals bring evil manners in their train; the political swindle
is reflected in everyday life."

Buck's voice had become stern. Now, for the first time, he
struck a note of pathos.

"I do not restrict myself, gentlemen, to the mechanical doc-
trine so dear to the so-called revolutionary party. The example of a great man can effect more changes in the world
than all the social legislation. But beware, if the example be
misunderstood! Then it may happen that a new type springs
up over the country, who sees in severity and repression, not
the sad transition to humane conditions, but the aim of life
itself. Weak and pacifistic by nature, he strives to appear a
man of iron because, in his conception, Bismarck was. Invoking without justification one higher than himself he becomes
noisy and unsafe. Without a doubt the victories of his vanity
will serve commercial ends. First his travesty of opinion
brings a man to prison for *lèse-majesté*. Afterwards he reaps
his profit."

Buck extended his arms as if his gown were to enfold the
whole world, and he had the intense expression of a leader of
men. He continued his discourse, putting every ounce of his
strength into it.

"You, gentlemen, wield sovereign power. Your sovereignty
is first and most powerful. The fate of the individual is in
your hands. You can give him life or moral death—a thing
no prince can do. But a generation is created according as
you approve or condemn. Thus your power extends to our
future. Upon you rests the tremendous responsibility whether,
in the future, men like the defendant shall fill the prisons,

while the governing class is composed of creatures like the witness Hessling. Choose between them! Make your choice between an upstart and a valuable citizen, between comedy and truth! Between a man who will sacrifice a victim to raise himself and one who will make sacrifices to advance the welfare of others. The defendant has done what few have dared; he has divested himself of his privileges; to those beneath him he has granted equal rights, comfort and the joy of hope. Can one who respects his neighbour as himself be guilty of disrespect for the person of the Emperor?"

The audience drew a deep breath. With changed feelings they stared at the accused, who sat with forehead resting on his hand, and at his wife, who stared steadily in front of her. Several people sobbed. Even the presiding judge was subdued. He had stopped blinking and sat there with wide-open eyes, as if Buck had fascinated him. Old Kühlemann nodded seriously and Jadassohn winced in spite of himself. But Buck spoiled his effect by allowing his excitement to carry him away. "The citizens are awake!" he shouted. "Real national opinion! The silent deed of one Lauer strengthens it more than a hundred noisy monologues, even though spoken by a crowned artist!"

Sprezius immediately began to blink again, and everybody looked at him. He had remembered the true state of affairs and resolved not to fall into the trap a second time. Jadassohn grinned, and in court there was a feeling that counsel for the defence had overplayed his part. Amidst general uneasiness the judge ordered him to end his eulogy of the accused.

When Buck sat down the actors tried to applaud, but Sprezius did not even snap at them. He merely gave them a bored glance and asked if the prosecution wished to reply. Jadassohn answered no, indifferently, and the Bench quickly withdrew. "It won't take long to reach a verdict," said Diederich shrugging his shoulders—although he was still terribly perturbed by Buck's speech. "Thank heaven!" said the Mayor's mother-in-law. "And to think that five minutes ago those people were getting the best of it." She pointed to Lauer, who was wiping his face, and to Buck whom the actors were actually congratulating. By this time the judges had returned and Sprezius was pronouncing the sentence: six months' imprisonment—which seemed to every one the most natural conclusion. In addition the accused was divested of the public offices which he held.

The presiding judge based the verdict on the fact that libellous intention was not essential to the establishment of guilt. Therefore the question of provocation did not arise. On the contrary, the fact that the accused had dared to speak in that fashion in the presence of loyal citizens must weigh against him. The defendant's plea that he had not meant the Emperor was held by the court to be untenable. "In view of the political sympathies of the listeners, and the known antimonarchical tendencies of the defendant, they could not but conclude that his utterances were directed against the Emperor. When the accused professes to have taken good care not to libel His Majesty, he merely proves his desire, not to avoid *lèse-majesté*, but to avoid its judicial consequences."

Everybody saw the force of this, and found that Lauer's conduct was natural, but not quite honest. The accused was at once arrested, and when the crowd had witnessed this final incident, it broke up, making unfavourable comments upon him. Now it was all over with Lauer, for what would become of his business during his six months in confinement? As a result of the sentence he was no longer a town-councillor. For the future he could neither help nor harm any one. As for the Buck clique, which talked so big, their number was up! People turned to look for the prisoner's wife, but she had disappeared. "She didn't even shake hands with him! A nice state of affairs!"

In the days that followed things happened which gave rise to even harsher judgments. Judith Lauer had packed her trunk

immediately and had gone off to the South. To the South!—
while her wedded husband sat up there in prison, with a sentry
marching beneath his barred window. And . . . a remarkable
coincidence!   Judge Fritzsche suddenly took leave. A card
from him, posted in Genoa, reached Dr. Heuteufel, who showed
it round, probably in order to make people forget his own conduct. It was hardly necessary to pump the Lauer servants
and the poor, forsaken children. People knew exactly what to
think. The scandal grew to such dimensions that the "Netzig
Journal" intervened with a warning to the upper ten not to
encourage revolutionary tendencies by shameless profligacy.
In a second article Rothgroschen set forth the unwisdom of
overpraising such reforms as Lauer had introduced into his
factory. What did the workers get out of profit-sharing? On
an average, according to Lauer's own showing, hardly eighty
marks a year. That might have been given to them in the
form of a Christmas present. But then, of course, it would no
longer be a demonstration against the existing social order!
Then the anti-monarchical views of the manufacturer, as established by the court, would derive no advantage! And if Herr'
Lauer had counted on the gratitude of the workers, he could
now learn better, provided, Rothgroschen added, that he was
allowed to read the Social Democratic newspaper in prison.
There they accused him of having endangered the existence of
several hundred working-class families by his irresponsible remarks about the Emperor.

The "Netzig Journal" took account of the changed circumstances in another very significant way. The manager, Tietz,
went to Hessling's factory for a portion of his paper supply.
They were printing more papers, and Gausenfeld, he said, had
more orders than could be filled. Diederich thought at once
that old Klüsing himself was behind this move. He was interested in the newspaper, and nothing happened there without
his consent. If he surrendered something it was obviously
because he was afraid he would otherwise lose even more. The

local papers! The government supplies! He was afraid of Wulckow, that was it. The old man must have heard, although he now rarely came into town, that Diederich had attracted the Governor's attention by his evidence. The old paper spider, back there in his web, which covered the whole province and more, felt danger and was uneasy. "He wants to feed me with the 'Netzig Journal'! But he won't get off as cheap as that, not in these hard times! If he only knew what plans I have! Wait until I have Wulckow behind me—I'll simply take over his entire business!" Diederich said these words aloud and struck the desk so that Sötbier jumped up in alarm. "Beware of undue excitement," Diederich mocked. "At your age, Sötbier. I admit that in former years you did a good deal for the firm. But that was a bad business with the cylinder machine. You took away my courage, and now I could use it for the 'Netzig Journal.' You had better take a rest. You are finished."

Amongst the results which the trial brought Diederich was a letter from Major Kunze. The latter wished to clear up a regrettable misunderstanding and informed him that there was now no obstacle to Dr. Hessling's admission to the Veterans' Association. Deeply moved by this triumph Diederich's impulse was to clasp the two hands of the old soldier. Fortunately, he made inquiries, and discovered that Governor von Wulckow was responsible for the letter! The Governor had honoured the club with a visit and expressed his amazement at not finding Dr. Hessling there. Then Diederich realised what a power he was, and acted accordingly. To the major's private letter he replied with an official communication to the Club, and requested that two members of the committee should call on him, Major Kunze and Professor Kühnchen. And they came. Diederich received them in his office, between business calls which he had purposely arranged for the same hour, and he dictated to them the form of an address, whose receipt he made a condition of accepting their flattering invitation. In it he had them assure him that he had vindicated his loyal and patriotic feelings, with brilliant fearlessness and in spite of slander and calumny. That his action had made it possible to administer a serious rebuff to the unpatriotic element in Netzig. That Diederich had emerged, a pure and true-blue German, from a struggle waged at great personal loss.

The occasion of his admission to the Association was festive, and Kunze read the address, while Diederich, with tears in his voice, confessed his unworthiness to receive such praise. If patriotism was gaining ground in Netzig, they should thank, after God, one higher than himself, whose gracious commands he executed in joyful obedience. . . . They were all moved, even Kunze and Kühnchen. It was a great evening. Diederich presented the club with a cup . . . and he made a speech in which he touched upon the difficulties with which the new Army Bill was meeting in the Reichstag. "Our sharp sword alone," cried Diederich, "assures our place in the world, and His Majesty the Emperor appeals to us to keep it sharp. When the Emperor commands it will fly from its sheath! Those politician fellows, who want to butt in with their talk, had better take care that they are not the first to feel it! You cannot fool with His Majesty, gentlemen, I can tell you that." Diederich glared and nodded weightily, as if he knew more than he could tell. At that moment he had a real inspiration. "Recently in the provincial legislature of Brandenburg the Emperor made his attitude clear to the Reichstag. He said: 'If these chaps refuse me my soldiers, I'll clear out the whole shop!'" The phrase aroused enthusiasm, and by the time Diederich had replied to every one who toasted him, he could not have said whether the words were his own or the Emperor's. . . . The next day the phrase appeared in the "Netzig Journal" and the same evening in the "Lokal-Anzeiger." The radical papers demanded an official denial, but none was forthcoming.

V

FEELINGS of exaltation were still swelling in Diederich's breast when Emma and Magda received an invitation to tea one afternoon from Frau von Wulckow. It could only be in connection with the play which the Governor's wife was having produced at the next entertainment of the Harmony Club. Emma and Magda were to have parts. They returned home flushed with pleasure. Frau von Wulckow had been exceedingly charming, with her own hands she had put cake after cake on their plates. Inge Tietz was mad! Some officers were going to take part in the play! Special costumes would be required; if Diederich thought they could do with their fifty marks. . . . But Diederich gave them unlimited credit. None of the things they bought were fine enough in his opinion. The sitting-room was strewn with ribbons and artificial flowers and the girls were bewildered by Diederich's interruptions and advice. Then a visitor called; it was Guste Daimchen.

"I haven't yet properly congratulated the happy bride," she said, trying to smile affectionately, but her eyes roved anxiously over the flowers and ribbons. "I suppose these are for the silly play?" she inquired. "Wolfgang heard about it. He says it is awfully silly." Magda replied: "He could hardly tell you anything else, since you are not acting in it." And Diederich declared: "That is just his way of excusing himself because, on his account, you are not invited to Wulckow's." Guste gave a contemptuous laugh. "We can do without the Wulckows, but we are going to the Club dance." Diederich asked: "Don't you think it would be better to wait until people have forgotten the trial?" He looked at her sympathetically. "Dear Fräulein Guste, we are old friends. You will allow me to warn you that your relations with the Bucks are not exactly a help to you in society just now." Guste's eyes flinched and it was evident that she herself had already arrived at the same conclusion. "Thank heaven," said Magda, "my Kienast is not like that." To which Emma retorted: "But Herr Buck is more interesting. I cried at his speech the other day, it was like being in the theatre."—"Why, of course!" cried Guste, taking courage. "Only yesterday he made me a present of this bag." She held up the gilt bag, at which Emma and Magda had been glancing for some time. Magda said snappishly: "I suppose he made a lot out of that brief. Kienast and I believe in economy." But Guste had had her revenge. "Well, I won't disturb you any longer," she concluded.

Diederich accompanied her downstairs. "I'll see you home, if you are good," he said, "but I must first look in at the factory. They will be breaking off work in a moment."— "But I can go with you," suggested Guste. In order to impress her he led the way to the big paper machine. "I am sure you have never seen anything like that before." He began self-importantly to explain to her the system of tanks, cutters and cylinders, through which the material passed the whole length of the room, first wet, then drier and drier, until at the end of the machine great rolls of finished paper came out. Guste shook her head. "What an idea! And the noise it makes! And the heat here!" Not yet satisfied with the effect he was making, Diederich found an excuse to thunder at the workers, and when Napoleon Fischer came up, he got all the blame.

Both shouted to drown the noise of the machine and Guste could not understand a word. But Diederich's secret fear saw beneath that straggly beard the peculiar grin which was a reminder of Fischer's complicity in the affair of the Double Cylinder, and was an open defiance of all authority. The more violent Diederich became the quieter was the other. That quietness was rebellious! Trembling and fuming Diederich opened the door of the packing-room and allowed Guste to enter. "That fellow is a Social Democrat!" he declared. "A chap like that is capable of setting fire to this place. But I' will not dismiss him, just for that reason! We'll see who is the stronger. I'll attend to the Social Democrats!" Guste gazed at him admiringly, as he continued: "I am sure you would never have guessed what dangerous posts people like myself must hold. Fearless and true is my motto. You see how I am defending our most sacred national possessions just like the Emperor. That requires more courage than making fine speeches in court."

Guste admitted it and her expression became thoughtful. "It is cooler here," she remarked, "after coming out of that inferno next door. The women in here should consider themselves lucky." "They?" queried Diederich. "They couldn't be better off!" He led Guste up to the table. One of the women was sorting the sheets, another checked them, and a third counted them up to five hundred. It was all done with incredible speed. The sheets flew one after another uninterruptedly, as if of their own accord, and without resisting the busy hands, which seemed to merge into the endless stream of paper that passed over them. Hands and arms, the woman herself, eyes and brain and heart. All that had come into being and lived so that the sheets might fly. . . .

Guste yawned; while Diederich explained the culpable negligence of the women who were working together. He was about to intervene because they passed a sheet from which the corner was torn, when Guste said rather spitefully: "You needn't imagine that Käthchen Zillich cares particularly for you . . . at least no more than for certain other people," she added. And her only reply to his bewildered question as to what she meant was to give a meaning smile. "But you must tell me," he repeated. Whereupon Guste assumed a most friendly air. "I am speaking only for your own good. I suppose you haven't noticed anything? For instance, with Herr

Jadassohn? But that's the sort of girl Käthchen Zillich is."
Here Guste laughed loudly, Diederich looked so flabbergasted.
She moved on and he followed her. "With Jadassohn?" he
asked anxiously. Then the noise of the machines stopped, the
bell rang to cease work, and the employés were already disappearing across the yard. Diederich shrugged his shoulders.
"What Fräulein Zillich does leaves me cold," he said. "At
most I am sorry for the old pastor, if that's the sort of person
she is. Are you quite sure of it?" Guste looked away. "You
can find that out for yourself!" Whereat Diederich felt flattered, and smiled.

"Leave the gas on," he shouted to the machinist, who was
passing. "I'll turn it off myself." The rag room just happened to be wide open to let the workers out. "Oh!" cried
Guste, "how romantic it looks in there." Back there in the
shadow she had caught a glimpse of grey mounds splashed
with many bright patches, and above these what seemed to be
a forest of branches. "Ah," she said, as she drew nearer, "it
is so dark here I thought . . .—But they are only heaps of
rags and hot water pipes. . . ." She made a grimace. Diederich drove off the women who were resting on the sacks, in spite
of orders. Several were knitting, although they had hardly
ceased work. Others were eating. "No doubt you find this
very comfortable!" he snorted. "Cadging heat at my expense!" They got up slowly, in silence, without a sign of
resistance, and passing the strange lady, at whom they all
turned to look curiously, they clattered out in their men's
boots, heavy as a herd of cattle and enveloped in the odour
in which they lived. Diederich kept a sharp watch on each
of them until they were outside. "Fischer!" he suddenly
shouted, "what has that fat one under her skirts?" With his
ambiguous grin the machinist answered. "That's only because
she is expecting a certain event." Whereupon Diederich turned
away dissatisfied and explained to Guste. "I thought I had
caught one of them. They steal rags, you know, to make chil-

dren's clothes." And when Guste turned up her nose: "It's too good for working-class brats."

With the tips of her glove Guste lifted one of the pieces from the floor. Immediately Diederich seized her wrist and kissed her hand greedily at the opening in her glove. She gave a frightened look round. "Oh, I see, they are all gone." She laughed confidently. "I guessed what you had still to do in the factory." Diederich looked at her defiantly. "Well, and what about yourself? Why did you come here at all to-day? You must have come to the conclusion that I was not after all, such an impossible person. Of course, your Wolf-gang—it is not everybody who can make such an ass of him-self as he did in court the other day." To which Guste re-torted indignantly: "Just you keep your mouth shut. You will never be half the man he is." But her eyes spoke differ-ently, as Diederich noticed. He laughed excitedly. "How anxious he is to have you! Do you know how he regards you? As the pot in which his meal is cooking and which I am to keep stirred for him!" Guste could have annihilated him. "You're a liar!" she said. But Diederich felt in good form. "All that worries him is that there is not enough in the pot. At first, of course, he also believed you had come into a million. But you can't get a man of that type for fifty thousand marks." Then Guste's rage boiled over. She looked so dangerous that Diederich shrank back. "Fifty thousand!. Are you crazy? Why must I listen to such talk? I, who have three hundred and fifty thousand in the bank in gilt edged securities. Fifty thousand! Whoever insults me by telling such stories around is open to an action for libel!" She had tears in her eyes, and Diederich stammered apologetically: "Don't mind such things," and Guste used her handkerchief. "Wolfgang knows exactly how I am situated. But you be-lieved the lie yourself. You had the impertinence to believe it," she cried. Her rosy cushions of fat quivered with rage, and her little snub nose had turned quite pale. He recovered his presence of mind. "That shows you that, even without money, I like you," he said insinuatingly. She bit her lips. "Who knows," she said, looking at him from under her eyelashes, pouting and uncertain. "Even fifty thousand is a lot of money for people like you."

Diederich tried to persuade himself that he was getting on with Guste, but his progress was admittedly slow. The events connected with the trial had made their impression, but that was not enough. Also, he heard nothing more from Wulckow. After the momentous action of the Governor at the Veterans' Association Diederich confidently expected further developments, an approach, a mark of friendship, he did not know exactly what. Perhaps it would happen at the Harmony Club ball. Otherwise, why had his sisters been given parts in the play of the Governor's wife? But it was all hanging fire too long for one of Diederich's active temper. It was a time of stress and unrest. He overflowed with hopes, plans and prospects. As each day came round he wanted to seize everything at one stroke. And at the end of each day he found himself empty-handed. Diederich was seized by a desire for movement. Several times he did not turn up at his *Stammtisch*, but went out walking aimlessly in the country, a thing he never did. He turned his back· on the centre of the town, tramped with energetic steps to the end of the empty Meisestrasse in the evenings, covered the whole length of Gäbbelchenstrasse, with its suburban inns, where drivers were yoking or unyoking their carts, and passed in front of the jail. Up there under the guard of a soldier and a barred window, sat Herr Lauer, who had never dreamt this would happen to him. "Pride goes before a fall," Diederich reflected. "As a man sows, so shall he reap." And although he was no stranger to the events which had brought the manufacturer to jail, Lauer now appeared to him as an uncanny creature, bearing the mark of

Cain. Once he fancied he saw a figure in the prison yard. It was dark at the time, but perhaps . . . ? A shudder ran through Diederich and he hurried away.

Beyond the city gate lay the country road to the hill on which stood Schweinichen Castle, where once upon a time little Diederich had shared with Frau Hessling the delightful thrill of the Castle ghost. That childishness was now far behind him. Now he preferred every time to turn sharply, on the other side of the gate, into the road leading to Gausenfeld. He had not intended to do so, and he hesitated, for he would not like any one to have caught him on this road. But he could not resist. The big paper factory drew him like a forbidden paradise. He simply had to go a few steps nearer to it, go round it, peep over the walls. . . . One evening Diederich was disturbed in this occupation by voices which were quite close in the dark. He had barely time to cower down in the ditch. While the people, probably employés of the factory who had stayed late, were passing his hiding place, Diederich closed his eyes, partly out of fear and partly because it seemed to him their covetous gleam might have betrayed him.

His heart was still beating when he returned to the city gate, and he looked round for a glass of beer. Right in the corner of the gateway stood the "Green Angel," one of the lowest inns, crooked with age, dirty and badly lighted. Just at that moment a woman's figure disappeared into the arched entrance. Seized with a desire for adventure Diederich hastened after her. As she passed the red light of a stable lantern she tried to hide her face, which was already veiled, with her muff. But Diederich had recognized her. "Good evening, Fräulein Zillich!"—"Good evening, Dr. Hessling." There they both stood with their mouths open. Käthchen Zillich was the first to speak, and she murmured something about children who lived in the house, and whom she was to take to her father's Sunday-school. Diederich began to talk, but she continued to chatter, faster and faster. No, as a matter of fact the children did not live there, but their parents frequented this bar, and they were not to know anything about the Sunday-school, for they were Social Democrats. . . . She lost her head, and Diederich, who had only thought at first of his own guilty conscience, began to realise that Käthchen was in an even more suspicious position. He did not therefore, trouble to explain his presence in the "Green Angel." He simply proposed that they should wait for the children in the coffee room. Käthchen nervously refused to take anything, but out of a sense of his own powerfulness Diederich ordered beer for her also. "Your health!" he said, and his ironical look was a reminder that they had almost become engaged at their last meeting in the comfortable sitting-room of the manse. Beneath her veil Käthchen turned red and pale and spilled her beer. Every now and then she fluttered up helplessly from her chair and tried to go, but Diederich had shoved her into the corner behind the table and spread himself out in front of her. "The children should be here any moment," he said amiably. Instead it was Jadassohn who came. He entered suddenly and stood as if he had been struck dumb. The two others did not move either. "Oh, I see!" thought Diederich. Jadassohn seemed to come to a similar conclusion. Neither of the gentlemen spoke a word. Käthchen began again about children and Sunday-school. Her voice was beseeching and she was almost in tears. Jadassohn listened to her impatiently, and even remarked that some tales were too involved for him—and he gave Diederich an inquisitorial glance.

"After all," Diederich interposed, "it's very simple. Fräulein Zillich is looking for children here and we two are going to help her." "Whether she will get one is another matter," added Jadassohn smartly. "And also, who shall assist me," retorted Käthchen.

The gentlemen set down their glasses in front of them. Käthchen had stopped crying and, throwing back her veil, she looked from one to the other, with remarkably bright eyes.

An open, frank tone had crept into her voice. "Well, now that you are both here," she said by way of explanation, as she took a cigarette from Jadassohn's case. Then she suddenly drank off the glass of cognac which was in front of Diederich. Now it was the latter's turn to lose his head. This other side of Käthchen did not seem unfamiliar to Jadassohn. The two of them continued to exchange double meaning witticisms until Diederich grew indignant with Käthchen. "This time I am seeing you in your true colours anyway!" he cried, striking the table. Käthchen at once resumed her most ladylike expression. "I do not understand what you mean, Dr. Hessling." Jadassohn continued: "I presume you do not intend any insinuation against the lady's honour!" Diederich stammered: "I only meant that I like Fräulein Zillich much better when she is like this." He rolled his eyes helplessly. "Recently, when we nearly became engaged, she did not appeal to me half so much." Then Käthchen laughed uproariously, with all her heart, in a way which Diederich had also never seen before. He began to feel warm and joined in her mirth, Jadassohn following, and all three rocked in the chairs with laughter and called for more cognac.

"Well, now I must be off," said Käthchen, "otherwise papa will get home before me. He has been paying sick calls, and then he always distributes pictures like these." She pulled two coloured pictures out of her leather bag. "There are some for you." Jadassohn received Magdalene the sinner, and Diederich the lamb with the shepherd. He was not satisfied. "I also want a sinful woman." Käthchen searched but could not find another. "You'll have to be content with a sheep," she decided, and they set off, Käthchen in the middle hanging on their arms. Making wide curves, all three staggered jerkily along the dimly lighted street, singing a hymn which Käthchen had started. When they came to a corner she said she would have to hurry and disappeared down a side street. "Good-bye, sheep!" she shouted to Diederich, who struggled in vain to follow her. Jadassohn held him tight, and suddenly began in authoritative tones to convince Diederich that this had all been a little fun and mere chance. "I wish to make it perfectly clear that there is absolutely no ground for misunderstanding."

"I had no idea of drawing improper conclusions," said Diederich. "And if I," continued Jadassohn, "had the privilege of being considered by the Zillich family in the light of a more intimate relationship, this accidental occurrence would not hold me back. I owe it to my sense of honour to tell you this."

Diederich replied: "I thoroughly appreciate the correctness of your conduct." Then the gentlemen clicked their heels together, shook hands and parted.

Käthchen and Jadassohn had exchanged a sign on parting, and Diederich was certain they would meet soon again at the "Green Angel." He loosened his overcoat and a feeling of pride filled him because he had stumbled into a dubious affair and had got out of it with all the rules of his code intact. He felt a certain respect and sympathy for Jadassohn. He too would have acted similarly. Men understood one another. But what a woman! That other side of Käthchen, the pastor's daughter whose face had unsuspectedly revealed the loose woman! This sly double-dealer, so remote from the simple integrity which lay at the root of his own character! He shuddered as if he had looked into an abyss. He buttoned up his coat again. He realised that outside the bourgeois world there were others beside that in which Herr Lauer now lived. He was fuming as he sat down to supper. His voice was so threatening that the three women maintained silence. Frau Hessling plucked up courage. "Don't you like your supper, my dear child?" Instead of answering Diederich began to browbeat his sisters. "I forbid you to have anything more to do with Käthchen Zillich!" As they stared at him, he blushed and exclaimed angrily: "She is an abandoned woman!" But they merely pursed their lips and did not seem particularly astonished by the fearful allusions into which he clumsily launched. "I suppose you are talking about Jadassohn?" Magda asked finally, with the utmost calm. Diederich started. So they were initiated and were in connivance; all the women probably. Guste Daimchen, too! She had once begun about it. He had to wipe the perspiration from his brow. Magda said: "If you by any chance had serious intentions with Käthchen, you never questioned us." At this Diederich, to keep himself in countenance, banged the table so that they all screamed. He forbade such insinuations, he shouted. He hoped that there were still a few decent girls left. Frau Hessling pleaded, trembling: "You have only to look at your own sisters, my dear son." And Diederich really looked at them and glared. For the first time he thought, not without fear, of what these female creatures, who were his sisters, might have been up to during their lives. . . . "Confound it all," he decided, pulling himself up stiffly, "the reins will simply have to be held more tightly over you. When I marry, my wife will know the reason why!" As the girls smiled at one another, he gave a start, for he remembered Guste Daimchen; were they thinking also of Guste when they smiled? He could trust nobody. He could see Guste in front of him, with her blonde white hair and plump, rosy cheeks. Her fleshy lips were parted and she was sticking out her tongue at him. That was what Käthchen Zillich had done a while back, when she shouted, "Good-bye, sheep!" And Guste, who was very similar to her in type, would have looked just like that, if she were half drunk and had her tongue out!

Magda was just saying: "Käthchen is awfully silly, but it is understandable when you have waited so long for a man and none comes." Emma at once interposed. "To whom do you refer, please? If Käthchen had been content with any Kienast she would also not have to wait any more."

Conscious that she had the facts on her side Magda did not reply, but her breast heaved.

"In any case," said Emma, rising and throwing her napkin down, "how can you believe so easily what the men say about Käthchen? It is disgusting. Are we all to remain defenceless against their gossip?" In high dudgeon she sat down in a corner and began to read. Magda simply shrugged her shoulders, while Diederich sought anxiously and in vain for a transition which would enable him to ask if Guste Daimchen also . . . ? With such a long engagement? "There are situations," he declared, "where it is no longer just gossip." Then Emma flung away her book.

"Well, what about it? Käthchen does what she thinks fit. We girls have just as much right as you men to live our own lives! You may consider yourselves lucky if you can get us at all afterwards!"

Diederich stood up. "I will not listen to such talk in my house," he said seriously, and he glared at Magda until she stopped laughing.

Frau Hessling brought him his cigar. "I know my little Diedel will never marry any one like that"—she stroked him consolingly. He replied with great emphasis: "Mother, I cannot imagine that a true German man ever did so."

She began to flatter him: "Oh, they are not all idealists, like my dear son. Many think more materially and with the money they take something else into the bargain, which makes people talk." Under his commanding glance she continued to chatter nervously. "For instance, Guste. God knows, he is dead now, and it can't make any difference to him, but at the time there was a great deal of talk." Now all three children looked at her inquiringly. "Yes, indeed," she said soberly, "that affair of Frau Daimchen and Herr Buck; Guste was born too soon."

After this statement Frau Hessling had to take refuge behind the screen in front of the stove, for the three of them pressed upon her at the same time. "This is startling news," cried Magda and Emma together. "How did it happen?" Diederich, in his turn, thundered against more of this women's tittle-tattle. "Well, we had to listen to your men's gossip," cried the girls, as they tried to shove him away from the screen. Wringing her hands the mother looked on at the struggle. "Children, I didn't say anything, only every one said so at the time, and Herr Buck also gave Frau Daimchen a present of her dowry."

"So that's the reason," said Magda. "That's the sort of rich uncles they have in the Daimchen family! That's where the gilt bags come from!"

Diederich defended Guste's inheritance. "It comes from Magdeburg!" "And the husband?" Emma asked. "Does he comes from Magdeburg, too?" Suddenly they were all silent and looked at each other as if they had been stunned. Then Emma went quietly back to the sofa and took up her book again. Magda began to clear the table. Diederich went up to the screen behind which Frau Hessling was hidden. "Now, mother, you do not mean to tell me that Wolfgang Buck is marrying his own sister." A tearful voice answered: "My dear child, I can't help it. I had long since forgotten the old story, and then it is not certain. No living soul knows anything about it." Raising her head from her book Emma interjected: "Old Herr Buck must know where he now gets the money for his son." And into the tablecloth which she was folding Magda said: "Strange things happen." Then Diederich raised his arms, as if to appeal to heaven. Just in time he suppressed the feeling of horror which threatened to overcome him. "Have I fallen into a den of thieves and murderers?" he asked in matter-of-fact tones, as he went stiffly towards the door. There he turned. "Of course, I cannot prevent you from hawking your remarkable wisdom about the town. So far as I am concerned, I declare that

I have nothing more to do with you. I'll put a notice to that effect in the papers!" He went out.

He avoided the Ratskeller, and at Klappsch's he reflected upon a world in which such horrors prevailed. The code of honour of his students' corps was obviously inadequate to such circumstances. Whoever wished to extract from the Bucks their shameful booty must not shrink from stern measures. "With mailed fist," he cried into his beer. As he clapped the lid for a fourth glass, it sounded like the rattle of swords. . . . After a while his stern demeanour relaxed; scruples presented themselves. His intervention would assuredly have the result that the whole town would point the finger of scorn at Guste Daimchen. No man of the slightest honour could then marry such a girl. Diederich's deepest feelings commanded him, his deeply grounded belief in manliness and idealism. What a shame! What a pity for Guste's three hundred and fifty thousand marks, which were now without a master and without an object. The opportunity would have been favourable to provide them with both. . . . Diederich rejected the thought with scorn. He was only doing his duty! A crime must be prevented. The woman would then see what her place was in the struggles of men. What did he care for any of these creatures who, for their part, as Diederich had learnt by experience, were capable of every treason. Only a fifth glass was now required and he had reached a decision.

On the evening of the following day all the looking-glasses in the house had been brought into the sitting-room. Emma, Magda and Inge Tietz were twisting and turning in front of them until they had pains in their necks. Then they sat down nervously on the edge of a chair. "Good Heavens, isn't it time to go!" But Diederich was determined not to arrive any earlier than he did at Lauer's trial. The impression one made went to the devil when one arrived too early. When they finally started Inge Tietz apologised again to Frau Hessling for taking her place in the carriage. Once more Frau Hessling repeated: "Why, it's a pleasure. An old woman like me is not equal to these affairs. Have a good time, children!" With tears in her eyes she embraced her daughters, who repelled her coldly. They knew that all their mother was afraid of was that the only subject of conversation would be the horrible, scandalous story for which she herself was responsible.

In the carriage Inge at once began again to talk about it. "What about the Bucks and the Daimchens? I wonder if they will really have the infernal cheek to show up?" Magda remarked quietly. "They must come, otherwise they would be admitting that it is true."—"Well, suppose it is," said Emma. "It is their own affair. I am not going to get excited about it."—"Nor I," added Diederich. "The first I heard of it was from you to-night, Fräulein Tietz."

At this Fräulein Tietz lost her temper. The scandal could not be regarded in this easy fashion. Did he mean to imply that she had invented the whole story? "The thing has been notorious so long that their own servants know about it." —"I see," said Diederich, "servants' gossip," while he returned the nudge which Magda gave him with her knee. Then they had to get out and go down the steps which connected the new section of Kaiser Wilhelmstrasse with the lower level of the old Riekestrasse. Diederich cursed, for it was beginning to rain and their dancing shoes were getting wet. In front of the place where the ball was being held working people had gathered and they indulged in hostile comment. Why hadn't this old rubbish heap been torn down when that quarter of the town had been levelled up. The historical Concert Hall might have been preserved—as if the town could not afford to build a modern first-class entertainment hall in a central position. In this old shanty everything was musty.

Right at the entrance the ladies always giggled because there was a statue of Friendship clothed in nothing more substantial than a wig. "Be careful," said Diederich on the stairs, "or we'll fall through." The two slender curves of the stairway stretched out like the skinny arms of an old man. The reddish brown of the woodwork had faded, but at the top, where they met, there smiled from the bannisters the white marble face of the bewigged mayor, who had left all this to the city, and whose name had been Buck. Diederich sullenly ignored him, as he passed.

In the long mirrored gallery all was quiet. A solitary lady was standing in the background and seemed to be peeping into the entertainment hall through a cleft in the door. Suddenly the girls were seized with horror: the play had begun! Magda ran along the gallery and burst into tears. Then the lady turned round and put her finger to her lips. It was Frau von Wulckow, the authoress. She smiled excitedly and whispered: "It's going splendidly. They like my play. You are just in time, Fräulein Hessling; go now and change your clothes." Of course! Emma and Magda did not appear until the second act. Diederich had also lost his head. While his sisters hurried off through the ante-rooms with Inge Tietz, who was to help them, he introduced himself to the Governor's wife and stood there not knowing what to do. "You can't go in now," she said, "it would disturb people." Diederich stammered his apologies and then rolled his eyes, and thus caught a glimpse of his mysteriously pale reflection among the gaudy rows of half-dulled mirrors. The tender yellow varnish of the walls played freakish tricks and the colours of flowers and faces were extinguished in the panels. . . . Frau von Wulckow shut a little door, through which somebody seemed to enter, a shepherdess with her beribboned staff.

She shut the door very carefully, so that the performance should not be disturbed, but a little cloud of dust arose, as if it was powder from the hair of the painted shepherdess.

"This house is so romantic," whispered Frau von Wulckow. "Don't you think so, Dr. Hessling? When one looks at oneself in the mirror here, one fancies one is wearing a hoop-petticoat." At this Diederich, more and more bewildered, looked at her evening gown. Her bare shoulders were hollow and rather stooped, her hair was extremely fair and she carried a pince-nez.

"You fit these surroundings perfectly, Madame . . . Countess," he corrected, and he was rewarded with a smile for this bold flattery. Not every one would have reminded Frau von Wulckow so aptly that she was born Countess Züsewitz!

"As a matter of fact," she said, "it is hard to believe that in its time this home was not built for distinguished society, instead of for the good burghers of Netzig." She smiled reflectively. "But to-day, Countess, you can doubtless feel quite at home here." "I am sure you have a feeling for the beautiful," Frau von Wulckow hazarded, and as Diederich admitted it, she declared he must not miss the first act altogether, but must look through the cleft in the door. For some time she had been showing obvious signs of impatience, and with her fan she pointed in the direction of the stage. "Major Kunze will go off in a moment. He is not very good, but it can't be helped, he is on the Club committee, and was the first to point out to these people the artistic significance of my work." While Diederich had no trouble in recognising the major, who had not changed his appearance in the least, the authoress with lightning fluency gave him a synopsis of what had gone before. The young peasant girl, with whom Kunze was speaking, was his natural daughter, that is, the daughter of a Count, and for that reason the play was called "The Secret Countess." As gruff as ever, he was just explaining the circumstances to her. He was also telling her of his intention to marry her to a poor cousin and leave her one-half of his possessions. On that account, after he had gone, there was great rejoicing on the part of the girl and her foster-mother, the honest herdsman's wife.

"Who is that dreadful person?" asked Diederich, without thinking. Frau Von Wulckow looked astonished.

"That's the comic female lead from the State Theatre. We had nobody else who could play the part, but my niece rather likes acting with her." Diederich started in horror, for it was the niece he had described as a dreadful person. "Your niece is absolutely charming," he hastened to assure her and smiled delightedly at the fat, red face, which seemed to rest directly on the shoulders—and they were Wulckow's shoulders! "And she has plenty of talent, too," he added for safety. Frau von Wulckow whispered: "Just watch"—and there came Jadassohn out from the wings. What a surprise. His clothes were freshly pressed and with his fashionably cut morning coat he wore an immense stock, in which a red stone of imposing dimensions glittered. But however bright its glow, Jadassohn's ears glowed even more brightly. As his head was closely cropped and very flat, his ears stood out and illuminated his grandeur like two lamps. He swung his yellow gloved hands about as if he were pleading for many years' imprisonment. As a matter of fact, he was saying the most terrible things to the niece, who seemed thunder-struck, and to the comic old lady who was yelling. . . . Frau von Wulckow whispered: "He is a bad character." "I should say he is," said Diederich with conviction. "Do you know my play?" "Oh, I see. No. But I can guess what he wants to do." The situation was that Jadassohn, who was the son and heir of the old Count Kunze, had been eavesdropping, and was not at all disposed to share with the niece the possessions with which God had endowed him. He imperatively commanded her to clear out, otherwise he would have her arrested as a fraudulent legatee and remove her from Kunze's guardianship.

"What a cad," said Diederich. "After all, she is his sister." The author explained to him:

"That is true, but, on the other hand, he is right in wanting to entail the estates. He is working for the good of the whole family, even though the individual should suffer. Of course, that is tragic for the secret countess."

"When you look at it properly—" Diederich was delighted. This aristocratic standpoint suited him perfectly, when he felt disinclined to give Magda a share in the business on her marriage.

"Countess, your play is excellent," he said, with deep conviction. But just then Frau von Wulckow anxiously seized his arm. There was a noise amongst the audience; chairs were scraped and people were sniggering and blowing their noses. "He is overdoing it," stormed the authoress. "I always told him so."

Jadassohn was really acting outrageously. He had cornered the niece, together with the comic lady, behind a table, and filled the whole stage with noisy demonstrations of his aristocratic personality. The more hostile the audience became, the more aggressively did he realise his part on the stage. Now they were actually hissing. Several people had even turned towards the door behind which Frau von Wulckow was trembling, and were hissing. Perhaps it was only because the door was squeaking—but the authoress drew back, lost her glasses, and in helpless horror clawed the air, until Diederich restored them to her. He tried to console her. "This doesn't matter. Jadassohn goes off very soon, doesn't he?" He was listening through the closed door. "Yes, thank Heaven!" she cried, while her teeth chattered. "Now he has finished. Now my niece flees with the comic old lady and then Kunze returns, you know, with the lieutenant."

"Is there a lieutenant in the play also?" asked Diederich,

obviously impressed. "Yes, that is to say, he is still at college; he is the son of Judge Sprezius. He is the poor relation, you know, whom the old Count wishes his daughter to marry. He promises the old man that he will search the whole world for the secret Countess."

"Very naturally," said Diederich. "It is in his own interest to do so."

"You will see, he is a noble character."

"But Jadassohn, Countess. If you will allow me to say so, you should not have given him a part," said Diederich reproachfully and with secret satisfaction. "If only on account of his ears."

Frau von Wulckow felt crushed, as she replied: "I did not think that they would have such an effect on the stage. Do you think it will be a failure?"

"Countess!" Diederich laid his hand on his heart. "A play like 'The Secret Countess' cannot be spoiled so easily! Isn't that so? In the theatre it is artistic significance that counts."

"Certainly. But it must be admitted a pair of ears like that have a great deal of influence"—Diederich looked thoughtful.

Frau von Wulckow cried pleadingly. "The second act is a great deal better. The scene takes place in the house of an upstart manufacturer, where the secret countess is engaged as housemaid. They have a music-teacher, a vulgar person, who has even kissed one of the daughters, and he now proposes to the Countess, but she naturally repulses him. A music-teacher! How could she?"

Diederich agreed that it was out of the question.

"But now you will see how tragic it becomes. The daughter who allowed the music-teacher to kiss her becomes engaged to a lieutenant at a dance, and when the lieutenant comes to the house, it is the same lieutenant who—"

"Good Heavens, Countess!" Diederich stretched out his

hands in self-defence, quite excited by so many complications. "How do you think of such things?"

The authoress smiled passionately. "Yes, it is that which is most interesting. Afterwards one doesn't know how it happens. It is worked out so mysteriously in one's mind! Sometimes I think I must have inherited the gift."

"Have you so many authors in your respected family?"

"Not exactly. But if my great ancestor had not won the battle of Kröchenwerda, who knows if I should have written 'The Secret Countess'? After all, it is always a question of birth."

Diederich bowed awkwardly when he heard the name of the battle and did not dare to continue the subject.

"Now the curtain ought to fall any moment," said Frau von Wulckow. "Do you hear anything?"

He could hear nothing.—The authoress alone was oblivious of the door and the walls. "Now the lieutenant is vowing eternal fidelity to the distant Countess," she whispered. "Now"—and all the blood rushed to her face. Immediately it flowed back with a rush. People were applauding, not violently but still it was applause. The door was opened from inside. In the background the curtain had risen again, and when young Sprezius and the Wulckows' niece came forward, the applause was more animated. Suddenly Jadassohn hastened out from the wings, planted himself in front of the pair and looked as if he would take their success for himself. At this the audience hissed. Frau von Wulckow turned away indignantly. To Mayor Scheffelweis's mother-in-law and to Frau Harnisch, who were congratulating her, she declared: "Herr Jadassohn is impossible as Public Prosecutor. I shall tell my husband so."

The phrase was at once repeated by the ladies and made a great hit. The gallery of mirrors was suddenly filled with groups adversely criticising Jadassohn's ears. "The play is well written, but Jadassohn's ears. . . ." But when it became known that he would not appear in the second act, people were disappointed. Wolfgang Buck, with Guste Daimchen, came up to Diederich. "Have you heard the latest?" he asked. "Jadassohn is to issue a writ and confiscate his ears." Diederich answered coldly: "I cannot see any joke in another's misfortune," and as he said this he carefully watched the glances which Buck and his companion exchanged. Every one brightened up at the sight of this couple. Jadassohn was forgotten. From the doorway the high-pitched voice of Professor Kühnchen was heard above the din saying something that sounded like "infernal outrage." When Frau Zillich laid her hand entreatingly upon his arm he turned in their direction, and could be heard distinctly: "It is an absolute outrage!"

Guste looked round and her eyes narrowed. "There they are talking about it also," she said mysteriously.

"About what?" stammered Diederich.

"Oh, we know all about that. And I also know who began it." Diederich broke into a perspiration. "What on earth is wrong with you?" asked Guste. Buck who was eyeing the refreshment room through a side-door, said calmly:

"Hessling is a cautious politician; he does not like to hear that, while the Mayor is a devoted husband, he cannot, at the same time, refuse his mother-in-law anything."

Diederich blushed deeply. "That is a mean thing to say! How can you be such a cad?"

Guste giggled violently, but Buck remained unmoved. "In the first place, it appears to be a fact that Her Ladyship caught the two of them by surprise and told a friend about it. But in any case, it was self-evident."

Guste remarked: "Well, Dr. Hessling, you would never have guessed such a thing, of course." As she said this she gave her fiancé a tender smile. Diederich looked daggers. "Huh," he said severely. "Anyway, I know enough now." And he turned on his heels. So they themselves were inventing scan-

dals, and about the Mayor, into the bargain! Diederich felt
he could hold his head high. He made for Kühnchen's group,
which was steering towards the refreshment room, leaving behind a wake of moral indignation. The Mayor's mother-in-
law, purple in the face, swore that "this crew" would in future see her house only from the outside. Several of the
ladies seconded the resolution, in spite of the defection of
Frau Cohn, who, in the absence of further information, doubted
the whole story, because a moral lapse of that kind by a
tried and true old Liberal like Herr Buck seemed inconceiv-
able. Professor Kühnchen was rather of the opinion that
morality was being threatened by exaggerated radicalism.
Even Dr. Heuteufel, although he had instituted the freethought
Sunday festivals, remarked that old Buck had never lacked
a sense of family, of nepotism, he might say. "You can all
easily recall cases in point. That he should now try to marry
his illegitimate with his legitimate offspring, in order to keep
the money in the family, I should diagnose medically as the
senile manifestation of a natural tendency hitherto repressed."
At this the ladies looked shocked and the Pastor's wife sent
Käthchen to the cloak-room to fetch her handkerchief.

On her way Käthchen passed Guste Daimchen, but she
hung down her head and did not salute her. Guste seemed
crushed. In the refreshment room people noticed this and
expressions of disapproval were mixed with sympathy. Guste
was now to learn what it meant to defy public morality. It
might have been remembered in her favour that she perhaps
had been deceived and influenced for evil. But Frau Daimchen knew the exact circumstances and she was warned! The
Mayor's mother-in-law related her visit to Guste's mother,
and her vain efforts, by pointed allusion, to wring a confession from the hardened old lady, whose youthful dream was
doubtless realised by this legitimate connection with the Buck
family!

"Well, but what about Herr Buck, barrister-at-law?"

screamed Kühnchen. As a matter of fact, who did he think
believed that he was not fully acquainted with this new scandal connected with his family? Was he not aware of the
offences of the Lauer household? And yet he did not hesitate
to wash the dirty linen of his sister and his brother-in-law
in open court, simply in order to get talked about. Dr. Heuteufel, who was still driven to try and justify belatedly his
own attitude during the trial, declared: "That man is no ad-
vocate, he is simply a comedian!" When Diederich raised
the point that Buck, after all, had definite, if arguable, views
in politics and morals he was told: "You, Dr. Hessling, are his
friend. That you should defend him is to your credit, but
you cannot teach us." Whereupon Diederich retired, with
a worried look, but not without a glance at the editor, Rothgroschen, who was modestly chewing a ham sandwich and
taking everything in.

All of a sudden there was dead silence, for in the room
near the stage old Herr Buck could be seen surrounded by a
group of young girls. Apparently he was explaining the
paintings on the walls, the life of former times, whose faded
gaiety enveloped the whole room; and the area of the city
as it used to be, with meadows and gardens now no more, and
all the people who once were the noisy masters of this festive
house, and were now banished into the depths of Beyond by
the generation which was at this moment so clamorous. . . .
Now it seemed as if the old man and the girls were imitating
the figures. Just above them was a picture of the city gate,
and a gentleman in his wig and chain of office was coming out,
the same who stood in marble at the head of the stairs. In
the lovely wood full of flowers, which had stood where the
Gausenfeld paper factory now was, bright children were dancing towards him, throwing a wreath about him, with which
they tried to turn him round. The reflection of rosy little
clouds fell upon his happy face. Just so happily old Buck
was smiling at that moment, as he let himself be dragged

hither and thither by the girls, who had encircled him like
a living wreath. His freedom from care was incomprehensible, and was a positive irritation. Had he stifled his conscience to such a degree that his illegitimate daughter . . .
"*Our* daughters are not illegitimate children," said Frau Cohn.
"My Sidonie arm in arm with Guste Daimchen!" . . . Buck
and his young friends did not notice that they had reached
the end of an empty space. In the forefront a hostile public
formed a wall. Eyes were gleaming and anger rose. "The
family has been on top far too long! One is now safe in jail.
The turn of number two will soon come!" Two ladies impetuously broke out of the crowd, made a run and crossed the
empty space. The wife of Councillor Harnisch, rolling along
in her red satin train, met Frau Cohn, in yellow, exactly at
their common goal. With the same gesture the one seized
her Sidonie and the other her Meta, and what satisfaction when
they returned to their starting point! "I nearly fainted," said
Frau Zillich, when Käthchen fortunately turned up. Good
humour was restored and people joked about the old sinner,
comparing him with the Count in Frau von Wulckow's play.
It is true, Guste was not a secret Countess; but one could
sympathise with such conditions in a story, in order to be
agreeable to the wife of the Governor. There the conditions
were tolerable, for the Countess was only going to marry her
cousin, whereas Guste . . . !

Old Buck looked puzzled when he became aware that there
was nobody near him except his prospective daughter-in-law
and one of his nieces. Indeed, he was obviously embarrassed
by the curious glances which were cast at him in his isolation. This was noticed and commented upon and even Diederich began to wonder if there wasn't, after all, some truth
in Frau Hessling's story of the scandal. He himself had become frightened, since he saw the phantom, which he had sent
forth into the world, taking tangible shape and becoming ever
more threatening. This time it was not a mere nobody like

Lauer. It was old Herr Buck, the most honourable figure of
Diederich's childhood, the great man of the town, and the
personification of its civic virtues—the man who had been
condemned to death in Forty-Eight! In his own heart Diederich felt a revulsion against what he had begun. Besides,
it was folly; it would take more than that to smash the old
man. But if it ever came out who had started it, then Diederich would have to be prepared to see every one turn against
him. . . . At all events, he had aimed a stroke and it had not
missed. Now it was not only the family which was shaky
and hung about the old man like a weight: the brother on the
verge of bankruptcy, the son-in-law in jail, the daughter away
on a trip with her lover, and of the two sons, one degraded
to the level of a peasant, and the other suspect on account of
his life and his opinions. Now he himself was beginning to
shake, for the first time. Down with him so that Diederich
might rise! Nevertheless, Diederich was frightened to the
very marrow of his bones. He got up to inspect the ante-
rooms. He ran, for the bell was ringing for the second act.

Wulckow appeared in the doorway. He came up, his paunch
swinging from side to side, laid his black paw on the shoulder
of Dr. Scheffelweis and said in stentorian tones: "Well, my
little Mayor, all alone here? I suppose your town councillors
have thrown you out?" Dr. Scheffelweis answered with a
feeble laugh. But Diederich looked round anxiously at the
door of the large room, which was still open. He went up
in front of Wulckow, so that the latter could not be seen from
the other room, and whispered something in his ear, with the
result that the Governor turned away and adjusted his clothing.
Then he said to Diederich: " 'Pon my soul, you really are
very serviceable, Doctor." Diederich felt flattered and smiled.
"Your appreciation, Governor, makes me happy."

Wulckow graciously remarked: "No doubt there are a lot
of other things you can tell me. We must talk things over together some time." He thrust forward his face, freckled

and with high Slavic cheekbones, and stared at Diederich from the depths of his Mongolian eyes, which were full of warm-blooded, impish strength. He stared until Diederich became breathless from sheer nervousness. This result seemed to satisfy Wulckow. He brushed his beard in front of the mirror, but immediately pressed it down on his shirt front, because his head looked like a bull's. "Well, let's go! The fool show has begun, hasn't it?" With Diederich and the Mayor on either side he set out energetically to disturb the performance. Then a piping voice from the refreshment room was heard:

"Good Heavens, Otto dear!"

"Oh, there she is," growled Wulckow, as he went to meet his wife. "I might have guessed. When it comes to the point she is afraid. More dash, my dear Frieda!"

"Gracious, Otto darling, I am so horribly frightened." Turning to the two other gentlemen, she chatted rapidly, although her teeth were chattering. "I know one ought to go into the battle with a more joyful heart."

"Especially," said Diederich with ready tact, "when it is already won," and he bowed politely. Frau von Wulckow tapped him with her fan.

"Dr. Hessling kept me company out here during the first act. He has feeling for the Beautiful, and even gives one useful hints."

"I have noticed that myself," said Wulckow, while Diederich kept bowing alternately to him and to his wife, overflowing with gratitude. "Why shouldn't we stay here near the supper-table?" the Governor asked.

"That was also my plan of campaign," confided Frau von Wulckow, "the more so as I have now discovered that there is a little door which opens into the large room. In this way we can enjoy the isolation from what is happening, which I need, and yet keep in touch with things."

"My little Mayor," said Wulckow, smacking his lips, "you

ought to get some of that lobster salad." He pulled Dr. Scheffelweis's ear, and added: "In that matter of the Labour Exchange, the town council has again cut a very poor figure."

The Mayor was eating obediently and listening obediently, while Diederich stood beside Frau von Wulckow and peeped out at the stage. There Magda Hessling was having a music lesson and the teacher, a black-haired virtuoso, was giving her passionate kisses, which she did not happen to resent particularly. "It's a good thing Kienast is not here," thought Diederich, but even on his own account he felt offended, and he remarked:

"Don't you think, Countess, that the music-teacher's acting is too realistic?"

The authoress answered coldly: "That was precisely my intention."

"I only meant . . ." Diederich stammered, and then he started, for Frau Hessling appeared in the doorway, or a lady who looked very like her. Emma also came, the couple were caught and were crying and screaming. Wulckow was obliged to raise his voice.

Dr. Scheffelweis tried to answer him, but Magda yelled that she had no intention of marrying the man, the servant was good enough for him. The authoress remarked: "She should say that in a much more vulgar way. They are only *parvenus.*"

Diederich smiled in agreement, although he was terribly humiliated by such a state of affairs in a home that was like his own. In his own mind he thought Emma was quite right, when she declared there must be no scandal, and sent for the servant. But when the latter appeared, hang it all, it was the secret Countess!

The Wulckows' niece addressed herself to the public, as the manufacturer's family was not supposed to hear.

"What! I, the daughter of a Count, am to marry a music-teacher? Far from me such a thought, even if they should promise me a trousseau. Others may debase themselves for money, but I know what I owe to my noble birth!"

At this there was applause. Frau Harnisch and Frau Tietz were observed wiping away the tears which the Countess's nobility of mind had provoked. But their tears flowed again when the niece said:

"But, alas, where shall I, as a servant, find one so well born as myself?"

"As an officer," said the lieutenant, "I cannot, my dear Magda, allow this girl to be badly treated, even if she is only a poor servant."

The lieutenant in the first act, the poor cousin, who was to marry the secret Countess, was Magda's fiancé! The audience was trembling with excitement. Even the authoress noticed it. "Inventiveness is one of my strongest points," she said to Diederich, who was absolutely flabbergasted. But Dr. Scheffelweis had no time to abandon himself to the emotions of the drama. He was defending himself against Wulckow.

The niece, on the other hand, was shouting to the public: "Surely he must see that I am a Countess, he who is sprung from the same noble line!"

"Oh, Countess," said Diederich, "now I really am curious to know if he will recognise the fact."

"Of course," replied the authoress. "They recognise each other because of their finer manners."

As a matter of fact, the lieutenant and the niece were exchanging glances, because Emma, Magda and Frau Hessling were eating cheese with a knife. Diederich was open-mouthed. The vulgar demeanour of the manufacturer's family evoked the greatest amusement in the audience. The Buck girls, Frau Cohn and Guste Daimchen were all delighted. Even Wulckow became interested. He licked the grease from his fingers and said:

"You're all right; they are laughing."

Then a laugh was heard of a different kind. It was quite

unrestrained and was obviously caused by some mishap. The authoress retreated precipitately behind the supper-table. She looked as if she would like to creep into the sideboard. "Gracious heavens," she whispered, "all is lost!" Her husband stood sternly at the door and said: "Come now, come now!" but even this could no longer check their mirth. Magda had said to the Countess: "Hurry up, now, you silly country lout, and see that the lieutenant gets his coffee." Another voice corrected, "tea," Madga repeated "coffee," the other insisted, and so did Magda. The public saw there was a misunderstanding between her and the prompter. Happily the lieutenant intervened, clicked his spurs and said: "I'll take both"—whereat the laughter became less confident. But the authoress was raging. "The public! It is and always will be a beast!" she snarled.

"My sister is a goose," said Diederich. "I shall tell her what I think of her afterwards."

Frau von Wulckow smiled deprecatingly. "The poor thing, she is doing her best. But the arrogance and impertinence of the crowd is really intolerable. Only a moment ago I had raised them to an enthusiasm for the ideal."

"Countess," said Diederich with conviction, "you are not only the one to have this bitter experience. It is the same everywhere in public life." He was thinking of the general exaltation at the time of his clash with the calumniator of His Majesty, and of the trials which he subsequently bore. "In the end the good cause triumphs," he said firmly.

"Isn't that so?" she agreed with a smile which seemed to pierce through the clouds. "The Good, the True, the Beautiful."

She held out her slender hand. "I believe, my friend, that we understand one another." Conscious of the occasion, Diederich boldly pressed it to his lips, and bowed. He placed his hand on his heart and declared from the depths of his soul: "You can trust me, Countess. . . ."

The curtain fell, the audience slowly emerged from its ecstasy, and expressed its feelings all the more deeply by applauding the servant and the lieutenant who, it was unfortunately evident, would have to bear still longer with the cruel fate of not being received at Court.

"It is really awful!" sighed Frau Harnisch and Frau Cohn. Meanwhile the Governor's wife was holding a reception in the mirrored gallery and receiving congratulations, while Diederich tried to work up the enthusiasm. Heuteufel, Cohn, Harnisch and several gentlemen made his task difficult, for they let it be understood, though cautiously, that they considered the whole thing piffle. Diederich had to give them hints about the absolutely first-rate third act, in order to shut them up. He dictated a detailed account of what the authoress had told him to Rothgroschen, who had to leave, as the paper was going to press. "If you write any nonsense, you damned penny-a-liner, I'll punch your head!" Rothgroschen thanked him and took his leave. Professor Kühnchen, who was listening, buttonholed Diederich and shrieked: "I say, old man, there's one thing you forgot to tell our gossip-monger." The editor, hearing himself mentioned, returned, and Kühnchen continued: "I mean that the magnificent invention of our honoured hostess has been anticipated, and from no less a person than Goethe in his 'Natürliche Tochter.' Now, that is the highest praise that can be given to the author!"

Diederich had his doubts about the appropriateness of Kühnchen's discovery, but deemed it unnecessary to state them. The little old man was already fighting his way through the throng, his hair streaming wildly, and he could be seen stopping in front of Frau von Wulckow and explaining to her the result of his researches into comparative literature. Such a fiasco as he experienced could not have been foreseen, even by Diederich. The authoress said in icy tones: "There must be some mistake in what you say, Professor. Is the 'Natürliche Tochter' by Goethe at all?" she asked, turning up her nose suspiciously. Kühnchen assured her it was, but in vain.

"In any case, you have read in the newspaper a novel by me, 'The Beloved Home,' and that is what I have now dramatised. My creations are all original work. Gentlemen"—she looked around her—"you will deny any malicious rumours to the contrary."

Thereupon Kühnchen was dismissed, and withdrew gasping. In a tone of condescending sympathy Diederich reminded him of Rothgroschen, who had gone off with his dangerous information, and Kühnchen tore after him to prevent the worst.

When Diederich turned round again, the scene in the room had altered. Not only the Governor's wife, but old Buck was holding a reception. It was amazing, but one learnt to know people as they really are. They could not bear the idea that they had previously given free rein to their instincts. With expressions of regret one after another came up to the old gentleman, and tried to look as if they had done nothing. Even after deep convulsions, such was the power of what is, and what has long been accepted. Diederich himself found it advisable not to remain too noticeably in the rear of the majority. After he had made sure that Wulckow was gone, he went up to pay his compliments. The old man was just sitting alone in an armchair which had been placed for him right up in front near the stage. He let his white hand hang very gently over the arm and looked up at Diederich.

"There you are, my dear Hessling. I have often regretted that you never came"—he said it so simply and considerately that Diederich felt tears again coming immediately to his eyes. He gave him his hand and was glad when Herr Buck held it a little longer than was necessary. He began to stammer something about business, troubles and "to tell the honest truth"—for he was seized with a strong desire for honour—about doubts and fears.

"It is fine of you," said the old man, "not to let me guess that, but to confess it. You are young and are probably affected by the impulses which men's minds follow nowadays. I will not give in to the impatience of old age."

Diederich's eyes were downcast, for he understood this was forgiveness for the trial which had taken away the civic honours of the old man's son-in-law. He felt uncomfortable in the face of such mildness, such self-forgetfulness. The old man continued:

"I respect the fight and know it too well to hate any one who is against my friends." At this Diederich, seized with fear lest this should lead too far, took refuge in denial. He hardly knew himself . . . you get into things. . . . The old man made it easy for him. "I know, you are seeking and have not yet found yourself."

His white curly beard was sunk in his silk neckerchief. When he raised his head Diederich saw that something new was coming.

"You haven't bought the house behind yours," said he. "I suppose you have changed your plans?"

Diederich thought: "He knows everything," and could see all his most secret calculations revealed.

Herr Buck smiled slily and kindly. "Perhaps you will shortly be moving the site of your factory, and then make your extensions. I can imagine you would like to sell the site and are waiting for a certain opportunity—of which, I, too, am taking account," he added, and with a glance at Diederich: "The town is thinking of erecting an Infants' Asylum."

"Not at all, Herr Buck. I will not surrender the family property."

Then the old man took his hand again. "I will not tempt you," he said. "Your family piety does you credit."

"Idiot!" thought Diederich.

"Then we must look for another site. Indeed, you perhaps will help us. We do not want to lose a distinterested desire to serve the common welfare, my dear Hessling, even though it seems momentarily to be working in the wrong direction.

He stood up.

"If you run for the Town Council I will support you." Diederich stared, unable to understand him. The old man's eyes were blue and deep, and he was just offering Diederich' the public office for which Diederich had ruined his son-in-law. He did not know whether to spit in disgust, or crawl away in shame. He decided it was preferable to click his heels and politely to tender his thanks.

"You see," the old man resumed, "a sense of the common welfare bridges the gap between young and old, and even extends beyond to those who are no longer with us."

He moved his hands in a circle over the walls where the people of former times seemed to step out of their painted background, faded but full of gaiety. He smiled at the young girls in their hoop skirts, and also at one of his nieces and Meta Harnisch, who were passing. When he turned his face towards the old Mayor, who was coming through the city gate, amidst flowers and children, Diederich noticed the similarity between them. Old Buck pointed out one person and then another amongst the people in the pictures.

"I have heard a great deal about that man. I used to know that lady. Doesn't the clergyman look like Pastor Zillich? No, there can never be a serious estrangement between us. For a long time past we have been jointly pledged to good-will and our common progress, also by those who bequeathed to us this Harmony Club."

"Nice harmony!" thought Diederich, as he looked about for an excuse to get away. The old gentleman, as usual, had made a transition from business to sentimental twaddle. "The literary gent is always in evidence," was Diederich's reflection.

Just then Guste Daimchen and Inge Tietz passed; Guste had taken her arm and Inge was bragging about her experiences behind the scenes. "We were awfully frightened when they kept on saying: 'tea, coffee, tea,'" Guste declared. "Next time Wolfgang will write a much finer play and I'll have a part." At this Inge disengaged her arm and assumed an expression of chaste repulsion. "Oh, indeed?" she said, and Guste's fat face at once lost its harmless air of enthusiasm.— "Why not, may I ask?" she said, tearfully indignant.—"What on earth is wrong with you again?" Diederich, who could' have told her, turned back hastily to old Buck, who talked on.

"We have the same friends nowadays as in former times, and the same enemies too. But he has almost faded out, that armoured knight, the children's bogey there in the niche near the gate. Don Antonio Manrique, you cruel cavalier, who laid poor Netzig under contribution in the Thirty Years' War, where would even the faintest echo of your fame be, if Riekestrasse had not been named after you? . . . He was another of those who did not like our sense of freedom and thought he could destroy us."

Suddenly a silent chuckle shook the old man. He took Diederich's hand: "Don't you think he looks like our Herr von Wulckow?"

Diederich looked very solemn, but the old man did not notice it. Now that he had once started, other things occurred to him. He motioned to Diederich to follow him behind a group of plants, and showed him two figures on the wall, a young shepherd, whose arms were opened longingly, and on the other side of the brook a shepherdess, who was preparing to jump across. Herr Buck whispered: "What do you think? Do you believe they will meet? Very few people know that now, but I still remember." He looked round to make sure he was not being watched, then suddenly he opened a little door which nobody would ever have discovered. The shepherdess on the door moved towards her lover. A little more, and she would lie in his arms in the dark behind the door. . . . The old man pointed to the room which he had revealed. "This is called the cabinet of love." The light of a lantern from some courtyard streamed through the uncur- tained window, lit up the mirror and the spindle-legged sofa. Mr. Buck took a long breath of the musty air which was wafted out after goodness knows how many years. He smiled absentmindedly and then shut the little door.

Diederich, who was not much interested in all this, ob- served the approach of something that promised to be much more exciting. It was Judge Fritzsche who had arrived. His leave was probably over, he was back from the south, and he had put in an appearance, though rather late, and also without Judith Lauer, whose holiday would last so long as her husband was in prison. As he approached, with a swinging stride which did not deceive the onlookers, there was a great deal of whispering, and every one whom he greeted stole a glance at old Herr Buck. Fritzsche doubtless realised that, in the circumstances, he would have to do something. He plucked up his courage and went ahead. The old man, who was still unaware of his presence, suddenly found Fritzsche in front of him. He turned very pale. Diederich was fright- ened and stretched out his arms, but nothing happened. The old man had recovered himself. He stood there, holding him- self so stiffly erect that his back was hollow, and looked calmly and steadily at the man who had seduced his daughter.

"Back so soon, Judge?" he asked in a loud tone. Fritzsche tried to laugh genially. "The weather was nicer down south, Herr Buck. And how is art?" "We have only a reflection of it here," and without taking his eyes off Fritzsche he mo- tioned towards the walls. His demeanour made an impres- sion on most of those who were watching eagerly for a sign of weakness. He held fast and did the honours in a situa- tion which would have rendered a certain lack of self-restraint explicable. He stood for the old dignity, he alone, on behalf of his ruined family, of his following, which was conspicu- ously absent. In that moment he gained the sympathies of

many, in place of the many he had lost. . . . Diederich heard
him saying, in clear, formal tones: "I succeeded in having
our modern street plan altered in order to spare this house
and these paintings. They have only the value of descriptive
records, it may be. But a picture which lends permanence to
its own times and manners may hope for permanence itself."
Then Diederich retreated; for he was ashamed on Fritzsche's
account.

The secret Countess had now married the music-teacher and
every one was impressed by her tragic fate. Frau Harnisch,
Frau Cohn and the Mayor's mother-in-law had been weeping.
Jadassohn, who had washed off the grease-paint, and come
to receive congratulations, was not well received by the ladies.
"It is your fault, Dr. Jadassohn, that this happened! After
all, she was your own sister." "I beg your pardon, ladies,"
and Jadassohn proceeded to defend his attitude as the legitimate heir to the count's possessions. Then Meta Harnisch
said: "Well, you did not have to be so nasty about it."
Immediately every one looked at his ears and sniggered.
Jadassohn, who kept asking in vain what was the matter, was
taken aside by Diederich. With a pleasant thrill of revenge
in his heart Diederich led him right up to where the Governor's wife was saying good-bye to Major Kunze, with the
liveliest expressions of thanks for his efforts on behalf of her
play. As soon as she saw Jadassohn she turned her back on
him. Jadassohn stood as if rooted to the spot. Diederich
did not bring him any further. "What's wrong?" he asked
hypocritically. "Oh, of course, Frau von Wulckow. You
have annoyed her. You are not to be made Public Prosecutor. Your ears are too prominent."
Whatever Diederich may have expected, Jadassohn's monstrous grimace was a surprise! Where was the lofty good
form to which he had dedicated his life? "I say I shall,"
was all he could say, quite softly, yet it seemed like a ter-

rible cry. Then he began to move, stamping with rage as he spoke: "You may laugh, my friend! You do not know what an asset your face is. If I only had your face I'd be a Cabinet Minister in ten years." "Come, come!" said Diederich. "You don't require the whole face, only the ears," he added.

"Will you sell them to me?" asked Jadassohn, with a look that frightened Diederich. "Is that possible?" he asked dubiously. With a cynical laugh Jadassohn went up to Heuteufel, who declared that, as a matter of fact, operations were performed, though so far only in Paris, by which the size of the ears could be reduced by one-half. "Why remove the lot?" he queried.—"You can keep half of them." Jadassohn had recovered himself. "That's a good joke! I'll tell it in court, you old rascal!" said he, digging Heuteufel in the ribs.

Meanwhile Diederich had gone off to meet his sisters, who had changed into their ball dresses and were coming out of the dressing room. They were greeted with applause on all sides, and gave their impressions of what had happened on the stage. "Tea—coffee: heavens, wasn't that exciting!" said Magda. As their brother, Diederich also received congratulations. He got between them, and Magda at once linked her arm in his, but he had to hold Emma tightly. "Stop this play-acting," she hissed. Between nods and smiles he snorted at her: "I know you had only a smart part, but consider yourself lucky to have had a part at all.—Look at Magda!" Magda nestled willingly against him and seemed ready to be a perambulating picture of the happy united family as long as ever he liked. "My dear little sister," he said, with tender respect, "you have had a success. But I can assure you so have I." He even began to pay her compliments. "You look stunning to-night. You are much too nice for Kienast." When the Governor's wife nodded to them graciously, as they were leaving, they met everywhere the most respectful glances.

The large room had been cleared, and behind a group of palms, a polonaise was being played. Diederich bowed to Magda with the utmost correctness and conducted her triumphantly to the dance, right after Major Kunze, who was leading. Thus they passed by Guste Daimchen, who was sitting out. She was beside the hunchbacked Fräulein Kühnchen, and she looked after them as if she had been struck. Her look moved Diederich as unpleasantly as that of Herr Lauer in prison.

"Poor Guste!" said Magda. Diederich frowned. "Yes, that is what happens."

"But, as a matter of fact . . ." Magda smiled with downcast eyes, "happens when?"

"That doesn't matter, my child, it is so now."

"Diedel, you should ask her for a waltz afterwards."

"I can't. A man must remember what he owes to himself."

Soon after he left the room. Young Sprezius, now no longer a lieutenant, was just inviting the hunchbacked Fräulein Kühnchen away from the wall. He was doubtless thinking of her father. Guste Daimchen was left in the lurch. . . . Diederich took a turn through the ante-rooms, where the elderly gentlemen were playing cards. When he surprised Käthchen Zillich behind a door with an actor, she made a face at him. He reached the refreshment room, and there was Wolfgang Buck, sitting at a little table and sketching in a note-book the mothers who were waiting around the dancing room.

"Very talented," said Diederich. "Have you drawn your future bride yet?"

"In this connection she does not interest me," retorted Buck stolidly.

"I can never make you out," said he disappointedly.

"I can always make you out," replied Buck. "I would like to have drawn you that time in court, when you were delivering your great monologue."

"Your speech was enough for me. It was an attempt,

though fortunately ineffective, to bring myself and my actions into discredit with the greatest publicity, and to make them contemptible."

Diederich glared, as Buck noticed with astonishment: "Apparently you are offended. And I made such a good speech." He wagged his head and smiled pensively, delighted with himself. "Won't you split a bottle of champagne with me?" he asked.

Diederich began: "Are you exactly the person I ought to—" But he gave in. "The decision of the court established the fact that your accusations were directed, not only against me, but against all right-thinking patriots. So I regard the matter as settled."

"I suppose we'll make it Heidsieck?" said Buck. He insisted on Diederich's clinking glasses with him. "You must admit, my dear Hessling, that nobody ever dealt so thoroughly with you as I did. Now I don't mind telling you that your rôle in court interested me much more than my own. Afterwards, when I got home, I imitated you in front of the glass."

"My rôle? You mean, I suppose, my convictions. I know, of course, that you regard the actor as the representative man of to-day."

"I said that in reference to . . . some one else. But you see how much nearer I have the type to study. If I had not to defend the washerwoman to-morrow, who is accused of having stolen a pair of drawers from Wulckow's, I might perhaps play *Hamlet. Prosit!*"

"*Prosit.* You do not need to have any convictions for that!"

"Good Lord, I have convictions. But are they always the same? So you would advise me to go on the stage?" asked Buck. Diederich had opened his mouth to advise him to do so, when Guste entered. Diederich blushed, for Buck's question had made him think of her. Buck remarked pensively:

"Meanwhile the pot in which my meal is cooking would boil over, and the food is good." Guste crept up softly from behind, pressed her hands over his eyes, and asked: "Who is that?"—"There she is," replied Buck, giving her a slap.

"You gentlemen are having an interesting talk, I suppose? Shall I leave you?" asked Guste. Diederich hastened to get her a chair, but in reality he would have preferred to be alone with Buck. The feverish brightness of Guste's eyes were not promising. She talked more freely than usual.

"You get on wonderfully together, if you were only not so formal."

"That is mutual respect," said Buck. Diederich was taken aback, and then he made a remark which astonished himself. "The fact is, every time I leave your fiancé I am mad with him, but when we next meet I am glad." He drew himself up. "If I were not already a loyal citizen he would make me one."

"And if I were," said Buck, smiling, "he would cure me of it. That is the charm of it."

But Guste had obviously other cares. She was pale and choking.

"Now I'll tell you something, Wolfgang. Will you bet you can't stand?"

"Mr. Rose, some of your Hennessy!" shouted Buck. While he mixed cognac and champagne, Diederich seized Guste's arm, and as the noise of the dance music grew very loud just then, he whispered entreatingly: "Don't do anything foolish." She laughed evasively. "Dr. Hessling is afraid! He thinks it's a vulgar story, but I find it terribly funny." She laughed loudly. "What do you think? They say your father and my mother . . . you understand, and consequently we are to . . . you know!"

Buck moved his head slowly, and then his lips curled. "Well, what about it?" Guste stopped laughing.

"How do you mean? What then?"

"I mean if the Netzig people believe such a thing, it must be a common occurrence amongst them, and therefore it doesn't matter."

"Soft words butter no parsnips," said Guste decisively. Diederich then felt it his duty to enter a protest.

"To err is human, but nobody can defy public opinion with impunity."

"He always thinks he is too good for this world," said Guste. And Diederich: "These are stern times. He who does not refute a charge must believe in it." Then Guste cried, full of painful enthusiasm:

"Dr. Hessling is not like you! He defended me. I have proof, I know it, from Meta Harnisch, because in the end she had to tell me what she knew. He was the only person of them all who took my defence. He, in your place, would let the people know what he thought of them, when they dared to gossip about me!"

Diederich nodded his head in approval, but Buck kept twisting his glass and looking at his reflection in it. Suddenly he put it down.

"How do you know I, too, wouldn't like sometime to give them a piece of my mind—to take one of them, without choosing particularly, for they are all about equally mean and stupid?" As he said this he shut his eyes. Guste shrugged her bare shoulders.

"That's what you say, but they are not so stupid, they know what they want. . . . The stupider they are the cleverer," she concluded challengingly, and Diederich nodded ironically. Then Buck looked at him with eyes which suddenly seemed to be those of a madman. His trembling hands convulsively fumbled at his neck; his voice was hoarse. "If I could only—if I only had one of them by the scruff of the neck, and knew that he had started the whole thing, that he embodied in himself all the hateful and evil qualities of the rest; if, if I could get hold of one who was the personification of all that is inhuman and sub-human—!" Diederich turned as pale as a sheet as he sidled from his chair and slowly drew back, step by step. "It's the cognac!" Diederich shouted to her. . . . But Buck's glance, filled with dreadful malice, inspired real terror, as it wavered between them. He blinked, and then his eyes shone clearer.

"Unfortunately I am accustomed to this mixture," he explained. "It was only to show you what I could do."

Diederich sat down again noisily. "After all, you are nothing but a play-actor," he said with an air of disappointment.

"Do you really think so?" Buck asked and his glance became even brighter. Guste turned up her nose. "Well, I hope you'll continue to enjoy yourselves," she said, preparing to leave them. But Judge Fritzsche had come along, and he bowed to her and also to Buck, and asked if he would allow him to have the pleasure of dancing the cotillion with his fiancée. He was exceedingly polite, almost entreating. Buck frowned and did not answer, but in the meantime Guste had taken Fritzsche's arm.

Buck looked after them, a heavy furrow between his eyebrows, and oblivious of everything. "Yes, indeed," thought Diederich, "it is not pleasant, my friend, to meet a man who has been off on a pleasure trip with your sister, and then he takes your fiancée away from the table, and you can do nothing, for that would only increase the scandal, because your engagement in itself is a scandal. . . ."

Rousing himself with a start, Buck said: "Do you know it is only now that I really feel as if I'd like to marry Fräulein Daimchen. I regarded the affair as . . . rather tame, but the inhabitants of Netzig have given it a really piquant flavour."

This effect left Diederich thunderstruck. "If you think so," he managed to ejaculate.

"Why not? You and I, though at opposite poles, are introducing here the advanced tendencies of an epoch of moral freedom. We are stirring things up. The spirit of the times still sneaks about the streets here in carpet slippers."

"We'll put spurs on them," declared Diederich.

"Your health!"

"Here's to you! But they'll be *my* spurs"—Diederich glared. "Your scepticism and your flabby point of view are out of date. Intellectual weapons"—he breathed heavily—"are no use to-day. National deeds"—he banged his fist on the table—"will win the future!"

To this Buck retorted with a pitying smile: "The future? That's just where you are mixed. National deeds have died out in the course of centuries. What we see, and what we shall still experience, is the spasmodic twitching and the odour of their corpse. It will not sweeten the air."

"From you I did not expect anything better than that you should drag what is most sacred into the dust!"

"Sacred! Unapproachable! Why not call it eternal and have done with it! Except in the realm of the ideal, your nationalism will never, never be seen again. Formerly, it may have been possible, in that dark period of history when you people were not yet born. But now you are here and the world has moved on to its goal. Darkness and hatred amongst nations, that is the end and you cannot avoid it."

"We are living in strenuous times," Diederich declared seriously.

"Not so much strenuous as conscienceless. . . . I am not sure that the people whose lot was cast in the period of the Thirty Years' War believed in the immutability of their by no means easy circumstances. And I am convinced that the fantastic obstinacy of those whom they overthrew was regarded as unconquerable. Otherwise, there would have been no revolution. Whereabouts, in those periods of history which we can still spiritually enter, is there an age which would have declared itself permanent, and prided itself before eternity on

its miserable limitations; which would have superstitiously cen-
sured every one who was not wholly identified with it? You
are filled with horror rather than hate when confronted by
a lack of red-blooded patriotism! But the men without a
country are on your tracks. Do you see them there in the
ballroom?"

Diederich turned round so suddenly that he spilled his
champagne. Had Napoleon Fischer and his comrades forced
their way in? . . . Buck laughed inwardly. "Don't get excited, I mean merely the silent folk on the walls. Why do
they look so gay? What gives them the right to flowered
paths, light footsteps and harmony? Ah, you friendly ones!"
Over the heads of the dancers Buck motioned with his glass.
"You friends of humanity, and of every future good, your
capacious hearts did not know the sordid selfishness of a
national family party. You citizens of the world, return!
Even amongst us there are still some who wait for you!"

He emptied his glass and Diederich noticed with contempt
that he was weeping. Then he looked very sly. "You, my
contemporaries, do not know, I am sure, what sort of a sash
the old Mayor is wearing, as he smiles there in the midst of
officials and shepherdesses. The colours have faded, and you
doubtless think they are yours? But it is the French tricolour.
Then the colours were new, and they did not belong to any
country, but heralded the universal dawn. To wear them was
the best badge of opinion. It was, as you would say, most
correct. *Prosit!*"

Diederich had surreptitiously drawn away his chair and
was looking about to see if any one was listening. "You're
drunk," he murmured, and in order to save the situation he
shouted: "Herr Rose, another bottle!" Thereupon he drew
up his chair again and looked most proper.

"You seem to forget that we have had a Bismarck since
then!"

"Not only one," said Buck. "On all sides Europe is being

driven along this road to national ruin. Let us suppose it could not have been avoided. Better times will come again. But did you follow your Bismarck so long as he was in the right? You allowed yourselves to be dragged on; you quarrelled with him. But now, when you think you can go beyond him, you cling to his powerless shadow! Your method of renewing your national forces is depressingly slow. By the time you have grasped the fact that a great man is amongst you, he has ceased to be great!"

"You will learn to know about him soon enough," Diederich assured him. "Blood and iron are still the most effective remedy! Might before might!" His head became heated at the utterance of this credo. But Buck also became excited. "Might! Might will not allow itself to be carried eternally on the bayonet's point like a skewered sausage. Nowadays the real power is peace. Play your comedy of force. Brag about your imaginary enemies at home and abroad. Fortunately, deeds are forbidden to you."

"Forbidden?" Diederich snorted with indignation. "His Majesty has said: We would rather leave our eighteen army corps and forty-two million inhabitants on the field . . ."

"Than that the German eagle—!" cried Buck impetuously, and then more mildly: "No parliamentary resolutions! The army is our only tower of strength."

Diederich would not be outdone. "You are called upon, in the first place, to defend me against my domestic and foreign enemies."

"To ward off a host of miserable traitors," yelled Buck.

"A gang of people—"

"Diederich concluded the sentence: "Unworthy to bear the name of Germans!"

Then both in chorus: "Shoot down your brothers and relatives!" Some of the dancers, who had come for refreshments, were attracted by the shouting, and fetched their womenfolk to contemplate this spectacle of heroic intoxication. Even the card-players put their heads in the doorway, and every one was astounded at the sight of Diederich and his partner, rolling in their chairs, clutching the table and hurling strong words at each other, with glassy eyes and snarling teeth.

"There is one enemy and he is my enemy!"

"There is only one master in my kingdom and I will endure no other!"

"I can be very unpleasant!"

They tried to shout one another down.

"Mistaken humanitarianism."

"Enemies of their own country and of the divine order of the world!"

"They must be exterminated to the last man."

A bottle crushed against the wall.

"I will smash!"

"German dust . . . from their shoes . . . glorious days!"

Just then some one with blindfolded eyes glided through the spectators. It was Guste Daimchen who had to find a gentleman this way. She came up behind Diederich and touched him, trying to make him stand up. He stiffened up and repeated threateningly: "Glorious days!" She pulled down the bandage, stared at him anxiously and went to get his sisters. Buck also saw that it was time to stop. In an unostentatious manner he assisted his friend to get away, but he could not prevent Diederich from turning at the door to the gaping crowd of dancers, and drawing himself up haughtily, though his eyes were too glassy to flash.

"I will smash!"

Then he was taken downstairs and put into the carriage.

When he came into the sitting-room towards midday, with a terrible headache, he was astonished to see Emma march out indignantly. But Magda had only to make a few cautious allusions for him to remember what was the matter. "Did I really do that? Well, I admit there were ladies present.

There are more ways than one for a true-born German to show himself. With ladies it is different. . . . In such cases, of course, one must lose no time in setting the matter to rights in the frankest and most correct fashion."

Although he could hardly see, he knew perfectly well what had to be done: While a two-horse Victoria was being sent for, he put on his frock-coat, white tie and silk hat. Then he handed the coachman the list which Magda had drawn up, and drove off. At each house he asked to see the ladies and disturbed many of them at lunch. Without being quite sure whether he was addressing Frau Harnisch, Frau Daimchen or Frau Tietz, he reeled off a statement in his hoarse voice of "the morning after": "I frankly confess . . . as a German gentleman, in the presence of ladies . . . in the fullest and most correct fashion . . ."

By half-past one he was back, and sat down to lunch with a sigh of relief: "It is all settled."

That afternoon he had a more difficult task before him. He sent for Napoleon Fischer to come up to the house.

"Herr Fischer," he said, offering him a chair, "I am receiving you here, instead of in the office, because our affairs are no concern of Herr Sötbier's. It is a question of politics, I ought to explain."

Napoleon Fischer nodded as if he had already guessed that. He now seemed to be accustomed to these confidential conversations. At Diederich's first nod he at once took a cigar, and he even crossed his legs. Diederich was far less sure of himself; he was breathing hard. Then he decided, without beating about the bush, to go straight to the point with brutal frankness. That is what Bismarck would have done.

"The fact is I want to get a seat on the Town Council," he explained, "and for that I will need you."

The machinist glanced up at him. "And I you," he said, "for I also want to be a municipal councillor."

"What! Come now! I was prepared for most things. . . ."

"I suppose you had another couple of twenty-mark pieces ready?"—and the proletarian bared his yellow teeth. He no longer concealed his grin and Diederich saw that he was not going to be as easy to deal with in this as in previous matters.

"I may tell you, Doctor," Napoleon began, "my party is dead sure of one of the two seats. The Liberals will probably get the other. If you want to kick them out, you will need us."

"I see that," said Diederich. "It is true, I have the support of old Buck. But his people are not all perhaps so confiding as to elect me if I went forward as a Liberal. It is safer to come to an understanding with you."

"And I have a very good idea how that can be arranged," declared Napoleon. "Because for a long time I have had my eye on you, wondering whether you would not soon be entering the political arena."

Napoleon began to blow smoke rings, he felt so elated.

"Your trial, Dr. Hessling, and then that business with the Veterans' Association, and so on, that was all excellent as an advertisement. But a politician must always ask: How many votes do I get?" And Napoleon gave him the benefit of his experience. When he referred to the "patriotic gang," Diederich tried to protest, but Napoleon shut him up.

"What do you mean? In my party we have a certain respect for the patriotic gang. It is easier to do business with them than with the Liberals. Soon the middle-class Democrats will all be able to fit into one cab."

"And we'll finish even them," cried Diederich. The allies laughed for joy. Diederich got a bottle of beer.

"But," insisted the Social Democrat, as he stated his terms; a trade union hall, which the town was to help the party to build. . . . Diederich jumped up from his chair. "And you have the cheek to demand that of a true patriot?"

The other remained cool and ironical. "If we do not help the true patriot to be elected, where will the true patriot be?"

In spite of his pleas and threats, Diederich finally had to sign a paper, pledging himself not only to vote for the hall, but to work up the councillors with whom he had influence. After that he bluntly declared the interview at an end and took the beer bottle out of the machinist's hand. But Napoleon Fischer had a twinkle in his eye. Dr. Hessling ought to be thankful that he was dealing with him and not with Rille, the party boss. Rille was trying to get into the running himself and would not have been agreeable to such a compromise. Opinion was divided amongst the party. Diederich therefore would have good reason to do something on behalf of Fischer's candidature in the press where he had influence. "If strangers, like Rille, for example, were to poke their noses into your affairs, Doctor, I am sure you would not like it. Between the two of us it is quite different. We have already turned a few tricks together." With this he left Diederich to his own feelings.

Some days later Emma and Magda were invited to tea at Frau von Wulckow's, and Diederich accompanied them. With their chins in the air the three of them marched along Kaiser Wilhelmstrasse, and Diederich raised his hat very calmly to the gentlemen on the steps of the Freemasons' Lodge, who stared in amazement as he entered the government building. He greeted the sentry with a genial wave of his hand. In the dressing room they met several officers and their wives, to whom the Fräulein Hesslings were already well known. Clicking his spurs, Lieutenant von Brietzen helped Emma off with her coat, and she thanked him over her shoulder like a countess. She nudged Diederich with her foot to draw his attention to the sacred ground on which they were treading. After they had given precedence to Herr von Brietzen on entering the drawing-room, had bowed and scraped ecstatically to the Governor's wife, and had been introduced to everybody—what a task it was, as dangerous as it was honourable, to sit on a little chair, squeezed in amongst the ladies, to balance one's teacup while passing round plates, and to offer the cakes with a respectful smile! And while eating it was necessary to say something touching about the successful performance of the "Secret Countess," and a word of appropriate recognition for the far-seeing administrative ability of the Governor, and something impressive about revolution and patriotism, and into the bargain, to feed the Wulckow's dog which was begging! Here there could be no question of the unpretentious gatherings in the Ratskeller and of the Veterans' Association. One had to gaze with a simulated smile into the pale blue eyes of Captain von Köckevitz, whose bald head was white, but whose face from the middle of his forehead down was a fiery red, and who talked about the training ground. And if one were already breaking into a sweat from anxiety lest the question be raised whether one had served in the army, there came the unexpected relief, that the lady at one's side, who combed her blond, white hair flat over the top of her head, and whose nose was freckled, began to talk about horses. . . . This time Emma saved Diederich with the aid of Herr von Brietzen, with whom she seemed to be on very familiar terms. Emma joined easily in the conversation about horses, used technical terms, and even went so far as to draw on her imagination about cross-country rides which she said she had taken on the estate of an aunt. When the lieutenant offered to go out riding with her, she pleaded poor Frau Hessling as an excuse, as she would not allow it. Diederich could hardly recognize Emma. Her uncanny talents left Magda altogether in the shade, although the latter had succeeded in capturing a husband. As on the occasion when he returned from the "Green Angel," Diederich reflected uneasily on the unaccountable ways which, when you were out of sight, a girl would . . . Then he noticed that he had not been listening to a question of Frau von Wulckow's, and that every one had stopped talking, so that he might reply. He gazed around him helplessly, looking for assistance, but his eyes met only the gaze of a forbidding portrait of a man, pale and unbending, in a red hussar's uniform, with his hand on his hip, his moustaches curling up to his eyes, who glared coldly over his shoulder! Diederich was trembling and nearly choked himself with his tea. Herr von Brietzen had to clap him on the back.

Now a lady who had previously done nothing but eat was going to sing. The guests drew together in the music room. Diederich stood at the door and was glancing surreptitiously at his watch when the Governor's wife gave a little cough behind him. "I know, my dear Dr. Hessling, that you cannot sacrifice your valuable time on our frivolous, our all-too-frivolous conversation. My husband is expecting you, come along." With her finger to her lips she preceded him along a passage and through an empty ante-room. She knocked very gently. As there was no reply, she looked anxiously at Diederich, who also felt uncomfortable. "Otto, dearest," she cried, nestling tenderly against the closed door. After they had listened for a while the terrible bass voice was heard inside. "Dearest Otto is not here! Tell those idiots to drink their tea slop without him!"—"He is so dreadfully busy," whispered Frau von Wulckow, turning a little paler. "His health is being undermined by the subversive elements. . . . Now, unfortunately, I must return to my guests, but the servant will announce you." And she disappeared. Diederich waited in vain many long minutes for the servant. Then the dog came along, went past Diederich full of immense contempt and scratched at the door. Immediately the voice within shouted: "Schnaps, come in here!"—Whereupon the great beast raised the latch. As it forgot to shut the door again Diederich took the liberty of creeping in behind the dog. Herr von Wulckow was sitting at his writing table, in a cloud of smoke, with his enormous back turned towards the intruder.

"Good day, sir," said Diederich, with an awkward bow. "Hello, have you learnt to babble, too, Schnaps?" asked

Wulckow, without looking round. He folded up a document and lit a fresh cigar. "Here it comes," thought Diederich, but Wulckow began to write something else. Only the dog took any notice of Diederich. It obviously found the visitor even more out of place here and its contempt turned to hostility. Showing its teeth it sniffed at Diederich's trousers, and almost went further than mere sniffing. Diederich hopped as quietly as possible from one leg to the other, and the dog growled threateningly but softly, knowing well that otherwise its master would intervene. Finally Diederich succeeded in interposing a chair between himself and his enemy, and clinging to this he twisted about, now quickly, now slowly, always on the lookout for Schnaps's flank attacks. Once he noticed Wulckow turning his head a little and he fancied he saw him grin. At length the dog grew tired of the game, and went to its master to be stroked. Encamped near Wulckow's chair, it measured Diederich with the keen eyes of a hunter, as he mopped up his perspiration.

"Well, my little Doctor," said Herr von Wulckow, turning round his chair, "what is the matter with you? You are becoming a real statesman. Won't you take this seat of honour?"

"If I may be so bold," stammered Diederich. "I have been able to do something for the national cause."

Wulckow blew an enormous volume of smoke into his face, then he came quite close to him with his hot-blooded, cynical eyes beneath their Oriental lids. "To start with, you have succeeded in getting into the Town Council. Well, we won't go into that. At all events, it will help you, for I understand your business is in a pretty bad way." Wulckow laughed boisterously as Diederich winced. "That's all right. You are the man for me. What do you think I have been writing here?" The huge sheet was hidden by the paper-weight which he placed upon it. "I have asked the minister for a little dicky bird for a certain Dr. Hessling, in recognition of his services on behalf of loyal opinion in Netzig. . . . I am sure you never thought I could be as nice as that," he added, for Diederich kept bowing from his chair, looking dazzled and seized with sudden weakness. "I can hardly say," he murmured, ". . . my modest services . . ."

"It, is the first step that counts," said Wulckow. "This is only a little encouragement. Your attitude in the Lauer trial was pretty good. Your call for cheers for the Emperor during the debate at the Council set the anti-monarchical press by the ears. In three different places around the country-side complaints of *lèse-majesté* have been raised on the head of it. We must, therefore, show you some mark of our appreciation."

Diederich cried: "My highest reward is the fact that the 'Lokal-Anzeiger' brought my humble name to the attention of His Gracious Majesty himself!"

"Well, now, won't you take a cigar?" Wulckow concluded, and Diederich understood that they were now coming to business. Already a doubt had arisen in the midst of his elation as to whether Wulckow's condescension had not some special motive. He said, as a feeler:

"The town, I am pretty sure will sanction its quota for the line to Ratzenhausen."

Wulckow thrust his head forward. "So much the better for you. Otherwise we have a much more inexpensive scheme, in which Netzig will not be involved at all. So see that those people learn sense. On that condition you will have the privilege of furnishing your light to the Quitzin estates."

"The Council doesn't want that." Diederich pleaded with his hands for consideration. "The town loses on the transaction, and Herr von Quitzin pays no taxes to us. . . . But now I am a municipal councillor as well as a loyal patriot. . . ."

"I must insist on that, otherwise my cousin, Herr von Quitzin, will simply instal his own electric plant. He can get that cheap, as you may imagine; two cabinet ministers come to his place for the hunting. Then he will undersell you here in Netzig itself."

Diederich straightened himself up. "Sir, I am determined, I am determined, despite all hostile attacks, to hold aloft the national banner in Netzig." Then, in softer tones : "In any case we can get rid of one enemy, indeed a particularly bad one, old Klüsing in Gausenfeld."

"That fellow?" Wulckow smiled contemptuously. "He eats out of my hand. He supplies paper to the official newspapers of the district." "Do you know whether he does not supply even more to the bad papers? On that score, with all due respect, I am probably better informed."

"The 'Netziger Journal' has become more reliable from the national standpoint."

"That is true"—Diederich nodded impressively—"since the day when old Klüsing allowed me to tender for part of the paper supply. Gausenfeld was supposed to be too full of orders. Of course, he was really afraid that I would become interested in a rival sheet on the national side. And perhaps he was also afraid"—a significant pause—"that the Governor might prefer to order the paper for the official press from a patriotic firm."

"So you now supply the 'Netziger Journal'?"

"Never will I so betray my patriotic convictions as to supply a paper so long as there is Liberal money behind it."

"Hm. Very good." Wulckow rested his hands on his thighs. "You needn't say anything more. You want the whole contract for the 'Netziger Journal.' You also want the official organs of the district. Probably also the supplies of paper for government use. Anything else?"

To which Diederich replied in practical tones:

"I, sir, am not like Klüsing. I have no truck with revolution. If you, sir, as President of the Bible Society, will give me your support, I may say that it can only be to the advantage of the national cause."

"Hm. Very good," repeated Wulckow, blinking. Diederich played his trump card.

"Under Klüsing, sir, Gausenfeld is a breeding ground of revolution. Amongst his eight hundred workmen there is not one who ever votes for any one but a Social Democrat."

"Well, and what about your men?"

Diederich struck his chest. "God is my witness that I' would rather shut the whole shop to-day, and go into poverty with my family, than keep one single man in my employment whom I knew to be unpatriotic."

"Most excellent sentiments," said Wulckow. Diederich looked at him with candid eyes. "I only take people who have been in the army. Forty of them served in the war. I no longer employ young men since that affair with the workman whom the sentry laid low on the field of honour, as His Majesty was pleased to state, after the fellow and his girl, behind my rags—"

Wulckow interrupted: "That's your funeral, my little man."

Diederich did not allow his plan to be spoiled. "There shall be no revolution hatched in my rags. In yours, I mean in politics, it is different. There we can use the revolution so that out of the rags of Liberalism, white patriotic paper may come." He looked exceedingly profound, but Wulckow did not seem impressed. His smile was terrible.

"My boy, I wasn't born yesterday. Let me hear what you have worked out with your machinist."

When he saw Diederich giving ground, Wulckow continued: "He is also one of your old soldiers, Mr. Councillor?"

Diederich gulped, but saw there was no use beating any more about the bush. He spoke with determination at first, but his voice became quick and nervous. "The man wants to go into the Reichstag, and from the national standpoint he is better than Heuteufel. In the first place, many Liberals will turn patriotic out of fear, and in the second, if Napoleon

Fischer is elected, we shall get a monument to Emperor William in Netzig. I have it in writing."

He spread out the paper in front of the Governor. Wulckow read it, then he stood up, kicked away his chair, and walked up and down the room, smoking like a chimney. "So Kühlemann snuffs out, and with his half million the town will build, not an Infant Asylum, but a monument to Emperor William." He stood still. "Mind you this, my friend, in your own interest. If Netzig afterwards has a Social Democrat in the Reichstag, but no William the Great, then I'll teach you a lesson. I'll smash you to pulp. I'll break you so small that they won't even admit you to the Infant Asylum!"

Diederich and his chair had both retreated against the wall. "Everything I am, my whole future, is staked on the national cause. The uncertainty of human affairs may affect me. . . ."

"Then, God help you!"

"Suppose Kühlemann again recovers from stone in the kidneys?"

"You are responsible! My reputation is also at stake!" Wulckow dropped heavily into his chair, and smoked furiously. When the clouds had dispersed he had cheered up again. "What I told you the night of the play is certain. This parliament will not last long. Get to work in the town here in advance. Help me against Buck and I'll help you against Klüsing."

Wulckow's smile filled Diederich with a great wave of hope. He could not contain himself. "If you would let him know on the quiet that you contemplated taking away the contracts from him! He will not make a row about it, you need not fear, but he will take measures accordingly. Perhaps he would negotiate—"

"With his successor," Wulckow concluded. Then it was Diederich's turn to jump up and walk up and down the room. "If you only knew, sir. . . . Gausenfeld is a machine of a thousand horse-power, so to speak, and there it stands rusting away, because the current is lacking, I mean, the modern, far-seeing mind!"

"You have that, apparently," insinuated Wulckow. "In the service of the national cause," Diederich assured him. He descended from the clouds. "The Kaiser Wilhelm Monument Committee will be most happy, if we succeed in inducing you to have the kindness to signify your esteemed interest by accepting the position of honorary chairman."

"Done!" said Wulckow.

"The Committee will duly appreciate the disinterested services of its honorary chairman."

"Be a little more explicit!" There was an ominous note in Wulckow's voice, but in his excitement Diederich failed to notice it.

"This idea has already given rise to certain discussions in committee. There is a desire to erect the monument on the most frequented site, and to surround it with a public park, so that the indissoluble bond between the ruler and his people may be prominently displayed. For that reason we thought of rather large pieces of property in the centre of the town, the adjoining houses are also available. It is in Meisestrasse."

"Oh, really? Meisestrasse." Wulckow's frown betokened a storm. Diederich was frightened, but he could not back out now.

"It occurred to us that, before the town looks into the matter more closely, we should make sure of the property in question, and thus anticipate undesirable speculations. Our honorary chairman, of course, would have the first right. . . ."

At this word Diederich retreated and the storm broke. "Sir! What do you take me for? Am I your business agent? This is intolerable; it is unbelievable! A damned tradesman has the cheek to presume that the representative of His Majesty the King will take a hand in his dirty deals!"

"You are guilty of libelling a government official, sir!"

Wulckow screamed, and Diederich, who was feeling behind his back for the table, could only wonder whether the dog or his master would be the first to seize him by the throat. His terrified glance strayed until it was held by a pale face on the wall which glared down threateningly at him. Now authority had caught him by the throat! He had dared to treat with authority on equal footing. That had proved his undoing. It broke upon him with all the terror of a cataclysm. . . . The door behind the writing table opened and some one in a police uniform entered. The demoralised Diederich was no longer capable of astonishment. The presence of the uniform suggested another fearful thought to Wulckow. "I could have you arrested this moment, you contemptible upstart, for attempted bribery of an official, bribery of the authorities, the highest authority in the district! I'll bring you to jail and ruin you for life!"

This last judgment was not far from having the same effect upon the gentleman from the police as upon Diederich. He laid the document which he had brought upon the table and disappeared. For the rest, Wulckow also turned around suddenly and lit his cigar again. Diederich no longer existed for him. Schnaps also left him alone, as if he had been made of air. Then Diederich ventured to fold his hands.

"Sir," he whispered shakily, "allow me, sir, to assure you; there is, if I may say so, a regrettable misunderstanding. With my well-known patriotic sentiments I would never . . . How could I?"

He waited, but nobody took any notice of him.

"If I were thinking of my own advantage," he resumed, a little more confidently, "instead of always having the national interest in view, I would not be here to-day, but at Herr Buck's. Herr Buck, I ought to tell you, proposed that I should sell my property to the town for the Liberal Infant Asylum. But I repelled the suggestion with indignation, and came straight to you. Better, I said, the Monument to Emperor

William the Great in the heart, than the Infant Asylum in the pocket, said I. I say it now with no uncertain voice!"

As Diederich actually did raise his voice, Wulckow turned to him. "Are you still here?" he asked. And Diederich again in mortal fear: "Sir. . . ."

"What are you waiting for? I do not know you at all. Have never had anything to do with you."

"Sir, in the national interest—"

"I can have no dealings with land sharks. Sell your plot of ground and good luck to you. Afterwards we can do business."

Diederich turned pale and felt as if he were being crushed against the wall. "In that case, do our conditions still hold good? The decoration? The hint to Klüsing? The honorary chairmanship?"

Wulckow made a wry face. "Well and good. But you must sell at once."

Diederich gasped for breath. "I will make the sacrifice," he declared. "The noblest possession of a loyal patriot, my fidelity to the Emperor, must be placed beyond suspicion."

"All right, then," said Wulckow, as Diederich withdrew, proud of his exit, though disturbed by the discovery that the Governor did not view him as an ally with any greater favour than he viewed his machinist.

In the drawing-room he found Emma and Magda all alone, turning over the pages of a magnificent looking volume. The visitors had all gone and Frau von Wulckow had left them, because she had to dress for a party given by the wife of Colonel von Haffke. "My interview with the Governor passed off quite satisfactorily for both of us," Diederich remarked. And when they were in the street, he added: "There you can see what it means when two honourable men negotiate. In the business world to-day that is unknown, there are so many Jews."

Emma was also greatly excited, and announced that she

would take riding lessons. "If I give you the money," said Deiderich, but only for form's sake, for he was proud of Emma. "Has Lieutenant von Brietzen no sisters?" he asked. "You ought to make their acquaintance and get invitations to Frau von Haffke's next party." The colonel just passed at that moment. Diederich stared after him for a long time. "I know," he said, "one shouldn't look back, but that represents, after all, what is highest. It draws you irresistibly."

This understanding with Wulckow, however, had only increased his troubles. The definite obligation to sell his house promised nothing more in return than hopes and prospects: vague prospects and hopes that were too bold. . . . It was freezing. On Sunday Diederich went to the park, where it was already growing dark, and on a lonely path he met Wolfgang Buck.

"I have made up my mind," Buck declared. "I am going on the stage."

"And what about your social position? And your marriage?"

"I have tried my best, but the theatre is preferable. There is less comedy, you know, people are more genuine. The women are also more beautiful."

"That is not a proper attitude," replied Diederich. But Buck was in earnest. "I must say the rumour about Guste and me amused me. On the other hand, silly as it is, the rumour exists. The girl is suffering under it and I cannot compromise her any longer."

Diederich gave him a look of scorn, for he had the impression that Buck was using the rumour as a pretext to escape. "No doubt," he said sternly. "You understand what you are about. Now, of course, it will not be easy for her to find another. It will take a man of the finest chivalry to marry her."

Buck admitted this. "It would be a special satisfaction," he said significantly, "to a really big, modern man to raise a girl up to his own level, under such circumstances, and to take her part. Here, where there is also money, nobility of mind would doubtless end by carrying the day. Remember the ordeal in Lohengrin."

"How do you mean, Lohengrin?"

Buck returned no answer to this. As they had reached the Saxon Gate he became uneasy. "Will you come in with me?" he asked. "In where?"—"Just here, 77 Schweinichen-strasse. I must tell her. Perhaps you could . . ." Then Diederich gave a whistle.

"You are really . . . Have you said nothing to her yet? You tell it all round the town first. That's your affair, my dear fellow, but leave me out of it. I am not in the habit of breaking off the engagements of other men's fiancées."

"Make an exception," begged Buck. "I cannot stand scenes."

"I have principles," said Diederich. Buck turned into the street.

"You need not say anything. You need only play a silent part, as moral support."

"Moral?" Diederich queried.

"As the spokesman, so to speak, of the fatal rumour."

"What does that mean?"

"I am only joking. Come on. Here we are."

Feeling touched by Buck's last allusion, Diederich accompanied him without another word.

Frau Daimchen was out, and Guste sent word to them to wait. Buck went to find out what was keeping her. Finally she came, but she was alone. "Wasn't Wolfgang here, too?" she asked.

Buck had decamped!

"I don't understand this," said Diederich. "He had something very urgent to tell you."

Guste blushed. Diederich turned towards the door. "Then I had better be going."

"What on earth did he want?" she inquired. "It doesn't often happen that he wants anything. And why did he bring you with him?"

"I don't understand that either. In fact, I may say that I decidedly object to his bringing witnesses in such a matter. It is not my fault. Good-bye."

The more embarrassed his manner became the more insistent was she.

"I must decline," he confessed finally, "to burn my fingers in the affairs of a third person, especially when the third party skedaddles and evades his most earnest obligations."

With eyes wide open Guste seemed to watch each word singly as it fell from Diederich's lips. When the last was uttered she remained motionless for a moment, and then buried her face in her hands. She was sobbing and he could see her swollen cheeks and the tears trickling between her fingers. She had no handkerchief, and Diederich affected by her sorrow, lent her his. "After all," said he, "he is not such a great loss." But then Guste arose in her wrath. "You dare say that! It was you who was attacking him. That he should send just you here seems to be more than strange."

"Kindly explain what you mean," demanded Diederich. "You must have known just as well as I, my dear young lady, what to expect from the gentleman in question. Where a man's opinions are feeble, everything else in him is equally so."

As she looked him up and down mockingly, he continued, all the more severely: "I told you beforehand exactly what would happen."

"Because you wanted it to happen," she replied venomously. And Diederich ironically: "He himself appointed me to keep his pot stirred. And if the pot had not been wrapped in a cloth, he would long since have let it boil over."

Then it burst from Guste, in spite of herself: "If you only knew. It is that which I cannot pardon in him, that *every-thing* was indifferent to him, even my money!"

Diederich was staggered. "One shouldn't have anything to do with such people," he said primly. "They have no backbone, and are as slippery as eels." He shook his head impressively. "The person who is indifferent to money does not understand life."

She gave a feeble laugh. "In that case, you understand it wonderfully."

"Let us hope so," he replied. She came closer to him and smiled at him through her tears.

"Well, you have been right all along. What am I to do now?" She turned down the corners of her mouth. "Anyway, I never loved him. I was only waiting for an opportunity to get rid of him. Now he shows what a cad he is by going off himself! . . . Let us get on without him," she added with an alluring glance. But Diederich merely took back his handkerchief, and seemed to have no wish for anything more.

"You are no doubt referring to the position in which I have been placed."

He declined to be drawn. "I did not say anything." Guste complained softly: "If people say dreadful things about me I cannot help it."

"Neither can I."

Guste bowed her head "Ah, yes, I suppose I shall have to give in. A person like me does not deserve to be taken by a really fine man with a serious view of life." As she said this she peeped at him from under her eyelashes to see the effect. Diederich snorted. "It is possible—" He began and he stopped. Guste held her breath. "Let us suppose," he said with sharp emphasis, "that some one, on the contrary, takes a most earnest view of life, sees things in a large modern fashion, is as fully conscious of his responsibilities to himself and his future children as to his King and country, and undertakes to protect the defenceless woman and to raise her up to his own level."

Guste's expression had become more and more solemn. She pressed her palms together, and looked at him, with her head on one side, fervently entreating him. This did not seem to be enough—he obviously demanded something quite unusual, so Guste fell plump upon her knees—then Diederich graciously approached her. "So shall it be," he said, his eyes flashing.

At this point Frau Daimchen entered. "Hello," she said, "what has happened?" With great presence of mind Guste replied: "Oh, mother, we are looking for my ring." Whereupon Frau Daimchen also got down on the ground. Diederich did not wish to be behind-hand. After they had all crawled about for a while in silence, Guste cried: "Here it is!" She stood up and said in resolute tones:

"In case you don't know, mother, I have changed my mind." Frau Daimchen, still out of breath, did not understand at first. Guste and Diederich united their efforts in making the matter clear to her. In the end she admitted that she herself had thought the same thing because of the way people were talking: "In any case, Wolfgang was too lackadaisical, except when he had had something to drink. The family was the only thing, on the other hand, the Hesslings don't amount to much."

Diederich said she would see, and announced that nothing could be taken as settled until the practical side of the question had been discussed. They had to produce documentary evidence of Guste's dowry, and then he insisted upon joint ownership of the property—then, whatever he did with the money afterwards, nobody would interfere! Every time they opposed him he took hold of the door handle, and each time Guste remonstrated with her mother in a beseeching whisper: "Do you want the whole town to be wagging their jaws tomorrow because I have got rid of one man and lost the other?"

When everything was settled Diederich became genial. He

stayed to supper with the ladies, and without waiting for their answer, he was on the point of sending the servant for champagne to celebrate the engagement. Frau Daimchen was offended at this, for of course she had some in the house, the officers who came to see them expected it. "The truth is you have more luck than cunning, for Lieutenant von Brietzen could also have had Guste." At this Diederich laughed goodhumouredly. Things were going swimmingly. He had the money and Emma had Lieutenant von Brietzen! . . . They grew very jolly. After the second bottle the happy couple were rolling up against one another on their chairs, their legs were intertwined up to the knee, and Diederich's hands were busy caressing Guste. Frau Daimchen sat twiddling her thumbs. Suddenly a loud report was heard for which Diederich at once accepted full responsibility, saying that it was the custom in aristocratic circles, that he was a frequent guest of the Wulckows.

What a surprise when Netzig learnt the strange turn the affair had taken. To the inquiries of his congratulating friends Diederich replied that he was quite undecided what he would do with his wife's million and a half. Perhaps he would move to Berlin, where there was more scope for big undertakings. In any case he thought he would sell his factory as opportunity offered. "The paper industry is going through a crisis anyhow; this little piece of property buried in the middle of Netzig is quite inadequate to my circumstances."

At home there was joy and sunshine. The girls received increased pocket-money, and Diederich allowed his mother as many embraces and tender scenes as her heart desired. He even accepted her blessing with good grace. Every time Guste came it was in the part of a good fairy, with her arms full of flowers, sweets and silver bags. By her side it seemed to Diederich he was walking along a flower-strewn path. The heavenly days passed quickly with purchases, champagne breakfasts and visits by the engaged couple, who sat inside the carriage busily absorbed in one another, while the box seat was occupied by a footman hired for the occasion.

Then came the wedding day; for they were both in a hurry, Guste because of the people, Diederich for political reasons. In order to make a bigger splash it had been arranged that Magda and Kienast should be married on the same day. Kienast had arrived and Diederich kept looking at him uneasily, for he had shaved his beard, turned up the points of his moustache and already learnt to flash his eyes. In the negotiations over Magda's share in the business he displayed a truly terrifying commercial sense. Not without anxiety for the ultimate issue of the whole thing, though determined to fulfil his duty to himself without flinching, Diederich was now more constantly absorbed in his account books. . . . Even on his wedding morning he was sitting in his office, in full dress, when a visiting card was presented: Karnauke, First Lieutenant, Retired. "What on earth does he want, Sötbier?" The old bookkeeper did not know either. "Well, it doesn't matter. I can't refuse to see an officer," and Diederich went himself to the door.

In the doorway, however, he met a gentleman who held himself unusually stiffly, in a green summer overcoat, which was dripping and was buttoned tightly around his neck. A pool of water formed at once underneath his patent leather shoes, and the rain fell from his green Tyrolese hat, which he had not removed, strange to say. "First let us get dried a bit," said the gentleman, moving towards the stove, before Diederich could speak. "For sale, what? Queer street, what?" At first Diederich did not grasp his meaning; then he glanced uneasily at Sötbier. The old fellow had resumed his letter. "You must have made a mistake in the number of the house," said Diederich in a conciliatory tone, but it was no use.

"Bosh, I know exactly. No nonsense. Superior orders. Sell and keep your mouth shut, or God help you."

This speech was too obvious. Diederich could no longer

ignore the fact that, in spite of his military past, the incredible stiffness of the gentleman's bearing was not natural, and that his eyes were glassy. Just as Diederich came to this conclusion the gentleman took his little green hat and shook the water out of it onto Diederich's dress shirt front. This drew a protest which the gentleman took in very bad part. "I am at your disposal," he snarled. "Herren von Quitzin and von Wulckow will call upon you as my seconds." He blinked strenuously at these words, and Diederich, upon whom an awful suspicion was dawning, forgot his anger, his sole thought being to get the first lieutenant out through the door. "We'll talk outside," he whispered to him, and to Sötbier, on the other side: "The man is helplessly drunk. I'll have to see how I can get rid of him." But Sötbier's lips were pressed together, his brow wrinkled, and this time he did not return to his letter.

The gentleman went straight out into the rain; Diederich following him. "No offence meant; we can talk things over." It was not until he was wet through that he succeeded in piloting the gentleman back into the house. Through the empty machine room the first lieutenant yelled: "A glass of brandy; I'll buy everything, including the brandy!" Although the workmen had the day off, on account of the wedding, Diederich looked anxiously around. He opened the little room where the sacks of chlorine were kept, and got the gentleman inside with a desperate shove. The stench was awful. The gentleman sniffed several times, and then said: "My name is Karnauke. Why do you stink so?"

"Who is backing you?" asked Diederich. This also irritated the gentleman. "What do you mean to insinuate? . . . Oh, I see. I'll buy the whole show." Following Diederich's glance he gazed at his dripping, light summer coat. "Temporarily embarrassed," he growled. "Am acting for honourable parties. Genuine offer."

"How much are you commissioned to offer?"

"A hundred and twenty for the lot."

Diederich grew indignant and angry by turns. The land alone was worth two hundred thousand. The lieutenant insisted: "A hundred and twenty for the lot."

"Nothing doing"—Diederich made an incautious move towards the door, whereupon the gentleman tackled him seriously. Diederich had to struggle, fell onto a sack of chlorine, and the other on top of him. "Get up," gasped Diederich, "we'll be bleached here." The lieutenant howled aloud as if it already burnt through his clothes—then he suddenly resumed his stiff demeanour. He blinked. "Governor von Wulckow will cut up nasty; if you don't sell, he'll do nothing for you. Cousin Quitzin is extending his property hereabouts. He's counting for a certain on your meeting his wishes. A hundred and twenty for the lot." Diederich turned whiter than if he had remained in the chlorine, and tried again: "One hundred and fifty"—but his voice failed him. It was too much for an honourable man! Wulckow insisting upon his official honour, as incorruptible as the Last Judgment! . . . Disconsolately he once again looked at the figure of this Karnauke, First Lieutenant, Retired. That was the man Wulckow sent; he put himself in the hands of such a person! Couldn't they recently have negotiated the deal between themselves, with all due precautions and with mutual respect? But these Junkers could only spring at your throat: they could not yet understand that business is business. "Just go on ahead to the notary's," whispered Diederich, "I'll be right after you." He showed him out, but when he himself was on the point of leaving, old Sötbier was standing there, with his lips still pursed. "What do you want?" Diederich was exhausted.

"Young master," began the old man in a hollow voice. "I can no longer be responsible for what you are now planning to do."

"You're not asked to be." Diederich recovered his composure. "I am the best judge of what I am doing." The old man raised his hands in dismay.

"You do not know, Master Diederich! It is the life work of your lamented father and myself that I am defending. Because we built up the business with industry and hard work, you have become big. If you buy expensive machinery at one time and decline contracts the next, that is a zig-zag course which will bring the business to ruin. And now you are selling the old house."

"You were listening at the keyhole. If anything happens without you, you still cannot stand the idea. Mind you don't catch cold here," Diederich sneered.

"You must not sell it!" moaned Sötbier. "I cannot look on and see the son and heir of my old master undermining the solid foundations of the firm and playing for heavy stakes."

Diederich gave him a pitying look. "In your time, Sötbier, big ideas were unknown. Nowadays people take risks. Push is the main thing. Later you will see what was the advantage in my selling the house."

"Yes, you will only see that later, too. Perhaps when you are bankrupt, or when your brother-in-law, Herr Kienast, brings a lawsuit against you. You have manipulated certain things to the prejudice of your sisters and your mother! If I were to tell Herr Kienast certain things—only I have a sense of family piety, I could get you into trouble!"

The old man was beside himself. He was screaming and there were tears of passion on his red eyelids. Diederich went up to him and held his clenched fist under his nose: "Just you try it! I will simply prove that you have been robbing the firm and always did. Do you imagine I haven't taken precautions?"

The old man also raised his trembling fist. They fumed at one another. Sötbier's bloodshot eyes were rolling. Diederich glared. Then the old fellow drew back. "No, this cannot happen. I was always a faithful servant of the old master. My conscience commands me to give my faithful services to his successors as long as possible."

"That would suit you very well," said Diederich harshly and coldly. "Consider yourself lucky that I don't fire you on the spot. You may send in your resignation, it is accepted." And he marched off.

At the notary's he asked that the purchaser in the agreement of sale be described as "unknown." Karnauke grinned. "Unknown is good. Don't we know Herr von Quitzin?" At this the notary also smiled. "I see," said he, "that Herr von Quitzin is spreading out. For a long time he owned in Meisestrasse only the little Cock tavern. But he is also in negotiations for the two pieces of property behind yours, Dr. Hessling. Then he will be on the borders of the park and will have room for immense buildings."

Diederich began to tremble again. In a whisper he begged the notary to be discreet as long as possible. Then he said good-bye, as he had no time to lose. "I know," said the first lieutenant holding him fast. "Day of joy. Luncheon at the Hotel Reichshof. I'm ready." He opened his green overcoat and pointed to his crumpled dress-suit. Diederich looked at him in horror, tried to put him off, but the lieutenant again threatened him with his backers.

The bride had been waiting for a long time, and the two mothers were drying their tears amidst the knowing smiles of the other ladies present. This bridegroom had also jumped the traces! Magda and Kienast were furious, and messengers were running between Schweinichenstrasse and Meisestrasse. . . . At last! Diederich came, though he was wearing his old dress-suit. He did not even condescend to explain. At the civil ceremony and in the church he was absent-minded. On all sides it was said that no blessing could rest upon a marriage consummated under such circumstances. Pastor Zillich even mentioned in his discourse that earthly possessions did not endure. His disappointment was comprehensible. Käthchen did not come at all.

At the wedding luncheon Diederich sat in silence, obviously

busied with other things. He even forgot to eat and stared
into space. First Lieutenant Karnauke alone had the faculty
of arousing his attention. The lieutenant admittedly did his
best. No sooner had the soup been removed than he proposed
a toast to the bride, making allusions which were excessive in
proportion to the amount of wine the rest of the company had
drunk. Diederich was more disturbed by certain references of
Karnauke's, which were accompanied by winks in his direction and which unfortunately sounded suspicious to Kienast.
The moment arrived which Diederich had foreseen with beating heart. Kienast stood up and asked him for a word in private. . . . Just then the first lieutenant tapped energetically
on his glass, and jumped up stiffly from his seat. The considerable noise of the party was hushed. A blue ribbon could be
seen hanging from Karnauke's pointed fingers, and beneath it
a cross, whose gold rim sparkled. . . . Ah, what an uproar
and congratulations! Diederich stretched out his two hands,
an ineffable joy flowed from his heart to his throat, and he began to speak involuntarily, before he knew what he was saying: "His Majesty . . . unprecedented graciousness . . . modest services . . . unshakable loyalty." He bowed and scraped,
and as Karnauke handed him the cross, he laid his hands on
his heart, closed his eyes and sank back, as if another stood
before him, the Donor himself. Basking in the royal approval
Diederich felt that salvation and victory were his. Wulckow
had kept his pact. Authority kept its pact with Diederich!
The Order of the Crown, fourth class, glittered. It was an
event, foreshadowing the William the Great monument and
Gausenfeld, business and glory!

It was time to break up. Kienast, though moved and impressed, succeeded in getting a few words from Diederich of
general significance, about the glorious days which he would
enjoy, and the great things which were in store for him and
the whole family—and then Diederich was off with Guste.

They got into a first-class carriage. He gave the porter

three marks and pulled down the blinds. Carried on the wings of happiness, his desire for action suffered no relaxation. Guste could never have expected so amorous a temperament. "You are not like Lohengrin," she said. As she swooned away and closed her eyes, Diederich got up again. Like a man of iron he stood before her, his order hanging on his breast; he glittered like steel. "Before we go any further," he said in martial tones, "let us think of His Majesty, our Gracious Emperor. We must keep before us the higher aim of doing honour to His Majesty, and of giving him capable soldiers." "Oh!" cried Guste, carried away into loftier splendours by the sparkling ornament on his breast, "Is it . . . really . . . you . . . my Diederich!" . . .

VI

HERR and Frau Dr. Hessling from Netzig looked at one another in the lift of the hotel in Zurich, for they were being taken up to the fourth floor. This was the result of the glance of quick, discreet appraisal which the clerk at the desk had given them. Diederich obediently filled up the form for visitors, but when the waiter had withdrawn, he relieved his feelings about the way things were done here, and about Zurich in general. His indignation increased more and more, and finally took shape in the resolve to write to Baedeker. As this relief meanwhile seemed a little too remote, he turned on Guste. It was all the fault of her hat. Guste, in her turn, blamed his German military cape. Thus they descended to lunch, both red with anger. At the door they stopped, and sniffed superciliously as they met the gaze of the hotel guests, Diederich in his dinner jacket, and Guste wearing a hat whose ribbons, feathers and buckle combined, certainly entitled her to the best floor in the hotel. Their earlier acquaintance, the waiter, conducted them in triumph to their seats.

That night they became reconciled both to Zurich and the hotel. In the first place their room on the fourth floor was cheap, if not distinguished. And then, just opposite the twin beds of the wedded couple there hung an almost life-size picture of an odalisque, whose brownish body reclined voluptuously on a pillow, her hands under her head, and her dark eyes full of languishing desire. The figure was cut off in the middle by the frame, a fact which moved them to joking comment. The next day they went about with eyelids heavy as lead, ate enormous meals, and wondered what would have happened if the odalisque had been entirely visible instead of being cut off from the waist. They were too tired to catch the train and re-

turned in the evening, as soon as possible, to their inexpensive
and inspiring room. There was no saying when this sort of
existence might have ended, if Diederich's heavy eyes had not
caught sight of an announcement in the newspaper that the
Emperor was on his way to Rome to visit the King of Italy.
He aroused himself in a flash. With elastic stride he went
from the hall-porter to the office, and from the office to the
lift, and though Guste wailed that her head was turning, the
trunks were made ready, and Diederich got Guste away. "Oh,
why," she complained "must we leave a place where the bed
is so comfortable?" But Diederich had only a mocking look
for the odalisque as they left. "Have a good time, by dear
young lady!"

For a long time he could not sleep from excitement. Guste
snored peaceably on his shoulder while Diederich, as the train
roared through the night, remembered how at that very moment, on another line, the Emperor himself was being carried
by a train which roared similarly, towards the same goal. The
Emperor and Diederich were having a race! And, as Diederich had more than once been privileged to utter thoughts
which seemed in some mystic way to coincide with those of the
All-Highest, perhaps at that hour His Majesty knew of Diederich, knew that his loyal servant was crossing the Alps by his
side, in order to show these degenerate Latins what loyalty to
king and country means. He glared at the sleepers on the
opposite seat, small, dark people, whose faces seemed haggard
in their sleep. They would see what Germanic valour was!

Passengers got out in the early morning at Milan, and at
Florence, about noon, to Diederich's astonishment. Without
any noticeable success he endeavoured to impress upon those
who remained what a great event awaited them in Rome. Two
Americans showed themselves somewhat more susceptible, at
which Diederich exclaimed triumphantly: "Ah, I am sure you
also envy us our Emperor." Then the Americans looked at
one another in a mute and vain interrogation. Before they

reached Rome Diederich's excitement was translated into a feverish desire to be up and doing. With his finger in a phrase-book he ran after the employés on the train, trying to find out who would arrive first, his Emperor or he. His enthusiasm had infected Guste. "Diedel!" she cried, "I feel like throwing my veil on the ground for him to walk on it and flinging the roses from my hat at him!"—"If he sees you and you make an impression on him?" asked Diederich, with a feverish smile. Guste's bosom began to heave and she dropped her eyes. Diederich, who was gasping, broke the fearful tension. "My manly honour is sacred, I must insist. But in such a case . . ." and he concluded with a brief gesture.

Then they arrived, but very differently from what they had imagined. In the greatest confusion the passengers were pushed by officials out of the station, over to the edge of a broad square and into the streets behind it, which were immediately closed off again. With unshakable enthusiasm Diederich broke through the barriers. Guste, who stretched out her arm in horror, was left standing there with all the hand-luggage, while he stormed blindly forward. He had got as far as the middle of the square, and two soldiers with plumed helmets were running after him so that the tails of their gaily-coloured dress tunics flapped in the breeze. Then several gentlemen walked down the sloping entrance to the station, and almost simultaneously Diederich saw a carriage driving towards him. He waved his hat and bawled so loudly that the gentlemen in the carriage interrupted their conversation. The one on the right leaned forward and—they were face to face, Diederich and his Emperor! The Emperor smiled coldly and critically, and the lines of his mouth relaxed slightly. Diederich ran along beside the carriage for a while, his eyes staring wildly, shouting continuously and waving his hat. For a few seconds, while the foreign crowd in the background applauded, the Emperor and his loyal subject were alone together, in the middle of the empty square, beneath the glaring blue sky.

The carriage had already disappeared along the streets hung with bunting, cheers could be heard in the distance, when Diederich heaved a great sigh and put on his hat.

Guste was beckoning to him frantically, and the people who were still standing around applauded, with looks of cheerful good nature. Even the soldiers who had previously followed him were now laughing. One of them showed his sympathy so far as to call a cab. As he drove off Diederich saluted the crowd. "They are like children," said his wife. "Yes, but correspondingly undisciplined," he added, and he admitted: "That could not have happened in Berlin. . . . When I think of the row Unter den Linden, order was much more sharply maintained." He tidied himself before they drove up to the hotel. Thanks to his manner, they were given a room on the second floor.

The early morning sun saw Diederich once more in the streets. "The Emperor is an early riser," he had informed Guste, who only grunted from the pillows. In any case she could not assist him in his task. Guiding himself with a plan of the city he arrived in front of the Quirinal, and took up his position. The quiet square gleamed bright gold under the oblique rays of the sun. Gaunt and massive the palace stood out against the empty sky—and opposite stood Diederich, awaiting His Majesty, the Order of the Crown, fourth class, on his protruding chest. A herd of goats tripped up the steps from the city, and disappeared behind the fountain and the statues of giant horse-breakers. Diederich did not look around. Two hours went by, more people began to pass, a sentry had come out of his box, in one of the portals a gatekeeper was moving about, and several persons went in and out. Diederich became uneasy. He approached the façade, moved slowly up and down, peeping anxiously inside. On his third appearance the gatekeeper touched his hat hesitatingly. When Diederich stopped and returned his salute, he became more confidential. "Everything in order," he said behind his hand, and Diederich received the information with an air of understanding. It seemed to him only natural that he should be informed of the Emperor's welfare. His questions, when the Emperor would be going out and where, were answered without hesitation. The gatekeeper himself got the idea that, in order to accompany the Emperor, Diederich would need a carriage and he sent for one. Meanwhile a knot of curious onlookers had formed, and then the gatekeeper stepped to one side. Behind an outrider, in an open carriage came the blond ruler of the North, beneath his flashing eagle-helmet. Diederich's hat was in the air and he shouted in Italian, with the precision of a pistol shot: "Long live the Emperor!" And obligingly the knot of people shouted with him.

In a jump Diederich had got into his one-horse carriage, which stood ready, and was off in pursuit, urging the coachman with hoarse cries and an ample tip. Now he stops, for the royal carriage is only just coming up. When the Emperor gets out there is another little knot of people, and again Diederich shouts in Italian. . . . Watch must be kept in front of the house where the Emperor lingers! With chest extended and flashing eyes: let him beware who ventures to come too near! In ten minutes the little group re-forms, the carriage drives out through the gate, and Diederich: "Long live the Emperor!" and the shout is echoed by the crowd, as the company rushes wildly back to the Quirinal. Guard is mounted. The Emperor in a shako. The little crowd. Another visit, another return, another uniform, and again Diederich, and again an enthusiastic reception. So it went, and never had Diederich enjoyed himself so much before. His friend the gatekeeper kept him reliably informed as to the Emperor's movements. It also happened that an official would salute and give him a message which he condescendingly received, or that another would ask for instructions, which Diederich gave in general terms, but in a commanding tone. The sun rose higher and higher. In front of the marble squares of the façade, behind which his Emperor was holding conversations covering the whole orbit of the world, Diederich was suffering hunger and thirst without flinching. Although he held himself firmly erect, he felt, nevertheless, as if his paunch were sinking to the pavement under the burden of noon, and his Order of the Crown, fourth class, were melting on his breast. . . . . The coachman, whose visits to the nearest tavern were becoming more frequent, finally was impressed by the German's heroic sense of duty and brought him back some wine. With a new fire in their veins the pair took part in the next race. The imperial horses ran quickly, in order to get there before them, it was necessary to plunge through side streets that looked like canals, and whose few pedestrians shrank back in terror against the walls. Or they had to get out and clamber madly up flights of steps. But Diederich was punctually at the head of his little crowd, watched for the seventh uniform emerging from the carriage, and shouted. Then the Emperor turned his head and smiled. He recognised him, his loyal subject! The one who shouted, who was always on the spot, like a devoted retainer. Diederich felt as if he were flying on the wings of elation because of the All Highest's attention. His eyes flashed at the people whose faces wore an expression of cheerful good nature.

Only when the gatekeeper assured him that His Majesty was now at lunch did Diederich allow himself to think of Guste. "What a sight you are!" she cried, drawing back against the wall, when she beheld him. He was as red as a tomato, soaked with perspiration, and his eyes were as bright and wild as those of a Germanic warrior of yore on a foray through the Latin territories. "This is a great day for the national cause!" he said furiously. "His Majesty and I are making moral conquests!" How fine he looked! Guste forgot her fright and her annoyance at the long wait. She came up with her arms affectionately outstretched and clung to him humbly.

Diederich, however, would hardly allow himself the brief

hour for lunch. He knew that the Emperor rested after eating. Then it was his duty to mount guard under his windows without shirking. He did not shirk his duty, and the result showed how well he had done. He had not been eighty minutes at his post opposite the portal of the palace, when a suspicious looking individual, profiting by the brief absence of the gate-keeper, slipped in, hid behind a pillar, and in the dark shadow concealed plans which could not be otherwise than dangerous. This was Diederich's opportunity! With a warlike cry he could be seen thundering across the square like a storm.' Startled people rushed after him, the guard hurried up, in the gateway servants were running about—and every one admired Diederich as he dragged some man forward, wildly struggling, who had hidden himself. The pair fought so fiercely that the armed guards did not even dare to approach. Suddenly Diederich's opponent, who had succeeded in freeing his right arm, was seen swinging a box. A breathless second—then the panic-stricken crowd rushed yelling to the gate. A bomb! He is going to throw it! . . . He had thrown it! In expectation of the explosion those nearest, threw themselves on the ground, moaning in advance. But Diederich, his face, shoulders and chest all white, stood there and sneezed. There was a strong smell of peppermint. The boldest returned and tested it with their sense of smell. A soldier, with waving plumes, gingerly dipped his moistened finger into it, and tasted it. Diederich grasped the situation and explained it to the crowd, whose expression of cheerful good humour returned, for he himself was no longer in doubt for some moments past that he was covered with tooth-powder. The bomb-thrower—absolutely in vain—tried to get past him and escape. Diederich's iron fist delivered him to the police. The latter ascertained that the man was a German, and asked Diederich to question him. In spite of the tooth-powder which covered him, he undertook this duty with the utmost dignity. The answers of the man, who, significantly enough, was an artist, had no particular political colour, but their abysmal lack of respect and moral sense betrayed only too clearly revolutionary tendencies. Therefore Diederich strongly urged that he should be arrested. The police led him off, and they did not forget to salute Diederich, who had only just time to get brushed by his friend the gatekeeper. For the Emperor was announced, and Diederich's personal service began again.

The following evening at the gala performance at the theatre the Emperor looked more serious than usual. Diederich noticed it, and said to Guste: "Now I know why I spent our good money coming here. Just watch, this will be an historic occasion!" His premonition did not deceive him. The evening papers spread round the theatre, and it was learned that the Emperor was going away that night, that he had dissolved the Reichstag. Diederich, no less serious than the Emperor, explained the significance of the event to every one near him. The revolutionaries had dared to vote against the Army Bill. The patriotic parties were entering upon a life and death struggle for their Emperor! He himself was returning home by the next train, he assured them, and they hastened to tell him at what hour it left.

. . . The person who was dissatisfied was Guste. "When one gets somewhere else, at last, and thank God, one has the money and can afford it, why should I, after moping for two days in the hotel, start back at once, just because—" She threw a glance of such disgust at the royal box that Diederich had to intervene with the utmost severity. Guste answered loudly, every one around them cried "sh!" and when Diederich turned round to glare at the objectors, they compelled him and Guste to leave, long before the train started. "That rabble has no manners," he remarked, snorting furiously, when they got outside. "Anyhow, what's the good of this place, I'd like to know. The weather is all right, I suppose . . . but just look at all that old junk about the place!" he insisted. Guste, who was once more pacified, said complainingly: "but I enjoy it." Then they departed at a respectful distance behind the Emperor's train. Guste had forgotten her sponge and brushes in their haste and at every station she wanted to get out. Diederich had to remind her ceaselessly of the national cause, in order to induce her to wait for thirty-six hours. When they finally arrived in Netzig, however, her first thought was for the sponge. Of course they had arrived on a Sunday! Fortunately, the apothecary's shop, at least, was open. While Diederich was waiting in the station for the luggage Guste went over to it. As she did not return, he went after her.

The door of the apothecary's was half open, and three youths were peeping in and laughing. Diederich looked over their shoulders and was amazed, for inside his old college friend, Gottlieb Hornung, was marching up and down behind the counter, with folded arms and gloomy countenance. Guste was just saying: "Now I'd really like to know when I am going to get my tooth-brush." Then Gottlieb Hornung stepped forward from behind the counter, with arms still crossed, and turned his melancholy gaze upon Guste. "You cannot fail," he began oratorically, "to have noticed by my expression that I have neither the will nor the power to sell you a tooth-brush." Guste drew back and said: "Really! But you have a whole showcase full." Gottlieb Hornung's smile was Mephistophelian. "My uncle upstairs"—he jerked up his head and pointed with his chin to the ceiling, above which his employer doubtless resided—"my uncle can huckster here as he likes. That does not concern me. I did not study for three years and belong to a swagger corps in order to come here and sell tooth-brushes."—"What are you here for, then?" asked Guste visibly impressed. Then Hornung replied with majestic emphasis: "I am here to attend exclusively to prescriptions!" Guste must have felt that she was beaten, for she turned to go. Then something else occurred to her: "I suppose it is the same with sponges?"—"Just the same," Hornung assured her. This was obviously what Guste had been waiting for, to lose her

temper properly. She stuck out her chest and was going to give
him a piece of her mind. Diederich had just time to intervene.
He agreed with his friend that the dignity of the Neo-Teutons
should be preserved and their banner held aloft. But if any
one wanted a sponge he could, after all, take it himself and
deposit the amount—which Diederich proceeded to do. Gottlieb Hornung, meanwhile, moved to one side and began to
whistle, as if he were quite alone. Then Diederich expressed
his interest in what his friend had been doing since they last
met. Unfortunately, it was a story of many mishaps, for, as
Hornung could never sell sponges and tooth-brushes, he had
already been dismissed by five apothecaries. Nevertheless he
was determined to stand by his convictions, at the risk of also
losing his present situation. "There you can see a real Neo-
Teuton!" said Diederich to Guste, who had a good look at him.

In his turn Diederich was not slow to relate all his experiences and achievements. He drew attention to his decoration, turned Guste round in front of Hornung, and named the
amount of her fortune. The Emperor, whose enemies and slan-
derers were behind lock and key, thanks to Diederich, had
recently escaped grave personal danger in Rome, also thanks
to Diederich. In order to avoid a panic in the courts of
Europe and on the stock exchange, the press had spoken only
of a silly trick played by a half-wit, "but between ourselves, I
have reason to believe that it was a widespread plot. You
will understand, Hornung, that the national interest commands the utmost discretion, for I am sure you, too, are a
loyal patriot." Of course, Hornung was, and so Diederich
could unburden himself about the highly important task which
had compelled him suddenly to return from his honeymoon.
It was a question of pushing through the national candidates
in Netzig. They must not underestimate the difficulties.
Netzig was a stronghold of Liberalism, and revolution was undermining the foundations. . . . At this stage Guste threatened to drive off home with the luggage. Diederich could only

invite his friend urgently to come to see him that very evening, as he had pressing matters to talk over with him. As he got into the cab he saw one of the young rascals, who had waited outside, going into the shop and asking for a tooth-brush. Diederich reflected that Gottlieb Hornung, just because of the aristocratic tendency which so sadly interfered with the sale of sponges and tooth-brushes, might be an invaluable ally in the fight against democracy. But this was the least of his immediate cares. He only gave old Frau Hessling an opportunity of shedding a few hasty tears; then she had to return to the top floor, formerly reserved for the servant and the washing, where Diederich had now dumped his mother and Emma. Without waiting to remove the dust of his journey he betook himself by devious ways to Governor von Wulckow's. Then with no less discretion he sent for Napoleon Fischer, and meanwhile took steps to arrange without delay a meeting with Kunze, Kühnchen and Zillich.

This was rendered more difficult because it was a Sunday afternoon. The major could be dragged only with the greatest difficulty from his game of nine-pins. The pastor had to be interrupted as he was preparing to go out on a family excursion with Käthchen and Jadassohn. The professor was in the hands of his two boarders, who had already got him half drunk. Finally he succeeded in getting them all into the club-room of the Veterans' Association, and Diederich explained to them, without further loss of time, that they would have to run a national candidate. And, as things were, there could be no question of any one but Major Kunze. "Hear! Hear!" cried Kühnchen, at once, but the major's expression threatened a storm. Did they take him for a fool? he snarled. Did they think he was anxious to put his foot in it? "A national candidate in Netzig—I have no doubts as to what will happen to him! If everything else were as certain as his defeat!" Diederich would not hear of this. "We have the Veterans' Association, you must take that into account, gentlemen. The

Veterans' Association is an invaluable basis of operations. From that point we can hit out in a straight line, so to speak, to the Emperor William Monument: there the battle will be won." "Hurrah!" cried Kühnchen again, but the other two wanted to know what was this business with the monument. Diederich initiated them into his idea, but preferred to gloss over the fact that it was the subject of a compact between himself and Napoleon Fischer. The Liberal Infant Asylum was not popular, so much he confided, and many voters would be drawn to the national cause, if they were promised an Emperor William Monument out of the Kühlemann bequest. In the first place, this would create more employment, and then it would bring business to the town, for the unveiling of such a monument drew people from far and wide. Netzig had a prospect of losing its bad reputation as a democratic hole and to bask in the sunshine of official favour. At this Diederich remembered his agreement with Wulckow, which he also preferred to leave unmentioned. "To the man who achieved and secured so much for us all"—he pointed enthusiastically to Kunze—"our dear old town will one day certainly erect a monument. He and Emperor William the Great will face one another—" "And stick out our tongues," concluded the major, whose scepticism was unshaken. "If you believe that the people of Netzig are only waiting for the great man to lead them, with bands playing, into the national camp, why do you not play the part of that great man yourself?" And his eyes looked squarely into Diederich's. But the latter only returned his gaze all the more virtuously and laid his hand on his heart! "Major, my well-known devotion to King and country has already imposed upon me trials more severe than a candidature to the Reichstag, and I think I may say, I have stood the test! And in so doing I was not afraid, as a pioneer in a good cause, to draw upon myself all the hatred of ill-disposed people, thereby making it impossible for me to reap myself the fruit of my sacrifice. Netzig would not vote for me, but it will vote for my cause. Therefore, I withdraw, for it is characteristic of a German to be practical, and I leave to you, Major, without envy, the joys and the honour!" General sensation! There were tears in Kühnchen's cheer, the pastor nodded solemnly, and Kunze stared at the ground, obviously shaken. Diederich felt relieved and virtuous; he had allowed his heart to speak and it had expressed loyalty, sacrifice and manly idealism. Diederich's hand, covered with fair hairs, was extended across the table and the major's, with its dark hairs, clasped his, hesitatingly yet warmly.

Now that the hearts of all four had spoken, reason again became articulate. The major inquired whether Diederich was prepared to compensate him for the material and spiritual losses that threatened him, in case he entered the lists against the candidate of the Liberal gang and was defeated. "Look here" —he pointed his finger at Diederich, who could not immediately find words to counter this directness—"the national cause does not seem to you as certain as all that, and as I know you, Dr. Hessling, the fact that you insist on bringing me into it is connected with some chicanery or other on your part, which a bluff old soldier like myself cannot, thank God, understand." Hereupon Diederich hastened to promise the bluff old soldier a decoration, and as he gave a hint of his understanding with Wulckow, the national candidate was finally won over completely. . . . Meanwhile Pastor Zillich had been debating whether his position in the town would permit of his being chairman of the national election committee. Was he to introduce dissensions among his flock? His own brother-in-law, Heuteufel, was the Liberal candidate! Of course, if a church were to be built instead of a monument! "Truly, the house of God is more necessary than ever, and my beloved St. Mary's is so neglected by the town that one of these days it will fall down about the ears of myself and my congregation." Without hesitation, Diederich guaranteed all the necessary repairs. The only condition he made was that the pastor should keep out of confidential positions in the new party all those who had aroused just doubts, by certain external evidence, as to the genuineness of their national sentiments. "Without wishing to interfere in family matters," Diederich added, looking hard at Käthchen's father, who had clearly understood, for he did not breathe a sound. . . . But Kühnchen who had long since ceased to shout hurrah, also presented himself. The two others had only kept him in his seat by force, while they were speaking. They had scarcely released him when he noisily assumed the centre of the debate. Where would national sentiment have its roots, above all? Amongst the youth? But how could that be, when the headmaster of the college was a friend of Herr Buck's? "I could talk myself hoarse about our glorious deeds in the year '70. . . ." Enough: Kühnchen wanted to be appointed headmaster, and Diederich magnanimously granted his request.

In due course the preparations had been made which the national committee considered necessary for the first election meeting of the "Emperor's Party." It was to take place at Klappsch's, who had patriotically thrown open his room. In the midst of green wreaths flaming mottoes were set. "The Will of the King is the Supreme Command." "You have only one Enemy, and He is Mine." "Leave the Social Democrats to Me." "Mine is the Right Course." "Citizens, awake from your Slumbers." Klappsch and his daughter saw to it that they were aroused by keeping them all constantly supplied with fresh beer, without being as particular as usual about the amount each one consumed. Thus, they were in a good mood to receive Kunze, when he was introduced by the chairman, Pastor Zillich. From behind the cloud of smoke in which the committee sat, Diederich, however, made the unpleasant discovery that Heuteufel, Cohn and some of their followers, had also gained admission. He took Gottlieb Hornung to task, for the latter was in charge of the arrangements. But he would not listen; he was irritated, the labour of bringing the people together had been too much.

There were now so many contractors for the Emperor William Monument, thanks to his efforts, that the town would never be able to pay them, not if old Kühlemann were to die and leave his money three times over! Hornung's hands· were swollen from shaking those of all the newly converted patriots! They had asked too much of him; that he should associate with druggists was the least of his grievances. But Gottlieb Hornung protested against this democratic lack of respect for rank. The proprietor of the pharmacy had just given him notice to leave, but he was more determined than ever to sell neither tooth-brushes nor combs. . . . Meanwhile Kunze was stammering through his speech. His gloomy air was proof to Diederich that the major was not at all sure of what he wanted to say, and that he was more embarrassed by the election than he would have been in a really grave crisis. He was saying: "The army, gentlemen, is our only support," but as a heckler in Heuteufel's neighbourhood shouted: "It is rotten!" Kunze immediately lost his head, and added: "But who pays for it? The citizens." At this the people near Heuteufel shouted bravo. Thereby forced into a false position, Kunze began to explain: "Therefore, we are all supports, on that we ·must insist, and woe to the King who—" "Hear! Hear!" replied the Liberal voters, and they were joined by the right-thinking patriots. The major wiped the perspiration from his brow. In spite of himself his speech was developing as if it had been addressed to a Liberal meeting. From behind Diederich kept pulling his coat-tails and begged him to stop, but it was in vain that Kunze essayed to do so. He could not make a transition to the electoral slogan of the Emperor's Party. Finally he lost patience, turned suddenly very red, and with unexpected ferocity, he yelled: "Stamp them out root and branch!" The Veterans' Association thundered its applause.

Whenever people were not applauding Klappsch and· his daughter hastened with beer, at a sign from Diederich.

Dr. Heuteufel at once asked for permission to take part in the discussion, but Gottlieb Hornung got in before him. Diederich, for his part, preferred to remain in the background, behind the cloud of smoke which enveloped the platform. He had promised Hornung ten marks and the latter was not in a position to refuse. Gnashing his teeth he stepped over to the edge of the platform, and began to explain the speech of the gallant major, by saying that the army, for which we are all prepared to make any sacrifice, was our bulwark against the turbid flood of democracy. "Democracy is the philosophy of the half-educated," said the apothecary. "It has been defeated by science." Some one shouted: "Hear! Hear!" It was the druggist who wished to associate with him: "There will always be masters and men," asserted Gottlieb Hornung, "for it is the same in nature. It is the one great truth, for each of us must have a superior to fear, and an inferior to frighten. What would become of us otherwise? If every nonentity believes that he is somebody, and that we are all equal! Unhappy the nation whose traditional and honourable social forms are broken up by the solvent of democracy, and which allows the disintegrating standpoint of personality to get the upper hand!"

Here Gottlieb Hornung folded his arms and thrust forward his head. "I," he cried, "who have been a member of a crack corps and know what it is to shed my blood gladly for the colours—I refuse to sell tooth-brushes!" "Or sponges, either?" asked a voice.

"Or sponges either!" said Hornung decisively. "I emphatically forbid any one else to ask that of me. People should always know with what sort of a person they are dealing. Honour to whom honour is due. And in that sense we give our votes to the one candidate who will allow the Emperor as many soldiers as he wants. Either we have an Emperor or we have not!"

Then Gottlieb Hornung stepped back and, with pugnaciously protruding jaw and wrinkled brow, gazed at the applauding audience. The Veterans' Association would not be deprived of the opportunity to march past him and Kunze with upraised beer glasses. Kunze received handshakes, Hornung stood there stolidly—and Diederich could not but feel rather bitterly that these two second-rate personalities had all the advantage of a situation which he had created. He had to leave to them the popular approval of the moment, for he knew better than these two simpletons where it was all going to lead. As the national candidate's sole reason for existence was to procure reinforcements for Napoleon Fischer, it was wiser not to go forward oneself. But Heuteufel was anxious to draw Diederich out. Pastor Zillich, the chairman, could not refuse any longer to allow him to take the floor. He began at once about the Infant Asylum; it was a matter of humanity and social conscience. What was the Emperor William Monument? A speculation, and vanity was not the most discreditable part of the speculators' calculations. . . . The contractors in the rear listened in a silence filled with painful feelings, which here and there found expression in a muffled murmur. Diederich was trembling. "There are people," Heuteufel declared, "who do not mind another million for the army, for they know how they can get some of it back to their own profit." Then Diederich jumped up. "I wish to say a word!" With cries of "Bravo!" "Ha, ha!" "Sit down," the contractors relieved their feelings. They yelled until Heuteufel made way for Diederich.

Diederich waited for some time before the storm of patriotic indignation had subsided. Then he began: "Gentlemen!" "Bravo!" shouted the contractors and Diederich had to wait again, in that atmosphere of feeling identical with his own, in which he breathed so easily. When they allowed him to speak he gave expression to the general indignation that the previous speaker had dared to cast suspicions upon the loyal sentiments of the meeting. "Shame!" cried the contractors. "This only proves," said Diederich, "how opportune has been the founding of the 'Emperor's Party—' The Emperor himself has commanded all those to join hands who, whether nobles or commoners, wish to free him from the revolutionary pest. That is our purpose, and therefore our loyal and patriotic sentiments are far above the suspicions of those who themselves are nothing but the forerunners of revolt!" Before the applause could break out, Heuteufel said in a very loud tone: "Wait until the second ballot!" Although the contractors immediately drowned the rest in the noise of their clapping, Diederich scented so much danger in these words that he hastened to change the subject. The Infant Asylum was on less treacherous ground. What? A matter of social conscience, they said! It was an encouragement to vice. "We Germans leave such things to the French, a decadent people!" Diederich had only to repeat an article he had sent to the "Netzig Journal." Pastor Zillich's Young Men's Christian Association and the Christian Clerks' Association applauded every word. "The Teuton is chaste," cried Diederich, "that is why we won in the year seventy!" Now it was the turn of the Veterans' Association to give the noisiest signs of enthusiasm. Kühnchen jumped up behind the chairman's table, waved his cigar and screamed: "We'll soon smash 'em again!" Diederich raised himself on his toes, "Gentlemen," he shouted, carried away on the tide of national emotion, "the Emperor William Monument shall be a mark of reverence for the noble grandfather whom we all, I think I may say, worship almost as a saint, and also a pledge to the noble nephew, our magnificent young Emperor, that we shall ever remain as we are, pure, liberty-loving, truthful, brave and true!"

Latterly Guste had begun to be peevish, and to have fits of

sickness, during which Frau Hessling had to take care of her in the bedroom. As soon as she felt better she would remind the old lady that everything there had been really paid with her money. Frau Hessling never failed to describe the marriage with her Diedel as a real mercy for Guste in the peculiar circumstances of her position at the time. The end would be that Guste's cheeks were swollen red with rage and she was fuming, while Frau Hessling shed tears. Diederich profited by this, for afterwards each of them was as affectionate as possible towards him, with the object, which he did not suspect, of bringing him onto her side.

So far as Emma was concerned, as was her custom, she simply slammed the door and went up to her room, which had a slanting roof. Guste kept wondering how she could drive her even out of that. Where were they to dry the washing when it rained? If Emma couldn't get a husband, because she had no money, they would simply have to marry her to some one beneath her socially, some honest artisan. But, as a matter of fact, she was the swell member of the family, she visited the Brietzens. . . . For it was this that embittered Guste most. Emma was invited by the Fräulein von Brietzen, although they had never set foot in her house. Their brother, the lieutenant, would at least have owed Guste a visit for the suppers her mother had given, but he condescended to visit only the second story of Hessling's house, it was absolutely notorious. . . . Her social successes, however, did not prevent Emma from having days of the utmost depression. Then she would not even leave her room for meals, which were eaten in common. Once Guste went up to her, out of pity and sheer boredom, but when Emma saw her she shut her eyes, and lay there, pale and motionless, in her flowing morning wrap. Getting no answer, Guste tried to exchange confidences about Diederich and her own condition. Then Emma's rigid face contracted suddenly, she turned on one of her arms and with the other pointed violently to the door. Guste did not fail to express her indignation. Emma jumped up impetuously, and clearly gave her to understand that she wished to be alone. When old Frau Hessling came up it was already decided that the two families in future would have their meals apart. When Guste came weeping to Diederich, he was unpleasantly disturbed by these women's quarrels. Fortunately he had an idea which seemed to promise immediate peace. He went to Emma and announced that he had decided to send her to stay for a while in Eschweiler with Magda. To his amazement, she declined to go. As he kept insisting, she was on the point of flaring up, but she was suddenly seized as if by some fear, and began to beg softly and entreatingly to be allowed to stay. Diederich, touched by an ill-defined emotion, looked helplessly around the room and then retreated.

The following day Emma appeared at lunch as if nothing had happened; her cheeks were freshly coloured and she was in the best of humours. Guste, who was all the more reserved, kept exchanging glances with Diederich. Thinking he understood, he raised his glass to Emma, and said teasingly: *"Prosit, Frau von Brietzen."* Emma turned deadly pale. "Don't make an ass of yourself," she cried angrily, throwing down her napkin and banging the door after her. "Hello!" growled Diederich, but Guste merely shrugged her shoulders. It was only after old Frau Hessling had gone that she gave Diederich a curious look and asked: "Do you really think . . .?" He winced, but looked inquiringly. "I mean," Guste explained, "that the lieutenant might at least salute me in the street. To-day he went out of his way to avoid me." Diederich thought this was all nonsense. Guste replied: "If I only imagine it, then I imagine other things as well, because at night I have many times heard something creeping through the house, and to-day Minna said—" Guste got no further. "Ah," Diederich fumed, "you are hobnobbing with the servants! Mother always used to do that. All I can tell you is, that I won't have it. I alone can watch over the honour of my family and do not need either Minna's assistance or yours. If you don't agree with me, then the pair of you know where the door is through which you came!" Naturally, Guste could only bow in the face of this virile attitude, but she smiled slily after him as he went out.

For his part, Diederich was happy at having disposed of the matter by his firm procedure. He could not allow his life to become any more complicated than it was at that time. His hoarseness, which had unfortunately kept him out of the struggle for three days, had not been overlooked by the enemy. In fact, Napoleon Fischer had told him only that morning that the "Emperor's Party" was getting too strong for him, and had been stirring up feeling against the Social Democrats too much lately. In these circumstances. . . . In order to quiet him Diederich had to promise to carry out his bargain that very day, and ask the town councillors to sanction the Social Democratic Trade Union Hall. . . . So, although his throat was not quite well, he went to the meeting—and there he discovered that the motion concerning the Trade Union Hall had just been introduced; by Messrs. Cohn and company, moreover! The Liberals voted for it, and it went through as smoothly as if it had been the most ordinary measure. Diederich who wished to scourge openly the national treason of Cohn and his comrades, could only bark hoarsely. This clever trick had once more robbed him of his voice. No sooner had he got home than he sent for Napoleon Fischer.

"You are dismissed!" Diederich bellowed. The machinist grinned ambiguously. "All right," said he, preparing to go. "Stop!" shouted Diederich. "Don't think you are going to get off so easily as that. If you join with the Liberals, then you may be sure I will make our agreement public! I'll show you!"

"Politics is politics," Napoleon remarked with a shrug, and as Diederich could not bellow any more in the face of such cynicism, Napoleon Fischer stepped nearer confidentially, and almost tapped Diederich on the shoulder. "Dr. Hessling," he said amiably, "Don't you do that. We two—yes, I say we two. . . ." His grin was so full of threats that Diederich shuddered. He quickly offered Napoleon Fischer a cigar. Fischer smoked . and said:

"If one of us two were to begin talking where would the other stop? Ain't I right, Dr. Hessling? But we are not a pair of old chatterboxes who have to blab everything immediately, like Herr Buck for example."

"What do you mean?" asked Diederich dully, as he fell into one fright after another. The machinist professed to be astonished. "Don't you know? Herr Buck goes about everywhere saying that you do not really mean all that patriotic stuff so badly. You simply want to get Gausenfeld cheap, and you think you will get it cheaper if Klüsing is frightened about certain contracts because he is not a patriot."

"Is that what he says?" asked Diederich, who felt stunned.

"That's what he says," Fischer repeated. "And he also says he will do you a favour and speak a word in your behalf to Klüsing. Then you will probably be quieter, he says."

Then a weight was lifted from Diederich's heart. "Fischer," he said with a short bark, "just you watch what happens. You will see old Buck standing in the gutter begging. That's what you'll see. I'll answer for it, Fischer. Good-bye."

Old Buck had blue eyes, a benevolent smile, and he was the most treacherous dog of all those who threatened the loyalists. The thought of old Buck held Diederich as if in a dream. The next evening, under the light of the domestic lamp, he was so busy with imaginary moves against old Buck that he did not hear the family when they spoke to him. He was particularly embittered because he had looked upon the old man as a toothless old chatterbox, and now he was showing his teeth. After all his humanitarian phrase-making it seemed a challenge to Diederich that he did not now allow himself to be simply gobbled up. The hypocritical gentleness with which he pretended he had forgiven Diederich the ruin of his son-in-law! Why had he protected him? Got him onto the Town Council? Only so that Diederich might give himself away and be more easily caught. The old man's question at that time, whether Diederich wanted to sell his property to the town, now appeared as the most dangerous trap. Diederich felt as if his game had been seen through all the time. He now felt as if old Buck had been present, invisible in the clouds of smoke, at his secret interview with Governor von Wulckow. When Diederich had crept along to Gausenfeld one dark winter's night, and had hidden in the ditch, shutting his eyes which had perhaps gleamed, old Buck had passed above him and peeped down at him. . . . In his imagination Diederich saw the old gentleman stooping over him, and stretching out his soft white hand to help him out of the ditch. The kindness in his face was simply mockery, it was more unbearable than anything else. He thought he could make Diederich docile, and with his tricks bring him back like the prodigal son. But they would see which of them would end by eating husks.

"What is the matter, my dear child?" asked Frau Hessling, for Diederich had groaned aloud from hate and fear. He gave a start. At that moment Emma was walking across the room, it seemed to Diederich that she had already done so several times. She went to the window, put her head out, sighed, as if there was nobody present, and walked back. Guste looked after her, and as Emma passed in front of Diederich, Guste's mocking look covered them both. And this startled Diederich more than ever, for this was the revolutionary smile which he had learnt to recognise in Napoleon Fischer. Guste was smiling in the same way. He wrinkled his brow in terror and shouted sharply: "What's the matter?" Immediately Guste was plunged in her darning, but Emma stood still and gazed at him with those dulled eyes which she now sometimes had. "What's wrong with you?" he asked, as she remained silent. "Whom are you looking for in the street?" She merely

shrugged her shoulders, but her face remained motionless.
"Well?" he repeated more softly, for her look, her demeanour,
which seemed remarkably indifferent and therefore, superior,
made it difficult for him to be rough. Finally she decided
to speak.

"It was possible that the two Fräulein von Britzens might
have come."

"So late at night?" asked Diederich. Then Guste said:
"Because we are not accustomed to that honour. And anyhow,
they went away yesterday with their mamma. If they do not
even say good-bye to people, because they do not even know
them, all one has to do is to go past their villa to know that
they are gone."

"What?" said Emma.

"Why, certainly!" Beaming with triumph Guste told her
the whole story. "The lieutenant will soon follow them. He
has been transferred." She paused, and looked up. "He has
had himself transferred." "You're a liar!" cried Emma. She
had swayed and was visibly holding herself erect. With her
head high she turned and let the curtain fall behind her.
There was silence in the room. Old Frau Hessling on the sofa
folded her hands, Guste looked defiantly at Diederich, who
rushed up and down fuming. When he reached the door again
he gave a start. Through the opening he caught a glimpse of
Emma who was sitting, or rather hanging, huddled up in a
chair, as if she had been tied up and thrown there. She quivered, then turned her face towards the lamp. Just before it
had been quite pale and it was now deep red. She was looking
with unseen eyes. Suddenly she sprang up, rushed off as if
she were on fire, and with angry, uncertain steps she dashed
out, knocking against things without feeling them, out as if
into a mist, into a fog. . . . With increasing anxiety Diederich
turned to his wife and his mother. As Guste seemed disposed
to be disrespectful he pulled himself together, with his accustomed good form, and marched stiffly after Emma.

He had not yet reached the stairs when the door above was closed noisily with lock and bolt. Then Diederich's heart began to beat so fast that he had to stop. By the time he reached the top the voice with which he asked permission to enter was weak and breathless. There was no answer, but he heard something rattle on the washstand—and suddenly he waved his arms, shouted, banged on the door and yelled madly. Because of his own noise he did not hear her opening the door, and he was still shouting when she stood before him. "What do you want?" she asked angrily, whereupon Diederich recovered himself. From the stairs Frau Hessling and Guste were peeping up, out of horrified curiosity. "Stay down!" he commanded, pushing Emma back into the room. He shut the door. "The others needn't smell this," he said sharply, and he took out of the wash-jug a small sponge dripping with chloroform. He held it away from him with outstretched arm and asked: "Where did you get this?" She tossed her head and looked at him without replying. The longer this lasted the more unimportant Diederich felt the question becoming, which should, by rights, have been the first. Finally, he simply went to the window and threw out the sponge into the dark courtyard. There was a splash. It had fallen into the brook. Diederich gave a sigh of relief.

Now it was Emma's turn to ask questions. "What do you think you are doing up here? Kindly allow me to do what I think fit." This came to him as a surprise. "Yes, but . . . what *are* you doing?" She looked away and replied with a shrug: "That doesn't matter." "Oh, come now!" Diederich was indignant. "If you no longer have any respect for your divine Judge, which I personally cannot approve of, you might, at least, have a little regard for us here. You are not alone in the world."

Her indifference wounded him deeply. "I will have no scandal in my house. I am the first person who will suffer."

Suddenly she looked at him. "And I?"

He snapped: "My honour—" but stopped suddenly. Her expression, which had never seemed to him so eloquent, seemed to accuse and to mock him at the same time. In confusion he went to the door. Here it dawned on him what he ought to have done.

"At all events, as your brother and a man of honour, I will, of course, do my duty. Meanwhile I expect you to impose upon yourself the utmost reserve." With a glance at the wash-jug, from which there was still a smell:

"Your word of honour!"

"Leave me alone," said Emma. Then Diederich came back.

"You do not seem to be aware of the seriousness of the situation. If what I fear is true, you have—"

"It is true," said Emma.

"Then you have not only risked your own existence, at least socially, but you have covered a whole family with shame."

"That is also possible," said Emma.

He was startled and was preparing to express his loathing of such cynicism, but it was too plain from Emma's face all that she had been through and had left behind her as useless.

Diederich shuddered at the superiority of her desperation. He felt as if certain artificial springs had snapped inside him. His legs trembled, he sat down, and managed to say: "Can't you just tell me—I will also—" He looked at Emma's appearance and the word pardon stuck in his throat. "I will help you," he said. "How can you make that right?" she answered wearily, as she leant against the wall.

He looked down in front of him. "Of course, you must give me some information, I mean, about certain details. I presume this has gone on since your riding-lessons?"

She allowed him to make further suppositions, which she neither confirmed nor denied. But when he raised his eyes to her, her lips were softly parted and she was gazing at him in wonder. He understood that she was wondering how he was relieving her of so much she had borne alone, merely because he mentioned it aloud. An unfamiliar pride possessed him. He stood up and said confidingly: "You can leave it to me. First thing to-morrow morning I'll go there."

"You don't understand. It is all over."

Then his voice·became·benevolent. "We are not absolutely without weapons. Wait until I see him!"

He gave her his hand as they parted. She called him back again.

"Are you going to challenge him?" Her eyes were staring wide open and she held her hands to her lips.

"Why do you ask?" said Diederich, for he ceased to think of this.

"Swear that you will not challenge him!"

He promised. At the same time he blushed, for he would like to have known for whom she feared, for him or the other. He would not have liked it to be the other, but he stifled the question, because it might have been painful for her to answer, and he tiptoed out of the room.

He ordered the two women, who still waited below, sternly to bed. He lay down beside Guste only after she had fallen asleep. He had to think over what he would do the next day. Make an impression, of course! Admit of no possible doubt as to the outcome of the affair! But instead of his own smart figure, Diederich saw again and again in his imagination a stout man with pale troubled eyes, who begged, raged and finally collapsed: Herr Göppel, Agnes Göppel's father. Now in his terrified soul Diederich understood what the father must then have felt. "You don't understand," said Emma. He did understand what he himself had done.

"God forbid!" he said aloud, as he turned over. "I won't be drawn into this business. Emma was only bluffing with the chloroform. Women are depraved enough for that. I'll throw her out, as she deserves!" Then Agnes appeared before him in the rainy street and stared up at his window, the pale reflection of the gas light on her face. He pulled the bedclothes

over his eyes. "I can't drive her onto the streets!" Morning
dawned and he was amazed at what had happened to him.

"Lieutenants get up early," he thought, and he slipped off
before Guste was awake. Beyond the Saxon Gate the gardens
were full of perfume and twittering, beneath the spring skies.
The villas, still closed up, looked as if they had been freshly
washed, and as if innumerable newly-married couples had
rented them. "Who knows," thought Diederich as he breathed
in the pure air, "perhaps it will not be difficult. They are
decent people. The circumstances also are essentially more
favourable than—" He preferred not to complete the thought.
There in the distance a cab stopped—before which house was
it? Yes, it was. The iron gate stood open and also the door.
The officer's servant came towards him. "It doesn't matter,"
said Diederich, "I'll see the lieutenant." Right in the room
facing them Herr von Brietzen was packing a trunk. "So
early," he was saying, let the lid of the trunk fall and caught
his finger. "Damn it!" was Diederich's discouraging reflection, "he, too, is busy packing."

"To what chance am I indebted—" began Herr von Brietzen,
but involuntarily Diederich made a movement which signified
that this was superfluous. Nevertheless, Herr von Brietzen denied everything. He denied even longer than Diederich had
done, and Diederich recognised this fact inwardly, for when a
girl's honour was at stake a lieutenant had to be several degrees more punctilious than a Neo-Teuton. When they had
finally got the whole situation straight, Herr von Brietzen at
once placed himself at Diederich's disposal, as was certainly
expected of him. But in spite of his deadly fear, Diederich
replied cheerfully that he hoped a decision with arms might
be unnecessary, provided Herr von Brietzen— And Herr von
Brietzen assumed exactly the expression Diederich had foreseen, and used exactly those expressions which Diederich had
heard in his imagination. When driven into a corner, he uttered the sentence which Diederich dreaded most, and which,

he admitted, could not be avoided. A girl who had lost her virtue could not be selected as the mother of one's children. Diederich replied to this as Herr Göppel had replied, and was as crushed as Herr Göppel. He did not get really angry until he came out with his big threat, the threat with which he had been promising himself success since yesterday.

"In view of your unchivalrous refusal, Lieutenant, I find myself unfortunately compelled to place your colonel in possession of the facts."

Herr von Brietzen really seemed to be hit in a vulnerable spot. He asked hesitatingly: "What good do you think that will do? Force me to listen to a moral lecture? Well, all right. But, in any case,"—Herr von Brietzen recovered his self-possession—"so far as chivalry is concerned, the colonel will probably have very different views from those of a gentleman who refuses to accept a challenge."

Then Diederich arose in his wrath. Herr von Brietzen would kindly hold his tongue, otherwise he might find that he would have to deal with the Neo-Teutons! He, Diederich, had proved by his scars that he had joyfully shed his blood for the honour of the colours! He could only wish that Lieutenant von Brietzen should find himself some time in a position where he would have to challenge a Graf von Tauern-Bärenheim! "I challenged him flatly!" And in the same breath he declared that he was far from recognising the right of an impertinent Junker to shoot down a decent burgher and the father of a family. "You'd no doubt like to seduce the sister and shoot the brother," he shouted, beside himself. In a similar state of rage Herr von Brietzen talked of having his servant smash the tradesman's face, and as the servant stood there ready, Diederich cleared out, but not without a parting shot. "If you think, because of your impertinence, we will pass the Army Bill! We'll show you what revolution is!"

Outside in the deserted avenue he continued to rage, shook his fist at the invisible enemy and uttered threats. "You will regret that some day, when we call a halt!" Suddenly he noticed that the gardens were still full of perfume and twittering beneath the spring skies, and it became clear to him that Nature itself, whether she smiled or snarled, was powerless before Authority, the authority above us, which is quite impregnable. It was easy to threaten revolution, but what about the Emperor William Monument? Wulckow and Gausenfeld? Whoever trampled others under foot must be prepared to be walked on, that was the iron law of might. After his attack of resistance, Diederich again felt the secret thrill of the man who is trampled upon. . . . A cab came along from behind, Herr von Brietzen and his trunk. Before he knew what he was doing Diederich faced about, ready to salute. But Herr von Brietzen looked the other way. In spite of everything Diederich rejoiced in the fresh, chivalrous young officer. "Nobody can duplicate that for us," he said with conviction.

Now, however, that he had entered Meisestrasse he felt embarrassed. From a distance he could see Emma looking out for him. All of a sudden he realised all that she must have gone through during the last hour, which had decided her fate. Poor Emma! Now it was decided. No doubt, Power was elevating, but when it hit one's own sister—"I did not know it would touch me so closely." He nodded up as encouragingly as possible. She had become much thinner, how was it nobody noticed it? She had big sleepless eyes beneath her pale shimmering hair; her lips twitched as he nodded to her. He noticed that also with the sharp eyes of fear. He almost crept up the stairs. On the first floor she came out of the room and went on in front of him to the floor above. When she was up she turned round—and when she saw his face she went inside without speaking, went to the window, and remained standing, with her face turned away. He pulled himself together and said aloud: "Oh! Nothing is lost yet." She shrank at this and closed her eyes. As he groaned audibly, she turned, came slowly towards him, laid her head on his shoulder, and they wept together.

Afterwards he had an encounter with Guste who wanted to nag. Diederich told her pointblank that she was only using Emma's misfortune in order to have her revenge for the not altogether auspicious circumstances under which she herself had got married. "Emma, at least, is not throwing herself at any one's head." Guste screamed: "Did I throw myself at yours?" He cut her short. "In any case, she is my sister!" . . . And as she was now living under his protection, he began to find her interesting, and to show her unusual respect. After meals, he used to kiss her hand, in spite of Guste's grins. He compared the two women. How much more common Guste was! Magda, even, whom he had favoured because she was successful, no longer compared in his memory with the abandoned Emma. Through her misfortune Emma had become more refined and, so to speak, more elusive. When her hand lay there, so white and so absent-mindedly, and Emma was sunk silently in her own thoughts, as if in an unknown abyss, Diederich felt touched by the premonition of a deeper world. The attribute of a fallen woman, unnatural and despicable in others, lent Emma, Diederich's sister, a strange shimmering air of questionable charm. Emma was now both more touching and more brilliant.

The lieutenant, who had caused all this, lost notably in comparison—and so did the Power, in whose name he had triumphed. Diederich discovered that Power could sometimes present a common and vulgar appearance, Power and everything that went with it, success, honour, loyalty. He looked at Emma and was forced to question the value of what he had attained or was still striving for; Guste and her money, the monument, the favour of the authorities, Gausenfeld, distinctions and high office. He looked at Emma and thought of Agnes. Agnes had cultivated tenderness and love in him, she had been the true thing in his life, he should have held it fast. Where was she now? Dead? Sometimes he used to sit, holding his head in his hands. What had he now? What were the rewards in the service of Power? Once more everything failed him, every one betrayed him, distorted his purest intentions, and old Buck was master of the situation. Agnes, who could only suffer—the thought insinuated itself, that she had won. He wrote to Berlin and made inquiries about her. She was married and in good health. This relieved him, but somehow, it also disappointed him.

While Diederich was lost in such reflections election day approached. Filled with a sense of the vanity of all things, Diederich took no notice of what was going on, not even of the increasingly hostile air of the machinist. On the day of the polls, while Diederich was still in bed, Napoleon Fischer came to see him. Without the least apology he began: "At the eleventh hour, Dr. Hessling, I have something serious to tell you." This time it was he who scented betrayal and recalled their agreement. "You are playing a double-faced game. You made certain promises to us, and being men of our word, we did not work against you, but only against the Liberals."

"So did we," declared Diederich.

"You know that's not true. You have been hobnobbing with Heuteufel. He has already agreed to your monument. If you do not go over to his side with full colours to-day, you will certainly do so on the second ballot, and shamefully betray the people."

With folded arms Napoleon Fischer took another long stride towards the bed. "All I want to tell you is that we are not blind."

Diederich found himself in bed and completely at the mercy of his political opponent. He tried to soothe him. "I know, Fischer, you are a great politician. You will certainly get into the Reichstag."

"That's right." Napoleon winked slily. "If I don't, there will be a strike in several factories in Netzig." He turned on his heel. At the door he held Diederich, who had sunk down under the bedclothes in terror, once more in his glance. "Therefore, long live international Social Democracy!" he shouted as he went out.

From beneath the bedclothes Diederich cried: "Hurrah for His Majesty the Emperor!" After that there was nothing to be done but to face the situation. It looked pretty threatening. Oppressed with misgivings he hastened out into the street, to the Veterans' Association, to Klappsch's and everywhere he was forced to admit that, during the days of his discouragement, the clever tactics of old Buck had achieved wide success. The Emperor's Party had been diluted by accretions from the Liberal ranks, and the difference between Kunze and Heuteufel was inconsiderable compared with the abyss between him and Napoleon Fischer. Pastor Zillich, who exchanged shy greetings with his brother-in-law, Heuteufel, asserted that the Emperor's Party ought to be satisfied with its success, for it had certainly strengthened the national conscience of the Liberal candidate, even if he eventually won. As Professor Kühnchen expressed the same opinion, the suspicion became insistent that they were not satisfied with the promises they had extracted from Diederich and Wulckow, and that they had allowed old Buck to win them over by promises of greater personal advantage. The corruption of the democratic gang was enough for anything! So far as Kunze was concerned, he wanted to be elected in any case; if necessary, with the help of the Liberals. His ambition had corrupted him, it had brought him to the point of promising to stand for the Infant Asylum. Diederich became indignant; Heuteufel was a hundred times worse than any proletarian, and he alluded to the terrible consequences which such an unpatriotic attitude would have. Unfortunately he could not be more specific—and with the picture of the strike before him,

the ruins of the Emperor William Monument, of Gausenfeld
and all his dreams, in his heart, he rushed about in the rain
from one polling-station to another, bringing up the loyal
voters, with the certainty that their loyalty was wasted and
would help the worst enemies of the Emperor. At Klappsch's
in the evening, splashed with mud to the neck, his nerves on
edge after the noise of the long day, the vast amount of beer
and the nearness of the final result, he heard the figures.
Against Heuteufel's eight thousand votes, Napoleon Fischer
had six thousand odd, but Kunze had three thousand six hundred and seventy-two. The second ballot was between Heuteufel and Fischer. "Hurrah!" shouted Diederich, for nothing was lost and they had gained time.

He returned to his office from which old Sötbier had vanished and where Diederich was now his own accountant, answerable only to his God, and where his weightiest decisions
were made. He went to the telephone and asked for Gausenfeld. Just then the door opened and the postman handed in
his packages. On the top Diederich noticed Gausenfeld. He
hung up the receiver again and, nodding like Destiny, he gazed
at the letter. The deed was done! The old chap had not
waited to be told; he understood that he no longer dared to
give money to Buck and his allies, and that if necessary, he
could personally be called to account. Diederich calmly tore
open the envelope—but after two lines he was reading fever-
ishly. What a surprise! Klüsing was ready to sell! He
was growing old and regarded Diederich as his natural successor!

What did it all mean? Diederich sat down in a corner to
think. First of all, it meant that Wulckow had intervened.
The old fellow was in mortal fear because of the government
contracts; and the strike, which Napoleon threatened, had
done the rest. Where was the time when he thought he could
get out of the dilemma by offering Diederich a share of the
paper for the "Netzig Journal"? Now he offered him the

whole of Gausenfeld! "I am a Power," Diederich declared, and it came upon him that Klüsing's idea, that he would buy the factory and pay its full value, was simply ridiculous, in view of the circumstances; and he actually laughed out loud. . . . Then he became aware that at the end of the letter, below the signature, there was something else, a postscript written smaller than the rest and so unnoticeable that Diederich had missed it before. He deciphered it—and his jaw dropped. Suddenly he leaped up. "So that's it!" he shouted, capering triumphantly about his empty office. "Now we have it!" Then he said, with great seriousness: "It is dreadful! An abyss!" He read again, word for word, the fateful postscript, placed the letter in the safe and shut the door sharply. In there the poison was simmering for Buck and his followers— supplied by their friend. Not only did Klüsing no longer furnish them with funds; he betrayed them also. But there was no doubt they deserved it; such depravity had probably disgusted even Klüsing. To spare them would be to share their guilt. Diederich examined his conscience. "Mercy would really be a crime. Let every man look to himself. This was a case where he must proceed without fear or favour, tear the mask from the conspiracy and clean it out ruthlessly! I undertake the task in the interest of the public welfare, my duty as a loyal patriot leaves me no choice. These are strenuous times."

The next evening there was a big, open public meeting, called by the Liberal election committee in the large Walhalla Theatre. With the active assistance of Gottlieb Hornung, Diederich had taken steps to ensure that the meeting was not confined to Heuteufel's supporters. He himself did not think it necessary to hear the speech of the candidate, and he did not go until the meeting was open for discussion. In an anteroom he ran into Kunze, who was in a bad humour. "A discharged assassin!" he shouted. "Look at me, sir, and tell me if I look like the sort of man who would allow himself

to be called that!" As he was too excited to explain himself
further, Kühnchen came to his assistance. "Heuteufel should
have said that to me!" he yelled. "I'd have shown him the
sort of man Kühnchen is!" Diederich strongly recommended
the major to sue his opponent. But Kunze needed no further
encouragement; he swore he would simply mash Heuteufel's
face for him. Diederich thought this a good idea, and he
agreed most emphatically when Kunze declared that, in the
circumstances, he preferred to side with the worst revolutionaries rather than with the Liberals. Kühnchen and Pastor
Zillich, who had joined them, opposed this view. The enemies of their country—and the Emperor's Party! "Corrupt
cowards!" said Diederich's look—while the major continued
to swear vengeance. These swine would weep tears of blood!
"And they'll do it to-night," said Diederich with such decision
that they were all astonished. He paused for a moment and
glared at each of them. "What would you say, Pastor, if
I were to prove certain machinations against your Liberal
friends? . . ." Pastor Zillich turned pale. Diederich turned
to Kühnchen: "Dishonest manipulation of public funds."
Kühnchen jumped. "They will wish themselves dead," he
shouted ferociously. Kunze bellowed: "Give me your hand!"
and he seized Diederich in his arms. "The shell may be rough,
but the kernel is sound. Prove the knavery of those swine
and Major Kunze is your friend, as though we had been
under fire together at Mars-la-Tour!"

The major had tears in his eyes, and so had Diederich,
and the exaltation of their souls was equalled only by that
of the meeting. On entering one could see arms being raised
everywhere, through the blue haze, and here and there shouts
arose: "Shame!" "Hear, hear!" or "Disgraceful!" The electoral contest was at its height. Diederich plunged in with
extraordinary bitterness, for in front of the table, at which
old Buck was presiding in person, who was standing at the
edge of the platform and speaking? Sötbier, Diederich's dis-

missed bookkeeper! Out of revenge Sötbier was making a
provocative speech, in which he uttered the most striking
judgments upon the alleged friendliness of certain gentlemen
for the workers. It was simply a demagogic stunt, by which,
for the sake of certain personal advantages, they wished to
divide the middle-classes and drive the voters onto the side
of revolution. Formerly the gentleman in question had said:
Whoever is born a slave must remain a slave. "Shame!"
yelled the organised workers. Diederich pushed his way
through until he was beside the platform. "A vulgar libel!"
he shouted into Sötbier's face. "You ought to be ashamed of
yourself! Since your dismissal you have joined the malcon-
tents." The Veterans' Association, under Kunze's command,
bawled like one man: "Disgraceful!" and "Hear, hear!"—
while the organised workers hissed and Sötbier shook a trembling fist at Diederich, who threatened to have him locked up.
Then old Buck stood up and rang his bell.

When silence had been restored he said in a gentle voice,
which rose and thrilled the hearers: "Fellow-citizens! Do not
give the personal ambition of individuals anything to feed on
by taking it seriously! What is the individual? What are
classes even? The people's interests are at stake, and the
people includes every one except those who want to be masters. We must stand together. We citizens must not again
make the mistake, which was made in my youth, of entrusting
our welfare to bayonets, as soon as the workers demand their
rights. Because we would never grant the workers their
rights, we have given the masters power to deprive us also
of our rights."

"Quite right!"

"We, the people, have all perhaps our last opportunity, in
the face of this demand upon us to increase the army, to assert
our freedom against our masters, who are arming us still more,
merely that we may be slaves. Whoever is born a slave must
remain a slave. That is not said only to you workers, it is

said to us all by the masters whose power we must pay for ever more dearly." "Quite right! Bravo! Not a man, not a cent!" Amidst enthusiastic approval old Buck sat down. Diederich, who was dripping with perspiration as he approached the final struggle, glanced over the audience and saw Gottlieb Hornung, in charge of the contractors for the Emperor William Monument. Pastor Zillich was busy among the Christian young men, and the Veterans' Association had rallied round Kunze. Then he launched forth. "Our hereditary foe is raising his head once more," he shouted defiantly. "A traitor to the Fatherland, who refuses our magnificent young Emperor what he—" "Ha, ha!" cried the traitors to the Fatherland, but amidst the applause of the loyalists Diederich continued to shout, although he was over-straining his throat: "A French general is asking for *revanche!*" From the platform some one asked: "How much is he getting for that from Berlin?" There was laughter, while Diederich clawed the air as if he wanted to climb up. "The flash of arms! Blood and iron! Manly ideals. A strong Empire!" His forcible phrases jostled, rattling against each other, amidst the din made by the right-thinking patriots. "A powerful regiment, a bulwark against the turbid stream of democracy."

"Wulckow is your bulwark!" cried the voice from the platform again. Diederich turned around and recognised Heuteufel. "Do you mean His Majesty's Government—?" "Another bulwark!" said Heuteufel. Diederich pointed his finger at him. "You have insulted the Emperor!" he shouted sharply. Behind him, however, some one yelled: "Informer!" It was Napoleon Fischer and his comrades repeated it with hoarse shouts. They had jumped up and surrounded Diederich in a fashion which boded him no good. "He is trying again to provoke some one! He wants to get some one else in jail! Throw him out!" They seized him. Horny hands were pressing his neck as he turned his face, distorted with terror, towards the chairman and begged chokingly for help. Old Buck granted his request; he rang his bell incessantly, and even sent some young men down to rescue Diederich from his enemies. No sooner was he free than Diederich pointed his finger at old Buck. "The corruptness of democracy," he shouted, dancing with passion. "I will prove it to him!" "Bravo!" "Let him speak"—and the camp of the loyalists was set in motion, poured over the tables and stood face to face with the revolutionaries. A free fight seemed imminent. The police officer on the platform caught hold of his helmet to protect himself; it was a critical moment. Then a command was heard: "Silence! Let him speak!" It was almost quiet, for people had become aware of an anger greater than any other present. Old Buck, looming above his table on the platform, was no longer a worthy old gentleman. Power seemed to give slenderness to his figure, he was pale with hatred, and he darted a glance at Diederich which caused the onlookers to hold their breath.

"Let him speak," the old man repeated. "Even traitors are allowed to speak before they are condemned. That is what traitors to the nation look like. They have changed only in externals since the time when my generation fought and died, and went to prison and the scaffold."

"Ha! ha!" cried Gottlieb Hornung, filled with superior mirth. Unfortunately for him, he was sitting within arm's reach of a powerful workman, who raised his arm so threateningly that, before the blow struck him, Hornung collapsed together with his chair.

"At that time also," shouted the old man, "there were such people who preferred profit to honour, and who found no domination humiliating, provided their pockets were the better of it. Servile materialism, the fruit and weapon of every tyranny, that was what defeated us, and you also, my fellow-citizens—"

The old man spread out his arms and nerved himself for the final cry of his conscience.

"Fellow-citizens, you also are in danger to-day of being betrayed by that materialism and of becoming its prey. Let this man speak."

"No!"

"He shall speak. Afterwards you can ask him how much in hard cash those opinions are worth, which he has the impertinence to call patriotic. Ask him who bought his house, for what purpose, and to whose advantage."

"Wulckow!" The word was shouted from the platform, but the audience took it up. Diederich was pushed against his will by irresistible hands up to the steps of the platform. He looked around in search of counsel. Old Buck was sitting motionless, his clenched fist resting on his knee, and his eyes never left Diederich. Heuteufel, Cohn, all the members of the committee, were waiting for his collapse, with an expression of cold eagerness on their faces. And the audience shouted, "Wulckow! Wulckow!" He stammered something about calumny, his heart was beating furiously, and for a moment he shut his eyes, in the hope that he was going to faint and would thus get out of the dilemma. But he did not faint, and, as there was no alternative, a terrible courage possessed him. He seized his pocketbook, to make sure of his weapon, and with something like the joy of battle he surveyed his enemy, that sly old man, who had at last torn off the mask of the paternal friend and confessed his hatred. Diederich glared at him and shook both his fists in front of him. Then he faced the audience aggressively.

"Do you want to earn some money?" he bawled, like a street-hawker above the din—and all was silent as if at a magic command. "Every one can earn some money from me," he yelled with undiminished violence. "To every one who can prove how much I made on the sale of my house I will pay the same again!"

Nobody seemed prepared for this. The contractors were the first to cry "Bravo!" Then the Christians and the war-

riors followed suit, but half-heartedly, for the shout of
"Wulckow!" had begun again, to the tapping of beer glasses
which were being knocked on the tables. Diederich saw that
this was a pre-arranged trick, and was directed not only against
himself but much higher authorities. He looked around uneasily, and the police officer was again clasping his helmet.
Diederich made a sign to him with his hand, as much as to
say he would attend to this, and bellowed:

"Not Wulckow, but very different people! The Liberal
Infant Asylum! They wanted me to give up my house for
that; that was proposed to me, I am ready to swear it. As a
loyal patriot I emphatically repudiated the suggestion that I
should cheat the town and share the spoil with an unprincipled municipal council."

"You lie!" cried old Buck, as he stood up flaming. But
Diederich flamed even more fiercely, in the consciousness of being right and of his moral mission. He plunged his hand into
his pocketbook, and in front of the hydra-headed monster
below whose venom bespattered him: "Liar! Swindler!" he
fearlessly waved his document. "Here's the proof!" he shouted,
waving the paper until they decided to listen to him.

"It did not work with me, but in Gausenfeld, it did, my fellow-citizens. In Gausenfeld . . . How can that be? I'll tell
you. Two gentlemen from the Liberal Party went to the
owner and tried to secure in advance purchase rights to a certain piece of property, in case the Infant Asylum should be
built there."

"Name! Name!"

Diederich slapped his chest, prepared to go to any length.
Klüsing had told him everything except the names. With
flashing eyes he stared at the members of the committee. One
seemed to grow pale. "Nothing venture, nothing win," thought
Diederich, and he shouted: "one was Cohn the owner of the
drapery stores!"

He stepped off the platform with the air of one whose duty

has been fulfilled. Down below Kunze received him and kissed him on both cheeks, oblivious of everything, whereat the loyalists applauded. The others shouted: "Proof!" or "Nonsense!" But "Let Cohn speak!" that was the general cry. It was impossible for Cohn to evade this invitation. Old Buck looked at him; his cheeks were quivering and he was rigid, and then he called upon him to speak. Cohn, pushed forward vigorously by Heuteufel, came out very indecisively from behind the long table of the committee, dragged his feet, and created a most unfavourable impression even before he started. He smiled apologetically. "Gentlemen, you will hardly believe what the previous speaker has said." He spoke so softly that hardly anybody understood. Yet Cohn fancied, even then, that he had gone too far. "I will not exactly contradict the previous speaker, but it was not the way he has described."

"Aha! He admits it!"—and suddenly there broke loose such an uproar that Cohn, who anticipated nothing, jumped backwards. The room was filled with noise and gesticulation. Here and there opponents were falling upon one another. "Hurra!" screamed Kühnchen as he rushed through the crowd, with streaming hair, swinging his fists and egging on the fight. . . . On the platform also every one had jumped up, except the police officer. Old Buck had left the chairman's seat, and with his back to the people, on whose deaf ears the last cry of his conscience had fallen, he turned away his eyes so that nobody could see he was weeping, forsaken and alone. Heuteufel spoke indignantly to the police officer, who did not move from his chair, but was told that the police alone decided if and when the meeting should be stopped. There was no necessity to do so just when the Liberals were getting the worst of it. Then Heuteufel went to the table and rang the bell, shouting, as he did so: "The second name!" And as every one on the platform joined in the cry, it was finally audible, and Heuteufel could continue.

THE PATRIOTEER

"The second person who was in Gausenfeld is Judge Kühlemann! That's true. Kühlemann himself. The same Kühlemann from whose bequest the Infant Asylum is to be built. Will any one pretend that Kühlemann was stealing from his own bequest? The conclusion is obvious!" Heuteufel shrugged his shoulders and there was approving laughter. But not for long; passions were soon kindled again. "Proof! Kühlemann himself should explain! Thieves!" Heuteufel explained that Kühlemann was dangerously ill. They were sending a messenger and had already telephoned. "Oh, damn!" whispered Kunze to his friend Diederich. "If it was Kühlemann then it is all over except the shouting." "Not by a long chalk," Diederich answered confidently. Pastor Zillich, for his part, had now no other hope than the hand of God. "We don't want that," said Diederich with great assurance, as he pounced upon a sceptic and talked him over. He egged on the loyalists to take a more decided stand, he even shook hands with Social Democrats in order to strengthen their hatred of the corrupt bourgeoisie, and everywhere he displayed Klüsing's letter. He beat on the paper so vigorously with the back of his hand that nobody could read it, and shouted: "Is Kühlemann there? It is Buck who is mentioned. If Kühlemann has a gasp left he will have to admit that it wasn't he. It was Buck!"

As he spoke he kept his eye on the platform, where a remarkable silence had ensued. The gentlemen of the committee were rushing about, but they talked in whispers. Old Buck was nowhere to be seen. "What is wrong?" The hall had also grown quieter, nobody knew why. Suddenly word came: "They say Kühlemann is dead!" Diederich felt it rather than heard it. He suddenly stopped talking and exerting himself. His face was twitching from excitement. He did not reply when he was asked a question, around him he could hear a vague buzzing of voices, and he no longer knew exactly where he was. Then Gottlieb Hornung came up and said: "God's truth, he's dead. I was up there; they telephoned. At that very moment he died."

"At the right moment," said Diederich, looking around him in astonishment, as if awaking from a dream. "The hand of God has again proved itself," Pastor Zillich affirmed, and Diederich became aware that this was a hand not to be despised. What, if it had given another turn to the wheel of fate? . . . The parties in the hall were dispersing. The intervention of death in politics had turned the parties into human beings. They spoke in lowered tones and withdrew. When Diederich reached the street he also heard that old Buck had had a stroke.

The final voting took place at three o'clock in the afternoon. An alarm was sounded in Kaiser Wilhelmstrasse, and every one rushed to the windows and shop doors to see where the fire was. It was the Veterans' Association marching past in uniform. Their flag pointed the way of honour. Kühnchen, who was in command, had his helmet on the back of his neck and was swinging his sword in a fearsome manner. Diederich with the rank and file tramped along, and rejoiced at the thought that now everything further would be done in line, mechanically and in obedience to superior orders. The march of Power had trampled old Buck into pulp! . . . At the other end of the street they received the new colours, which were presented with thunderous music and cheers of pride. The procession, lengthened by unlimited reinforcements of patriots, reached Klappsch's premises. Here they formed into sections and Kühnchen gave the command: "To the urns." The election committee, with Pastor Zillich at the head, was waiting in the hall, festively attired. Kühnchen issued his commands in martial tones. "On, comrades, to the poll! We vote for Fischer!" Whereupon the music crashed and they marched from the left wing into the polling-booth. The entire procession followed the Veterans' Association. Klappsch was not prepared for so much enthusiasm, and had run out of beer. Finally, when the national cause seemed to have thrown up all that it was capable of producing, Mayor Scheffelweis arrived amidst cheers. He quite frankly allowed a red ticket to be thrust into his hand, and when he returned from casting his vote it was plain he was agreeably moved. "At last!" he said, pressing Diederich's hand: "We have this day conquered the dragon." Diederich's reply was merciless. "You, Mr. Mayor? Why, you are still halfway down its throat. Mind it doesn't take you with it when it dies!" As Dr. Scheffelweis paled, another cheer arose. Wulckow! . . .

Five thousand odd votes for Fischer! Heuteufel, with barely three thousand, was swept aside by the patriotic tide, and the Social Democrat went to the Reichstag. The "Netzig Journal" insisted upon a victory for the "Emperor's Party," for thanks to the latter, a fortress of Liberalism had fallen. With this, however, Rothgroschen aroused neither great satisfaction nor definite contradiction. Every one found the accomplished fact natural but uninteresting. After the uproar of election time it was now a question of making some more money. The Emperor William Monument, only yesterday the centre of a civil war, no longer aroused the slightest excitement. Old Kühlemann had left the town six hundred thousand marks, for public purposes; very decent. An asylum or a monument, that was the same as sponges and tooth-brushes to Gottlieb Hornung. At the decisive meeting of the town councillors it turned out that the Social Democrats were in favour of the monument; well and good. Somebody proposed that a committee be formed at once, and that the honorary chairmanship be offered to Governor von Wulckow. Here Heuteufel, who was probably annoyed, after all, by his defeat, got up and expressed a doubt as to whether the Governor, who was mixed up in a certain property deal, would himself think it fitting that he should vote for the site on which the monument was to stand. There were grins and winks, and Diederich had a cold shiver down his spine as he waited to see if the scandal would now come out. He waited in silence, secretly thrilled at the thought of what would happen to Authority, if somebody uncovered the scandal. He could not have said what he really wished. As nothing happened, he stood up, very straight, and protested, without exaggerated effort, against the insinuation which he had once already publicly refuted. The other side, on the contrary, had not invalidated in the least the charges of irregularity which had been brought against them. "Don't you worry," replied Heuteufel, "You will soon be satisfied. A complaint has already been lodged."

This, at least, caused a sensation, but the impression was weakened when Heuteufel admitted that his friend Buck had taken action, not against Councillor Hessling, but merely against the socialist paper. "Hessling knows too much," people said—and after Wulckow, who was made honorary chairman, Diederich was appointed chairman of the Monument Committee. In the Council these decisions received the warmest support from Mayor Scheffelweis; they were passed in the noticeable absence of old Buck. If he himself did not think more of his own cause! Heuteufel said: "Is he to look on in person at dirty work which he cannot prevent?" This merely harmed Heuteufel himself. As old Buck in recent times had suffered two defeats, it was expected that his action against the newspaper would be the third. The statements which had to be made in court were adapted by every one in advance to fit the given circumstances. Of course, Hessling had gone too far, the more reasonable people said. Old Buck, who was long known to them all, was not a swindler and a cheat. He may have been guilty of imprudence, especially now, when he was paying his brother's debts, and was himself up to his neck in debt. Did he really go with Cohn to Klüsing about the site? It was a good stroke of business—only it should not have been found out. And why should Kühlemann die exactly at the moment when he ought to have declared his friend's innocence? Such bad luck was not without cause. Herr Tietz, the business manager of the "Netzig Journal," who had the run of Gausenfeld, said pointblank that it was a crime against oneself to take up the defence of people who had shot their bolt. Tietz also drew attention to the fact that old Klüsing, who could have ended the whole thing with a word, took good care to say nothing. He was ill, and, only on his account, the hearing was postponed indefinitely.

That, however, did not prevent him from selling his factory. This was the latest, the "significant changes in a large enterprise of the utmost importance to the industrial life of Netzig," to which the "Netzig Journal" made occult reference. Klüsing had joined a Berlin syndicate. When asked why he did not take any action, Diederich produced the letter in which Klüsing offered him the sale before any one else. "And on absolutely unique terms," he added. "Unfortunately, I am deeply engaged with my brother-in-law in Eschweiler, I am not even sure that I shall not have to leave Netzig." But as an expert he answered an inquiry of Rothgroschen's, who made the reply public, that the prospectus was, if anything, an understatement of the facts. Gausenfeld, as a matter of fact, was a gold mine. The purchase of shares, which were put on the open market, could be strongly recommended. And, it so happened, there was a great demand for the shares in Netzig. How impartial and uninfluenced by his personal interests Diederich's opinion was, came out under special circumstances, to wit, when old Buck was looking for money. The latter had gone so far, his family and his sense of public duty had brought him to such a point, that even his friends refused to encourage him any further. Then Diederich intervened. He gave the old man a second mortgage on his house in the Fleischhauergrube. "He must have been desperately in need of the money," Diederich used to remark whenever he told the story. "When he accepts it from me, his strongest political opponent! Who would have believed it once upon a time?" Diederich gratefully contemplated fate. . . . He added that the house would be an expensive luxury if it came into his hands. Of course, he would soon have to leave his own, and this also showed that he was not counting on Gausenfeld. "But," declared Diederich, "the old man is not on a bed of roses. Who knows how his lawsuit will end. And just because I have to fight him politically, I want to show—you understand." People understood and congratulated Diederich on his more than creditable action. Diederich modestly demurred. "He accused me of lacking idealism, and I had to prove that he was wrong." A note of virile emotion trembled in his voice.

The Fates pursued their course, and if in many cases they encountered difficulties, it was all the more pleasant to find them running smoothly in one's own case. Diederich fully realised this on the day Napoleon Fischer left for Berlin to vote against the Army Bill. The Socialist paper had announced a monster demonstration, and the station was to be occupied by the police. It was the duty of every loyal citizen to be present. Diederich ran into Jadassohn *en route*. They greeted one another formally as befitted the coolness which had sprung up between them. "Are you also going to have a look at the show?" asked Diederich.

"I am going on a holiday—to Paris." As a matter of fact Jadassohn was wearing knickerbockers. "If only to avoid the political imbecilities which have been going on here," he added.

Diederich resolved to ignore loftily the spite of a man who had had no success. "It has been said that you were now going to settle down."

"I? Why so?"

"Isn't Fräulein Zillich away at her aunt's?"

"Her aunt's is good!" Jadassohn grinned. "And people thought . . . I suppose you did, too?"

"Leave me out of it." Diederich looked very knowing. "But why is her aunt's good? Where has she gone, then?"

"Kicked over the traces," said Jadassohn. Then Diederich

stood still and gasped. Käthchen Zillich had run away! In what adventures he might have been involved! . . . Jadassohn spoke as a man of the world.

"Yes, she's gone to Berlin. Her fond parents are still in ignorance. I have no quarrel with her, you understand; there had to be a crash, sooner or later."

"In one way or another," Diederich added, having recovered himself.

"I prefer this way to any other," Jadassohn declared. To which Diederich replied in a confidential whisper: "I don't mind telling you now that it always looked as if that girl was rather sweet on you."

Jadassohn denied it, but not without a touch of *amour-propre*. "What do you take me for? I myself gave her letters of introduction. Just you wait. She will be a big success in Berlin."

"I do not doubt it." Diederich winked. "I know her good points. . . . You certainly thought I was very innocent." He would not listen to Jadassohn's defence. "You thought me very innocent, but at the same time I put a damned big spoke in your wheel, I can tell you." He gave the other, who was becoming more and more uneasy, an account of an adventure he had with Käthchen at the Harmony Club dance—an account which was much more detailed than the facts warranted. With a smile of satisfied vengeance he watched Jadassohn, who was obviously in doubt as to whether his honour were not involved. Finally he decided to slap Diederich on the shoulder, and in the friendliest manner they drew the obvious conclusions. "Of course, the matter is strictly between ourselves. . . . Such a girl must be judged fairly, for where would the better *demi-monde* get recruits. . . . Her address? Well, as a favour to you. If you happen to be in Berlin, then you know where you are." "It would even have a certain charm," Diederich said reflectively. And as Jadassohn espied his luggage, they said good-bye. "We have unfortunately been rather separated in politics, but, thank God, we can come together in human affairs. Have a good time in Paris."

"It is not a pleasure trip." Jadassohn turned round, with an expression as if he were about to trap a witness. When he saw how disturbed Diederich looked he came back. "In four weeks you will see it for yourself," he said with remarkable solemnity. "Perhaps it would be better if you were now to prepare the public." Impressed, in spite of himself, Diederich asked: "What do you propose to do?" Jadassohn answered very seriously and with a smile of resigned determination: "I am about to adapt my outward appearance more appropriately to my patriotic convictions. . . ." When Diederich grasped the significance of these words, he could only incline his head respectfully. Jadassohn had already gone. In the background as he entered the station, his ears glowed once more—for the last time!—like two church windows in the light of the setting sun.

A group of men was approaching the station, a banner flying in their midst. A few policemen came heavily down the steps and faced them. Immediately the group began to sing the International. At the same time their advance was successfully repelled by the representatives of law and order. Some, it is true, got through and crowded around Napoleon Fischer, whose arms were so long that he seemed to drag his carpet bag almost along the ground. The men were recovering themselves in the refreshment room after their exertions in the July sun on behalf of the revolution. As the train was late Napoleon Fischer tried to make a speech on the platform, but the parliamentary representative was forbidden to do so by a policeman. Napoleon put down his carpet bag and bared his teeth. As Diederich knew him, he was evidently on the point of resisting the power of the State. Fortunately for him the train drew up. Only then Diederich noticed a low-sized gentleman, who turned away whenever people passed

near him. He was holding a large bouquet in front of him
and looking in the direction of the train. Those shoulders
seemed familiar to Diederich. . . . That was the devil himself! Judith Lauer nodded from a carriage, her husband
helped her out, and actually handed her the bouquet, which
she accepted with that serious smile of hers. As the pair
turned towards the exit, Diederich hastened, fuming, to get
out of their way. The devil had nothing to do with it. Lauer's
term was up simply; he was a free man once more. Not that
there was anything further to fear from him, but one would
have to become accustomed again to the thought that he was
at large. . . . And he received her with flowers! Did he not
know anything? Surely he had had time to reflect. And she
returned to him after he had served his sentence! There were
situations of which no decent men would even dream. In any
case, the matter did not concern Diederich any more than
every one else. He had only done his duty on that occasion.
"Everybody will be as painfully affected as myself. Everywhere they will give him to understand that he had better remain quiet. . . . He has made his bed and must lie on it."
Käthchen Zillich had understood that and drawn the right
conclusion. What was right in her case applied to others, and
not only to Herr Lauer.

Diederich himself, who walked through the town to the accompaniment of respectful greetings, now assumed in the most
natural way the position to which his services had entitled him.
During those strenuous times he had fought his way through
so hard that it now only remained for him to reap his reward.
Others had begun to believe in him, and forthwith his own
doubts vanished. . . . Lately there had been unfavourable
rumours about Gausenfeld, and the shares fell. How had
people heard that the government had withdrawn its contracts
and entrusted them to Hessling's firm? Diederich had not
breathed a word about it, but it became known even before
the dismissal of the workmen, which the "Netzig Journal" re-

gretted so deeply. Old Buck, as chairman of the board of directors, had to take personal action, which injured him generally. Presumably it was only because of old Buck that the government was acting so harshly. It had been a mistake to elect him chairman. In any case, he should have paid his debts with the money Hessling had so decently given him, instead of buying Gausenfeld shares. Diederich himself repeatedly expressed this opinion. "Who ever would have believed it once upon a time," he remarked again in this connection; and again he thoughtfully contemplated his fate. "It is easily seen what a man is capable of when he feels the ground slipping from beneath his feet." This gave everybody the unpleasant impression that old Buck would drag them down, as shareholders, in his own ruin. For the shares were falling. As a result of the dismissals, a strike was threatened, and they fell still further. . . . At this juncture Kienast made a number of friends. Kienast had arrived unexpectedly in Netzig, for a rest, as he said. Nobody liked admitting that they had Gausenfeld shares and had been taken in. Kienast told one that the other had already sold out. His personal opinion was that it was high time to do so. A broker, whom he did not know, by the way, came into the cafés from time to time and bought stock. Some months later the newspaper published a daily advertisement of the banking house of Sanft and Co. Any one who still had Gausenfeld shares could unload them here without any trouble. As a matter of fact at the beginning of the autumn not a soul held any more of those rotten stocks. But there was talk of an amalgamation of Hessling and Gausenfeld. Diederich professed to be amazed. "What about old Herr Buck?" he asked. "As chairman of the board of directors he will certainly have something to say in the matter. Or has he also sold out?" Then it was said: "He has more troubles," for his action for libel against the socialist paper had now come up for hearing. "He will probably lose," people said, and Diederich, with perfect impartiality: "It is a pity. In that case he will never sit on another board of directors."

With this idea every one went to the trial. The witnesses who appeared could remember nothing. Klüsing had long since spoken to every one about the sale of the factory. Did he specially mention the site? And had he mentioned old Buck as the go-between? All this remained doubtful. In municipal circles it was known that the site was under discussion for the then projected Infant Asylum. Had Buck been in favour of it? Certainly, he had not opposed it. Several people had been struck by his lively interest in that site. Klüsing himself, who was still ill, had declared in his affidavit that his friend Buck had been in and out a good deal a short while before. If Buck had spoken to him about an option on the ground he had certainly not understood it in any sense detrimental to Buck's honour. . . . The plaintiff, Buck, wished to establish the fact that it was the late Kühlemann who had negotiated with Klüsing: Kühlemann himself, the donor of the money, but the point was not proven. In this also Klüsing's testimony was indecisive. That Cohn said so was immaterial, as Cohn was interested in proving that his own visit to Gausenfeld was innocent. Diederich remained as the most important witness. Klüsing had written to him and immediately afterwards had had a conversation with him. Was any name mentioned on that occasion? Diederich testified:

"I had no wish to learn one name or another. I declare, as all the witnesses can confirm, that I have never publicly mentioned the name of Herr Buck. My sole interest in the matter was that of the town, which must not be injured by the actions of individuals. I intervened on behalf of political morality: I bear no personal malice whatever, and I should be sorry if the plaintiff did not leave this court without a stain on his character."

A murmur of approval greeted his words. Only Buck seemed dissatisfied. He jumped up, red in the face . . .

Diederich was now asked for his personal view of the matter. He was preparing to speak, when old Buck stepped forward, holding himself erect, and his eyes flashing as they did at that fateful election meeting.

"I forbid this witness to give a favourable testimony to myself and my life. He is not qualified to do so. His success has been attained by methods very different from mine, and they have a very different aim. My house was always open and free to every one, including the witness. For more than fifty years my life has not been my own, it has been devoted to one idea, which was shared by many in my time, to justice and the common welfare. I was well off when I entered public life; when I leave it I shall be poor. I need no defence."

He was silent and his face trembled—but Diederich merely shrugged his shoulders. On what success was the old man counting? He had long since failed, and now he was spinning sonorous phrases, which inspired no confidence. He pretended to be superior, but he was already in the dust. How could a man so misunderstand his position? "If one of us is to condescend to the other"—Diederich glared. The old man flamed up in vain, he simply glared him down, and with him justice and the common welfare. Every man for himself—and whatever succeeded was right! . . . He felt clearly that this was definitely true. The old man felt it also; he sat down, his shoulders hunched, and in his face there was a look of something like shame. Turning to the magistrates he said: "I do not claim any privileged position. I submit to the judgment of my fellow-citizens."

As if nothing had happened, Diederich continued his testimony. It was really very favourable and made an excellent impression. Since the Lauer trial people found him changed for the better, he had acquired a quiet superiority, which was, after all, nothing wonderful, for he was now a man of some importance and dignity. It was just striking midday when the latest news from the "Netzig Journal" spread through the courtroom. It was a fact, Hessling was the largest share-holder in Gausenfeld and had been made general director of the company. . . . The crowd gazed at him with great curiosity, and contrasted him with old Buck, at whose expense he had prospered. He now got back with a hundred per cent. interest the last twenty thousand which he had lent the old man, and yet retained his reputation for virtue. That the latter should have invested the money in Gausenfeld precisely, was regarded as a good joke on Hessling's part, and was a momentary consolation to many for their own losses. When Diederich left he did so amidst a respectful silence. He was greeted with that degree of respect which is almost servility. The cheated were saluting success.

They were by no means so lenient with old Buck. When the presiding magistrate pronounced the verdict, there was applause. The newspaper was fined only fifty marks! The case was not proven and the plea of good faith was admitted. The legal view was that this was damning to the plaintiff, and as Buck left the courthouse even his friends cut him. Humble folks, who had lost their savings in Gausenfeld, shook their fists after him. This verdict convinced them all that they had long since formed their own opinion of old Buck. A deal like that of the site for the Infant Asylum ought, at least, to be successful; the utterance was Diederich's, and it fitted the case. But that was just it. All his life nothing had ever succeeded with old Buck. He thought himself a wonder because as a city father and party leader he was retiring in debt. There were plenty of other good-for-nothing customers. His questionable business capacity had its counterpart in morals, the proof of which was that still unexplained story of the engagement of his son, who was now hanging around the theatre. And Buck's politics? An international standpoint, always demanding sacrifices for demagogic purposes, and on the worst terms with the government, which in its turn, had a bad effect on business. That was the policy of a man who had nothing more to lose, and is destitute of a good citizen's sense of responsibility in regard to investments. With indignation people recognised that they had delivered themselves entirely into the hands of an adventurer. There was a general, heartfelt desire to prevent him from doing further harm. As he himself did not draw the obvious conclusion from the damaging verdict, it became necessary for others to drive it home. The right to hold administrative office must surely be conditioned by the provision that a public official must prove himself worthy of the dignity demanded by his position, by his conduct both in and out of office. Did old Buck fulfil this condition? To ask the question was to answer it, as the "Netzig Journal" observed, of course, without mentioning names.

But things had reached such a point that the matter was brought to the attention of the Municipal Council. Then in the end, one day before the discussion, the obstinate old man became reasonable and resigned his position as town councillor. After that his political friends could not risk losing their remaining supporters by retaining him as the leader of the party. It appeared that he did not make their task any easier. Several visits and some gentle pressure were necessary before a letter appeared in the press, saying that he placed the welfare of democracy above his own. As the former was threatened with harm, through his name, owing to the influence of passions which he hoped were only temporary, he would retire. "If the general good demands it, I am prepared to bear the unjustified slur which a deceived public opinion has put upon me, in the belief that the eternal justice of people will one day absolve me again."

This was regarded as superiority and hypocrisy. Wellwishers excused it on the ground of old age. In any case what he wrote or did not write was of no consequence, for what was he now? People who were under obligations to him looked him in the face without raising their hats, many laughed and made audible remarks. There were people who had never had to deal with him, but who were, nevertheless, very respectful as long as he enjoyed general esteem. Instead of the old friends whom he never encountered on his daily walk, new and strange friends appeared. They met him as he was returning home, when twilight was coming on; sometimes it was a small tradesman with haggard eyes, threatened with bankruptcy; at others a furtive drunkard or some shadowy figure slinking along by the walls of the houses. They would slow up and look at him with shy or bold confidence. They lifted their hats, no doubt reluctantly, and then old Buck would nod to them, shaking the hand extended towards him, no matter whose it might be.

As time went on people even ceased to hate him. Those who had purposely cut him now passed him indifferently, and sometimes he would salute again out of old habit. Fathers with their young sons looked serious, and when they had passed him, they would explain to their children: "Did you see that old gentleman creeping all alone and looking at nobody? Remember all your life what disgrace can do to a man." Henceforward at the sight of old Buck the children were seized with a mysterious thrill of horror, just as the older generation, when it was young, had a feeling of instinctive pride on seeing him. There were, it is true, young people who did not follow the prevailing opinion. Sometimes, as the old man left the house, school was just over. The rising generation would trot off in droves, stepping respectfully aside to make room for their teachers; and Kühnchen, now a thorough-going patriot, or Pastor Zillich, more moral than ever since Käthchen's misfortune, would hurry on, without even a glance at the man in disgrace. Then these few youngsters would stop on the road, each for himself, and apparently of his own initiative. Their brows were not so smooth as most; they had expression in their eyes when they turned their backs on Kühnchen and Zillich and took off their caps to old Buck. Involuntarily he would stop and gaze into these faces pregnant with the future, inspired once more by the hope with which, all his life long, he had looked into the face of every fellow-creature.

In the meantime Diederich had really little time to pay attention to the minor accompaniments of his progress. The "Netzig Journal," now unreservedly at Diederich's disposal, established the fact that it was Herr Buck himself who, prior to his resignation as chairman of the board of directors, had to propose the appointment of Dr. Hessling as general director. The fact seemed rather peculiar to many people. But Rothsgroschen drew attention to Dr. Hessling's great and undeniable services to the community in that capacity. But for him, who had quietly acquired more than half the shares, they would certainly have fallen still more, and a great many families had only Dr. Hessling to thank if they were saved from ruin. The strike had been prevented by the energetic action of the new chairman. His loyalty to King and country was a guarantee that for the future the sun of governmental approval would never set on Gausenfeld. In brief, glorious days were dawning for the industrial life of Netzig, and especially for the paper industry—the more so, as the rumour of an amalgamation of Hessling's business and Gausenfeld proved to be true. Rothgroschen was able to state that only on this condition could Dr. Hessling be prevailed upon to take charge of Gausenfeld.

As a matter of fact Diederich lost no time in increasing the share capital. The Hessling factory was put in as new capital. Diederich did an excellent stroke of business. Success had crowned his first deal with the government. He was master of the situation, with his docile board of directors, and could proceed to impress his commanding personality upon the internal organisation of the business. At the outset he assembled the entire staff of workers and employés. "Some of you," he said, "already know me from the Hessling factory. Well, the rest of you will soon know me better! Whoever is prepared to co-operate with me is welcome, but I will stand no radicalism! Barely two years ago I said that to a few of you, and now you can see how many I have under my orders. You may be proud to have such a master! You can rely upon me, I will undertake the responsibility of arousing you to a sense of patriotism, and of making you faithful supporters of the existing order." He promised them dwellings, sick relief and cheaper necessities of life. "But I forbid socialistic agitation! In the future you can vote as I tell you, or leave!" Diederich also said that he was determined to curb irreligion. He would note every Sunday who went to church and who did not. "So long as the world is unredeemed from sin, there will be war and hatred, envy and discord. Therefore, there must be one master!"

In order to enforce this fundamental principle every room in the factory was adorned with inscriptions to drive it home: No thoroughfare! It is strictly prohibited to fetch water in the buckets for use in case of fire! They were not allowed to send out for bottles of beer, for Diederich had not failed to make a contract with a brewery which ensured him a profit on what his employés consumed. . . . Eating, sleeping, smoking, children, "Courting, flirting, lovemaking, in fact, every vice," was strictly prohibited! In the workmen's dwellings, even before they were built, foster-children were forbidden. An unmarried couple living together, who had evaded detection for ten years under Klüsing, were solemnly dismissed. This occurrence even inspired Diederich to invent a new means of raising the moral tone of the people. In the appropriate places he had paper hung up, which was manufactured in Gausenfeld itself, and nobody could use it without noticing the moral and patriotic maxims with which it was adorned. At times he would hear the men shouting some august saying which they had learnt in this fashion, or singing a patriotic song which had been impressed upon their memory on a like occasion. Encouraged by this success Diederich put his in-

vention on the market. It appeared under the name of "World
Power," and, as a grandiloquent advertisement announced, it
carried the German spirit, supported by German workmanship,
in triumph all over the world.

Even this educational toilet-paper could not remove all pos-
sibility of conflict between master and men. One day Diederich was compelled to issue a warning that he would pay only
for dental treatment, but not for new teeth, out of the insurance fund. One man had had an entire set made. As Diederich insisted upon his warning, which was issued after the
event, the man sued him, and by some miracle won his case.
His faith in the existing order thereby shaken, he became an
agitator, his morals declined, and he would certainly have
been dismissed under normal circumstances. But Diederich
could not bring himself to abandon the set of teeth, which had
cost him so much. Therefore he retained the man. . . . He
did not conceal from himself that the whole business was most
injurious to the spirit of the working classes. Added to this
came the influence of dangerous political events. When several Social Democrats in the newly opened Reichstag building
remained seated while cheers for the Emperor were called,
there was no longer any doubt that the necessity for anti-
revolutionary legislation was established. Diederich publicly
advocated the idea, and prepared his employés for it in an address which was received in gloomy silence. The majority
in the Reichstag was so unprincipled as to defeat the measure,
and the result was not long in making itself known; an industrial magnate was murdered. Murdered! An industrial magnate! The assassin declared he was not a Social Democrat,
but Diederich knew what that meant from his own work-
people. The murdered man was supposed to have been well
disposed towards the workers, but Diederich knew what that
meant from his own experience. For days and weeks he never
opened a door without the fear that a drawn dagger was behind it. His office was fitted with automatic locks, and in

Guste's company he crawled every evening around the bedroom and made a search. His telegrams to the Emperor, whether emanating from the Town Council, the committee of the "Emperor's Party," the Employers' Association, or the Veterans' Association, the telegrams with which Diederich bombarded the All-Highest shouted for help against the revolutionary movement, fanned by the Socialists, which had claimed another victim; for relief from this pest; for immediate legal action and military protection for authority and property; for the imprisonment of strikers who prevented any one from working. . . . The "Netzig Journal," which duly reported all this, never forgot to add how great were the services of Dr. Hessling in the cause of social peace and the welfare of the workers. Every new workman's dwelling Diederich built was published by Rothgroschen in a highly flattering picture and was made the subject of a laudatory article. Certain other employers, whose influence in Netzig fortunately was no longer of any account, might encourage subversive tendencies in their employés by sharing profits with them. The principles for which Dr. Hessling stood established the best possible relationship between employer and employed, such as His Majesty the Emperor wished to see everywhere in German industry. Strong resistance to the unjust demands of the workers, together with joint action on the part of the employers, were a part, as every one knew, of the Emperor's social programme, which it was the honourable ambition of Dr. Hessling also to carry out. Beside this stood a picture of Diederich.

Such recognition was a spur to ever greater activities—in spite of the unredeemed sins, whose powerful effects were visible not only in business but also in domestic life, and in the latter, unfortunately, it was Kienast who sowed envy and discord. He declared that but for him and his discreet assistance in the purchase of the shares Diederich could never have attained his brilliant position. To this Diederich retorted that

Kienast had been compensated by a number of shares proportionate to his means. His brother-in-law would not admit this, and professed, on the contrary, to have real grounds for his unconscionable demands. Was he not, as Magda's husband, part-owner of the old Hessling factory, to the extent of one-eighth of its value? The factory was sold and Diederich had received ready money and preferred Gausenfeld shares in exchange. Kienast demanded one-eighth of the capital income and of the yearly dividends from the preferred shares. To this unheard of presumption Diederich replied emphatically that he owed nothing more either to his sister or his brother-in-law. "I was bound to pay you only your share of the annual profits of my factory. My factory is sold. Gausenfeld does not belong to me but to a company of shareholders. So far as the capital is concerned, that is my private fortune. You have no claim on it." Kienast called this barefaced robbery. Fully convinced by his own argument Diederich talked of blackmail, and then came a lawsuit.

The lawsuit lasted three years. It was fought with increasing bitterness, especially by Kienast, who gave up his post in Eschweiler and moved with Magda to Netzig, in order to devote himself entirely to it. As chief witness against Diederich he had cited old Sötbier, who, in his desire for vengeance, was actually prepared to prove that even earlier Diederich had not given his relations the money which was due to them. Kienast also bethought himself of the idea of showing up certain incidents in Diederich's past, with the assistance of Napoleon Fischer, now a deputy in the Reichstag. In this, however, he never quite succeeded. Nevertheless, those tactics compelled Diederich on different occasions to pay over considerable sums to the party funds of the Social Democrats. And he told himself that his personal loss grieved him less than the injury which the national cause thereby suffered. Guste, who could not see quite so far, egged on the men in their fight rather from feminine motives. Her first child was a girl, and she could not forgive Magda for having a boy. Magda, who was at first mildly interested in the money question, traced the beginning of hostilities to the time when Emma appeared with a daring hat from Berlin. Magda remarked that Emma was now favoured by Diederich in the most shameful fashion. Emma had her own flat in Gausenfeld where she gave tea parties. The amount of her dress allowance was nothing less than an insult to her married sister. Magda had to witness the advantage which her marriage had conferred upon her being turned into the very opposite, and she accused Diederich of having meanly got rid of her just before his success had begun. If Emma could still not find a husband there appeared to be good reasons for it—which were even being whispered about in Netzig. Magda saw no reason why she should not say them out loud. Inge Tietz brought the story to Gausenfeld, but at the same time she brought with her a weapon against Magda, because she happened to meet the midwife at the Kienasts', and the first child was born hardly six months after they were married. A terrible commotion ensued, telephonic vituperation from one house to the other, threats of legal proceedings, for which material was collected by each lady's acquiring the other's servants.

In due course Diederich was once more in a position to say: "My house is my castle." The family quarrels were settled and the household flourished exceedingly. After Gretchen, who was born in 1894, and Horst in 1895, came Kraft in 1896. Like a model father, Diederich kept an account for every child, even before it was born, and the first thing he entered up was the cost of the midwife and the expenses of providing for each child. His view of married life was very strict. Horst came into the world with great difficulty. When it was all over Diederich informed his wife that, if it had been necessary to choose, he would simply have allowed her to die, "painful as that course would have been," he added. "But the race is more important, and I am responsible to the Emperor for my sons." Women were there to produce children and Diederich refused them any licence for frivolity and impropriety, although he graciously allowed them opportunities for recreation and improvement. "Keep to woman's sphere," he would say to Guste, "religion, cooking and children." On the red check tablecloth, with the imperial eagle and royal crown on each square, the Bible always lay beside the coffee-pot, and it was Guste's duty to read a passage from it every morning. On Sundays they went to church. "The authorities wish it," said Diederich seriously, when Guste was recalcitrant. As Diederich lived in the fear of his master, so Guste had to live in the fear of hers. When they entered a room she knew that the right of precedence properly belonged to her husband. The children, in turn, had to treat her with respect, and Männe, the dachshund, had to obey every one. At meals, therefore, the children and the dog had to keep quiet. Guste's duty was to discern from the wrinkles upon her husband's brow whether it was advisable to leave him undisturbed, or to drive away his cares with chatter. Certain dishes were prepared only for the master of the house, and when he was in a good humour Diederich would throw a piece across the table and, laughing heartily, would watch to see who caught it, Gretchen, Guste or the dog. His siesta was often troubled by gastronomical disturbances, and Guste's duty then commanded her to put warm poultices on his stomach. Groaning and terribly frightened he used to say he would make his will and appoint a trustee. Guste would not be allowed to touch a penny. "I have worked for my sons, not in order that you may amuse yourself after I am gone!" Guste objected that her own fortune was the foundation of everything, but it availed her nothing. . . . Of course, when Guste had a cold, she did not expect that Diederich, in his turn, would nurse her. Then she had to keep as far away from him as possible, for Diederich was determined not to have any germs near him. He would not go into the factory unless he had antiseptic tablets in his mouth, and one night there was a great disturbance because the cook had come down with influenza, and had a fever temperature. "Out of the house with the beastly thing at once!" Diederich commanded, and when she had gone he wandered about the house for a long time spraying it with disinfecting fluids.

When he read the "Lokal-Anzeiger" in the evening he would constantly say to his wife that Germany could cease to live, but she could not do without a merchant marine—to which Guste agreed, for the simple reason that she did not like the Empress Friedrich, who was betraying us to England, as every one knew, quite apart from certain domestic conditions in Friedrichskron Castle, of which Guste strongly disapproved. We needed a strong fleet against England, which must be absolutely smashed; it was the deadliest enemy of the Emperor. And why? In Netzig, they knew all about it. Simply because His Majesty had once, in a lively mood, given the Prince of Wales a friendly kick in a tempting portion of his anatomy. Besides, certain kinds of paper came from England, whose importation could best be stopped by a victorious war. Looking over the top of his paper Diederich used to say to Guste: "I hate England as only Frederick the Great hated that nation of thieves and tradesmen. Those are His Majesty's sentiments and I subscribe to them." He subscribed to every word in every speech of the Emperor's, and always in their first and strongest form, not in the modified version which appeared the next day. All these keywords to the character of Germany and of the times—Diederich lived, moved and had his being in them, as if they had been manifestations of his own nature; they remained in his memory as if he himself had spoken them. Sometimes he really had already said such things. He mixed some of them, on public occasions, with his own inventions, and neither he nor anybody else could tell what came from him and what from one more exalted. . . .

"This is sweet," said Guste who was reading the miscellaneous column. "We must grasp the trident," declared Diederich resolutely, while Guste read out some adventure of the Empress which filled her with deep satisfaction. At Hubertus-stock the exalted lady liked to dress in simple, almost middle-class style. A postman to whom she revealed her identity on the country road did not believe who she was and laughed in her face. Afterwards he was overwhelmed and fell upon his knees, only to be rewarded with a mark. This also delighted Diederich, just as his heart was touched when the Emperor went out into the street on Christmas Eve, with fifty-seven marks in newly-minted money, to give the poor of Berlin a happy Christmas; as when an ominous thrill ran through him on learning that the Emperor had become an Honorary Bailiff of the Knights of Saint John. The "Lokal-Anzeiger" opened up new worlds, and then, again, it brought the highest rulers comfortably close to one. There in the alcove the three-quarter life-size figures in bronze of their Majesties seemed to move smilingly closer, and the Trumpeter of Säckingen, who accompanied them, could be heard blowing a cordial blast. "It must be heavenly on washing-day at the Emperor's," said Guste, "when there are a lot of clothes. They have a hundred people for washing!" Diederich, on the other hand, was filled with profound pleasure because the Emperor's dachshunds were not obliged to respect the trains of the court ladies. He conceived the plan of giving full liberty to his own Männe in this respect at their next evening party. But a telegram in the next column made him uneasy, because it was still uncertain whether the Emperor and the Tsar would meet. "If it doesn't happen soon," said Diederich importantly, "we shall have to be prepared for the worst. One cannot trifle with world history." He liked to linger over imminent catastrophes, for "the German spirit is serious, almost tragic," he would declare.

On the whole, Diederich's relations with Jadassohn turned

out very well. The erstwhile rivals had become more mature
and more advanced in the sphere of life that satisfied them,
and they interfered with one another neither politically nor
socially, nor in that discreet villa which Diederich visited one
evening in the week when, without Guste's knowledge, he
did not appear at the *Stammtisch*. It lay beyond the Saxon
Gate, and was inhabited by a single lady, who was rarely seen
in public, and then never on foot. In a stage box at the Valhalla Theatre she sometimes sat in great state, was subjected
to general scrutiny with opera-glasses, but was never saluted
by any one. For her own part she behaved like a queen pre-
serving her incognito. In spite of her splendour, everybody
knew that it was Käthchen Zillich who had trained for her
profession in Berlin, and now followed it successfully in the
villa the von Brietzens used to have. Nobody denied that this
fact was not calculated to enhance the prestige of Pastor Zillich. His parishioners were deeply offended, not to mention
the sceptics, who were delighted. In order to obviate a catastrophe the Pastor appealed to the police to put an end to the
scandal, but he encountered opposition which could only be explained by reference to certain connections between the von
Brietzen villa and the highest offices in the town. Doubting
of human no less than divine justice, the father swore he
would discharge the duties of a judge himself, and one afternoon he was really supposed to have inflicted chastisement on
his daughter, as she lay in bed. Only for her mother, who
guessed everything and followed him, Käthchen would not have
got off with her life, the parish declared. It was said that the
mother still had a reprehensible weakness for the daughter in
her wicked splendour. So far as the Pastor was concerned,
he declared from the pulpit that Käthchen was dead and
buried, thus saving himself from the intervention of the eccle-
siastical court. In time this trial increased his authority. . . .
Among the gentlemen who had an investment interest in Käthchen's career Diederich knew officially only Jadassohn, al-

though the latter had invested less money than any one, none at all, in fact, Diederich suspected. Jadassohn's relations with Käthchen, from former times, were a sort of mortgage on the enterprise. So Diederich had no scruples in discussing with Jadassohn the anxiety it caused him. At the *Stammtisch* the pair pulled their chairs together in a corner, over which the motto stood: "What lovely woman does for love of man must e'er succeed accordingly to plan." With due respect for Pastor Zillich, who was discoursing not far off upon the canons of Christianity, they discussed the affairs of the villa. Diederich complained of Käthchen's rapacious demands upon his purse, and he expected Jadassohn to exercise a restraining influence upon her. But Jadassohn merely said: "Why do you keep her then? Isn't she supposed to be most expensive?" And this was also true. After his first fleeting satisfaction at having got Käthchen in this fashion, Diederich had come to regard her practically as an item, an imposing item, in his advertising account. "My position," he said to Jadassohn, "obliges me to do things on a large scale. Otherwise I would—honestly—drop the whole thing, for, between ourselves, Käthchen does not offer enough attraction." At this Jadassohn smiled eloquently, but said nothing. "In any case," continued Diederich, "she is the same type as my wife, and my wife"—here he whispered behind his hand—"has a better technique. You see there is no resisting her temperament, and after every escapade at the von Brietzen villa I have the feeling that I owe my wife something. You may laugh, but as a matter of fact, I always make her a present. Provided she doesn't notice anything!" Jadassohn laughed with more reason than Diederich suspected, for he had long since regarded it as his moral duty to enlighten Frau Hessling about this relationship.

In political matters a similarly advantageous co-operation was established between Diederich and Jadassohn as in the case of Käthchen. They jointly did their utmost to purge the town of unpatriotic elements, especially of those who spread the plague of *lèse-majesté*. With his many connections Diederich discovered the offenders, while Jadassohn led them to the slaughter. When the Song to Ægir appeared their activities proved especially fruitful. In Diederich's own house the piano-teacher, with whom Guste practised, spoke disrespectfully of the Song to Ægir and endured appropriate punishment. . . . Even Wolfgang Buck, who had latterly come to live in Netzig again, declared that the punishment was quite just, for it satisfied monarchial sentiment. "People would not have understood a pardon," he said at the *Stammtisch*. "The monarchy is in politics what the exigent and energetic women are in love. Whoever is built that way will insist on something being done and cannot be satisfied with half measures." Diederich blushed at this. . . . Unfortunately, Buck confessed to such sentiments only so long as he was sober. Later on he gave sufficient grounds for being excluded from all decent society by his well-known way of dragging the most sacred things in the dust. It was Diederich who saved him from that fate. He defended his friend. "You must remember, gentlemen, that he has an hereditary taint, for the family shows signs of already advanced degeneracy. On the other hand, a proof of the healthy kernel in him is the fact that he was not satisfied with an actor's existence and has resumed his profession as a lawyer." The reply was that it looked suspicious that Buck should preserve such absolute silence concerning his experiences of almost three years on the stage. Was he, after all, still a man of honour? Diederich could not answer this question. A profound impulse, indefensible in logic, always drove him to the son of old Buck. Every time he eagerly renewed a discussion which abruptly terminated on each occasion, after having revealed irreconcilable divergencies of opinion. But if Buck came at first merely for the sake of a particularly good glass of cognac, he was soon coming obviously on account of Emma. They both understood one

another without reference to Diederich, and in a way that offended him. They carried on clever and caustic conversations,
apparently without the spirit and the other factors which nor-
mally stimulated the intercourse of the sexes. When they
lowered their voices and became confidential Diederich found
them absolutely sinister. He had the choice of interfering
and bringing about more formal relations, or of simply leaving
the room. To his own astonishment he chose the latter.
"They have both, so to speak, fulfilled their fate, if fate it
can be called," he said to himself with a sense of superiority
which overwhelmed him. He hardly noticed that, at bottom,
he was proud of Emma, because his own sister, Emma, was
smart enough, peculiar enough, indeed, unusual enough, to
get on with Wolfgang Buck. "Who knows?" he thought hesitatingly, and finally decided: "Why not! Bismarck did the
same thing with Austria; first a defeat and then an alliance!"

These obscure reflections prompted Diederich again to take
a certain interest in Wolfgang's father. Old Buck's heart was
affected and he was now rarely seen, and when he was, he
was usually standing in front of a shop-window apparently
absorbed in the display, but in reality solely concerned to
conceal the fact that he could not breathe. What did he
think? How did he judge the new commercial prosperity of
Netzig, the renaissance of patriotism, and those who now exercised authority? Was he convinced and inwardly vanquished?
It happened that Dr. Hessling, the most powerful person in
the community, would slip surreptitiously through a certain
doorway, and then creep along unobserved behind this powerless half-forgotten old man. In his elevated position he was
mysteriously disturbed by a dying man. . . . As old Buck
was in arrears with the interest on his mortgage, Diederich proposed to the son that he should take over the house. Of course
he would allow the old gentleman to occupy it so long as he
was alive. Diederich wanted also to buy the furniture and
pay for it at once. Wolfgang induced his father to accept.

Meanwhile the 22nd of March passed, William the Great was a hundred years old and his monument had not yet been erected in the public park. Questions without end were asked at the meetings of the Town Council, several times additional credits were sanctioned after great difficulty, only to be vetoed again. The worst blow the community received was when His Majesty refused to have his lamented grandfather on foot and commanded an equestrian statue. Spurred on by his impatience Diederich often went to Meisestrasse in the evening to see how the work was progressing. It was the month of May and unpleasantly warm even in the twilight, but there was a breeze blowing through the deserted, newly planted area of the public park. With feelings of irritation Diederich thought again of the excellent stroke of business which the lord of the manor, Herr von Quitzin, had done here. That fellow had it all his own way! It was not very difficult to speculate in landed property when one's cousin was Governor! The town had no alternative but to take over the whole lot for the monument and pay whatever he demanded. . . . Then two figures appeared. Diederich saw in time who it was, and drew back among the shrubbery.

"We can breathe here," said old Buck. His son answered: "Unless the place takes away all desire to do so. They have contracted a debt of a million and a half to create this dumping ground for rubbish." And he pointed to the unfinished erection of stone pedestals, eagles, circular seats, lions, temples and figures. With beating wings the eagles had planted their talons on the still empty pedestal, others were perched on top of those temples which were set at symmetrical distances in the circular seats; behind, lions were crouching ready to spring into the foreground, where there was enough movement caused by fluttering flags and people in violent agitation. Napoleon III, in the crushed attitude of Wilhelmshöhe, adorned the rear of the pedestal, as the vanquished in the rear of the triumphal chariot. He was also threatened with an attack from one of the lions, which was humping its back ferociously on the steps of the monument just behind him. Bismarck and the other paladins, very much at home in the midst of this menagerie, stretched up their hands from the base of the pedestal in order to share in the deeds of the as yet absent ruler.

"Who ought to jump into that vacant place up there?" asked Wolfgang Buck. "The old man was merely a forerunner. Afterwards this mystic-heroic spectacle will be shut off with chains, and we shall have something to gape at—which was the main object of the whole thing. Melodrama, and no good, at that."

After a while—as twilight deepened—the father said: "And you, my son? Acting also seemed to you to be the main object."

"As it does to all my generation. We are no good for anything else. We should not take ourselves too seriously nowadays. That is the safest attitude in view of the future, and I will not deny that it was for no other reason than vanity, that I abandoned the stage again. It is laughable, father. I left because once, when I was acting, a chief of police wept. But can you imagine that being tolerable? I represent the last degree of refinement, an insight into the heart of man, lofty morality, the intellect and soul of a modern man, to people who seem to be my equals, because they nod to me and look as if they felt something. But afterwards they pursue revolutionaries and fire on strikers, for my chief of police is typical of them all."

Here Buck turned straight towards the bush which concealed Diederich. "Art is art, and the whole tumult of the soul never touches your lives. On the day the masters of your culture understood that, as I do, they would leave you alone with your wild animals, as I do." As he pointed to the lions and eagles, the old man also looked at the monument and said:

"They have become more powerful, but their power has

brought neither more intelligence nor more kindness into the world. It has been in vain. We also were born in vain, apparently." He glanced at his son. "Nevertheless you should not leave them a clear field."

Wolfgang sighed heavily. "What is there to hope for, father? They take good care not to push things too far, like the privileged classes before the revolution. History has unfortunately taught them moderation. Their social legislation prepares the way and corrupts. They satisfy the mob just enough to make it not worth while to fight them seriously for bread, not to mention freedom. Who is left to testify against them?"

Then the old man drew himself up, and his voice had its old sonorousness. "The spirit of humanity," he said, and, after a moment, as the younger man held his head down: "You must believe in that, my son. When the catastrophe is over which they think they can avoid, you may be sure that humanity will not consider the causes leading to the first revolution more shameless and stupid than the conditions which were ours."

Softly as a voice from the distance he said: "Who would have lived who lived only in the present."

Suddenly he seemed to totter. The son hastened to catch him and on his arm the old man disappeared in the darkness, with bowed figure and halting step. Diederich, who hurried off by a different route, had the sensation of emerging from a bad but largely incomprehensible dream, in which the very foundations had been shaken. And in spite of the unreality of all that he had heard, it seemed to shake more profoundly than the tremors of the revolution as he had known it. The days of one of this pair were numbered, the other had not very much to look forward to, yet Diederich felt it would have been better if they had stirred up a healthy uproar in the country, than to have whispered, here in the dark, things which were concerned only with the soul and the future.

The present certainly offered more tangible matters. Together with the creator of the monument Diederich planned artistic arrangements for the unveiling ceremony, in which the creator proved to be more accommodating than might have been expected of him. Generally speaking, he had so far shown only the good side of his profession, namely genius and a dignified point of view, while, for the rest, he turned out to be polite and competent. The young man, a nephew of Mayor Scheffelweis, was a proof that, in spite of obsolete prejudices, there were decent people in every walk of life, and that there is no need to despair of a young man who is too lazy to earn an honest living and becomes an artist. The first time he returned from Berlin to Netzig he still wore a velvet jacket, which only exposed his family to unpleasant remarks. But on his second visit he was already the proud possessor of a silk hat, and very soon he was discovered by His Majesty, and was permitted to make the successful likeness of the Margrave Hatto the Powerful for the Siegesallee, together with the likenesses of his two most important contemporaries, the monk Tassilo, who could drink one hundred litres of beer in a day, and the Knight Klitzenzitz, who introduced compulsory labour amongst the inhabitants of Berlin, although they hung him afterwards. His Majesty had drawn the special attention of the Lord Mayor to the achievements of the Knight Klitzenzitz, and this had again redounded to the advantage of the sculptor's career. One could not do too much for a man who basked in the direct rays of the imperial sunshine. Diederich placed his house at his disposal, he also hired the horse which the artist required to keep in good health. And what ambitions were conceived when the famous guest described as very promising little Horst's first attempts to sketch! Diederich decided on the spot that Horst should follow art, that most opportune career.

Wulckow, who had no feeling for art, and did not know, what to say to His Majesty's favourite, received from the monument committee a presentation of 2000 marks, to which he was entitled as honorary chairman. The oration to be made at the unveiling was entrusted by the Committee to the ordinary chairman, the spiritual creator of the monument and the founder of the national movement which had led to its erection, Dr. Hessling, Municipal Councillor and Managing Director of Gausenfeld, hurrah! Moved and elated, Diederich saw himself on the eve of further promotion. The Governor-General himself was expected. Diederich would have to speak before His Excellency; what results that promised! Wulckow, it is true, tried to thwart them. He was irritated because he had been ignored, and went so far as to refuse to admit Guste to the stand with the officials' wives. Diederich on this account, had an interview with him which was stormy, but fruitless. Fuming with rage he returned home to Guste. "He won't budge. He says you are not the wife of an official. We shall see who is more official, you or he! He shall beg you to come! Thank Heaven I have no longer need of him, but he may need me"— And so it was, for when the next number of "Die Woche" appeared, what did it contain besides the usual pictures of the Emperor? The reproduction of two portraits, one showing the creator of the Emperor William Monument in Netzig, as he was just putting the final touches to his work, the other showing the chairman of the committee and his wife, Diederich and Guste together. Not a mention of Wulckow— which was widely noticed and regarded as a sign that his position had been weakened. He must have felt it himself, for he took steps to get into "Die Woche." He called on Diederich, but Diederich sent word he was not at home. The artist made excuses. Then it happened that Wulckow actually went up to Guste in the street. That business about the seat with the officials' wives was all a misunderstanding. "He begged like our dachshund," Guste reported. "Just for that very reason, no!" decided Diederich, and he had no scruples in telling the story around to everybody. "Should I do violence to my feel-

ings, when the man is in my power?" he said to Wolfgang
Buck. "Colonel von Haffke is also throwing him over." He
calmly added: "Now he sees that there are people more powerful than himself. To his own disadvantage Wulckow did not
learn in time to adapt himself to the modern conditions of
large scale publicity, which have left their mark on our present course!" "Absolutism tempered by the craving for no-
toriety," added Buck.

In view of Wulckow's downfall Diederich began to find that
speculation in land values, which had been so disadvantageous
to himself, more and more offensive. His indignation grew to
such a point that the visit which Reichstag Deputy Napoleon
Fischer just happened to be paying to Netzig, became a real
opportunity for Diederich to relieve his feelings. Parliamentary immunity had its advantages, after all! For Napoleon
Fischer repaired immediately to the Reichstag and made revelations. In perfect safety he exposed the manœuvres of Governor von Wulckow in Netzig, his net profit on the site of the
Emperor William Monument, which, Napoleon declared, had
been extracted from the town, and the presentation of 5000
marks, which he described as "palm grease." According to the
press this caused an enormous sensation amongst the representatives of the people. It is true, they weren't excited against
Wulckow but against the man who had exposed him. There
was a furious demand for proofs and witnesses. Diederich
trembled lest the next line should mention his name. Happily
it did not appear. Napoleon Fischer did not betray the duty
of his office. Instead the minister spoke. He left to the judgment of the House this unheard-of attack, unfortunately made
under cover of immunity, against one who was absent and
could not defend himself. The House gave judgment by applauding the minister. The matter was at an end, so far as
Parliament was concerned, and it remained only for the press
also to express its horror and, where it was not entirely ir-
reproachable, to wink its eye gently. Several Social Demo-

cratic papers, which had been incautious, had to surrender the responsible editors to the courts, including the Netzig organ. Diederich seized this occasion to draw a sharp line between himself and those who had doubted Governor von Wulckow. He and Guste called on the Wulckows. "I know at first hand," he said afterwards, "that the man is assured of a brilliant future. He was hunting lately with His Majesty and brought off an excellent joke." A week later "Die Woche" published a full-page portrait, a bald head and beard in one half, a paunch in the other, and underneath the legend "Governor von Wulckow, the spiritual creator of the Emperor William Monument in Netzig, who was recently the object of an attack in the Reichstag which excited universal indignation, and whose appointment as Governor-General is expected. . . ." The picture of Dr. Hessling and his wife had only been given a quarter page. Diederich was satisfied that due proportions in rank had been restored. Authority remained as impregnable as ever, even under modern conditions of large-scale publicity. In spite of everything he was profoundly contented. In this way he was spiritually prepared most appropriately for his oration.

The latter was conceived during the ambitious visions of nights snatched from sleep, and as a result of a constant exchange of ideas with Wolfgang Buck, and especially Käthchen Zillich, who showed a remarkably clear perception of the importance of the approaching event. On the fateful day, when Diederich, his heart beating against the copy of his speech, drove up with his wife at half-past ten to the festive scene, the latter presented an as yet unanimated, but all the more orderly spectacle. Above all, the military cordon had already been drawn up, and when one got through, only after giving all the required credentials, there was here also an impressive barrier against the unprivileged mob, who had to crane their perspiring necks in the sun behind our soldiers and at the foot of a huge, black partition. The stands to the right and left of the long white cloths behind which William the Great could be divined, were sheltered by awnings and innumerable flags. On the left-hand side, as Diederich noticed, the officers and gentlemen were permitted to look after themselves and their ladies without the interference of strangers, thanks to the sense of discipline, which was in their very blood. All the rigours of police supervision were transferred to the right-hand side where the civilians scrambled for the seats. Then Guste expressed dissatisfaction with hers. It seemed to her that only the official marquee, facing the statue, was fit to receive her. She was an official lady; Wulckow had admitted it. Diederich had to go there with her, or appear a coward, but, of course, his daring assault was repulsed as emphatically as he had anticipated. For form's sake, and so that Guste should not lose faith in him, he protested against the tone of the police officer, and was almost arrested. His order of the Crown, fourth class, his black-white-and-red sash and his speech, which he produced, just saved him, but they could never pass as a satisfactory substitute for a uniform, either in his own eyes or those of the world. This one real distinction was lacking, and Diederich was once more compelled to notice that without a uniform one went through life with a bad conscience, notwithstanding one's other first-class qualifications.

In a state of disorganisation the Hesslings beat a retreat, which attracted general attention, Guste looking blue and swollen in her feathers, lace and diamonds. Diederich was fuming and shoved forward as much as possible his paunch with its sash, as if he were spreading the national colours over his defeat. Thus they passed between the Veterans' Association with wreaths of oak around their tall hats, who were placed in the lower half of the military stand, under the command of Kühnchen, as a Landwehr lieutenant, and the maids of honour in white, with black-white-and-red sashes, under the orders of Pastor Zillich, in his official robes. But when they reached their places, who was sitting, with the air of a queen, in Guste's seat? They were flabbergasted: Käthchen Zillich! Here Diederich felt bound to speak authoritatively in his turn. "This lady has made a mistake; the seat is not for her," he said, not to Käthchen Zillich, whom he appeared to take for a stranger, no less than for a doubtful character, but to the official in charge—and even if public opinion about him had not supported him, Diederich represented in this matter the inarticulate power of order, morals and law. Rather should the stand collapse than that Käthchen Zillich should remain there.

Nevertheless, the incredible occurred. The steward shrugged his shoulders, while Käthchen smiled ironically, and even the policeman whom Diederich had called, merely gave further support to this irruption of immorality. Diederich was stunned by a world whose normal laws appeared to be suspended, and he submitted when Guste was moved up to a row away at the top, meanwhile exchanging sharp words with Käthchen Zillich concerning their contrasted treatment. The argument spread to other people and threatened to break out, when the band began to crash out a march from "Lohengrin," for the procession to the official marquee was actually in progress; Wulckow at the head, unmistakable in spite of his red hussar uniform, with an important general on one side of him, and on the other, a gentleman in a dress-suit with decorations. Was it possible? Two more important generals! And their adjutants, uniforms of every colour, glittering orders and tremendously tall men. "Who is that tall one in yellow?" asked Guste anxiously. "Isn't he a fine man!"—"Would you kindly not walk on my feet!" Diederich demanded, for his neighbour had jumped up; everybody was straining forward, exalted and excited. "Just look at them, Guste! Emma is silly not to have come. This is the only first-class theatre. It is superb; there is no denying it!"—"But that one with the yellow facings!" Guste raved. "That slim man! He must be a real aristocrat. I can see it at once." Diederich laughed rapturously. "There is not one of them who isn't a blue-blooded aristocrat, you can bet your life. When I tell you that His Majesty's aide-de-camp is here!"—"The one in yellow!"—"Here in person!"

People were getting the story right. "The aide-de-camp! Two major-generals! By Jove!" And the graceful smartness of the salutes! Even Mayor Scheffelweis was dragged out of his modest obscurity and could stand stiffly in front of his superiors in the uniform of a lieutenant in the Army Service Corps Reserve. Dressed as a lancer Herr von Quitzin thoroughly examined through his monocle the place which had temporarily belonged to him. But Wulckow, the red hussar, only now brought into evidence the full significance of what a Governor was, as he saluted, thrusting forward the profile of his paunch framed with cords. "Those are the pillars of our strength!" shouted Diederich, his words drowned by the powerful sounds of the march. "So long as we have such rulers we shall be the terror of the world!" Driven by an overpowering impulse, in the belief that his hour had come, he rushed down towards the speaker's platform. But the policeman on guard intercepted him. "No, no! It ain't your turn yet," said the policeman. Suddenly checked in his course, he ran into a steward, who had been keeping an eye on him, the same one as before, a municipal employé, who assured him that he knew very well that the seat of the lady with the yellow hair belonged to Diederich, "but the lady got it according to superior orders." The rest was told in a faint whisper, and Diederich let him go with a gesture implying: "Of course, in that case!" His Majesty's aide-de-camp! Of course, in that case! Diederich wondered whether it would not be well to turn around and openly pay his homage to Käthchen Zillich.

He did not have time to do so. Colonel von Haffke commanded the colour guard to stand at ease, and Kühnchen gave his warriors the same command. Behind the marquee the regimental band played a call to prayers, which was obeyed by the maids of honour and the Veterans' Association. Kühnchen in his historical Landwehr uniform, which was decorated not only with an iron cross but also with a glorious patch—where a French bullet had penetrated—met Pastor Zillich attired in his robes in the middle of the open space. The colour guard also fell in and, under Zillich's guidance, they did honour to their ancient Ally. On the stand for the civilians the public were compelled by the officials to get up. The officers and gentlemen did so of their own accord. Then the band played "Ein' feste Burg." Zillich seemed anxious to do something more, but the Governor-General, obviously convinced that the ancient Ally had had enough, fell back in his seat very bored, with the aide-de-camp on his right and the Major-Generals on his left. When the whole company had formed groups, according to their natural laws, in the official marquee, Governor von Wulckow was seen to give a sign, as a result of which a policeman was set in motion. He betook himself to his colleague in charge of the speaker's platform, whereupon the latter passed the word to Diederich. "Come on, it's your turn," said the policeman.

Diederich took care not to stumble as he climbed up, for his legs had suddenly become weak, and everything swam before his eyes. After gasping for a moment, he distinguished in the bare circle around him a little tree, which had no leaves, but was covered with black-white-and-red paper flowers. The sight of the little tree brought back his strength and his memory. He began: "Your Excellencies, my Lords and gentlemen, it is a hundred years since the great Emperor, whose monument is being unveiled by His Majesty's representative, was given to us and to his country. At the same time—to lend more significance to this hour—it is almost a decade since his great grandson ascended the throne. Why should we not first of all cast back a proud and grateful glance over the great times which we ourselves have been privileged to experience?"

Diederich glanced back. He alternately celebrated the unparalleled development of commerce and loyalty. He lingered over the ocean for a considerable time. "The ocean is indispensable to the greatness of Germany. In the ocean we have a proof that there can be no decision, on the seas or beyond them, without Germany and the German Emperor, for to-day the business of the world is our chief concern." Not only from an industrial standpoint, however, but even more from a moral and intellectual standpoint, their advance could be described as unique. What was our former condition? Diederich drew an unflattering picture of the previous generation which, led away with perilous beliefs by a one-sided humanitarian education, had no sense of dignity in national affairs. If that had now been fundamentally changed, if we now formed one single national party, in the just consciousness that we were the most efficient people in Europe and the whole world, despite mean-spirited and captious critics—whom had we to thank for it? Only His Majesty, Diederich answered. "He aroused the citizen from his slumbers, his lofty example has made us what we are." As he said this he struck himself on the chest. "His personality, his unique, incomparable personality, is so powerful that we can all creep up by it, like the clinging ivy!" he shouted, although this was not in the draft he had written. "In whatever His Majesty the Emperor decides for the good of the German people, we will joyfully co-operate, without distinction of creed and class. The plain man from the workshop is also welcome!" he again added at the inspiration of the moment, suddenly stimulated by the smell of the perspiring populace behind the military cordon, which was borne in his direction by the wind.

"Rendered efficient to an astonishing degree, full of the highest moral strength for positive action, and in our shining armour, the terror of all the enemies who enviously threaten us, we are the *élite* among the nations. In us German master-culture has for the first time attained heights which will never be surpassed by any people, be they who they may!"

At this point the Governor-General was observed to make a sign with his head, while the aide-de-camp moved his hands against one another. Then the applause broke out in the stands. Handkerchiefs were waved amongst the civilians. Guste allowed hers to flutter in the breeze, and so did Käthchen Zillich, in spite of the earlier unpleasantness. His heart as light as the fluttering handkerchiefs, Diederich resumed his lofty flight.

"A master-nation, however, does not achieve such an incomparable flowering in the slackness of peaceful ease. No. Our ancient Ally has deemed it necessary to test the German gold with fire. We had to pass through the fiery furnaces of Jena and Tilsit, and in the end we have been able to plant our victorious colours everywhere, and to forge the imperial crown of Germany upon the field of battle."

He recalled the many trials in the life of William the Great, from which, Diederich asserted, we could see that the Creator does not lose sight of His chosen people, and that He builds up the instrument suitable to His purpose. The great Emperor, however, had never been mistaken about this, as was particularly noticeable on that great historic occasion when, as King by the grace of God, with his sceptre in one hand and his imperial sword in the other, he paid honour only unto God and received his throne from Him. With a lofty sense of duty he had scorned to pay honour to the people and to accept the Crown at their hands. Nor was he dismayed by the responsibility to God alone, from which no minister and no parliament could relieve him. Diederich's voice trembled with emotion. "The people themselves recognise that, when they almost worship the personality of the deceased Emperor. Did he not succeed? And where success is, there is God! In the Middle Ages William the Great would have been canonised. To-day we erect a magnificent monument to his memory."

Again the Governor-General made a sign, which was again the signal for enthusiastic applause. The sun had disappeared and it grew colder, and as if inspired by the lowering skies Diederich turned to a deeper question. "Who, then, stood in the way of his exalted purpose? Who was the enemy of the great Emperor and of his loyal people? Napoleon, whom he had happily laid low, held his crown not from God but from the people. The fact itself was eloquent. That gives to the judgment of history its eternal and overpowering significance." Then Diederich essayed to depict conditions in the empire of Napoleon III, poisoned by democracy and therefore abandoned by God. Crass materialism, concealed by hollow religiosity, had exaggerated an undoubted business sense. This contempt for the soul was naturally allied with a degraded lust for pleasure. The craving for advertisement was the essence of publicity, and at every moment it degenerated into a mania for persecution. Relying outwardly upon prestige, but inwardly upon the police, with no other remedy but force, one strove only for theatrical effects, making great pomp with the heroic periods of the past, but chauvinism was the only goal which was ever reached. . . . Of all that we know nothing," cried Diederich raising his hand towards the witnesses above. "Therefore, there can never, never be for us that terrible end which awaited the empire of our hereditary foe."

At this point there was a flash of lightning. Between the military cordon and the partition, in the neighbourhood of what he vaguely guessed to be the crowd, there was a lurid flash in the dark cloud, and a peal of thunder followed, which was obviously going too far. The gentlemen in the official marquee began to look uncomfortable and the Governor-General had winced. On the stand reserved for the officers there was, naturally, no falling off of discipline, though amongst the civilians a certain uneasiness was visible. Diederich dominated the noise, for he shouted, thundering likewise: "Our ancient Ally proves it! We are not like others. We are serious, loyal and true! To be a German is to do a thing for its own sake. Who amongst us has ever made money out of his loyalty? Where could corrupt officials be found? Here masculine honesty is united with feminine purity, for woman leads us ever onward and is not the tool of vulgar pleasure. This radiant picture of true German character, however, rests upon the solid earth of Christianity, and that is the only true foundation; for every heathen civilisation, however beautiful and fine, will collapse at the first breath of disaster. And the soul of the German being is respect for power, power transmitted and hallowed by God, against which it is impossible to revolt. Therefore we must, now as always, regard the defence of our country as the highest duty, the King's uniform as the supreme distinction, and the making of arms as the most dignified labour." The thunder rumbled, though apparently intimidated by Diederich's increasingly powerful voice. But drops began to fall, which could be heard separately, they were so large. "The turbid stream of democracy," Diederich shouted, "flows unceasingly from the land of our hereditary foe and German manliness and German idealism alone can dam the tide. The unpatriotic enemies of the divine world order, however, who wish to undermine our political system,—they must be exterminated, root and branch, in order that, one day when we are called before our heavenly Judge, each of us can appear with an easy conscience in the presence of his God and his old Emperor; so that when asked if he has worked wholeheartedly for the welfare of the Empire, he can strike his chest and answer frankly: 'Yes.' "

At these words Diederich hit his chest so hard that he was winded. The civilian stand profited by the unavoidable pause which ensued to show by its restlessness that it regarded the speech as finished. The storm had now come up right over the heads of the festive gathering, and in the mephitic light these raindrops, as big as a hen's egg, kept falling singly, slowly, like a warning. . . . Diederich had recovered his breath.

"Now, when this monument is unveiled," he began with renewed vigour, "when flags and standards are drooped in reverence, swords are lowered and bayonets flash at the command: present arms—" Just at this moment there was such a formidable crash in the heavens that Diederich ducked his head, and before he knew what he was doing he had crept under the reading-desk. Fortunately he emerged again before any one had noticed him disappear, for everybody had done the same. They scarcely paid any attention as Diederich requested His Excellency, the Governor-General, to be so kind as to order that the monument be unveiled. However, the Governor-General stepped out in front of the official marquee, his face was a shade yellower than usual and the glitter of his star was extinguished. In a feeble voice he said: "In the name of His Majesty I declare this monument to be unveiled"—and the covering fell, to the strains of "Die Wacht am Rhein." The loyal subjects were once more steeled against the threats from heaven by the spectacle of William the Great, riding through the air, looking like a good paterfamilias, though surrounded by all the terrors of authority. They joined heartily in the cheers of the Governor-General for the Emperor. The air of the national anthem was the cue for His Excellency to go up to the foot of the monument, examine it and to reward the expectant sculptor with a few appropriate words of recognition. People found it natural that this exalted personage should glance up dubiously at the sky, but, as might be expected, his sense of duty triumphed— a victory all the more brilliant because amongst that crowd of gallant soldiers he was the only civilian in a dress-suit. He ventured boldly forth, advancing beneath those huge, slow drops of rain, surrounded by lancers, cuirassiers and army service corps. . . . The inscription "William the Great" had already been inspected, the sculptor had been favoured with a few words and received his decoration, and it was just the turn of Hessling to be introduced as the spiritual creator of the monument, and to be decorated, when the heavens burst. They burst all at once with such force as to suggest a long-delayed explosion. Before the gentlemen could turn around they were up to their ankles in water, and His Excellency's sleeves and trousers were dripping. The stands disappeared beneath the downpour, and as if on a distant billowing sea it could be seen that the awnings had collapsed beneath the fury of the cloud-burst. Shrieking crowds struggled right and left in their moist embrace. The civilians scrambled down, like a grey, writhing serpent, bathing in the flooded field with spasmodic twists.

In the circumstances, the Governor-General consented to omit the remainder of the festive programme for reasons of expediency. While the lightning flashed all round him, and water sprang from him as from a fountain, he beat a hasty retreat, with the aide-de-camp, the two major-generals, dragoons, hussars, lancers and army service corps in the rear. On the way His Excellency remembered that the decoration for the spiritual creator was still hanging from his finger. Faithful to his duty in the extreme, but determined not to be detained, he passed it on, as he ran in his dripping clothes to Governor von Wulckow. Wulckow, in his turn, met a policeman, who was still clinging to his post, and entrusted him with the bestowal of this sign of the All Highest's approval. Whereupon the policeman wandered through storm and rain in search of Diederich. Finally he found him crouching in the water underneath the reading-desk. "Here y'are, the order of William," said the policeman, making off, for just then a flash of lightning came so near that it seemed as if it would prevent the decoration from being bestowed. Diederich could only heave a sigh.

When he finally ventured to peep halfway out at the world,

it presented a spectacle of increasing ruin. The huge black
partition opposite was swaying and threatened to topple over,
with the house behind it. Above a seething mass of people,
in the ghostly light of sulphur-yellow and blue, the carriage
horses reared and dashed away. Happy were the unprivileged
crowd outside who had decamped. The cultivated and pos-
sessing classes, on the other hand, were in such a position
that they could feel the fragments of the ruin falling about
their heads, and fire from heaven. It was hardly surprising
that their behaviour was governed accordingly and many ladies were hurled back from the exit in the most ungentlemanly
fashion, and simply rolled over one another. The officers,
relying upon their bravery alone, made use of their weapons
of offence against every one who opposed them, while flags,
torn by the storm from what remained of the stands and the
official marquee, whistled through the air, black-white-and-red,
about the ears of the strugglers. Hopeless though everything
was, the regimental band continued to play the national
anthem, even after the military cordon and the world order
had been dispersed. They played like the orchestra on a
sinking ship to ward off terror and the inevitable end. Another burst of the hurricane demoralised even them. Diederich closed his eyes, and to his dazed senses the end of everything seemed imminent. He sank back into the cool depths
below the desk, to which he clung like a drowning man to a
log. His farewell glance had embraced something that passed
all understanding: the fence hung with black-white-and-red,
which enclosed the park, had collapsed beneath the weight of
the people on it, followed by this clambering up and down,
this rolling about, this ebb and fall of people, standing on
their heads and getting in one another's way—and then being
lashed by whips from above, these streams of fire, this breaking up like the end of a drunken masquerade: nobles and commoners, the most distinguished uniform and the citizen
aroused from his slumbers, pillars of the state and heaven-sent

statesmen, ideal riches, hussars, lancers, dragoons and army service corps!

The horsemen of the apocalypse rode on, however, as Diederich noticed. They had only held manœuvres for the Judgment Day; the supreme crisis was not yet. With great precautions he left his hiding-place and discovered that it was now only raining, and that Emperor William the Great was, still there, with all the paraphernalia of power. All the time Diederich had had a feeling that the monument had been smashed and carried away. The scene of the festivities certainly looked like a desolate memory; not a soul stirred amongst the ruins. But, yes, there was some one moving in the background, some one wearing a lancer's uniform. It was Herr von Quitzin, who was examining the house that had collapsed. It had been struck by lightning and was smoking behind the remains of the huge, black partition. In the general exodus only Herr von Quitzin had stood his ground, for an idea had given him strength. Diederich read his mind. Herr von Quitzin was thinking: "We should also have planted that house on those fellows. But nothing could be done, in spite of the strongest pressure. But now I'll get the insurance money. There is a God!" And then he went in the direction of the fire-brigade which could not now intervene with any effect in the matter.

Encouraged by this example Diederich also set out. He had lost his hat, his shoes were full of water, and in the seat of his trousers he carried a puddle with him. As no conveyance seemed to be available he decided to cut through the centre of the town. The corners of the old streets shielded him from the wind and he felt warmer. "There is no danger of catarrh. I'll get Guste to put a poultice on my stomach. If she will only be good enough not to bring influenza into the house!" After this worry he remembered his decoration. "The order of William, created by His Majesty, is given only for exceptional services on behalf of the welfare and im-

provement of the people. . . . That's what I've got!" said
Diederich out loud in the empty street. "Even if the heavens
fall!" Nature had attempted to upset authority with inadequate means. Diederich called upon Heaven to observe his
order of William and said, "Sold again!" Whereupon he
pinned it on, beside the order of the Crown, fourth class.

In the Fleischhauergrube several carriages had stopped,
curiously enough, in front of old Buck's house. One of them,
moreover, was a country cart. Was he by any chance . . . ?
Diederich peered into the house. The glass door stood open,
strange to say, as if some one were expected who did not
often come. A religious quiet prevailed in the wide hall; it
was only when he crept past the kitchen that he heard sobbing: the old servant, with her face resting on her arms.
"So things are as bad as that!"—Diederich suddenly shuddered and stopped, ready to retreat. "This is no place for
me. . . . Yet, my place is here, for everything here is mine,
and it is my duty to see that they do not take anything away
afterwards." But this was not the only thing that impelled
him. Something less obvious and more profound made him
gasp for breath and caught him in the stomach. He stepped
carefully up the flat old stairs and thought: "Respect for a
brave enemy when he stands on the field of honour! God
has judged him. Yes, indeed, such is life. Nobody can tell
whether some day— But, come now, there is a difference,
either a thing is right or it isn't. One must neglect nothing
that can add to the fame of what is right. Our old Emperor
probably had also to make an effort when he went to
Wilhelmshöhe to meet the utterly defeated Napoleon."

By this time he had reached the mezzanine floor, and he
walked cautiously along the lengthy corridor at the end of
which the door—here also—stood open. He kept close up
against the wall and peeped in. A bed with the foot turned
towards him, and in it old Buck was reclining against a heap
of pillows, apparently out of his mind. Not a sound. Was

he alone? He moved carefully to the other side. Now he could see the curtained windows and, in front of them, the family in a semi-circle. Judith Lauer was sitting motionless, nearest the bed, then Wolfgang, with an expression on his face which nobody would have expected. Between the windows was huddled the herd of five daughters and their bankrupt father, who no longer even preserved outward appearances; further off stood the countrified son and his dull-looking wife, and finally Lauer, who had sat down. With good reason they all kept so quiet, at that moment they were losing their last prospect of ever having a say in anything again! They had been very uppish and very sure of themselves, so long as the old man held out. He had fallen and they with him; he was disappearing and so were all of them. He had always built upon quicksands, for he had not relied upon Power! The spirit was useless, for it left behind it but decay. The delusion of every ambition which had no fists nor money in those fists!

Why did Wolfgang look like that? It did not look like grief, although tears were falling from his yearning eyes; it looked like envy, bitter envy. What was wrong with the others? Judith Lauer, whose brows frowned darkly; her husband who was sighing aloud—even the eldest son's wife had folded in front of her face her working-woman's hands. Diederich stepped into the centre of the doorway in a determined attitude. It was dark in the passage and they could see nothing even if they wanted to; but what of the old man? His face was turned exactly in that direction, and where his eyes were fixed one divined more than was actually there, visions which nobody could obstruct. As they reappeared before his astonished eyes he opened out his arms on the pillows, tried to lift them, and did so, moving them in a gesture of welcome. Who was it? How many were there to whom he made these prolonged signs of welcome? A whole nation, apparently, but of what character, that its coming should awaken this spiritual joy in the countenance of old Buck?

Then he suddenly gave a start, as if he had met a stranger with a message of terror. He was frightened, and struggled for breath. Facing him, Diederich held himself even more stiffly, puffed out his chest with its black-white-and-red sash and its decorations, and glared, on general principles. Suddenly the old man's head dropped; he fell forward, right over, as though he had been broken. His family shrieked. In a horrified whisper the eldest son's wife cried: "He has seen something! He has seen the devil!" Judith Lauer got up slowly and shut the door. Diederich had vanished.